Pride Publishing books by T. Strange

Bound to the Spirits
Rattling Chains
Cold Blood

Bound to the Spirits

COLD BLOOD

T. STRANGE

Cold Blood
ISBN # 978-1-83943-776-2
©Copyright T. Strange 2022
Cover Art by Erin Dameron-Hill ©Copyright March 2022
Interior text design by Claire Siemaszkiewicz
Pride Publishing

COLD BLOOD

Dedication

For M.

Chapter One

Hamilton sighed as he lowered himself into the driver's seat of their police cruiser, settling in much more heavily than usual. "Matthew wants to meet you."

Harlan was relieved that he was already struggling with his seatbelt. It gave him a moment to think about what Hamilton had just said.

Matthew? Do I know a Matthew? Hamilton's — and, by extension, Harlan's — sergeant was named *Matthews*, but Harlan had already met her.

The seatbelt clicked into place. He was out of time.

Hamilton sighed again, this time with an edge of laughter. "Matthew is my..." He mumbled something Harlan couldn't make out. "You haven't met him," he added in his regular speaking voice.

Harlan waited, hoping Hamilton would elaborate, repeat himself or that the words would finally click into place as he ran them over and over in his mind.

Silence. Silence that he had to break if he was going to get anything else.

"Sorry... I didn't quite —"

"Boyfriend!" Too loud this time, loud and sudden enough that it startled Harlan. "Matthew is my *boyfriend*. He wants to meet you." Hamilton slid his gaze over to Harlan, a sly smile on his thin lips. "You *can* say no," he added, making it clear he would prefer that.

Harlan would prefer that as well, so it worked out nicely.

Before Harlan could assure him that he was, of course, in complete agreement, Hamilton shook his head and sighed for a third time that morning. "Nah, I think we're past that. At this point, it would just be a delaying tactic. He's made up his mind."

Harlan glanced sideways at Hamilton. *Is Hamilton actually blushing?* He hadn't thought Hamilton was physically capable of doing that, never mind imagined that it might actually happen.

"And I've met *your* boyfriend," Hamilton shot back, even though Harlan hadn't spoken.

Technically true, but they hadn't exactly met over dinner or another social event. Did life-and-death situations count more or less than sitting down for a meal together?

"And, by the way" — the blush Harlan had probably imagined was gone, and Hamilton was definitely smirking now — "I *knew* I recognized him from somewhere."

Shit. Harlan had been dreading this conversation, hoping it wouldn't happen. He'd hoped that Hamilton wouldn't connect Charles, Harlan's ghost-repelling boyfriend, to Mr. Moore, owner of Rattling Chains, a formerly haunted BDSM club. Apparently, that had been too much to ask for.

Hamilton opened his mouth, started to say something then seemed to reconsider when he saw Harlan's pained expression. "I'm glad you've got someone," he said, just as gruffly as usual, but with a hint of genuine fondness and even warmth. "You don't have a lot of people." He looked away while he took a left-hand turn, then laughed. "Of course you'd meet someone on the job."

Harlan looked down at his lap. Yeah. It was pretty pathetic. Sure, he'd started going to the occasional police-medium group—basically a coffee klatch, not everyone sitting in a circle sharing their feelings the way he'd been dreading—but that was *still* connected to the police. He hadn't even realized that Charles had the same connection. *Fuck.* Somehow, without realizing it, he'd become one of those adults who only lived for his job.

He blinked. *Maybe it isn't just me.*

"What does Matthew do?" he asked, fully expecting he already knew the answer.

He was wrong.

"He's an advertising consultant." Hamilton shrugged. "I don't know what that means, either." He paused, then added, as though he'd read Harlan's mind—more likely his expression—"I did meet him through a case, though."

Harlan wasn't sure if that made him feel better or worse. He didn't know exactly how old Hamilton was, but he guessed his police partner was at least a few years older than he was. Was that what he had to look forward to—all his personal connections coming from his work for the rest of his life? He wasn't sure why it bothered him, but it did. Maybe it was like that for everyone, and he just didn't know — not that there was anyone he could ask.

Maybe Charles... He'd met a few of Charles' friends, more or less in passing. He certainly hadn't sat down and had dinner with any of them, the way Hamilton seemed to be proposing that he do with Matthew. He'd always assumed it was because he and Charles were still fairly new as a couple and — knowing Harlan — Charles hadn't wanted to overwhelm him with a bunch of people all at once — but maybe he'd been wrong. Maybe he just didn't *want* to introduce Harlan to anyone else in his life.

Knowing he was starting to spiral, he was relieved when Hamilton continued.

"I told him you don't do phone calls and you wouldn't want to text someone you don't know" — *Wow, Hamilton really will make a great detective one day* — "so you can just let me know when *you* decide. Here." He fished a piece of paper out of his breast pocket and handed it to Harlan. "This is Matthew's number so you can give it to Charles. He's invited too, if he'd like." His smirk was back. "I think he still has a choice, unlike you."

"Where are we going today?" Normally Hamilton didn't tell him, and he didn't ask, but it was the only change of topic Harlan could think of. "Is it another one of Samuel's ghosts?" Killing the warped medium and serial killer Samuel Harkness had released most of the spirits under his control, but even eight months later they were still finding stragglers, like the ones that had led Harlan to their killer in the first place.

Interestingly, Harlan and Hamilton had found — and freed — almost three times as many wanderers as the other three medium pairs put together. It was as if even though he'd never met them, these spirits felt a connection to him for killing the man who had been controlling them.

This part of the job was a lot less glamorous when the ghosts they worked with weren't leading him to a serial killer.

"Kid," Hamilton had laughed after a sweaty, dusty and frustrated Harlan had snapped something along those lines after a very long, hot day crammed in the crawlspace of an old house, trying to coax an especially nervous ghost close enough for him to either grab or calm it down enough for it to cross over on its own, *"that's the job. It's not bringing down bad guys and epic showdowns. It's...this. Hey, you've got a cobweb on your face."*

Harlan couldn't help feeling that he'd peaked too soon, experienced more police-medium excitement than most of his colleagues got in a lifetime.

Crucially, he'd survived. Most police mediums didn't live long enough to retire.

He still liked his job and found it fulfilling, rewarding and *blah blah,* but he couldn't help feeling a little...let down. Restless, maybe. Not that he wanted to face anything like Samuel ever again! But...*something.* Something more than finding ghost, freeing ghost, next. Day in, day out, week after week. Just a little.

"Nah. Well—not as far as I know," Hamilton amended. "Though apparently this is kinda a weird one."

Harlan couldn't help brightening, sitting forward in his seat a little. In light of what he'd been thinking, 'weird' was good. "Really?"

"Yeah, yeah, keep it in your pants." Hamilton laughed.

"You gonna tell me or is it gonna be a surprise?" Even a few months ago Harlan wouldn't have dared ask for information about the scene they were going to, and he certainly wouldn't have expected an answer.

Now, it was almost like a game between the two of them — if Harlan *really* wanted to know, Hamilton would tell him, and if Hamilton *really* wanted to keep him in the dark until they got there — and Harlan was beginning to think that, sometimes at least, walking in without any preconceptions was helpful — he wouldn't. And, occasionally, Hamilton himself knew very little or nothing about the haunting situation. Harlan was starting to suspect that was one of the reasons Hamilton hadn't filled Harlan in ahead of time in the past. Hamilton didn't like admitting when he didn't know something.

"Mmm, this time I think I'll let you see for yourself. Besides, we're almost there." Hamilton pulled up beside a record store, one of those hipster places that had been popping up in the most gentrified parts of the city. He got out, coming around the other side of the car and opening Harlan's door when he didn't get out immediately.

Harlan stepped onto the sidewalk to take a better look around. Hauntings — the ones not related to violent crime, which he doubted was the case here — tended to be in residential buildings. People died where they lived, not where they bought vinyl.

He glanced across the street — more shops, and they didn't look like they had apartments over them. Neither did the record store or the others around it.

"There's a haunting *here*?"

"I can double-check the address if you'd like," Hamilton offered, smirking a little.

"No. That's fine." As far as Harlan knew, Hamilton had never got an address wrong.

Maybe the dispatcher had been wrong?

A young white man stepped out of the shop, waving at them. "Are you with the Graveyard Crew?"

It was a nickname for Toronto police mediums that Harlan didn't really like — and, by the look on Hamilton's face, he didn't care for it either.

Hamilton pointedly glanced down at his uniform and badge. "We're with the police."

"Oh, good! C'mon in. We've been expecting you." He turned and disappeared into the shop.

Harlan shot Hamilton a questioning glance.

Hamilton shrugged one shoulder, extending a hand to say *after you*.

He was suddenly hit by a barrage of noise — apparently the door was surprisingly soundproof. Harlan always thought the music in these types of places sounded bad, but this *was* bad.

Hamilton, never one to fuck around, headed straight to the man who'd welcomed them. "Can you turn the music down? Or off, maybe?" He had to raise his voice to be heard over the din.

The man shook his head. "No! That's the problem." He didn't have Hamilton's loud 'cop voice' and he was practically screaming.

Rolling his eyes, Hamilton motioned Harlan closer. "You go do your woo-woo, and I'll see if I can turn this noise down so we can think straight."

He hurried after the shopkeeper just as Harlan said, "I think they're connected..." He thought he'd figured out just why the music was so awful, because it wasn't just one song playing. It sounded like at least three, maybe as many as five. Harlan didn't know any of them, and at first, he'd assumed he was hearing something 'experimental' or something, but after listening for a few minutes, he'd come to a different conclusion.

Shaking his head, Harlan followed the other two men. There was a bank of five record players against one wall, with oversize old – or at least made to look old – headphones hanging from a hook beside each of them. Harlan assumed this was so shoppers could listen to the record they wanted before they bought it.

There was a spinning record on each of them.

He glanced around. There was no one else in the store. *Not exactly surprising.* "How long has this been going on?"

"A few days now." The man extended his hand. "I'm Simon, by the way," he added, his voice a little less shrill now that they were standing closer to him.

Harlan glanced at Simon's hand. Usually Hamilton did this kind of thing, but he wasn't paying attention. "Harlan," he said, shaking for the shortest amount of time he thought he could get away with without seeming rude.

Simon glanced at Hamilton's back.

Fuck. Harlan hated doing introductions. "And this is my partner, Hamilton."

Apparently satisfied, Simon backed off a little. "I called as soon as it started, but they told me I was 'low priority'. And, like, I get it, but..." He opened his arms to gesture at his empty shop.

"Yeah," was the only response Harlan could come up with. He could see both sides of the problem. Obviously, it wasn't great for Simon as a small-business owner—at least Harlan assumed he was the owner, since he was the only one who was here willingly—but by police-medium standards, it was *definitely* low priority. No one was being hurt or driven off or being frightened—just annoyed. Very, very annoyed.

The odd thing was that Harlan hadn't seen any sign of an actual ghost so far, not so much as a sparkle at the edges of his vision.

Hamilton, who'd been bent over one of the record players, abruptly straightened. Harlan could see that he'd been holding something, but he dropped it before Harlan could see what it was.

"Yeah, we tried that," Simon said dryly. "Didn't work."

Harlan wandered closer to Hamilton to see what he'd been doing.

"Unplugged. They're all unplugged." Looking stunned, Hamilton pointed at the cable dangling from each player.

Harlan frowned. He didn't know much about records or record players. A year ago, he never would have asked, but now he trusted Hamilton enough to suggest, "Maybe they don't need to be plugged in all the time? Maybe they can run off a-a battery or something?"

Hamilton blinked thoughtfully. "Maybe." He turned to Simon. "These need power to work, right?"

"Yep."

As one, Harlan and Hamilton turned back to the row of spinning records.

"Well, that's creepy," Hamilton said, deadpan.

Harlan nodded. "It is, but it's actually not all that uncommon." He'd almost got used to the noise. Barely noticed it anymore.

"Not uncommon?" Hamilton waved a hand at the players.

"Well, not this, specifically... I just mean, ghosts are very good at manipulating energy, especially electricity. They can make electronics — even broken or unplugged ones — turn on, but not usually for this long. It takes a lot out of them to interact with the physical world."

"Like he said, the call came in a few days ago, but no one was able to get to it until now."

Harlan hadn't thought Hamilton had been listening when Simon said that, but apparently Hamilton had heard *everything*. "That's the weird part. A few hours, maybe. A few days, even if the ghost is only doing it while people are here and resting when it's alone? Very weird."

"Where is the ghost, anyway? I don't know about you, but I'd really like to get outta here."

"That's another weird part."

"Great. *More* weirdness. My favourite."

Harlan ignored him. "I still haven't seen it." He let his eyes slightly un-focus and turned in a slow circle, without looking at anything in particular. His gaze was drawn to a pair of large speakers, one in each of the back corners of the shop. The music was blaring through them, but he could see their power cords hanging limp beside them.

Brushing past Hamilton and Simon, he inspected the turntables. All the headphones were connected.

"The music from the record players is only supposed to play through the headphones, right?"

"Yeah."

Harlan tried to lift the needle off one of the records. It didn't want to come, and he was afraid he would break it before it finally did, which wasn't helped by Simon making little 'gluhhh!' noises of protest behind him. The record kept spinning—Harlan wasn't sure if that was supposed to happen—but it sounded like there was one less song blasting out of the speakers. "That's something, anyway," he said, quietly enough that the others wouldn't hear. He was making little enough progress otherwise.

He got his fingers under the spinning disc and tried to lift the record off the turntable, but it felt like something heavy was sitting on top of it or like it was glued down. He pulled harder, ignoring Simon's increasingly frantic sounds. He wasn't sure why he was bothering with this—it almost certainly wouldn't solve the haunting—but he was stubbornly hoping that a series of small victories would add up and he'd be able to figure out how to stop it—or at least buy himself time.

Just as he was afraid the record was going to snap in half from the strain, it abruptly sped up. He pulled back with a hiss. Looking down at his hands, he could see a small friction burn on each finger.

"Are you okay?" Hamilton rushed over, and Harlan didn't think he was imagining the way Hamilton's elbow kept brushing his holster. *If only this was a problem Hamilton could solve with his gun.*

"I'm fine." Knowing Hamilton wouldn't let up until he'd seen the damage for himself, Harlan held out his hands.

Hamilton gave them a brief glance, then nodded. "What next?"

What next, indeed? Harlan was asking himself the same question. He just had to *think* for a minute, but it was so hard with all this music playing. When he'd first started working as a police medium, he probably would have stayed, telling himself he had to 'tough it out', but he knew that overstimulating himself would only be counterproductive. "I'm just going to step outside—"

Hamilton and Simon were right behind him. He didn't know how Simon had stayed sane after a few days of this.

Once outside, Harlan stepped around a corner into an alley, stopping where he could still see Hamilton, just in case. Of course, he promptly closed his eyes, but he was relying on the fact that Hamilton could see him, too.

The turntables were unplugged. The speakers were unplugged. It had been hard to lift the needle but raising it had stopped the music coming from that turntable. He couldn't tell how new or old any of the records or players were, but the turntables all matched, as though they'd been bought at or near the same time.

He hadn't been able to lift the record off.

Okay... That was the closest thing he had to a clue.

He opened his eyes and walked back to the shop. "Where do you get your records?"

Simon blinked. "Uh...all kinds of places. We order them online. People bring them in to sell or trade..."

Harlan shook his head. "Have you got any in the last few days?" Hopefully they hadn't been scattered around the store's stock already and were still sitting in the back waiting for...whatever needed to be done to them before they could be sold.

"Lemme check."

Harlan was afraid they'd have to go back inside so Simon could look at his computer, but he just pulled out his phone and started scrolling through. "Ah, here we go. This woman brought in her dad's old collection. If I'm thinking of the right person—she's not a regular—he passed away recently, and she was clearing out his house. Really sad for her, but great for us. There was some really primo shit."

Harlan and Hamilton exchanged glances. *Bingo.*

Hamilton definitely had an air of *Couldn't you have told us this half an hour ago?* but Harlan was just glad they were making progress.

"I don't suppose you could show us those records?" Harlan asked.

"Ohh-h! Yeah, that probably has something to do with it, eh?"

Harlan steeled himself and went back inside. It was even louder than before, and he groaned when he saw that the needle he'd managed to lift had dropped again, adding another song to the horrible medley.

He and Hamilton followed Simon as he darted them through the store like a hummingbird, flicking through boxes and displays of records and showing them the newest additions. Hamilton glanced at Harlan after each one, and Harlan had to keep shaking his head over and over. None of them held a hint of ghostly sparkle.

"That's all of 'em." Simon slid his phone back into his pocket. "Is this going to take much longer?"

Harlan groaned in the quiet of his mind. They had to be missing something. *He* had to be missing something—but what?

"Hmm." Simon nibbled his lip thoughtfully. "Wait a second. I wasn't actually here the day they came in. Let me call Brianne. She's the one who received them." He flitted outside and had a brief, animated phone call with lots of hand gestures. "Okay, you guys, this might be it." He led them to an office at the back of the store and opened a filing cabinet behind the overflowing desk. "Here we go." He held up a record. It wasn't in a sleeve, was bright blue and didn't have a label. *Definitely weird.*

Harlan, who'd been straining his psychic senses since entering the shop, was nearly blinded by the ghostly sparks shooting from the vinyl. He blinked rapidly, knowing it wouldn't really help, because it wasn't his actual vision that was being overwhelmed. He dialled his senses way back — the psychic equivalent of squinting. "Oh, yeah. That's it." He held out his hands.

Simon glanced down at the record he was holding, a strange mix of horror and reverence on his face. He quickly handed it over.

The music stopped.

Simon threw his hands in the air. "Oh, thank *fucking* God!" He immediately looked ashamed for his outburst, but at least Harlan and Hamilton weren't customers. Harlan also thought he was entitled to at *least* that after putting up with the non-stop blended music for days.

Hamilton grinned at Harlan and gave him a little golf clap.

Harlan turned away from both of them, concentrating on the disc. *Come out,* he told the spirit sternly. He was not in the mood for messing around with this haunting any longer, even if it was quiet now.

A long-haired young white man wearing clothes that looked like they were from the sixties or seventies slowly materialized. His arms were crossed, and he looked very unimpressed. "Dude, you're like, *majorly* harshing the vibe here."

Harlan wasn't surprised that the ghost didn't look old. It was pretty common for the deceased to appear as younger versions of themselves. "Good. The vibe is harshed. What were you *doing*?" He wasn't usually this abrupt with ghosts, but he could feel a major headache coming on and didn't feel like holding the ghost's hand. Besides, anyone—living or dead—who would do something *this* annoying probably needed a firm touch.

The ghost sighed heavily. "I asked, like, a *million* times for them to put on the records I wanted to listen to, but everyone just ignored me. Then I realized I could do it myself. I realized I could listen to *all* my favourites, *all* at once." He grinned dopily.

"I'm Harlan. I'm a medium, and I'm here to help you pass on today." Emphasis on *today*. "What's your name?" Harlan wasn't sure why, but he hated introductions a lot less with ghosts than with living people. He also tended to remember their names more easily. Though he also didn't have to remember their names for very *long*.

"Groovy. I'm Mike." He held out a hand, but Harlan didn't take it. He *could* have given him a handshake—unlike non-mediums, whose hands would have gone right through—but he already had enough nerve damage from touching ghosts, and he didn't want to add more for something so pointless.

Mike didn't seem offended and slowly pulled his hand back.

"It's time for you to go," Harlan told him solemnly.

"But I haven't listened to—"

"You do realize you're going to...a good place, right?" Harlan didn't like saying 'heaven,' and he didn't think it was entirely accurate. "You'll be able to listen to all the music you want."

"You mean it?"

"I mean it," Harlan agreed gently. He could afford to be gentle now that he was this close to sending the idiot on.

"Groovy," Mike said again.

Harlan opened the veil, blinking at the bright swirl of colours on the other side. He'd never seen a portal quite so...psychedelic. He was sure Mike was going to be just fine.

After one final glance back at the record store, Mike stepped through to his final resting place. Harlan wasn't sure if he imagined a sudden swell of sitar music as the vortex closed behind Mike.

Harlan took a deep, steadying breath, then turned back to Simon and Hamilton—who, he realized uncomfortably, had apparently just been standing there watching him the whole time. "He's gone," he assured Simon. "But you should make sure this gets back to its rightful owner."

"The dead guy?"

"No. His daughter. He had his ashes mixed in with the vinyl, and either she didn't know or she got it mixed up with the others. It looks like it didn't get a label by mistake." Or she'd just thought it was creepy and wanted to get rid of it.

Hamilton took a surreptitious step back. Harlan didn't think he'd even touched it.

"Cool..." Simon said.

Harlan could see him wiping his hands on his pants as if the ashes had left some kind of residue.

Mentally rolling his eyes at both of them, he handed the blue record back to Simon, who took it—though he held it at arm's length, like it was a dead rat.

"Do you still have that Advil in your car?" Harlan asked Hamilton, both because his head was killing him and because he wanted to get out of there.

"Yeah, I think so." Hamilton turned to Simon. "Feel free to call if you have any more problems, but you should be good to go." He barely waited for Simon's answering, "Thank you!" before striding toward the front door with Harlan hurrying to keep up with him.

There was plenty of Advil in the cruiser, but the only thing to drink was a miraculously unfinished cup of Tim Hortons coffee Hamilton had got before work. It was unpleasantly warm—worse than actually being cold—and Harlan didn't like Tim Hortons coffee, even when it was fresh. He was pretty sure that made him a Bad Canadian, but it was true. But he gulped it down, only grimacing a little at the taste. "Thanks."

"You know, we could've stopped somewhere and got you something to drink," Hamilton laughed, shaking his head as he popped the pill bottle back in the glove compartment and started the car.

"Yeah, but..." He couldn't explain that he'd, for some reason, decided using the coffee was a kind of personal challenge, because that sounded stupid, even to him. He grinned, changing the subject. "Well, you were right. That was a weird one."

Chapter Two

Harlan realized that it was silly but, based on Matthew's job description, Harlan hadn't been able to picture him as anything but a white man in a three-piece suit and tie and shiny black shoes, even in his own home.

The man who opened the door could hardly have been more different. He was a tall Native man wearing well-worn blue jeans and a faded T-shirt with a logo for what Harlan assumed was a band. If it was, it was one that he'd never heard of.

"Welcome! You must be Harlan. I've heard so much about you. Hamilton said you probably wouldn't want a hug."

Harlan found it pretty funny that even his boyfriend called him 'Hamilton'.

Harlan nodded, unexpectedly touched that Hamilton had noticed his preference and told Matthew, and that Matthew had asked rather than assuming. Harlan didn't even like hugs from people he knew well, and he *really* didn't like surprise hugs.

"Come in. Come in! Dinner is almost ready." Matthew led Harlan to a large kitchen that had a distressed-wood island with a neat line of bar stools on one side.

"Can I get you something to drink? We've got water, wine, beer, pop, juice..."

Feeling a little overwhelmed, Harlan concentrated on the list. He could cross wine and beer off immediately. He occasionally had a glass of either, but alcohol tended to fuck with his mood the next day, so he generally avoided it. He wouldn't have minded a pop, but he didn't know what varieties Matthew had and he didn't want to ask for something they didn't have and make it awkward. "I'll have a juice...please." There were definitely juices that Harlan liked and ones he didn't, but he could spend the rest of the evening sipping on a single glass of gross juice if he had to.

"Coming right up. We have strawberry passionfruit and good ol' orange." When Matthew turned, Harlan could see he had a long black braid down his back.

"Strawberry would be great."

Something Matthew had said snagged in Harlan's mind—"we've *got*." He'd assumed they were meeting at Matthew's apartment, not at Hamilton's, but it hadn't occurred to him that it might be *both*.

After bringing Harlan his glass, Matthew went back to cooking and Hamilton disappeared into the other room, calling out high- and lowlights of the day to his boyfriend. Finding himself alone, Harlan took a sneaky glance around, looking for signs of Hamilton in this condo. Of course, it would be easiest to check the bathroom—count toothbrushes, that sort of thing—but that almost seemed like cheating. And he didn't have to pee, at least not yet. He was a terrible liar, and he couldn't help thinking that Matthew would somehow *know* that he didn't really need to go and was only using it as an excuse to snoop.

There. Hanging on the wall in the living room was some sort of official-looking police award covered in seals and signatures. He doubted Hamilton would give it to his boyfriend to hang in an apartment he didn't live in. Once again, Harlan was stunned by how close Hamilton played his cards to his chest. He'd had no idea Hamilton *had* a boyfriend until the invitation the other day, let alone that they lived together.

Pleased with his little bit of deduction, Harlan took a sip of his juice and remembered he had a message to pass on. "Charles is running a little late. He got stuck at the club and now he's dealing with traffic," he told Matthew. Too late, Harlan realized what that meant. He was alone in unfamiliar territory, without Charles — who was almost as good at being Harlan's people-buffer as he was at being his ghost-buffer. All of Hamilton and Matthew's attention would be on him. Just him.

As though he'd sensed Harlan's insecurity, Matthew turned from the stove with a big smile. "Oh good! Everything can simmer for a while, and we can chat a little. It's so nice to meet you, finally! I've heard so much about you!"

"Oh. I, uh…"

Matthew laughed, bright and open. "That's about what I expected. I didn't think he'd told you much about me," he assured Harlan.

At that moment Hamilton emerged from the bedroom wearing a crisp white T-shirt and jeans that were just as pressed as his uniform pants. He looked like he was wearing another uniform, actually—off-duty-cop chic.

He was also doing a terrible job of trying to hide his grin. He swept up to Matthew and gave his hand a brief squeeze, looking Harlan right in the eye as he said, "Why don't we play a game or something instead?"

A game almost sounded more anxiety-inducing than having two people focusing only on him, but he dutifully took his glass of juice and followed his hosts into the living room, making a beeline for the armchair in the farthest corner.

Turning, almost in slow motion like he was in a horror movie, Harlan saw that Matthew and Hamilton had an entire shelf of boardgames. He'd never heard of any of them. No *Clue*. No *Monopoly*. There was nothing he'd played before, even a little, nothing he had even a passing familiarity with. He hadn't particularly enjoyed playing those games, but at least he wouldn't be a total beginner. It would be awkward enough, even if he wasn't at a complete disadvantage.

Hamilton ambled over and sat in the middle of the couch, facing Harlan. He smirked, probably at the look on Harlan's face. Harlan probably would have smirked too, if he could see it as an outsider.

Hamilton leaned forward, tapping a much smaller and more manageable stack of games on the coffee table. Harlan hadn't even noticed them.

"Don't worry. I grabbed a few that are easy to pick up right away and don't involve a lot of talking," he whispered, giving Harlan a conspiratorial wink.

Harlan leaned back with a tiny sigh of relief. Hamilton really did have his back, even off the job. The armchair, which was the colour of an eggplant— though it was fancy enough that it might be referred to as 'aubergine' — was very plush and comfortable. Harlan suspected it was something Matthew had chosen, not Hamilton.

Hamilton sprawled his arm across the back of the couch just as Matthew came over to join them. He sat on the end closest to Hamilton.

Hamilton's arm slowly dipped until it was draped over Matthew's shoulder.

"See anything you like?" Matthew asked Harlan, setting his glass of wine on a coaster on the end table beside him.

Catching Harlan's eye, Hamilton gave a tiny shrug. Either he couldn't or wouldn't offer any more help.

Harlan leaned forward and pretended to study the boxes. He didn't bother turning them over to read their descriptions, because he was already feeling overwhelmed enough, even with Hamilton's limited selection.

He picked one more or less at random, tapping the box and nudging it slightly closer to the other two.

"Great choice! This one's a lot of fun," Matthew assured him.

They'd just got the game set up and started explaining the rules to Harlan when the buzzer sounded. Hamilton buzzed Charles in while Matthew darted into the kitchen to stir — or whatever it was he had to do — and Harlan gave a silent *thank you* to whoever was looking out for him.

"Hey, everyone, sorry I was late. I was a little tied up."

Charles said it casually enough that it could have been an innocent comment — coming from someone else.

Harlan blushed and ducked his head, and he heard Hamilton snort from across the living room. Charles laughed at his own double entendre and, to Harlan's horrified surprise, so did Matthew. Did Matthew *know* what line of work Charles was in?

Harlan shot Hamilton a sharp look, and the policeman shrugged, palms out, in a gesture of *don't blame me!* Harlan couldn't decide if that meant he *had* told Matthew about Charles' profession and didn't see a problem with doing so, if he hadn't told Matthew but his boyfriend had figured it out on his own or that Hamilton and Matthew were both completely innocent and Matthew had only laughed at what was simply — as far as he knew — a common saying.

Harlan doubted very much it was the third option, and he fully intended to interrogate Hamilton about it later.

"Just let me wipe the secret blend of herbs and spices off my hands!" Matthew called to Charles. "Then I'll come say hi… And cat hair. Sorry! That stuff gets everywhere."

Harlan heard the sound of running water.

So far there had been no sign of cats — or *a* cat — but Harlan looked around with renewed interest. Pets were always a great distraction from having to be social. Maybe *he* should get a cat.

"Hey!" Hamilton and Charles exchanged a very manly half-hug, half vigorous back-clap that made Harlan feel weirdly excluded from 'the boys' club'. "Good to see you!"

"You too, man!"

Harlan was a little surprised by how warmly they'd greeted each other, but then again, they had met under the kinds of circumstances that forged bands of brothers.

Where had *that* thought come from?

Still drying his hands on a brightly coloured dish cloth, Matthew swept out of the kitchen. He threw the towel over his shoulder and approached Charles with partially open arms, clearly inviting a hug but also giving Charles space to decline and go for a handshake or something instead.

Harlan wasn't surprised when Charles went in for a hug, this time without the back-slapping camaraderie.

"It's very nice to meet you at last—both of you. You have no idea what I've had to do to make this dinner happen," Matthew laughed.

"Okay, okay, we've all met, and everyone's buddy-buddy. Back you go." Cheeks ever-so-slightly red, Hamilton shooed Matthew back into the kitchen, following right behind him.

"You weren't really...*really* tied up, were you?" Harlan asked softly.

"No. Maybe just a little wishful thinking," Charles assured him with a kiss.

A moment later Harlan heard clothing rustle, followed by a tiny moan.

"I think they're making out," Charles whispered.

Harlan nodded, grinning.

"Holy shit, they're so in love that they can't keep their—" Charles cut himself off when Hamilton reappeared, his face redder and his tie askew.

"What can I get you to drink?" Hamilton asked a little breathlessly, straightening his clothing.

"I'd take a beer, if you've got one."

"Coming right up." He returned a moment later with two beers with the caps already off.

Harlan didn't recognize the brand — not that he knew a lot about beer — but they looked artisanal and he suspected they were Matthew's choice. He doubted Hamilton was that particular about what he drank.

"Can I give either of you a hand in the kitchen?" Charles offered.

Hamilton laughed, passing Charles one of the beers. "Nah. I just tried to help, and I got booted back out here. But he said it won't be long."

"Not long at all!" Matthew announced. "Let's eat."

* * * *

"How did you and Matthew meet?" Charles asked.

Harlan swallowed his mouthful. It was such a nice, normal question to ask when meeting someone — one that never would have occurred to him.

Matthew and Hamilton turned and smiled at each other, actually holding hands on top of the table. Even more surprising, it was Hamilton who'd reached for Matthew.

"I volunteer with a trans youth-mentoring program," Hamilton said, which was news to Harlan. Harlan didn't have much of a personal life, aside from Charles, and he'd kind of assumed, based on Hamilton's silence, that his was the same. *Apparently not.*

"Oh, that's fantastic! I donate to them."

Hamilton glanced at Charles, then at Harlan. He grinned. "Holy shit, you didn't tell him!" he crowed, slapping the table with one hand and startling Harlan and Matthew a little.

"Tell him...?" Harlan asked, his eyes bouncing between the other three men.

"About me. You didn't tell him about me."

"Oh! No, of course not! I assumed you told me that in confidence."

Hamilton laughed, shaking his head. "I assumed you'd tell *Charles*!" He turned to Charles. "I'm trans."

Harlan noticed that Matthew was completely focused on Charles, waiting for his reaction.

Charles grinned, half-standing and reaching across the table to give Hamilton a clap on the shoulder. "Hey, that's awesome!" He sat down again. "I'm glad you trust me enough to tell me that."

Hamilton nodded at him. "Still can't believe you never told him. Good job, Brand." He managed to make it sound both sincere and teasing at the same time.

"Matthew is Two-Spirit, not trans, but he goes there at least a few times a year to do a presentation about mental health and speak to the Indigenous youth. When we met, my mentee was Indigenous, and we met through him. She's moved on, but we still keep in touch. Maybe one day I'll even let you meet him, Brand. And you, Charles."

"Do you have pictures?" Charles asked eagerly. Another normal question that Harlan never would have asked.

Hamilton whipped out his phone, quickly scrolled through and handed it to Charles.

Harlan could just see a picture of Hamilton standing with his hand resting on the shoulder of a smiling young woman.

"That's Tabitha." He took his phone back and scrolled again. "And this is my current youth, Hank."

Harlan wanted to look through this unexpected window into Hamilton's life while he could. He peered over Charles' shoulder. This picture showed Hamilton with a tall young man who looked East Asian.

Hamilton and Charles happily chatted about Hamilton's volunteer work for a while—the volunteer work Harlan had known nothing about, but that Charles had learned about within half an hour of talking to him in a non-life-or-death situation.

Harlan was happy to let the conversation flow over him without being forced to add to it.

He wasn't sure how the topic of Charles' ability had come up while they were eating. Matthew already seemed to know about it. Harlan liked Matthew, and clearly Hamilton trusted him—which was quite the feat—but he'd only just met the man, only found out that he existed a few days ago. He found himself feeling strangely protective of Charles' as-far-as-he-knew-unique power.

"You've really never heard of anyone else with this ability?" Matthew asked.

Hamilton shrugged, and everyone's gaze turned to Harlan.

He tried not to flinch, concentrating on chasing and pinning down a suddenly all-important grain of rice on his plate.

He'd spent the better part of two decades at the Centre. If anyone had asked him, before he'd met Charles, he would've said he knew every type of psychic ability there was—most of them from personal experience, some just from reading. Each gifted person's ability was a little different, of course, but they tended to fall into broad categories—mediumship, telepathy, telekinesis, clairvoyance, technology manipulation and pyrokinesis. There was a fair bit of overlap between the categories.

He'd never heard of an *anti*-ability like Charles'.

Pretending the single grain filled his mouth and kept him from talking, Harlan shook his head while he 'chewed' it.

"Have you asked anyone at the Centre for Psychic Education and Research here in Toronto?" Matthew suggested.

Hamilton choked a little, pointedly staring down at his plate and not looking at Harlan.

It was the Centre's full name, but no one ever called it that.

A moment later, Harlan, Hamilton and Charles exchanged identical expressions of disbelief that none of them had thought of that. Harlan mentally kicked himself. Of *course*! How could he not have thought of that before? After he'd got over his strange unwillingness to talk about Charles' ability to suppress ghosts around Harlan, he'd asked the other police mediums during their support group and they'd all agreed they'd never heard of a power like Charles', and Harlan had left it at that. Well, if he were being honest, he'd *never* have told anyone but Hamilton about Charles' power, but the other police mediums knew both that Harlan had got through a choking fogbank of ghosts and that he'd brought his boyfriend into the situation, so it hadn't taken much for them to put two and two together and ask the right questions.

The Centre had all kinds of resources, including an extensive library with both modern studies and data and all kinds of historical documents about psychics. They also had connections to similar schools and facilities around the world. If anyone could help them with the mystery that was Charles, it would be the Centre.

Of course, there were reasons it hadn't occurred to Harlan to ask anyone at the Centre for advice. He hadn't been back since he'd begun his new life. He'd only spoken to Tom — the history teacher and student counsellor — a handful of times on the phone. He wanted to prove, to himself and to them, that he *could* live independently, that he didn't need babysitting.

Even, apparently, when their help would have been useful.

"I'll take that as a no," Matthew chuckled.

"That's a really good idea. Thank you." Harlan's already-high estimation of Matthew went up even more.

Matthew grinned, giving a little bow from the neck. "My pleasure. Sometimes all you need is a different perspective. Now. Who wants dessert?"

Harlan was stuffed — the meal had been amazing, as they'd all said more than once — but if the dessert was half as good, there was no way he could turn it down. All three of them raised their hands.

* * * *

Hamilton had taken Harlan home with him after work, but he got a ride back to his apartment from Charles.

"What did you think?" Charles asked, reaching between the seats to give Harlan's thigh a fond squeeze.

"The food was so good. I don't think I've ever eaten that well in my life."

Charles laughed. "I mean, I agree with you, and I think this means we need to go out for a nice dinner with them sometime, but that's not what I meant."

"You're a good cook," Harlan assured him.

"Eh. I can manage a few basic things, but nothing like that. I'd rather take them to a restaurant than try to match that."

"I don't think you *have* to match it." Though Harlan wasn't completely sure about that. Maybe it was yet another of those Obscure Adult Rules he was slowly picking up on.

Charles squeezed his leg again. "Thank you, and that's very sweet of you, but I meant what did you think of Matthew?"

"Oh!" Harlan was glad the dim light in the car hid his blush. Of *course* that was what Charles had meant! "I like him."

"I'm sensing a 'but'…"

"No! I— Maybe. Are you sure you don't have any telepathic ability? You haven't been holding out on me?" Harlan laughed nervously.

"Pretty sure. You still haven't actually said what the 'but' is."

"But…I can't believe this is the first time I've heard about him! And Hamilton didn't even tell me they *live* together! And," he quickly added to lighten the mood, realizing he'd spoken a little more emphatically than he'd meant to, "Matthew calls him 'Hamilton,' too. Not 'Curt.'"

Charles snorted. "That doesn't really surprise me." He gave Harlan a quick glance, sliding his hand down from Harlan's thigh to his hand. He wrapped his short, powerful fingers gently around Harlan's much longer, thinner ones. "It doesn't *really* surprise you, does it? Hamilton keeping stuff—personal stuff—from you?"

"No." Realizing he sounded like he was sulking, Harlan forced himself to continue. "It's just…I thought we were past that. That he was really starting to open up to me. That we were starting to be—"

"Harlan, I think this *is* him opening up to you."

Harlan blinked. "Well, yeah, I guess, but…" He threw up his hands in exasperation.

"He invited you over. For dinner. With his boyfriend. To *their* place," Charles pointed out.

"He said *Matthew* insisted on meeting me."

"I'm sure he did. It might even be one-hundred percent true, but that doesn't change the outcome."

"You're too fucking good at this…people stuff!" But Harlan couldn't help laughing at himself. "And I just suck at it. You're right. I know you're right." He turned to give Charles a thoughtful glance. "It's Sunday night."

"It is," Charles agreed.

"You don't work tomorrow." Normally Charles would have been at the club on a Sunday night, but he'd got someone to cover for him so he could make their dinner. Matthew, unlike the rest of them, worked a regular nine-to-five, Monday-to-Friday week and his schedule was less flexible.

"Indeed I don't."

"Oh my God, stop torturing me. You know what I want!" Harlan laughed. "That's *my* job, remember?"

He could just see Charles' lopsided grin by the dashboard light.

"Of course I'll spend the night." Charles followed Harlan into his apartment.

They couldn't play too hard because Harlan worked the next day, but Harlan pulled Charles down across his lap for a quick spanking, which left them both achingly hard. Charles sucked Harlan off, his dark eyes sparkling mischievously the whole time. They lay curled together on the bed, Harlan stroking Charles until he came with a hoarse shout.

Harlan was tired after the dinner, and he quickly started feeling sleepy. Charles relaxed against him and started snoring softly.

Chapter Three

Harlan hadn't been able to find a direct number to the Centre's library, and he didn't want to go there in person unannounced. He called the only number listed online. He'd searched his apartment for a phonebook and had been about to give up in frustration when he remembered he had the phonebook—along with everything else he could ever possibly want to know—in his pocket.

Except what he wanted to know about Charles' ability, apparently.

He reached one of the admin staff, a man whose name he hadn't known and didn't remember, even though he'd just heard it.

The man had remembered him, and he'd insisted on passing the phone around so everyone could say hi and ask how he was doing. He'd already been on the phone about a hundred times longer than he wanted—well, any phone conversation was too long, in his opinion—by the time he was finally transferred to the library. If he had to say, *'Fine, how about you?'* one more time he was going to scream — or hang up…or scream *then* hang up. Possibly the other way around.

"Harlan! Or should I say Mr. Brand?" The familiar voice of Eileen, the Centre's elderly librarian, was comforting. Harlan had never been much of a reader, but he had spent a lot of time in the library in order to avoid people when he wasn't allowed to just hide in his room.

"Just 'Harlan' is fine." She hadn't asked The Question…at least not yet. Hopefully it would stay that way. He'd hate to scream or hang up now that he'd finally got through to the person he was trying to talk to, especially because he hadn't got her extension.

"It's funny that you should call. I've been putting something together and I was planning to contact *you* in the next few days."

"Really?" Harlan felt a pit in his stomach. Just how far had word of Charles' ability spread?

"Yes. I heard all about that awful business with Samuel Harkness, of course, and, well, it got me thinking."

Harlan couldn't help flinching at the name of the serial killer who he, Charles and Hamilton had helped take down eight months earlier, even though he *knew* the man's foul spirit was gone from the world. He'd ripped it out himself.

"I knew I'd seen a few mentions of mediums doing things like that, draining the life from people, in some of our archived letters and journals and even a few newspaper clippings, but I never paid them much heed. I thought… Well, mediums and other psychics didn't always have the same status they do now, did they?"

Harlan — whose parents had abandoned him to be raised by the Centre when they'd found out he was a

40

medium — might have argued that they *still* didn't have that 'status', at least not universally. He stayed quiet.

"I thought they were just rumours, exaggerations... fearmongering. I didn't think there was any truth to them. But since his story came to light, I've been re-examining the information I have. Collating it. I've been emailing with some of the older schools across the world" — it was funny to imagine a woman Eileen's age using email, but in reality, she was better with computers than Harlan — "and speaking with Native Elders across Canada and the United States."

"And?" He couldn't contain his excitement. He'd thought Samuel's secrets had died with him, dispersed like his ghosts. It wasn't that Harlan wanted to learn how to use any of his evil, twisted power — he hoped that was gone for good — but he couldn't help being curious about the man himself.

She hummed thoughtfully. "He was clever. Samuel Harkness — the name you and the public know him by — does appear to be his birth name. But he went by many, many other names wherever he travelled."

"So he wasn't in Toronto for long."

"No, I don't believe so."

That made Harlan feel a little better about the fact that no one had realized there was a serial killer stalking the city until he'd come up with his theory, but it also filled him with dread. What if Samuel had simply moved on while Harlan had been trying to find him? He could have disappeared, begun hunting in a new city while Harlan came to believe, like everyone else, that he'd been wrong.

"I can't be certain that all these records are accurate or that they all refer to the same person, but I believe I've managed to trace most of his movements over the past eighty years or so."

41

"Wow."

"I've *also* come up with a handful of similar occurrences in medieval Europe, the Mali Empire and the Ming Dynasty in China. A few of the Elders in Quebec told me they've heard stories about similar powers — stealing the life-force from the living, using it to bind and control the spirits of those they've killed — since the beginning of the European colonization. I doubt that any of those refer to our Mr. Harkness — if he was, as the reports say, born in 1927 — but it does seem to indicate that he was, perhaps, not the first of his kind." She paused. "Hopefully the last."

"Hopefully the last," he echoed, as if it was a kind of charm. *"Wow,"* he repeated, knowing he sounded like an idiot. His brain was still trying to process everything she'd said, and he couldn't come up with anything more profound.

"Would you be interested in seeing what I've gathered?" She sounded almost shy, and he wondered how much, if any, her employers knew about her side project.

"Yes! Yes, of course, thank you!" He paused. "You haven't found out anything about Charles Moore, have you?"

"Who, dear?"

Right. Hamilton had been able to keep Charles' name out of the media. She'd probably never heard of him, and he wanted to keep it that way. Let her think his curiosity about this anti-ability was academic. It was even better that he had an unrelated excuse to visit her.

Now it was her turn to sound excited. "Is that one of the aliases he went by?"

"N-No, sorry. It's unrelated. Do you mind if I bring my partner? My *police* partner," he quickly added.

Normally he doubted Hamilton would be very enthusiastic about being volunteered to go to a library, but Harlan was sure Hamilton was just as curious to find out more about Samuel.

"Of course. I'm here all the time."

* * * *

"So, this is where you grew up." Hamilton looked around the Centre's lobby. "Nice."

It wasn't, not particularly. It looked like a middle-of-the-road hotel lobby at best.

Harlan was glad Eileen had told him about her research, making this police business so he could bring Hamilton. He'd planned on taking Charles when it had just been researching Charles' power, just so he wouldn't have to come back here alone, but he was glad it was Hamilton instead. Hamilton might not have ever seen the Centre before, but he knew this part of Harlan — the young, scared, insecure part. He didn't want Charles to see who or what he'd been before — only what he was now.

It wasn't that he was ashamed of coming from here, but he just... Well, he wasn't sure what he felt, but he didn't *think* it was shame.

Harlan hadn't spent much time in this part of the building since he'd first walked through the front doors almost seventeen years earlier. He'd come in with his parents, and they'd gone out without him. But he hadn't minded then. Didn't mind *now*, he told himself stubbornly, his nails biting into his palms. His life was unquestionably better than it would have been if they'd kept him, but that knowledge could never completely drive away the hurt of being abandoned.

He'd never met his younger brother, who'd been born after Harlan had 'left.' He'd never tried to contact him, didn't even know if their parents had told him he had an older brother.

"Brand." Harlan could tell from his tone that Hamilton had already said it a few times. "You good?"

One of those strange, sourceless shivers everyone seemed to get from time to time rolled from the top of his head down to his feet. "Fine," Harlan replied, a little more sharply than he'd intended.

"All right." Hamilton didn't sound like he believed him, but he was apparently willing to let it go. Hamilton wasn't one to get into a conversation about emotions, never mind *start* one, if he didn't have to. "After you. I wanna get outta here ASAP. This place gives me the creeps." He rubbed his arms for effect.

"Gee, thanks." Growing up, Harlan had always seen it as a sanctuary. With the tiny trace of mediumship ability he suspected Hamilton possessed, he probably hadn't felt the constantly renewed ghost wards ringing the Centre as anything more than a prickle. To Harlan, even though he was getting used to having ghosts around him all the time, crossing the barrier felt the same way it had when he'd first arrived — like walking into silence and solitude after a lifetime of noise and crowds.

Hamilton playfully punched his arm. "Any time, bud."

"The library is this way." He was pretty sure. He would've been able to find it from the dorms, no problem, but he had no business there. He was surprised — and, if he was being honest with himself, a little hurt — that no one had been waiting to greet him, but he pushed that thought aside. Maybe Eileen hadn't told anyone he was coming.

He almost offered to show Hamilton his old room but realized in time that someone else was almost certainly living there by now. The Centre usually ran near capacity, with a short waiting list. Even if he hadn't taken all his personal possessions, it wouldn't have been the same room.

He got turned around twice and pretended not to see Hamilton snickering before they finally found the library.

"Harlan!" Eileen greeted them with open arms, lowering them when she saw Harlan's expression. "Right, you're not much of a hugger, are you? In any case, it's good to see you. And who's this?"

Hamilton stepped forward before Harlan had to fumble his way through introductions. "I'm Officer Curt Hamilton, Brand's partner."

Eileen covered her mouth with both hands, then fanned her face. "Ooh, *Brand*! So formal! I'm glad to see you've found a place in the world, Harlan. And it's *very* nice to meet you, Curt."

Harlan definitely expected Hamilton to correct her — especially because even Matthew called him Hamilton, and *especially* because Eileen was clearly flirting with him — but he just grinned and offered his hand.

She gave a little curtsy while she shook it. "Now, then, I suppose you boys want to look at my little folder, hmm?"

"That is why we're here, ma'am," Hamilton said in his best talking-to-civilians voice, clearly playing along.

"Right this way." She got a file from behind her desk and led them through the library.

As they passed, a few heads popped up from behind books. Harlan didn't recognize any of them.

They followed her to a small study room, where she set the folder down on the table. "Well, I'd best leave you to it. Come let me know if you have any questions," she said, without showing any sign of actually leaving.

Hamilton glanced at Harlan, grinning. "Why don't you stay and show us what you've found, Ms....?"

She immediately sat beside him. "Oh, Eileen is fine, dear." She lightly patted his shoulder. "Now then." As soon as she'd swept the file closer to herself, she was all business. "Here on the first page is my timeline of Mr. Harkness' travels, or at least what I've been able to make of them." She traced her finger from a dot labelled 'Death – 2020' all the way back to the first dot, 'Birth – 1927.'

The information was all laid out, year by year, in the timeline, but Eileen turned out to be a gifted storyteller and turned the dry, historical facts into a narrative.

"He was born in Walworth in England in 1927. His father and uncle were tailors. His uncle moved to Canada when Samuel was very young, and the rest of the family followed when Samuel was ten years old. His uncle and father opened a tailor shop in Toronto, where they were quite successful."

It was strange for Harlan to hear her call him Samuel. He'd never really considered that the monster he'd destroyed had been a child at some point, with a family and a past beyond mayhem and slaughter. Maybe they should have asked her to go and read the file on their own.

Hamilton's expression was still perfectly neutral. Harlan couldn't tell if it was getting to him as well.

"He came full circle, then," Hamilton said thoughtfully. "He came back to Toronto."

Eileen nodded. "That's right. And I don't think it was the first time – but I'm getting ahead of myself.

Now, a few years later, when Samuel was about twelve or thirteen, his younger sister died suddenly, and her cause of death was only listed as 'accidental.' Apparently, she and Samuel had been quite close. Now this is speculation on my part—"

"Do you think *he* killed her?" Harlan blurted.

She gave him the sort of frown that only an elderly librarian can achieve, and he leaned back in his chair again. "This is a bit of speculation on my part," she repeated, "but no, I don't believe he did—at least not intentionally. Shortly after her death, all record of Samuel disappears from the family's history, and I strongly suspect he was...encouraged...to leave town. I believe he tried to put his sister's spirit into either her own corpse or another girl's. The Centre possesses—ha, no pun intended!—the journals of several of Toronto's former mediums. There's an entry from about the time in question where the medium prevents just such a thing from happening, though no names are mentioned."

For some reason, the thought made Harlan's neck prickle. Mediums from the past, doing the same or similar work as him, leaving their legacies behind. His would only be police reports and memes sifted from his Tumblr.

Should I start writing a diary?

"The next trace of Samuel I found isn't until after the war. How he spent those years is unclear, but in late 1945, there's a record of him joining a small-time travelling circus in New York, where he apprenticed to a woman with the stage name Madame Lupei. She was a medium of some renown in her day, though she left New York in a hurry after some sort of scandal.

"That is the last time his name appears in any official capacity until his body was identified last year."

Harlan frowned then turned to Hamilton. "How *did* they identify his body?" He'd wondered from time to time but had never got around to asking.

Eileen answered before Hamilton could. "They found a mourning photograph of him with his sister's body in his pocket. Their names were written on the back. I have a copy of it, if you'd like to see it."

Harlan shook his head, feeling a little sick. He didn't want to see a picture of Harkness. A deep, primal, superstitious part of him worried it would somehow invoke him.

"You said that's the last we know about him, but there's way more on the timeline," Hamilton pointed out.

"Correct, young man." Eileen graced him with an approving smile. "He's not mentioned by *name*, but I was able to trace a series of mysterious deaths and disappearances. It appears that he left the circus in Chicago. *Incidentally*, an obituary for Madame Lupei is printed in the *Chicago Tribune* at around that time."

"You think he killed *her*," Harlan guessed, hoping he was actually right this time. Maybe he wanted a 'good-boy' smile too.

"Yes, I do," Eileen agreed. "I believe she was one of the first spirits he bound to him and — because she was a medium — she substantially increased his power."

Harlan felt even more queasy. He could only be glad that he'd freed her, along with all the others, when he'd killed Harkness.

"The next time I can be reasonably certain of his involvement was a series of deaths and disappearances across Iowa — in small towns, where that sort of thing was noticed, unlike here. Then North Dakota, a few years later. It appears he then returned to Canada, because I was able to track down a string of mysterious bodies found in northern Manitoba."

"Why do you think they're all related to Harkness?" Hamilton asked.

"We can never be certain about the disappearances, of course, but for all of the *deaths* I've mentioned, the bodies were described as 'mummified'."

Harlan and Hamilton exchanged glances.

"Yeah, that sounds about right," Hamilton agreed.

"Thank you," Eileen said dryly, then ruined the effect by winking at him. "Then there's a rather large gap, either in his activity or in the records I could obtain, but the next place he surfaces is right back here in Toronto in 1955." She flipped through the folder, wetting her fingertip with her tongue between each page. "Ah, here it is." She turned the file towards Harlan and Hamilton, showing them a newspaper clipping with the headline "Preserved Bodies Found in Warehouse."

Hamilton whistled softly. "Yep, that sounds like him."

"I'm glad you agree with me, Curt," she teased.

He grinned in response.

"Then he gets even more difficult to follow, either because he got better at covering his tracks or, possibly, stopped killing for a while."

Harlan shook his head. "I don't think so. Maybe about either of those."

She shrugged one bony shoulder. "Or there could be some other explanation," she agreed. "It does seem that he visited Toronto at least once more before his most recent incursion." She flipped back to the timeline, tapping dots as she spoke. "There are traces of him across Ontario, Quebec, even into New Brunswick and Maine."

Harlan couldn't wait any longer to ask, "If this was all here, just sitting out there for someone to find it... Why did it take this long?"

Harlan could feel Hamilton bristle beside him at the insinuation that the police hadn't done their jobs properly.

Eileen held up her hands. "Harlan, that's not fair. Yes, most of what I've told you is a matter of public record, or drawn from the Centre's archives, but I had to do some *serious* digging to put it all together. I dedicated a lot of time to this little passion project." She laughed. "Besides, I already knew I was looking for something, and more or less what that something was." She turned to smile at Hamilton, who smiled back at her.

Harlan looked away. "You're right. I'm sorry."

She patted his hand, and Hamilton stopped frowning at him.

"Well, I should really go check on those hooligans out there." She stood slowly, stiffly.

Hamilton jumped to his feet and offered her a hand, which she accepted with a titter. "Thank you, young man." She gave his hand a little squeeze. "I'll leave the file with you for now, in case you want to look at anything. Just give it back to me before you go. This is *my* research, and it doesn't leave this building without my permission. Understood?"

Harlan and Hamilton nodded meekly.

Harlan held up a hand. "Wait! Before you go..." He glanced at Hamilton, unsure if he should ask what he'd originally called her to find out, especially in front of Hamilton.

She paused with her hand on the knob. "Yes?"

"Have you ever heard of someone with an...anti-medium ability?" he asked slowly. "That's why I originally called you, but then, when you told me about your research, I forgot to ask you."

She frowned. "Ah. You're talking about the young man who helped you defeat Samuel."

Hamilton shot both of them a suspicious glance.

Harlan threw his hands up. "Hey, I haven't been going around telling people!"

Eileen laughed. "Let's just say I'm very good at collecting information and making connections. If I understand correctly, Harlan—ghosts cannot appear around you as long as Charles Moore is in your vicinity?" She grinned. "I looked him up after you mentioned his name the last time we spoke."

He nodded.

"Hmm." She tilted her head thoughtfully. "I must say that I never have come across information about such an ability before, but I'll definitely let you know if I do."

Something about her smile made Harlan think she'd *already* started looking.

She nodded decisively and left, closing the door behind her.

Holding the folder Eileen had put together, Harlan couldn't help thinking of the lives that might have been spared, families who wouldn't have wondered what had happened to their loved ones until the day they'd died, if someone had put all this together sooner— someone competent, like Eileen, who wouldn't just blunder through the way *he* had.

"Hey." Hamilton rested a hand on his shoulder. "You can't think about shit like that. It'll drive you nuts."

"Yeah? What am I thinking?" Harlan snapped, pulling away.

"Whoa…okay." Hamilton took a step back, hands up.

Harlan sighed. "Sorry. I didn't mean to… I just felt… I *feel* so —"

"Guilty?"

Harlan nodded silently.

"That's the job," Hamilton said, more gently than Harlan had ever heard him before. "That's it, kid."

Chapter Four

They were just about to leave the Centre when Harlan heard rapid footsteps behind them.

"Harlan!"

He turned to see Tom hurrying across the lobby.

"I'm glad I caught you in time!" Tom doubled over, hands braced on his knees, one finger raised in a silent plea for them to wait.

Hamilton shot him a questioning frown, and Harlan could only shrug in response.

After a few long, panting breaths, Tom straightened. "I meant to be here to meet you when I heard you were coming, but we had a bit of a...situation today."

"A situation?"

Tom shook his head, holding up his hands on either side of his reddened face and waving them dismissively. "Oh, no! It's nothing. It's just a little prank, that's all." He laughed, a little too loudly, the sound echoing in the empty lobby.

God. Has he always been that annoying?

"What kind of 'prank'?" Hamilton asked.

"Ah... Since you're here, maybe you could help us with this!" Tom told Harlan. "Put some of your new skills to work for your old home, eh?"

Tom's smile seemed almost sickly sweet to Harlan now, and he couldn't believe he'd ever found it comforting as a kid.

Without waiting for a response from Harlan, he turned to Hamilton, offering his hand. "I'm Tomas Addison. I've known Harlan here a *long* time. Isn't that right?" He said it almost possessively, reaching out with his free hand to squeeze Harlan's arm. It was probably meant to be friendly, but it was a little too strong, bordering on painful.

He's probably just stressed about this 'incident', whatever it is, Harlan decided.

"And you are, Officer...?" Tom shot Harlan a disapproving look, making it clear *he* should have been the one to do the introductions. He'd always been a stickler about that kind of thing. Some of the other kids had called him *Anal Addison* behind his back.

"Hamilton." Apparently he wasn't taken in by Tom's overeager charm. He shook Tom's hand as briefly as possible before practically dropping it. "What can Brand do?"

Tom gave him a long, slow smile, as though they'd just shared a joke. Harlan knew Hamilton hadn't meant to imply that he was useless. He thought that was exactly how Tom had chosen to interpret it. "Well, I suppose that remains to be seen. This way, please."

"Mr. Addison, we're police officers, not maintenance men or what-have-you. Did you place a nine-one-one call?"

Harlan couldn't help a little thrill of delight at Hamilton referring to him as a police officer, which he technically wasn't. In fact, 'maintenance man' was much closer to his job description—but he still liked hearing Hamilton say it.

Tom did his dismissive hand-flapping thing again. "Oh, no! No, no, it's nothing that serious," he assured Hamilton. "It's just that you're *here*. And I thought it might be good training for Harlan to take a look."

"Brand?" Hamilton asked, leaving the decision up to Harlan.

Harlan got the feeling Hamilton was fully prepared to back him up if he said he wanted to just leave, which gave Harlan the confidence to ask, "What exactly is this 'incident', Tom?" *Or should I go back to calling him Mr. Addison, since I'm here on official business? Kind of.*

Tom glanced around the empty lobby, then shook his head. "No. Not here. My office, please." He turned on his heel, clearly expecting them to follow.

Harlan couldn't help bristling a little. Tom was still treating him like a child.

He relaxed slightly when he noticed that Hamilton just looked amused.

Hamilton gave a mock-bow, extending his arms to usher Harlan ahead of him.

Rolling his eyes, Harlan followed Tom into the administrative section of the building. He stopped in front of Tom's door—each teacher at the Centre had their own office. He frowned when Tom continued past it to another doorway. "That's the *director's* office."

Tom paused, his hand on the knob. "Oh. I'm so sorry. Did no one tell you? Ms. Hill passed away several months ago. You should have been informed of that."

Harlan bristled again at the watered-down euphemism for 'died'. He really hadn't missed *that* about the Centre.

"Oh." Harlan hadn't known the director well — he'd known her predecessor, Dr. Cunningham, much better — but it still stung to know the place he'd spent most of his life was going on without him, going through major changes he didn't know about. "So...you're the new director?"

"Sure am! C'mon in." Tom beckoned them into the office and closed the door behind himself.

Harlan had been in the director's office a few times. Eyeing the built-in oak shelves, wing-back chair and wide desk, a cynical part of him couldn't help thinking what an upgrade this office was from Tom's prior, much more utilitarian one.

There was a large, noticeable new addition since the last time Harlan had been inside — a large picture in an ornate frame of Tom standing in front of his house. The only word that came to mind was 'pretentious'. He wouldn't have guessed that was Tom's style. Tom had always seemed — or at least *acted* — very down to earth.

Tom sat behind the — behind *his* — desk, gesturing for Harlan and Hamilton to take the two seats opposite him.

Sitting in front of that desk, Harlan couldn't help feeling like a kid again, getting in trouble because he hadn't done his homework for a week. It was like being a teenager called to the director's office for skipping a meal.

He realized he was slouching and forced himself to sit straight, copying Hamilton's ever-perfect posture. He *wasn't* a kid. This place had no power over him anymore. They'd asked for him. They needed *his* help this time.

"So?" Hamilton asked. He tended to turn monosyllabic when he wanted to hurry things along or get someone to start talking.

"So?" Tom repeated. He met Hamilton's eyes with a flash of challenge, just for a moment, before he dropped his gaze and was mild-mannered Mr. Addison again.

Harlan frowned. Hamilton could be...abrasive, but Tom's reaction had seemed oddly strong.

Tom laced his fingers over his blotter. "So...we had a bit of a... Well, no sense beating about the bush, not with you." He smiled at Hamilton. "A section of our ghost wards failed this morning, and we had an uninvited guest as a result that frightened a few of the children. They're all fine!" he assured them quickly, as though they'd questioned him. He waved his hands beside his head again.

Had he always done that, and Harlan had never noticed or forgot — or was this something new? Harlan had spent most of his life looking down, so either possibility was just as likely.

He focused on the important part, what Tom had said. "*Our ghost wards failed.*" It was a phrase straight out of Harlan's worst nightmares. He'd arrived at the Centre as a little boy, jumping at shadows because he'd already learned they sometimes had teeth. Stepping into the ghost-warded building had been like being able to breathe freely for the first time in his life, but he'd always had nightmares about the wards failing and ghosts pouring in. He *still* did, though they were usually set at the Centre rather than his apartment, which he was grateful for.

Although, a ghost had actually got into his apartment. One of the other tenants in the building had died and found a way past his wards. He'd had nearly died of hypothermia and Charles had rescued him. It had taken him a long time to feel completely secure alone in his apartment again.

Despite his nightmares, the Centre had always been safe…at least until today.

As though he'd either noticed or anticipated Harlan's reaction, Hamilton leaned over and gave him a subtle, reassuring nudge with his elbow.

Harlan took a deep breath, then another. "And you think it was a prank?" He couldn't imagine any of the mediumship students doing such a thing, and most of the other kids wouldn't be able to see the wards to destroy them. But what other explanation could there be?

Tom nodded.

"And you want us to take a look?"

"That's right. If you have time." Once again, he was looking at Hamilton, not Harlan. "We have a ward-painter on the way, but I think it would reassure the kids to have one of their own—*a former*—reassure them."

Hamilton shrugged, turning to Harlan.

"Okay." Harlan wasn't sure how 'comforting' he'd be. He wasn't a comforting person or a kid-person to begin with, and when he'd left the Centre almost a year earlier, all the mediumship students had been way younger than him. He hadn't known any of them well, hadn't spoken to them outside of class. Even *in* class he'd mostly ignored them.

"Great!" Tom tapped his fingertips on his blotter a few times, then stood. "That's just great."

They followed him to the dormitories. Harlan couldn't even identify all the emotions swirling through him when he saw the door to his old room — the room he'd lived in most of his life — and he was relieved when they passed it.

"This is where the ward failed." Tom ushered them into a room where a little Black girl sat on one of the two beds, holding a stuffed rabbit and absently petting the top of its head. She didn't look up when they entered.

She was a medium. Harlan could see a *shiver* around her, something like an aura or heatwaves off hot pavement, but it was faint, not much stronger than the inkling of power he suspected Hamilton possessed, really. He was slightly surprised that someone with so little ability was living at the Centre, but mediums were always in high demand, even relatively weak ones.

He couldn't help wondering if her parents had abandoned her the way his own had when he had been even younger than her. He wanted to ask her, tell her things got better, but he wasn't there to be a guidance counsellor. He had a job to do, but hopefully just the sight of him doing it would help her, show her a tiny window to what her life might be like once she left the Centre.

Surprisingly, Tom didn't introduce her or make her introduce herself. She ignored Harlan, so he was happy to ignore her in return.

He turned his attention to the ghost wards. Ward-painters were few and far between, and the wards needed to be redone frequently, making them costly to maintain. Even the oil used to paint them had to be specially prepared, usually by the warders themselves.

Because of this, wards were only used where absolutely necessary.

On the other hand, if they were more common, he and the other police mediums might be out of a job.

While he couldn't paint them and have them work, he could see them if he concentrated. Normally they were as invisible to him as they were to anyone without any mediumship, which he appreciated. When he *did* look at them, they were blindingly bright.

A special *blink* and there they were—a wide band of loops and spirals and spiky runes that meant nothing to him on their own but were familiar to him from a lifetime under their protection. He spun in a slow circle, following them around the room. Only the mediums had warding on their interior walls, more for their peace of mind than because there was actually a threat of ghosts coming from inside the Centre.

He came to an abrupt stop when he reached the outer wall. There, where the protection should have been strongest, was a gaping hole. He'd been expecting maybe a pinprick, a tiny break in the sigil where a child had chipped away the paint. A prank, like Tom had said.

Instead, the ward was just...gone. There was no trace of it on the wall's entire surface, not even the glow of a depleted ward that needed to be repainted. The edges of the break were perfectly straight, as though that section had been cut out.

Harlan blinked until the room returned to normal and approached the wall. There were no marks on it, no signs of cutting or scraping or scrubbing on the regular paint. "A student did this?"

Tom shrugged. "Must have been."

Harlan nibbled his forefinger, an old nervous habit he'd mostly stopped doing. He wasn't surprised that this place brought back old behaviours, things he thought he'd left behind.

He tried to come up with a theory about what had happened. A student must have been messing around with their power, made a mistake and hadn't told anyone so they wouldn't get in trouble.

He looked around the room with his regular vision. There were pictures and other personal belongings on Rabbit Girl's side, but the other bed was stripped and there was no sign of another child living there. "You're lucky to have a room to yourself," he said, more to himself than to her.

She looked up at Tom, and whatever she saw on his face made her eyes widen a little, and she quickly shook her head.

Harlan wished he could've turned in time to see Tom's reaction without being noticed.

"Her roommate was recently offered a position at an exclusive school in Europe," Tom told him.

Something about that seemed odd to Harlan. Tom had always been the Centre's biggest fan, and it surprised him that Tom would suggest there was a better school anywhere on Earth.

He glanced back at the girl. She met his eyes for just a moment, then shrugged and looked away.

He stood. "Well, there's no ghost here now." He closed his eyes and reached out with his ability. With the ghost wards surrounding him on three sides, he felt like his ears were stuffed with cotton, but his senses could pass through the outer wall. The closest spirit was several blocks away—a harmless repeater, so old and worn that it didn't even react to him brushing it with his power. It wouldn't leave its place. It wouldn't enter the school.

"You're safe," he told the girl.

She nodded again, not looking up from her rabbit.

There was a soft knock on the door, and a woman who looked East Indian came in a moment later. She carried a wooden toolbox full of tiny jars of oil, and a canvas roll he assumed held her brushes. "Hi!" she said, smiling cheerily at everyone. "Is this where I'm meant to be?" She had a faint British accent. "Ooh!" Looking at the section of un-warded wall, she grimaced. "Yeah, I'll say it is. It's all right, love," she told the girl. "I'll get this patched up in just a tick and you'll be all right."

She got to work, whistling to herself as she unscrewed the tops of several jars and selected a brush.

"What could have done this?" Harlan asked, hoping he wouldn't distract her.

"I'm not sure," she admitted, glancing over her shoulder at him. She looked a little surprised, as though she expected *him* to know. "I've never seen anything like it."

He shivered, trying to convince himself this *had* just been some kind of accident. A prank, like Tom had said, at worst. The wards would be back in place in a few hours, and if a ghost had got out of the room and into the Centre at large, someone would notice it in no time and an instructor would dispel it.

Still… He couldn't shake his sense of foreboding.

"Well. If that's all…?" Tom broke the silence.

Harlan nodded.

Hamilton nudged him with his elbow, tilting his head in the girl's direction.

It took Harlan a moment to figure out what he wanted.

He stopped in the doorway and turned back. "It's all right," he assured the girl, echoing the warder's words. "You'll be okay."

Chapter Five

"I have...a bit of an unusual idea for our date tonight," Charles confessed.

The only thing Charles had told him ahead of time was to wear sturdy shoes. Not that Harlan had any other kind...or maybe he did. *What makes a shoe qualify as 'sturdy'?*

Charles already had Harlan in the car and was driving towards whatever their mystery destination was, which Harlan thought was unfair. He could at least have said something before Harlan had left his apartment, so he could attempt to psych himself up for...whatever was happening. During his childhood and teenage years, a lot of people at the Centre had tried to get him to do new things in order to 'get him out of his comfort zone'. He'd hated all of the activities and it had only made him resentful and more determined to be by himself as often as possible. One of the best parts about being an adult, of being out on his own, was being able to *stay* in his comfort zone. He liked his comfort zone. He could choose when and where and how he wanted to come out of it, and it hurt a little that Charles had made a unilateral decision to take him out of it. He didn't, as a rule, like surprises — even 'good' ones.

He shook his head, a physical resetting of his thoughts. No, Charles knew him. Charles wouldn't set him up to fail. It might be unusual, but Charles had picked it because he thought Harlan would like it.

Charles glanced over at him briefly, lightly resting a hand on Harlan's thigh as he drove. "Hey, are you okay? I'm sorry, this was a dumb idea. I should've told you ahead of time. I can tell you now, if you'd like."

Harlan shook his head again, giving Charles' hand a squeeze. "No. I'm fine. I...I want it to be a surprise." He usually liked Charles' surprises. He realized he'd actually liked all of them so far.

"Okay. If you hate it, or even if you just hate me surprising you, I won't do it again."

Harlan laughed, shaking his head. "Deal. But" — he bit his lip — "I bet I'll like it."

"I hope so." Charles grinned. "Like I said, it's kinda weird, but I hope it'll be good-weird."

"I'm sure it will," Harlan assured him. He wasn't sure. Not at all.

Charles stopped in front of a building with a yellow-and-black sign that said 'Smash City'. "We're here."

The name didn't mean anything to Harlan, and he was tempted to sneakily take his phone out of his pocket and google it, but he didn't.

Charles was clearly excited about whatever they were about to do, and just as clearly trying to hide it. Harlan was pretty sure it was because he didn't want Harlan to feel pressured to enjoy it, which Harlan thought was sweet. He got out of the car and followed Charles inside.

"I'm booked under Charles Moore," Charles told the man at the front desk, who nodded and said, "Room three."

Charles led them to a small room, gesturing grandly with his arm out to usher Harlan inside.

He stepped into the room. He couldn't help peering around anxiously, but nothing jumped out at him or whatever he'd been afraid of. The walls were painted black and yellow, like the sign. The only things in the room were a stack of tires with a piece of plywood covering the hole, a white ceramic vase on top of that and a plastic tub full of what seemed to be random objects. There was also a printer and an old computer monitor.

He turned to Charles, confused.

Charles grinned at him and handed him a pair of safety goggles. "Baseball bat or crowbar?" he asked after Harlan put them on.

"What?"

"It's a rage room. We get to break all this stuff. I know you've had a lot of stress at work lately, and I thought this might help." Charles slipped on his own goggles, then bent to pick up a crowbar in one hand and a wooden bat in the other, offering them both to Harlan.

"Break...?" Harlan glanced between Charles and the white vase. "Um...crowbar?"

"Good choice." Charles handed it to him and stepped back. "They let you play music, but I thought that might be a bit overwhelming."

As if to prove his point, Harlan stared between the bar in his hands and the vase. It just seemed so...wrong.

Wasteful, maybe. Could he really just swing the crowbar and smash the vase?

"Want some help?" Charles purred, stepping up behind him.

"Sure?" Harlan wished he could stop saying everything as a question, but he couldn't seem to.

Charles gently placed his hands over Harlan's more delicate ones, guiding his arms and the crowbar so they were level with the top of the stack of tires.

He twisted Harlan, using his hips to guide him, then straightened them out again. The tip of the crowbar hit the edge of the vase. It teetered for a moment—Harlan realized he was holding his breath for some reason—and then toppled off the side. It only broke into a few large pieces, but...Harlan couldn't deny that it had been deeply, primally satisfying.

He turned to grin at Charles, who'd taken a step back.

Charles inclined his head in the direction of the bin, and Harlan nodded. Charles picked out an ugly porcelain figurine of a donkey with two baskets attached to it and set it on top of the tires.

Harlan took a deep breath and brought the crowbar straight down on top of the tacky thing. It exploded, startling him a little and showering him with ceramic chips. He realized he was grinning—practically beaming.

"Great job!"

With anyone else, Harlan might have felt patronized, but he could tell Charles was genuinely encouraging him. "Thanks."

"Want another?"

Harlan nodded eagerly, barely hesitating as he smashed a beer stein.

He worked his way through several more objects, surprised to realize he was panting a little. His arms were actually starting to get a little tired, but he didn't want to stop. He glanced in the plastic tub and was relieved to see that there was still plenty more to break.

"Baseball bat?" he asked, almost shyly, but he couldn't stop grinning.

"Here you go." Charles took the crowbar and set it aside, then put a large glass on the plywood.

Harlan took his best 'baseball' stance, which was probably completely stupid looking, but he was too pumped to really care.

He swung at the glass and knocked it right off the stack of tires and into the wall behind it. He had mostly asked for the bat on a lark and to give himself a tiny rest. He hadn't expected it to really feel any different than the crowbar, but it did. He could feel the impact differently through the wood than through the metal, and he wasn't sure which he preferred. He'd just have to break a few more things and find out.

"Here... Take a look at this." Charles held out his phone.

Harlan took it and saw that Charles had taken a video of him. He hadn't even noticed—which was good, because if he *had*, he would have been self-conscious about it. He pressed play and watched himself, in slow motion, hit the glass and shatter it into a million pieces. "Whoa," he said, turning to Charles. "That's so cool!"

"Want to keep going?"

Harlan nodded, then frowned. "But you haven't done any yet."

"I'm enjoying watching you," Charles assured him.

"Okay, but promise you'll do at least one."

"I promise." Charles set the printer down for him to destroy next.

This one took several strikes, even with Harlan hitting harder with each swing. Finally it lay in pieces around him, and he was breathing hard now but nowhere near done.

Charles set up the monitor then a series of more small, breakable items.

Harlan switched back to the crowbar and decided he liked it better.

After a few minutes of breaking things as quickly as Charles could set them in place and get out of the way, Harlan emerged from his berserker state long enough to glance in the bin. There were only a few objects left.

Really panting now, he held out the crowbar to Charles.

"Are you sure? I really don't mind just watching you go to town." There was a deep rumble in Charles' voice that made Harlan think *just* how much he didn't mind, and what they might get up to after they were done at Smash City.

"I'm sure." He set up a porcelain figurine of a boy and a girl holding hands and got out of range.

Grinning, Charles brought the crowbar straight down, sending bits of face and clothing flying in all directions. The base was still intact, so Charles swung again, pulverizing it. "Wow. This is actually really fun."

"It is," Harlan agreed. "Thanks." He made a mental note. He wanted to remember this the next time Charles wanted to surprise him, so he could at least try to be excited *as well as* freaked out.

Now that he'd come back to himself, he realized his arms were aching. He suspected he'd be sore in the morning, and Hamilton would probably tease him about it. What would he tell Hamilton he'd been doing? *Maybe just the truth.*

He set a beer glass on the plywood, and Charles handily smashed it. "Want to switch to the bat?" Harlan offered. He was feeling a little guilty that he'd broken so many things and only left Charles with a few — not that Charles seemed to mind.

Not that I do, either, he thought as he passed Charles the bat and took the bar. He seemed to be having the same reaction as Charles. Watching his boyfriend destroy stuff was unexpectedly turning him on. Now he was glad there were only a few objects left and he wouldn't have to wait long. Too bad they'd have to drive to Harlan's apartment before they could do anything.

"I think I like the bat better," Charles announced, after driving a vase into the wall.

"And I like the crowbar." Harlan grabbed the last item in the bin — a ceramic windmill — then held up his free hand. "Oh, one sec." He set the tacky thing down and reached into his pocket for his phone.

"Gonna take a slow-mo video?"

"Yeah. I want you to have one too."

"Ready?"

Harlan started recording, then nodded. "Ready."

Charles hammed it up a little for the camera, swinging from way behind his back, breaking the windmill even before it hit the wall.

"Whew." Charles wiped mostly imaginary sweat off his brow. He glanced in the bin. "I guess that's it."

"Yeah. Sorry I did so many of them."

Charles grinned at him. "Like I said, I *really* enjoyed watching."

Harlan looked down and smirked. "Yeah, I can tell."

"Should we get outta here?"

Harlan glanced around at the debris-covered floor. "Do we have to clean up?"

"Nope! Cleanup is included. We just have to leave everything here and we're good to go."

"Let's go, then." Harlan took off his goggles and set them on the stack of tires, giving Charles a little nudge to hurry him along.

Charles laughed. "Well, I'm glad I'm not the only one who's a little excited. Your place, I assume?"

It was closer. "Yeah."

They could barely keep their hands off each other during the drive, but they managed to limit themselves to Charles' hand resting on Harlan's thigh—his *outer* thigh—while he drove. Harlan had seen the ghosts of too many mangled car-crash victims to risk doing anything more, and Charles was a cautious, careful person. It was one of the things Harlan lo—*liked* about him.

Finally they were up the stairs and unlocking the apartment door and only making out a *little* in the hallway. Harlan's weird neighbour, who apparently still had a thing for him, even after the number of times he'd seen Harlan with Charles, frowned at them before disappearing into his own suite.

He had an uncanny ability to be lurking in the hall just as Harlan got home or left. *Hmm.*

But that wasn't important.

Charles slammed the door behind them, and they crashed against it together, their bodies already intertwined. They kissed, long and deep, then Charles pulled back for a breath.

"We should probably…"

Harlan nodded. This was only keeping the edge off. They were wearing way too much for true satisfaction.

He twisted free and started pulling off his clothes, even as he ran to the bedroom. It was a miracle that he didn't trip himself.

"Someone's eager," Charles laughed. "And I'm glad it's not just me." He followed a little more slowly, almost stalking towards Harlan. He was just as naked by the time he crossed the threshold. "What were you —?"

"Get on all fours on the bed," Harlan told him. He was getting better at giving 'orders', and they rarely ended in a question anymore.

"Yes, Sir," Charles purred, doing what he was told. He leaned forward with his forehead touching the sheets — Harlan rarely bothered making his bed — and his knees spread with his ass way up in the air.

Harlan groaned.

"What? What's wrong?"

Harlan set a hand firmly on Charles' hip to keep him from flipping over to look at him. "I just can't decide what to do to you first."

"Ohhh… Fuck, you can't just say something like that and keep me waiting!" Charles squirmed, dropping his elbows and forearms onto the bed as well, offering himself up completely.

Harlan shivered with delight. He still couldn't believe that this broad, strong man would give himself up whenever he asked, surrender himself and let him drive them both mad with pleasure.

In response, Harlan put his other hand on Charles' opposite hip, then slid both palms down across the muscular swell of Charles' ass.

Charles moaned again, and he didn't say anything this time.

"Good," Harlan praised him, stroking Charles' hot skin a few more times while deciding what he wanted to do — not that he was going to tell Charles he'd made up his mind.

He lifted one hand and felt Charles tense and shift under him. Harlan knew he had probably given himself away already, but that was all right.

Keeping one hand firmly planted on Charles' hip, he lifted his free one and brought it down in a wide, stinging slap on Charles' ass cheek.

Charles arched and bucked beneath him, crying out softly.

Grinning, Harlan raised his hand again, giving Charles a series of quick swats that rocked him forward each time, even though he was braced on his knees, forehead and forearms. He got louder and louder with each strike, spreading his legs wider.

Harlan switched to his right hand and spanked Charles' other cheek so he wouldn't be uneven — and because his arm was starting to hurt already from breaking things earlier.

"That's it. That's it..." Charles moaned. "Yes!"

Harlan took a tiny step back so he could see more of Charles. He loved the way the root of Charles' thick, flushed cock jerked and bobbed beneath him every time Harlan struck, how close his heavy balls were drawn to his body.

Harlan shook out his hand, hoping Charles wouldn't notice, and he winced a little.

Charles' ass was nice and red, and Harlan thought he could get away with switching gears without disappointing Charles. He slid a hand between Charles' legs, gently cupping his balls and stroking them with his thumb.

Charles groaned and melted, spreading his knees even farther. If he minded that Harlan had stopped spanking him, he didn't say it out loud. Somehow, Harlan didn't think he minded all that much.

"What do you want?" he asked, stretching out one finger to trace the underside of Charles' cock.

It took Charles a few breathless seconds to answer in anything but moans. "You."

Harlan shivered at his reply, beaming down at Charles' back and kind of glad Charles couldn't see his probably dopey expression right now.

"I'd love to fuck you, to feel your hot ass against my thighs, but I think you're too close for that, aren't you?" It was only recently that Harlan had been able to start saying things like that without blushing or feeling like an idiot. Well, he might be blushing a little, but Charles couldn't see him.

"Mm-hmm," Charles agreed.

"How about this?" Harlan gently pulled Charles over onto his side, then kept rolling him until he was on his back.

Charles stretched out, extending his arms across the bed and letting his legs hang over the side.

Harlan grabbed his ankles to pull him a little farther down, so his ass was right on the corner of the mattress. He knelt between Charles' thighs, stroking a thumb over a vein that pulsed with Charles' heartbeat. He leaned forward, gently breathing on the glistening head of Charles' erection. "This way, your raw ass still gets rubbed against the sheets, and you don't have to last."

"Ohh-h…" Charles groaned, his whole body tensing for a moment.

Looking up, Harlan could just see that Charles' fists were clenched in the blankets.

Deciding he'd teased Charles—and himself—long enough, he slid his lips down past Charles' flared crown, letting them form a seal on the shaft just beneath Charles' head. He just held him there for a moment, feeling the weight, the heat in his mouth, tasting Charles' light sweat mixed with the still-faint salty tang of his pre-cum.

Charles' upper body collapsed onto the bed, and Harlan had to grab him by the ankles again to pull him back down within easy reach. He dropped one hand to wrap around Charles' shaft, but he had an especially wicked thought. He slid his other hand up Charles' short, stocky leg and down his inner thigh. He wedged his hand beneath Charles' ass and rubbed at the heated, sensitive skin there. He gave it a gentle squeeze to start, bobbing his head a little deeper until he could just feel Charles brushing the back of his throat.

He settled into a rhythm, taking Charles deep and nearly letting him pop free at the height of his stroke. Once he felt Charles sync with him, his hips moving in expectant counterpoint, rising each time Harlan dipped, falling each time Harlan rose, and once he was sure Charles was good and distracted and thought he knew exactly what was coming next, Harlan dug his nails into Charles' spanked ass cheek.

Charles howled, his whole body rising off the bed for a second like he was levitating or like Harlan had electrocuted him. The sheets shifted as Charles tightened his grip on them.

Harlan pulled back enough that he could lick Charles' tip, barely darting his tongue into the tiny hole at its centre. He could taste how close Charles was, and he smiled to himself as another thought occurred to him.

Ignoring Charles' wordless cry of dismay, Harlan let Charles' cock slide out of his mouth, the head passing his lips with a filthy *pop*. He looked up at Charles, still damp, the taste of him still on his tongue. He couldn't really see past Charles' hips, but he had a lovely view right where he was.

"Come," he said, very deliberately. He wasn't sure his voice could quite reach 'commanding', but he did his best. They'd done this a few times, and while it didn't always work, Harlan thought it was hot as hell when it did.

As soon as the word was out, he dropped his mouth around Charles' erection again and dug his nails into Charles' sore ass.

He didn't have long to wait. Charles thrashed like he was trying to throw Harlan off—though Harlan was sure he wanted the exact opposite of that. He cried out over and over, thrusting as hard and deep against Harlan's mouth as Harlan would let him, and he was glad he had a hand wrapped around the base of Charles' shaft. Charles came in long spurts down his throat, over and over, until he collapsed on the bed.

Harlan held on just a moment longer, swallowing the last of Charles' cum and breathing deeply through his nose.

Charles let out a soft sound, almost a whimper, and Harlan pulled free, letting Charles' overstimulated cock rest between his thighs. With a final gentle squeeze, Harlan slid his hand out from beneath Charles' ass, stroking his thighs and watching him come down from his peak. There was so much more he could do—that he *wanted* to do, especially after the thrill of Charles coming when he told him to — but he knew Charles was done for now.

He pushed aside the thought that it didn't really count, that Charles had been ready to pop at any second. He counted it as a win, though, and he couldn't wait to try it again next time.

"Wow. That was…" Charles blindly reached down with one hand and almost poked Harlan in the eye.

Harlan managed to duck his head in time and Charles' large, blunt fingers slid into his hair instead. "Yeah. For me too."

"C'mere," Charles rumbled.

His voice was so much more suited to being in control, of ordering men to come, but he let Harlan control him instead. Harlan felt another little thrill, as he always did when he was reminded that he was allowed to take charge of the big, handsome man above him. There were still times that he didn't feel worthy of it, that he was worried Charles would just laugh, but he was getting better at ignoring those thoughts and focusing on reality, where Charles was just as eager as he was.

Feeling a little limp himself, Harlan crawled up and over the corner of the bed, worming his way across the mattress until he came to rest at Charles' side.

Charles reached out one powerful arm and pulled Harlan against him. They both sighed together, breathing deeply in then out, their bodies finding a rhythm without either of them meaning to.

They both laughed, and Harlan buried his face in Charles' hairy, sweaty chest. "Mm-m," he hummed.

"Mm-m," Charles agreed, kissing the top of Harlan's head. "Do you need anything?"

He was still hard, but... "My arms are really sore." And it was so nice to just be held by Charles, to get Charles' scent all over his skin and to mark Charles in the same way.

Charles laughed. "Yeah, mine too. And I didn't even hit as many things as you did." Almost poking Harlan in the eye again with his unsteady hand, Charles reached across his chest and stroked Harlan's hair. "Would it be bad if we had a nap?" he asked, yawning as though to emphasize his point.

"Absolutely." Harlan yawned. "Let's do it anyway." His eyes were already floating shut. "Thank you," he whispered, just before he drifted off to sleep.

Chapter Six

"Harlan Brand?"

There was a ghost across the street, slowly ambling up and down the sidewalk as though window shopping. Based on his old-fashioned clothing, Harlan doubted the ghost was seeing the same items on display that Harlan was, Ghosts were, in their simplest form, memories. They saw what they expected to see, especially the older ones, unless someone or something jarred them badly enough to break through. That was when they got dangerous.

This ghost seemed content enough with his reality. He hadn't spoken.

Harlan couldn't help grinning as he saw Charles walking towards him, and he gave him a little wave, speeding up to meet him. "Hey! What're you doing here? Not that I'm not happy to see you," he added quickly. But something was strange. Why had Charles said his name like that? There was something else, something Harlan couldn't quite put his finger on, but it made every hair on his arms and the back of his neck stand on end.

He glanced across the street again.

The ghost was still there. It was well within range of Charles' ability, and he *shouldn't* have been able to see it, but the ghost was still there.

A cold weight of dread slid down Harlan's throat and into his stomach.

"Oh! I'm so sorry!" The world twitched — that was the only way Harlan could make sense of what happened — and Charles was…gone. In his place was a vaguely familiar white woman, about his height and at least a few years older than him, with auburn hair just long enough to tie back into a high ponytail.

"I was upset, then I saw you and I got distracted. Maybe you don't remember me. You are Harlan, right? Harlan Brand?" Her gaze kept darting around like she thought she was being followed or something, and Harlan had to keep himself from looking around as well.

He nodded, slowly.

"Oh, good. I'm Morgan. I was at the Centre?"

Now Harlan recognized her. No, he corrected himself, *them.* They were wearing a button that said *They/Them.*

It shouldn't have taken him that long to realize where he knew them from. There were only so many places he could have met someone. In his defence, they were quite a bit older than him and had left when he was ten or so. *What* is *their ability?* He knew it was something unusual, something more than just looking like other people, but he couldn't quite put his finger on it.

"You're with the police, right? I read this thing online about you stopping a serial killer or something, and I thought I recognized your name. Then I saw you just now and..."

They raised an eyebrow, and Harlan realized they were waiting for a response. "Oh. Uh, yeah. Kinda."

"Okay, good, because I didn't know where else to go. C'mon... Let's go get coffee or something. My treat." For a moment the hand reaching back was Charles', then just as quickly it wasn't. Their actual nails were painted deep copper. "Sorry. My control is bad today. I'm usually—well, you get better at controlling it, right?" They glanced across the street at the place Harlan had been looking, though Harlan didn't think they could see the ghost. "Or maybe— Sorry." They laughed, more of a sigh than anything. "I'm really sorry. I'm not usually this... I'm just scared right now."

Harlan gave a mental sigh of his own, then made a decision. They really did seem frightened. "Why don't you come to my apartment? It's only a few blocks away." He didn't really want to bring someone he barely knew into his space, but he also thought the last thing Morgan needed right now was caffeine, when they were already so full of nervous energy there were almost sparks flying off them. Even Harlan was picking up on it.

"Really? Thank you! You have no idea how glad I am I ran into you!"

Apparently he wasn't going to make it to the grocery store. He turned around and led them back the way he'd come.

"Would you like some water or something?" Harlan asked once he'd got his unexpected guest seated on the couch. At least he usually kept his living room tidy — if only because he spent most of his time in the bedroom — so he didn't have to worry about looking like a slob.

"That would be great. Thanks."

Harlan filled a glass, taking his time so he could adjust to the sudden upset in his day that having someone who was basically a stranger in his apartment represented.

He brought the water out to the living room and set it in front of them, then sat on an armchair facing them.

They'd been playing with their necklace, a pendant he couldn't quite see, but they tucked it back into their shirt and picked up the glass in its place. They didn't drink anything, just slowly rolled it between their palms, looking at their reflection rather than up at Harlan. "I don't know how well you remember me," they began slowly. "You might've been too young for this, but I know some of the other kids called me a slut and said I'd become a hooker when I left." They took a deep breath and added, "I can look like anyone's ideal romantic and-or sexual partner. Sorry about earlier."

Harlan's embarrassment was kept at bay by his racing thoughts. *Ideal partner.* And they'd looked like *Charles.* Not just a Frankenstein-collage of traits Harlan found attractive in a guy, but *Charles*, specifically. What did that mean?

Am I in love with Charles?

Before he could follow this thought, Morgan leaned forward, linked their fingers and rested their wrists on their knees. They looked like they were about to say something very serious and important, and Harlan was positive he wouldn't like it.

"I'm not a hooker," they continued. "Not that I'm against sex workers! I'm not a SWERF. I'm an accountant, and I *never* use my power…intentionally," they added quickly. "But sometimes it just *happens*, and it's usually not a big deal. I don't tell people why I look a certain way to them. Let them think it's just random, right? But a few days ago" —they swallowed hard, picking up the glass again and spinning it first one way, then the other—"I was walking home and I realized this guy was following me. I thought he was just being a creep and I got out my phone to pretend to call someone so he'd go away, but my phone was…really big?"

They looked at him like they expected this to mean something.

He shook his head.

"I realized I was a little girl," they explained.

"Oh." Harlan's eyes widened and he had to swallow down bile. "Oh my God."

"It gets worse," they said, very softly. "I saw my reflection in my phone. And I *recognized* me. *Her*." They shook their head. "Here." They pulled out their phone and fiddled with it for a second before passing it to him. "I looked like her."

On their screen was a picture of a little blonde girl with pigtails, maybe seven or eight years old. Above her was the word '*Missing*', and there was more information below the image. Harlan really didn't want to read it.

He passed the phone back, feeling hollow and numb. He'd seen some horrible things, heard some of the worst humanity did to itself because of working with ghosts, but this…

He shivered, wrapped his arms around himself and found himself leaning away from them, like they were the source of this awfulness.

"So, uh, anyway..." They fanned their face with one hand, looking like they were trying not to cry. "I shifted the fuck out of that shape and turned around to get a better look at him — to like, ID him, right? But that was really dumb of me, because now he's seen me — what I really look like — and I'm scared he's gonna come after me. I think she's dead. When I looked like her, he looked like he'd seen..." They managed a very thin smile. "Well, a ghost. I think he killed her."

Harlan realized he was gripping the arms of his chair as though he needed to keep himself from floating away.

"And I've been so scared ever since," they continued softly. "I've hardly left the house, but then I needed groceries and I saw you and I thought maybe you could help me." They looked so expectant, terrified and exhausted, and he knew he couldn't let them down.

"I'm not with the police...exactly."

Their face went blank. For a moment he was worried they were going to just get up and leave.

"But I think I can help you!" he quickly continued.

Their expression stayed neutral, but they didn't stand, though they were still leaning forward.

"I need to call my partner."

They bit their lip, hooking the necklace chain from beneath their shirt and running it through their fingers before finally nodding. "Okay... If you think you can trust them."

"With my life," he assured them. He was about to text Hamilton when he remembered that, while he had the day off, Hamilton was on patrol for at least the next three hours. It was rare, but sometimes Hamilton worked without him. "We'll have to wait a bit," he told them, apologetically.

They nodded, lowering their head until a few strands of auburn hair fell across their face. "I can come back later." Their eyes were wide and never still, even in the safety of the apartment.

Harlan shook his head. "It might be better if you wait here," he told them, in his best impression of Hamilton's police-officer voice.

"If you say so." They said it with a shrug, but they were obviously relieved that he wasn't sending them back out alone.

Harlan couldn't imagine how frightened he would feel if he thought a child molester—and a murderer— was after him. It occurred to him that he might have led said molester directly to his apartment, but as long as Morgan felt a little safer there, they were welcome to stay.

Except…Charles was coming over.

He texted Charles to let him know about the change of plans, but he didn't get a response. It wasn't surprising, because Charles didn't check his phone all that often, and he usually had it on silent so it wouldn't interrupt scenes at the club. He usually forgot to turn the ringer on again when he was done with work.

Before he could even tell Morgan that Charles was coming, there was a soft knock on the apartment door, exactly when Charles had said he'd arrive. Harlan loved that Charles was punctual.

He'd given Charles a key to the building, but not to his suite. Not yet. He wasn't really sure why, but thinking about it at all gave him a stomach ache, so he just…didn't think about it. Giving Charles the single key had been difficult enough.

Morgan stiffened.

"It's all right," he assured them, getting up to unlock the door.

"Is that your partner?"

Shit. He hadn't even called Hamilton yet, never mind told them Charles was due to arrive any minute. "No… I mean, yes." Realizing he was close to tying himself in verbal knots, he shook his head and started over. "The man at the door is Charles, my…romantic partner. The man I'm going to call is Hamilton, my police partner."

They were still eyeing the door nervously.

"I can ask him to come back later, if you'd like?" he offered. He really didn't want to. He'd been looking forward to some intimate time with Charles, and it was clear he wasn't going to get that. He didn't want to go without seeing Charles at *all.*

Morgan took a slow, deep breath. Harlan recognized the meditation training from at the Centre. It was similar to the way he calmed himself down.

They shook their head. "No. It's okay. You trust him."

"With my life," Harlan repeated. "You're sure?" He didn't really want to give them a second chance to say no, but he knew all too well how it felt to agree to an uncomfortable or even frightening experience but feeling like he couldn't say no.

"Yeah."

Charles' fist was raised to knock again when Harlan opened the door. He grinned, wrapped his arms around Harlan and kissed him deeply. "Hey! Everything all right?"

Blushing, Harlan barely managed to keep himself from wiping his lips with the back of his hand. But why should he be ashamed about his boyfriend kissing him in his own apartment? Well, not quite in. He saw his neighbour, the one Charles was convinced had a thing for him, hurry down the hallway with his head down. *Whoops.*

"Yeah, everything's fine. Come in." He stepped aside.

Charles' eyebrows rose comically high when he saw Morgan. "Ah. I see you have a visitor. Is this a bad time? I can come back later."

Harlan wasn't surprised by Charles' reaction. Harlan never had company. Harlan didn't think he'd ever invited anyone but Charles and maintenance people in — the latter only reluctantly, because he'd had to.

Harlan was mentally kicking himself for this situation when he remembered he *had* let Charles know. Only a few minutes ago, but he'd tried. "I texted you about it, but you probably haven't checked your phone."

"Ah." Charles set down the bags he was carrying and pulled his phone out of his pocket. The bags smelled amazing. As usual, Charles had brought food.

Grinning a little guiltily, Charles flicked his phone out of silent mode but didn't read the text.

Harlan let his shoulders relax a little. Morgan's obvious fear was making *him* anxious, and even though the thing they were afraid of wasn't a ghost, something Charles could protect them from without risking himself, he felt safer with Charles there.

Charles, wisely, didn't wait for Harlan to make introductions. He walked over to the couch and offered his hand to Morgan. "Hi. I'm Charles."

They shook it. "Morgan Vermeer. They/them."

"He/him," Charles added.

As usual, Harlan couldn't help admiring and maybe feeling a little jealous of the way Charles effortlessly got to know people and immediately put them at ease — which was probably a good trait in a man who owned a BDSM club. Harlan couldn't imagine having that ability, but he could see that Morgan was sitting a little less stiffly and their eyes were mostly focused on Charles rather than flying around the room.

Charles sat on the armchair on the other side of the couch.

Harlan regretted giving Morgan the couch. Now, instead of sitting all snugged up together the way they usually did, he and Charles were on opposite sides of the room.

"How do you know Harlan?"

"We grew up at the Centre together…sort of. I'm a little older."

"Oh!" Charles leaned forward, giving Morgan his full attention.

Harlan knew from experience how intense the force of that attention was — or maybe that was just him.

"I've never met anyone else from there before. It's nice to meet you."

Morgan laughed. "Well, if Harlan is anything like me, we don't tend to talk about it much — or really keep in contact with each other after we leave."

"Morgan is here about a case!" Harlan quickly interjected. He was starting to feel uncomfortable, but he couldn't have said why.

"Oh? You don't usually bring cases home." Charles blinked, then chuckled. "Except me, I guess. Well, I'll let the two of you work, but I want to point out that I brought Chinese food. I tend to get too much, so feel free to help yourself, Morgan."

He got up and started grabbing plates and cutlery.

Harlan listened to him puttering around in the kitchen, awkwardly trying to avoid looking at Morgan. He let his mind wander so he wouldn't have to try and think of something to talk about. Was he just being silly? *Should* he just give Charles the damn key?

Charles came back, gesturing for Harlan to sit—he realized he'd still been standing awkwardly, looming over Morgan—and set out plates for each of them. He started pulling containers out of the bag, opening them and putting them in the middle of the coffee table. "Dig in. I can take off after we eat if you guys are busy."

Morgan shook their head. "No. It's not really a case. Not yet, anyway. Just...a frightening experience, and I thought Harlan might be able to help."

At the mention of the word 'frightening', Harlan noticed Charles stiffen a bit, going into 'protective mode'. Harlan blushed slightly. Charles was *very* good at protecting.

Charles nodded slowly. "I'm sure he can. Can I ask what happened?"

They glanced at Harlan, then back to Charles. "My ability is kind of...unusual."

Harlan was a little surprised that they were sharing this with someone they'd just met, but Charles *was* very easy to talk to. And they'd been so scared that it was probably good for them to vent a little. They'd already told Harlan, but he wasn't very good at comforting people. It was also probably a good idea for them to tell their story a few times before they had to repeat it to Hamilton and other police officers later.

Harlan filled a plate with steaming rice, meat and vegetables, mouthing *thank you* to Charles. He hadn't realized how hungry he was until he'd started eating — with a fork. He'd never really mastered chopsticks, and he didn't feel like covering himself in rice in front of Morgan.

"My ability is unusual, too."

Harlan couldn't help shooting Charles a look of surprise. He'd never heard Charles refer to it as his 'ability' before. Now that he thought of it, *he'd* never really considered it in those terms. More as an *anti-ability*. But Charles was totally right. Harlan was glad Charles had arrived at that conclusion on his own, especially because apparently Harlan wouldn't have.

Harlan had been surrounded by people who were open about their abilities, or acknowledged that others had them, since he was very young. He wondered if Charles' private realization had made him feel isolated. Should he offer to go to a psychic support or recreation group with Charles, or at least take him for his semi-weekly coffee with the other police mediums? Not that Charles was a medium, exactly. Or was that exactly what he was? *Fuck.*

Whether Charles was technically a medium or not, he didn't think the other police mediums would mind him joining them for coffee, and honestly, Harlan would be happier if he was there.

He was less keen on the idea of joining another group, especially if they did anything more than drink coffee and eat pastries. But he'd do it for Charles, if Charles needed his support, especially the first few times. Hopefully after that Charles would be confident enough to go on his own and Harlan could just…drift away. Although, because of their schedules, any time Charles spent at a group would be time he could have potentially spent with Harlan, so maybe it was better to be there with him? Not that he expected Charles to spend every possible minute with him.

Also, not that he would be much help if Charles was nervous about going to a new place that Harlan had *also* never been to. He wouldn't be much help even bringing Charles to the coffee group he was already a part of.

"Unusual?" Morgan asked softly, interrupting Harlan's thoughts.

Charles glanced at Harlan.

Harlan nodded.

"I…" Charles laughed. "I don't know what to call it, how to describe it. It doesn't work on everyone — so far it only works with Harlan, as far as we know — but something about my ability…blocks his? He can't see ghosts when I'm around." He paused. "Unless there are a *lot* of them."

Morgan leaned forward. "You were there, weren't you? When Harlan took out Samuel Harkness?"

Harlan was glad that Charles was distracting them from their own fear, but talking about Harkness still made Harlan a little afraid. He hoped they'd change the subject soon.

Besides… "It wasn't me!" he protested. Maybe that wasn't giving himself enough credit. He'd been working on that with his therapist, but it was still hard. "It wasn't *just* me," he amended, but he didn't want to say anything more about it.

Anyway, they were there to talk about Morgan, not him.

Charles glanced at Harlan again, then back to Morgan. "I was. But it's not widely known, so I'd appreciate..."

"Oh, of course! I won't tell anyone. What was it like? How does it *work*?"

"It was terrifying."

Harlan loved that Charles was secure enough in his masculinity that he didn't pretend he hadn't been afraid.

"And..." Charles laughed. "Honestly, we have no idea how it works.

Morgan nodded, a little of their own fear back in their eyes. "Of course." They leaned back, running their fingers through their hair.

"I'm a shapeshifter." They laughed, a little harshly. "I can't...change into an animal or grow wings or what have you. No, nothing like that. I can take on the appearance of someone's ideal sexual or romantic partner." They said it very matter-of-factly, using more or less the same words they'd used with Harlan.

Harlan wondered if he should tell Charles that Morgan had first appeared as him. He decided not to, at least not yet.

Charles nodded. "All right. I think I understand."

They leaned forward again briefly, then rocked back until their posture was perfect again. "My control is normally really good these days. It hardly ever happens by mistake." They said it almost defensively, as though they felt like they had to justify themself to Charles.

Charles only nodded again, beginning to close the containers of Chinese food they hadn't polished off.

"I don't use it very often at all."

Harlan couldn't imagine never using his ability. He'd hated his power most of his life, until very recently, but he also couldn't imagine life without it. The thought of tamping it down all the time, ignoring every spirit he saw, made his guts clench. It would be like in the old days, when they tied left-handed people's hands behind their backs to force them to use their right. He would adjust to it, but he would never be wholly himself, not using his full potential.

He'd got better at control since his parents had left him at the Centre, and even better after leaving it — not letting ghosts' emotions bleed into his own mental state, and ignoring them, even if they were trying to get his attention — but for them to be gone entirely...? The world would be so much...*flatter* without ghosts in it.

That being said, he didn't envy Morgan's position.

"But sometimes... Sometimes it still gets away from me." They explained about the suspected pedophile they'd encountered all in a rush, fists clenched, staring at the floor.

Charles whistled, lacing his fingers behind his neck and looking up at the ceiling. "Wow. Holy shit. That's a lot."

Morgan lifted their gaze, looking so relieved that Harlan was worried they might cry. "You think so? You think it's something?"

"Of course!"

Nibbling their lip, Morgan glanced at Harlan. "Sorry, Harlan. I didn't mean to imply that your opinion..."

Harlan shook his head. *He* didn't even trust his opinion, so why would anyone else?

Although he was also working on that.

"So, what next?" Now it was Charles' turn to lean forward with obvious excitement.

"I'm going to text Hamilton. He should be done in a few hours, and hopefully he'll come straight here." The sooner the better, as far as Harlan was concerned. It would mean one more person in his apartment, but hopefully it would lead to *no one* in his apartment soon after...besides Charles.

Charles nodded. "That sounds like a good starting point. Although..."

"What?" Harlan asked.

"Well, he didn't exactly believe you when you told him there was a serial killer."

"True. You're right. But I think things are different now."

Charles nodded. "I think so too. I just worry. In any case, I think this is the best, most logical next step." He slapped his palms on his knees and leaned forward as though he was about to stand. "So, I should probably..."

Harlan said, "No," just as Morgan said, "Please, stay."

"You're sure?" Charles looked to Harlan first, then Morgan.

They both nodded.

"Do they teach you how to be synchronized like that at that school of yours?" Charles laughed. "Okay. I can tell when I *am* wanted. I'll stay." He crossed his legs decisively.

An awkward silence fell, or at least it felt awkward to Harlan. It didn't take long for his foot to start tapping, then he started rocking it from heel to toe and back. It had taken him a while to adjust to having just

Charles in his space for very long, and he knew Charles a lot better than Morgan—and more intimately.

He liked Morgan and sympathized with their fear, but he was rapidly getting peopled-out and wanted to be alone. He didn't think he could—or maybe *should*—abandon Charles in the living room and retreat to the privacy of his bedroom with the door closed without feeling like a complete asshole, but he was tempted.

He'd really been looking forward to some alone time with Charles. It could sometimes be hard to find with their conflicting schedules. He couldn't help resenting Morgan a little for interrupting it, even though he knew they hadn't done it on purpose and that they had an excellent reason to be in his apartment.

"So, Morgan, what do you do?" Charles easily drew them into a conversation about their work, asking lots of questions and listening with genuine interest as they answered, the way he did with seemingly everyone he met.

Harlan was, as always, a little in awe of Charles' skill, but mostly he was just grateful and relieved that the silence had been broken and no one's attention was on him. He pulled his phone out of his pocket, completely guilt-free, and fooled around on it after texting Hamilton, without worrying he was being a dick or a bad host. Charles had the situation under control.

Since Harlan had been lulled by the gentle rise and fall of Charles and Morgan's conversation, getting a text startled him so badly that he almost dropped his phone. "It's Hamilton," he told the others, hoping they hadn't heard his little squeak of surprise over the sound of the text tone. "He's downstairs."

Charles stood. "I'll go get him." He gave Harlan's shoulder a gentle squeeze as he passed.

Morgan whipped around to face Harlan as soon as the door closed. Their face was a little pale, and there were dark circles under their eyes.

"Do you think I should do this?"

Harlan, who'd been thinking pretty much the exact same thing, forced himself to nod stiffly. "Absolutely," he said, with as much authority and conviction as he could, which wasn't much. "We've gotta... We've gotta catch this guy. Right?"

Morgan didn't look very convinced or reassured, but they didn't get up and leave, either.

A few moments later Harlan heard Charles and Hamilton in the hall. Charles was laughing, probably at something Hamilton had said.

Harlan couldn't help a small smile at hearing his two very different partners together. When he'd first left the Centre, Harlan had wanted to keep his personal and private bubbles separate, but more and more they kept blending around him.

Is Hamilton my friend?

Did Hamilton consider *him* a friend? No way Harlan would ever ask. Hopefully he'd be able to figure it out on his own somehow. He wasn't honestly sure which option he'd prefer. Was he a terrible person if he knew he'd be hurt if Hamilton told him they weren't friends, but he wasn't sure he considered Hamilton one?

Probably.

"Hamilton, this is Morgan. Morgan, Hamilton."

Harlan was relieved that Charles handled the introductions. Harlan always got in his own head too much and worried about messing up his own name to the point that he could never remember the name of the person he'd been introduced to after three seconds. Having to introduce people to each other was even worse.

If Morgan found it odd that Hamilton had been introduced by his last name only, they didn't let it show as they stood and shook his hand.

Charles gave Harlan's hand a quick squeeze and kissed the top of his head — something he could only do because Harlan was still sitting. "I'm going to take off for a while."

It was all Harlan could do not to let out a whine of disappointment.

"Call me when you three are done?"

Harlan nodded, wishing he could go with Charles instead of staying.

Charles waved at the room, then left.

"So, Harlan tells me you've got something you'd like to report?" Hamilton got out his pen and notepad in anticipation. While other cops might use their phones or tablets, Hamilton preferred good old-fashioned ink and paper. He stole Charles' armchair, forcing Harlan to sit on the couch beside Morgan. Hamilton had a way of immediately taking command of any room he entered, drawing all eyes to him.

"Yes, I think so." They quickly explained their power, their eyes darting between Hamilton and their lap. They told Hamilton about their recent incident — for the third time that day, Harlan realized. He knew it must have been exhausting to repeat it over and over. He wasn't sure if the repetition would make it more or less difficult. Easier, he decided, seeing a new lightness in Morgan's body language.

"Fuck," Hamilton said after he wrote the last word and looked up.

Morgan looked a little startled by Hamilton's reaction, but it was about what Harlan had expected — had maybe even hoped for.

"*Fuck,*" Hamilton said again, with even more feeling. He flipped back and forth through his notes for several minutes, moving his lips silently as he read and thought.

Chapter Seven

Hamilton glanced between them, his jaw working from side to side as he thought. "Can you do it again?"

"What?"

"Can you change your appearance to look like her again, since you've done it before?"

"Yes. Just to be clear" — they glanced at Hamilton, then at Harlan — "I *cannot* just change into anyone I want. I can't fake this. But, once I've taken on someone's appearance, I can do it again whenever I like."

Harlan, the image of them appearing as his own ideal sexual or romantic partner fresh in his memory, couldn't help feeling unsettled by the thought that they could turn into Charles at any time.

Without pulling out their phone to look at the picture — which Harlan thought made their story more believable, and hopefully Hamilton would agree — Morgan closed their eyes.

A moment later the girl from the missing poster was standing in Harlan's living room, in full three-dimensional life.

Every hair on Harlan's body stood on end. He wanted to look away, but he couldn't.

Hamilton started asking, "Now wh—?" but before he could finish, Morgan—probably still adjusting to their new size and shape—stumbled.

Harlan was closest and he reached out to steady them. The moment their skin made contact, a beyond-physical force threw him back, almost launching him over the top of the armchair.

Morgan landed on their butt on the carpet, in their own form again.

Harlan's ears were ringing and, based on the way both Morgan and Hamilton were tilting their heads from side to side, he assumed theirs were as well.

Hamilton was the first to collect himself. "What *happened*?"

At least, that was what Harlan thought he'd said. He still couldn't hear properly.

Harlan shook his head, sliding down into his armchair again. He immediately jumped to his feet, his eyes wide with shock and horror. He looked at Morgan. They were still the same, an adult, but standing beside them was a figure he immediately recognized as Monica. His skin crawled, something he'd always thought was just a saying, but it actually felt like it was trying to leave.

"What?" Hamilton asked, seeing how frightened Harlan was but not what he was afraid of.

"Is that—? Oh my God." Morgan sank back onto the couch.

"You can see her?" Harlan asked, without looking away from Monica.

"See what? See who? What's going on?" Hamilton demanded. He turned. "Oh, fuck. Holy fucking shit." He actually stumbled back a step before collecting himself.

Harlan ignored them both and concentrated on Monica. As soon as he did, he knew exactly what she was—a ghost. He had no idea how she'd got in there, past the ghost wards, or how both Morgan and Hamilton could see her, but she was there, and she was a ghost.

His breathing started coming too quick, too shallow. There was a ghost. In his apartment. Again. His ghost-warded apartment, where there should never *ever* be one.

Morgan turned away from Monica and set a hand on Harlan's shoulder. "What is it? What's wrong?"

Hamilton appeared, his movements seeming jerky, like frames were missing. He knelt in front of Harlan. "I think you're having a panic attack. You're hyperventilating." He set one hand on each of Harlan's knees. "Breathe with me. We'll deal with her, whatever she is, in a minute, but for now we've got to steady your breathing or you're gonna pass out." He didn't tell Harlan to just 'calm down', which even in this state, Harlan appreciated.

"Innn..." Hamilton drew an exaggerated breath, nostrils flaring. "Ouuuuut..." He blew a slow stream of air that Harlan could feel on his face. Hamilton's breath smelled like coffee, and somehow that helped bring Harlan back to himself.

Harlan closed his eyes. He hadn't needed to do this for…a long time. *Months? Maybe.* It was difficult to say, especially now, in the moment of fear.

Morgan backed away, giving the two of them space.

Harlan felt something change in the room, but he focused on Hamilton's warm hands on his knees, his clothing against his skin, all the sensations grounding him in his body.

In.

Out.

In, slow.

Out, slower.

It took several repetitions, but at last he opened his eyes and nodded. "I'm okay. Sorry."

"You're sure?"

Harlan nodded.

"Okay. Next problem— How the fuck is she here?" Hamilton didn't look away from Harlan.

Harlan's jaw was tight as he answered, "I don't know."

"What do you mean?" Morgan asked, looking between the two of them.

Hamilton shook his head vigorously, like he was shaking his thoughts loose. "She shouldn't be in here."

"What? Why?"

"She's gone."

Morgan turned around, their back stiffening when they realized what Harlan had already seen. "She's gone," they repeated, rubbing their arms.

Suddenly exhausted, Harlan rested his elbows on his thighs and buried his face in his hands, kneading his eyes and forehead as he tried to think. "I'm not…" *Okay. One thing at a time.* "My apartment is ghost-warded. *Heavily*," he explained to Morgan.

"There's no fucking way she should've been able to get in here if she really is..." Hamilton agreed. He stood up, tense and alert, ready to defend against a danger that was already gone.

"She was," Harlan assured him. "I just don't know *how*."

"Do you need me to call the...ward...guy?" Hamilton asked.

"No. Not yet. I... We have to figure this out." He motioned for Hamilton to sit on one of the armchairs opposite the couch. His restless pacing was starting to make Harlan nervous.

Where to start?

The wards. Had they been broken, like the ones at the Centre, or was something even worse, even stranger, going on?

He did his special *blink* and the wards snapped into sight. They were solid and whole and bright as the day they'd been painted. It didn't make sense. None of what had just happened made sense.

He blinked again. "It's not the wards. They're fine."

Hamilton raised an eyebrow. "It's not like...?"

"No."

If it wasn't the wards, what was the next step?

He turned to Morgan. "Okay. You were in Monica's form."

They nodded.

He shook his head slowly as he thought it through. "Then you *weren't*, and she *was*. Here, I mean."

"Should I try it again?" Morgan asked. "To make sure it wasn't a fluke or something?" They frowned. "She was gone so quickly, but I had this feeling... Like she wanted to tell me something."

Harlan shivered, swallowing hard. "I felt it too," he admitted reluctantly.

Hamilton was looking back and forth between the two of them like he was watching a tennis game he didn't understand — but he didn't interrupt.

When no one else spoke up or offered any suggestions, Harlan sighed. "All right. Let's try it again."

They stood in front of each other beside the coffee table. Harlan wondered if they felt as awkward and uncertain as he did.

He could see Morgan concentrating — Harlan imagined he looked similar when he *blinked* — and they turned into Monica.

Just Monica. Harlan reached out with his psychic senses — no ghost, just Morgan in a different form. "It didn't work."

Morgan groaned. "What else was...? Oh!" They reached out and touched Harlan's hand.

Morgan snapped back to their own form, and once again Monica — spectral Monica — was beside them. The feeling of force, of energy, wasn't as strong this time — or maybe Harlan was just expecting it and had braced himself. He held on grimly to Morgan's hand. Their copper nails dug into his skin.

Again, he sensed that the girl's spirit was trying to communicate, even though she stayed still and quiet. Just as he was thinking about speaking to her, Morgan let go of his hand and the girl flashed out of existence.

He hadn't seen a sign on her 'body' of what had killed her, but that wasn't unusual. For every ghost that appeared in full bloody, bloated horror, there was another that looked completely untouched.

"Whoa." Morgan laughed, a little too high-pitched. "That was… Whoa."

Harlan nodded slowly in agreement, hoping they didn't notice him rubbing the half-moon marks they'd left on the back of his hand.

"Maybe I don't even need to take her form first. Maybe I can just…" They grabbed Harlan's hand again without warning.

He winced at the sudden spark of power that flew between them like a static shock, but he was distracted from the unexpected pain by Monica's reappearance.

She looked more irritated than sad this time, and he wondered if it was as unnerving for her as it was for them, being called from…wherever she was…to a strange place with strange people.

She clasped her hands together, looking at Morgan and Harlan pointedly.

Morgan dug her nails in again, and Harlan thought he understood what Monica wanted. This time, they wouldn't let go until she'd given them her message.

She opened her mouth.

As Harlan had expected, no sound came out.

Monica looked increasingly annoyed, then almost frantic, but no matter how hard she tried, they couldn't hear her. She stomped her foot, glaring at the three of them.

She looked around the room and grinned when she spotted a pencil on the coffee table.

"That won't—" Harlan tried to warn her, but she was already reaching for it.

Her hand passed right through the pencil—and the table beneath it. It took a lot of energy—and usually a lot of practice—before a spirit could interact with physical objects, and Monica had neither. She managed to rock the pencil slightly, and he was impressed, but she just looked even more miserable.

"What are you trying to tell us?" Harlan asked softly.

She looked around again, frowning. She closed her eyes, and he was afraid she was going to disappear, but she only spun in a slow circle with her arm out, her finger pointing. She stopped, opened her eyes, and nodded, stabbing her finger a few times in the direction she was facing.

"You want us to follow you?" Morgan guessed.

Still pointing, she looked over her shoulder and nodded enthusiastically, grinning at them.

Morgan looked a little queasy, but they asked, "Will we...find your — *you* — if we go in that direction?"

She nodded again, looking like she might cry with relief.

"We'll help you if we can," Morgan told her, and Harlan noticed that they hadn't actually promised anything.

"We have to prepare first," Hamilton interjected before they could say more.

Monica slowly lowered her arm to her side, nodding sadly and staring at the three adults.

Morgan glanced at Hamilton and nodded. They swallowed hard, giving Harlan's hand another big squeeze. "We're going to stop touching now, and you're going to disappear," they explained. "But we're going to try to get you help."

She nodded again.

"Let go," Hamilton said.

They dropped each other's hands at the same time, and Monica disappeared again.

"Holy shit. Did you know you could do that?" Hamilton asked.

It wasn't clear which of them he was addressing, and they answered together, "No."

Harlan felt cold and numb and at a distance from his body.

"What does that mean?" Morgan asked, rubbing their arms.

Hamilton glanced at Harlan, who shook his head. "I don't know."

Morgan turned to Harlan, their eyes enormous. "Holy. Shit. If we're right, if we can do this *again*, we can help find her and do it for other missing people. Harlan, think of all the people we can—"

"No," Hamilton cut them off.

Harlan and Morgan stared at him.

"No!" Hamilton repeated, more forcefully. "I can't—I *won't*—stop you, but I think that's a bad idea."

"Why?" Morgan demanded.

Hamilton sighed. "Look," he said, his voice softer. "I get that you both want to help people, I really do. And that's admirable. But there's a reason there's a whole *team* of police psychics—all flavours, not just mediums. Burnout. If you two go off announcing your as-far-as-we-know-unique talent—if this is even something you can do again reliably—everyone in the city is going to be coming for you, wanting you to find Grandma's missing pooch."

"How would that—?" Morgan began indignantly, just as Harlan started saying, "And why shouldn't—?"

Hamilton cut them off again. "Trust me on this. These things need to be done delicately." He fished his phone out of its holster and turned away from them to make his call.

Morgan and Harlan exchanged grins — *The Wizard of Oz* had been one of the few movies in the Centre's very small collection. Harlan couldn't have said how many times he'd seen it.

As though sensing the amusement happening behind him, a frowning Hamilton turned, flapped a hand at them and pointedly gave them his back again.

Morgan rolled their eyes but sat on the couch.

After a moment's hesitation — Harlan usually only sat that close to Charles — he joined them.

While Hamilton was distracted, they leaned over and whispered, "Is Captain Sourpuss saying we *shouldn't* try to find old ladies' missing dogs?" They blinked. "Not that I could," they added.

Harlan couldn't help snorting at the nickname. He'd come up with plenty of his own when he'd first met Hamilton. "No, of course not!" he whispered back.

Well...maybe.

"He's just looking out for us. Burnout, like he said."

"Uh-huh."

Hamilton slammed his phone back into its case. "I got us a meeting to share your theory. If we" — Harlan found it incredibly touching that Hamilton included himself — "can convince them you're on to something, we'll be authorized to search for the body."

"What?" Morgan stood up. At Hamilton's expression, even though they were taller than him, they took a step back and sat down again.

"What?" Harlan echoed. "I thought we'd be going right now!"

Hamilton shrugged, but he seemed disappointed too. "Sorry. If it was up to me, we'd be in the cruiser already with the lights and siren going. But it's *not* up to me." He looked between them, then grinned. "What?

Do they teach you Advanced Pouting at the Centre, along with all the freaky shit? You're making the exact same face."

He held up his hands, addressing Harlan first. "Look. This isn't going to be like last time. I'm not going to *let* it be like last time." He turned to Morgan. "I get the feeling you've been let down—or worse—by the cops before, and I don't want to be another disappointment. I'm going to keep pushing on this, but it'll take *time*. There are official channels we have to go through. Besides, if she's really—" He shook his head, seeming to decide against continuing that thought out loud. "Besides...there's something else."

Morgan groaned, throwing a hand over their eyes.

"And this one I kinda agree with."

He was met only by silence.

"This is, as far as we know—and you can fucking bet we've got people looking into this right now while we're talking—the first time psychics have used... combined, whatever, their power in this way. We have no idea if what we saw was real—"

"What? Mass hysteria? Please." Morgan snorted.

"No, no, nothing like that. I just mean... We all saw the same thing, we did, but we don't know if it was really her. If she's really—"

"It was her ghost," Harlan said firmly.

Hamilton sighed but nodded. "Look. You're both too young to remember this—so am I, but on days like today it sure as fuck doesn't feel like it—but it wasn't that long ago that psychic cops had to act like they just got really good hunches, and everyone pretended to believe them. Open psychics got shitty assignments, passed over for promotion or just...not hired. The Centre was where people sent their—well, it's only in the last twenty years or so that police forces started accepting that psychics are a good forensic tool. Sorry, Brand, Morgan.

"But this psychic...stuff...still makes a lot of people nervous. And that's stuff they've *studied*, that they've seen work over and over, the same-ish way time after time. Something completely new, like this? I'd consider ourselves lucky that we got a meeting." He laughed. "I'm honestly not sure if having Brand involved will help us or hurt us."

"Why?" Morgan asked, before Harlan could.

"He made some...pretty big impressions with that whole Harkness thing—not all of them good," Hamilton replied, the most diplomatic response Harlan had ever heard from him.

Chapter Eight

Harlan almost never went to the police station. He'd found out — probably much later than he should have — that Hamilton took care of and shielded him from paperwork and other parts of the job that didn't directly involve ghosts.

He and Morgan fell back a step, letting Hamilton take the lead. Harlan tried to keep his gaze down and ignore the heads that raised as he walked by and the whispers that cut off abruptly as he passed. He knew, from the other police mediums, that some of the regular police officers were unhappy that a complete newbie medium had discovered and stopped a serial killer that no one else had even been aware of.

As far as Harlan was concerned, it didn't matter who discovered a problem as long as it got solved. He hadn't kept his theory a secret. Hamilton had told him that he'd informed his superiors of Harlan's hunch, and they'd told him to drop it.

None of the mediums seemed to hold it against him, at least not openly.

He was beginning to regret offering to go to the station with Morgan—like Hamilton had said, it might have been easier without him—but the way he kept catching Morgan shooting him nervous little sidelong glances made him glad he'd come along.

Hamilton led them into an office and shut the door behind them.

Sitting behind it was a Black woman whose short hair was almost completely grey. A nameplate on her desk read Captain Sullivan. Her neutral expression didn't change when she saw Harlan, and he couldn't decide if that was good or bad.

"You said you had information about a missing child?" she prompted Hamilton.

"Yes, ma'am. I think so."

This was the closest to flustered Harlan had ever seen him, and he began to suspect that Hamilton was putting himself on the line for him and Morgan. Now he could only hope their theory was correct.

"Brand and Mx. Vermeer believe she is dead. And they're hoping that they can locate her remains. Through…unconventional means."

"I see." She steepled her fingers on her blotter. "Does Mx. Vermeer have any qualifications I should know about?"

Hamilton swallowed hard, and Harlan could almost see him edging out on a limb he wasn't convinced would take his weight. "No, ma'am. Other than being a psychic, trained at the Centre."

"I don't suppose I could get a demonstration of this 'unconventional method' before I make my decision?" she asked.

Morgan nodded, rolling up onto their toes and back like they were stretching or warming up.

Harlan was far less enthusiastic. He didn't like dragging a ghost to him, away from wherever she was supposed to be, over and over again. He'd been relieved when they'd broken contact and released her.

Still... If there was any chance they could bring closure to Monica's family, they owed it to her and to them to try.

He nodded.

Hamilton looked him directly in the eyes, then nodded. He brushed past them and closed the blinds over the windows facing the bullpen.

Harlan immediately began feeling something akin to claustrophobia, which wasn't normally a problem for him. He realized it was more a sense of finality. What if they couldn't make her appear again?

Morgan took his hand, and this time it came even more quickly—that sense of being drawn tight, stretched until some force slammed into him, *through* him, then there she was. Morgan gave his hand an extra squeeze, their nails digging in a little. He didn't pull away, concentrating on the translucent girl in front of them, afraid she'd vanish if he stopped paying attention.

He heard a soft gasp from Captain Sullivan.

Just like before, the girl showed no visual signs of injury or whatever might have caused her death.

She looked around slowly, as though getting her bearings, then pointed to the rear wall of the office, looking in that direction as well.

Harlan tried to do a quick mental visualization. He got turned around inside buildings, especially ones as large as the police station, but he *thought* it was the same way she'd pointed in his apartment.

"Well." Captain Sullivan's voice, sounding a little unsteady, broke the heavy silence filling the room. "And you believe you can follow this…apparition…to the girl's remains?" Her eyes widened and she shot an almost-guilty look at Monica.

Monica didn't move or react to her words. She just kept pointing.

"Yes, ma'am."

Hamilton sounded so *certain*. It sent a hot rush of emotion through Harlan—pride that Hamilton had such faith in him, equally matched with the terror of disappointing him and losing that faith forever.

The captain came out from behind her desk and cautiously approached the girl, who still didn't move. "What do you need?" she asked Hamilton, softly.

"I want to keep this small to begin with—just me, Brand and Mx. Vermeer. We'll follow the ghost and see what, if anything, she leads us to. If it's nothing, no one outside this room has to know."

It was almost a question, and the captain nodded in response.

"If we *do* find her body, we'll proceed from there."

"Do it." They'd clearly been dismissed.

Morgan released Harlan's hand and the ghost immediately vanished. The room seemed to fill up with air again. They took deep, simultaneous breaths.

Hamilton opened the blinds, and the office felt even less oppressive. He nodded to the captain, turned on his heel and left. Harlan and Morgan fell into step behind him as he led them back to the cruiser.

Hamilton leaned on the car and tapped a finger impatiently on its roof for the few seconds it took them to catch up. "How are we gonna do this?" he asked.

"You two have to keep holding hands or at least be touching, right?"

Harlan hadn't really thought, in detail, about how they'd follow Monica's ghost. He'd sort of imagined them holding hands and walking.

Morgan opened their mouth, then closed it again.

"Yeah, that's about what I thought." Hamilton sighed. "All right, how about this... You two sit in the back of the cruiser. Will she be able to keep up with the car, or will she...lag?"

They both turned to Harlan again, and he ducked his head. "I think she can keep up. Even though they can pass through material barriers, they tend to stay more or less fully inside a room, not standing half in the floor or whatever. I haven't tried it" —and, honestly, the thought of being stuck in a car with a ghost, even that of a completely non-threatening little girl, was terrifying, but at least he wouldn't be alone—"but I think she'll stay in the car with us."

"All right. Good." He glanced at the two of them. "Vermeer, you're ready" —Harlan found it interesting that he'd dropped the 'Mx.' —"but you're not, Brand. We'll drop by your apartment to get you some warmer clothes."

Harlan opened his mouth to protest, but Hamilton cut him off.

"People don't usually dump a body within walking distance of a police station. Chances are we'll have to go a ways, and we might have to wander around outside."

Harlan nodded reluctantly. *Hamilton has a point.*

"C'mon, then."

After grabbing a warmer coat and a bright-red scarf Charles had given him, Harlan climbed into the back seat beside Morgan.

"Ready?" Hamilton was behind the wheel already, drumming it with his fingers. He started the car and pulled away from the curb with his usual stomach-lurching speed.

Harlan was used to it, but Morgan let out a little squeak.

He wasn't sure where Hamilton was going, since the ghost wasn't there to guide them yet, but that had never stopped his partner before. They *might* be heading in the direction the ghost had pointed – if it had even been the same both times – but Harlan wasn't sure about that either.

He knew he should get it over with and take Morgan's hand, but he wanted a little more time to settle in and mentally prepare.

He'd never been in the back of this or any other police car. It was uncomfortable having a metal grille between him and Hamilton, and the matching grilles on the side windows set off more of the not-quite-claustrophobia that had bothered him in the office.

Deciding he was ready – or at least that he could keep stalling forever if he didn't do it now – Harlan took a deep, steadying breath and reached out for Morgan's hand. It was already halfway there to meet him.

This time the connection came even harder and faster than before, the force of it – combined with Hamilton taking an abrupt turn – making him cry out and slamming him against his seat.

When Monica appeared, she was pointing more or less in the direction Hamilton was driving. She was humming with energy.

Harlan caught Hamilton glancing back at her in the rear-view mirror before looking straight ahead again. "Let me know if she starts pointing a different direction. I've gotta focus on the road." He sounded like he was talking more to himself than them, and Harlan noticed his hands flex on the wheel. His voice held the same energy as the spirit, the energy that filled everyone in the car.

"Please do." Morgan's voice was tight and afraid, and Harlan hoped they'd be able to see this through to the end.

He could feel Monica draining his energy, even more than his usual interactions with ghosts, and he was sure Morgan was feeling the same strain—maybe worse. Harlan used his gift almost every day, but Morgan had made it sound like they rarely used theirs. And this was a way they'd never used it before. He hoped they wouldn't have to follow the ghost for much longer.

Chapter Nine

Monica led them by pointing as the crow flew, making Hamilton curse whenever the road they were following ended or changed direction and he had to try and find another route. They didn't want to stop and take the time to look at a map in case they lost the connection — although Harlan suspected they would have saved time if they *had* just stopped.

"She's like the world's worst GPS voice navigator!" Hamilton laughed, but his teeth were gritted.

Harlan could feel Morgan trembling where their hands met, their grip almost painfully tight. He didn't want to complain about it in case he broke their concentration. When he glanced at them, he saw that they were biting their lip, their eyes fixed and staring straight ahead.

Hurry, he silently urged Hamilton. *Please be patient,* he begged the girl.

They left the Greater Toronto Area behind, and the buildings gave way to farmland sprinkled with widely spaced houses and sparse trees. For some reason the open landscape made Harlan deeply uncomfortable. He'd spent his whole life in Toronto, barring a few Centre fieldtrips and a half-remembered trip to…somewhere…with his parents when he was very young. While he still felt safest indoors — mainly because only buildings could be ghost-warded — he was *comfortable* in the city, surrounded by people and traffic, light and noise.

Here, in the emptiness, he felt vulnerable. Exposed. His reaction surprised him a little. He didn't like crowds, not at all, but he realized that he liked being surrounded by nameless, interchangeable *people*.

Although, he supposed, fewer people probably meant fewer ghosts.

He shivered, abruptly wishing Charles was with him.

Monica's arm swung in a sharp arc, and Harlan couldn't help ducking instinctively. It would have passed right through his head, of course, but it was an automatic reaction. And having her icy-cold hand inside his skull, even for a second, would have been uncomfortable.

"She's saying we need to go left," Morgan piped up.

"We might have to take gravel roads if we get off the highway," Hamilton grumbled.

"Then by all means, let's just turn around and go back!"

Hamilton's short, broad fingers straightened before curling around the wheel again. "All right. I guess we're going for a jaunt through the country. Nothing had better happen to my car!"

He turned and kept going as the ghost directed them until Harlan murmured, "Stop."

For once, Hamilton braked slowly rather than coming to his usual abrupt, screeching halt. Was this how he would drive with any child?

Harlan couldn't help wondering if it was out of respect for their ghostly passenger.

"What now?" Hamilton asked.

"I-I think we have to walk from here?" Harlan glanced at Morgan for assurance.

They nodded. Not that they knew anything he didn't, or the other way around, but it *felt* right.

"Great. It's going to be dark soon, and I definitely want to go slogging around in mud that I'll have to clean off my shoes—and out of my car—later." Apparently, Hamilton was as much of a city boy as Harlan, which helped explain his move from Calgary to Toronto.

Harlan had always thought it was a missed opportunity that he hadn't moved to Hamilton, Ontario. He could admit, secretly to himself, that his partner's discomfort made him feel a little less silly about his own.

Hamilton cleared his throat. "Right. Let's get moving."

Getting out of the car while holding hands with Morgan was awkward, but Harlan was afraid of breaking contact and possibly losing her forever—or that she'd have to start at the beginning and they'd have to follow her all over again. The sun was going down and Harlan just wanted to go home, back to his apartment, civilization and Charles.

With a great deal of bending, wiggling and maneuvering, he and Morgan managed to slide out on the same side.

At last they were standing side by side in a field, their fingers linked.

"Ready?"

Harlan nodded.

"Which way?" Hamilton asked.

Monica's ghost pointed straight ahead of them, away from the road, in the direction of a thin patch of trees.

A chill ran up Harlan's spine and Morgan squeezed his hand. He wasn't sure if it was to comfort him or out of fear.

Hamilton broke the silence. "Yeah, that's creepy as fuck." Even the birds and wind seemed hushed, or maybe it was always this quiet and still in the stupid country. "Y'all ready?"

That startled a laugh out of Harlan. As far as he knew, the closest Hamilton had ever got to the American South was...Toronto. "'Y'all'?"

"I say 'y'all' when I'm feeling sassy! And scared, apparently," Hamilton admitted. "And I'm from Alberta. We're the Texas of Canada."

"True." Harlan wished they could just stand there by the road, which was at least a sign of civilization, and continue this dumb conversation. He didn't want to see what the ghost was leading them to. He wanted to let go of Morgan's increasingly clammy hand, get back in the car without touching them again and go home—to Charles...and popcorn...and all the lights on. Why was a single ghost in the wild so much spookier than a city full of them? At least the others seemed as freaked out as him.

Monica's spectral form flickered.

Harlan shook his head. This was where he was needed.

He and Morgan stepped forward at the same time. They set off across the field.

Monica led the way, slightly in front of Harlan and Morgan, with Hamilton bringing up the rear.

As Harlan had expected—*feared?*—she led them straight for the trees on the far side of the field. Each step felt more reluctant than the last, and only the knowledge that they must, finally, be getting close kept him going. He was running on adrenaline alone, and he was sure Morgan was just as exhausted as he was.

The sun was even lower, dusk creeping up around them incredibly fast. And it was *dark* in the country, dark in a way Harlan had never experienced and didn't like at all. In his selfish heart of hearts, he now cared less about finding her remains than about getting back to the city where he belonged.

As soon as they stepped past the first tree, Monica disappeared. Even worse, it somehow got *darker* and Harlan realized she'd been casting a faint glow, at least for him. Harlan was almost completely blind now. The last of the fading sun was blocked by the trees, which suddenly seemed darker, thicker and more menacing. Harlan cursed as he tripped over a root—*or a body*, his treacherous mind suggested. He couldn't see, and he pulled his hand free of Morgan's. They frantically reached out for each other in the darkness, Morgan groping around in a way that made Harlan think the ghost had shone for them as well.

They clasped hands again, but nothing happened. They squeezed each other's hands at the same time, as though there might be a bad connection or something.

Harlan shook his head. "I don't think she's coming back."

"Good," Hamilton said. "She shouldn't have to see this...whatever we find. I know she's already been through it, and I know it probably doesn't make a damn bit of difference, but I'm glad she's not around while we..."

Morgan let go of Harlan's hand, slowly.

He flexed it to get the sensation back. It was full of pins and needles.

They shook their head. "I can't. I can't. I'm...sorry."

Hamilton caught up. "Hey, you've done your part. *More* than." He glanced over at Harlan, who nodded. "You wait here." He turned on a flashlight and beckoned Harlan forward with a tilt of his head.

Harlan frowned. "Why didn't you turn that on earlier?"

Hamilton shrugged. "I didn't want to mess up your...ghost stuff."

Harlan shook his head but didn't say anything. He wished very much that he could stay there with Morgan—he was so exhausted—but he knew he had to follow.

Hamilton forced his way through the dense underbrush like a bull moose, the yellow circle of his flashlight bouncing along in front of him, while Harlan scrambled after him, tripping over everything. Thorns scratched his face and hands and caught on his scarf. Several times he was whipped by branches that Hamilton released in front of him, and Hamilton's grunted warnings didn't help when Harlan couldn't see them.

Even though the night was cool, he was sweating already, and he felt like he'd only taken three steps into the woods.

He was never leaving the city again. Not for anyone, human or ghost.

"Stop." Hamilton came to a halt so abruptly that Harlan walked into him. He held his arms out, completely blocking Harlan.

"What is it?" Harlan stepped on a dry twig and of course it snapped so loudly it was like he was in a fucking cartoon.

Hamilton turned to frown at him but lowered his arms. "Give me your scarf."

"What?" Harlan clutched it. Charles had given it to him. It was one of the few brightly coloured things he owned that hadn't come with his apartment.

"Brand, please." Hamilton's voice was almost a growl. "I'm standing over the body of a little girl, it's pitch black, we have no jurisdiction here, we need to call the OPP, we're probably going to be here all night and we need to flag this spot so we can find it again. Give me your *damn* scarf."

Harlan handed it over without another word, stumbling back a few steps. He didn't want to see her body if he didn't have to. He didn't know how long she'd been dead, but he was relieved that he didn't smell anything—and that he didn't have to see her ghost while standing at the site where her body had been dumped like garbage. He wanted Charles more than ever, but the best he could do was dig his nails into his palms.

"*Thank* you," Hamilton said, pointedly, tying the scarf around a tree. He shooed Harlan back along the path he'd made, which Harlan's blundering had widened.

They gathered Morgan as they passed, the three of them retreating to the car.

Hamilton radioed in that they'd found a body outside the GTA and needed the Ontario Provincial Police. As soon as he'd finished, he leaned against the car with a sigh. "Like I told Harlan, we're probably going to be here all night explaining this mess. You two can fight each other for the back seat until the OPP gets here."

Morgan's lips were pressed together so tight that they were white at the edges. Harlan could see their hands shaking, even from several feet away in the dark. Their hair colour and length kept changing, and he saw them close their eyes and clench their fists each time it happened, like they were fighting to control their power. Every time they started looking Charles-ish, he felt a little queasy. As much as he would have liked to lie down, at the moment he just wanted to stop looking at them.

"I'm fine. You lie down and rest while you can." He felt about as crappy as they looked, but their power running wild made him worry that they were about to collapse or something. Besides, this wasn't their job.

"If you're sure..." They tried to look reluctant, but their eyes kept darting towards the car.

"G'wan." Hamilton hooked a thumb over his shoulder.

That seemed to be the only encouragement they needed. They climbed into the back seat and shut the door behind them.

Hamilton turned to Harlan. "You look like shit."

"Gee, thanks." Harlan was sure it was true, and he knew this was how Hamilton showed affection. "Would you mind if I...?" He wasn't really sure what he was asking, but he knew he couldn't stand in the road much longer.

"Knock yourself out." Hamilton's eyes widened, just for a second. "But please don't."

Harlan nodded, already thinking about his options. He considered trying to curl up in his seat in the cruiser, but he didn't want to disturb Morgan by opening the car door, and even the comfiest position in a car seat wasn't *very* comfy.

The grass — or hay, straw, wheat, or whatever... He had no idea — in the field looked like the most promising place to rest. People slept on that all the time in movies.

He took a step off the road, realized he was walking towards Monica's body, turned on his heel, and crossed to the other side. The grass over there was just as soft. *Probably.*

Hamilton watched him with an expression that was equal parts amusement, concern and confusion.

Harlan found himself wondering, for the first time, how odd their exhaustion must look to someone with no — or very little — psychic ability. From Hamilton's perspective, all he and Morgan had done was hold hands for a few hours.

Harlan flattened a patch of grass and lay down.

Movies lied. The grass was itchy, prickly and full of bugs. He would have to start keeping a blanket or something in the car in case there was a next time. He seriously hoped there wouldn't be.

Fuck it. Morgan could share. Even the passenger seat had to be better than this.

The next thing he knew was Hamilton shaking him awake. He didn't feel refreshed. He was cold and still itchy. His head was pounding.

"C'mon."

"What?" he asked, barely keeping himself from snapping at Hamilton. He wanted to be back in the city, in his own bed, with Charles, after a long hot shower. He was never coming to the country again. Ghosts outside of the city were on their own.

Hamilton was crouched in front of him, his hands hanging between his legs, vibrating with energy. "OPP's here."

"So?" He could just roll over and go back to sleep. This spot wasn't so bad. It definitely beat anything else he'd have to do. Almost certainly he'd have to talk to strangers. He yawned. "You know where the body is. I want my scarf back. No, I don't. Yes, I do." It hadn't touched the body. It was fine. No. It was ruined. It would always make him think of this now, not Charles.

"Sorry, bud. They need to talk to us."

"Right now?" He knew he was whining a little, but at this point he didn't care. He thought he'd earned at least a little whining.

Somehow he managed to sit up, rubbing his eyes. He felt little bits of grass getting ground into them and immediately sneezed. How had people survived before cities? He definitely deserved a medal for this.

"'fraid so, kiddo. I held them off as long as I could, but they're…a little freaked out by what the two of you did."

Harlan got up. He was swaying a little, but he didn't think he'd fall over.

Hamilton stood up more slowly, but with his usual grace.

Stupid not-exhausted Hamilton.

"They at least want to get statements from each of us before they'll let us go."

"Fine." This wasn't Hamilton's fault, but he knew Hamilton could handle some misdirected grumpiness.

The cruiser seemed to have sheltered him from what was happening on its far side better than he'd expected. Once he was on the other side, everything was light and noise and ordered chaos. There were two OPP vehicles and a hearse. There was a whole string of people between the trees and the road, more than the number of cars suggested, or at least it seemed that way to Harlan. *Maybe they carpooled,* he thought, his exhaustion shifting from surly to giddy.

They'd set up floodlights in the trees, and the whole place was ringed with yellow police tape.

Two men in scrubs were carrying a pitifully small shape suspended in a body bag between them, and Harlan's mood shifted again. He was tired and itchy, but a little girl was dead. He'd done his part to make sure she saw justice.

He watched them load the bag into the hearse and drive away. He saw no sign of her ghost, and he was glad.

Morgan got out of the car and shook their head. "I-I don't think I want to help Grandma look for Fido anymore."

Chapter Ten

It was after two a.m. by the time the OPP finished questioning them.

One of the OPP officers, seeing how tired the three of them were — especially Morgan, who looked wilted — suggested they spend the night at the nearby Elora Mill Inn. Harlan wanted to be home more than anything, but he didn't want to have to *travel* there, even though he wouldn't be the one driving. The last thing he wanted to do that night was dispel a spirit. He'd got so used to sleeping in ghost-warded rooms — or with Charles.

Harlan stumbled through the hotel's front door. Hamilton checked them in, handed each of them a key card and shooed in the direction of their rooms. Harlan only saw one ghost on the way, a simple repeater who seemed completely unaware of him or anyone else.

A lot of repeaters acted out their deaths over and over, and it was horrible to watch. Some — like the ghost girl he'd named Libby, who haunted the lobby of his apartment building—looped something that had taken place immediately before or led to their death. She'd never so much as looked at him, so he let her stay. He knew nothing about who she was—who she'd *been*—but from her retro clothes, he guessed she'd died in the sixties or seventies.

Or the week before he'd moved in, on her way to a costume party.

Even rarer were repeaters like the one in the Mill, who performed an action they'd done frequently in life that seemed to have nothing to do with their death. Harlan had always found those repeaters interesting. They were a tiny window into history, ordinary people going about their lives. Well…scenes from their lives, even if those lives were over.

It was hard to tell exactly what he was doing, because whatever objects he thought he was interacting with were long gone and had turned to dust, but after Harlan watched him for a while, he decided the ghost was unloading something heavy from a wagon and heaving it into a pile against a wall that no longer existed. He was whistling as he worked, but Harlan couldn't hear it—not without focusing, and he wasn't wasting his little remaining energy on *that*.

He was too tired for even that to hold his attention long, and he sighed with relief as his door shut behind him and locked automatically.

He wanted to crawl directly into the plush bed, but the memory of the tiny form in a flapping black body bag—not to mention his nap in the hay—forced him into the shower. He scrubbed himself thoroughly, trying to visualize the day running down the drain, comforting himself with the thought of his own bed the next day. Hopefully with Charles, too.

He didn't have deodorant or a toothbrush. He'd never stayed in a hotel before. Based on movies, he thought they would provide them if he asked, but that would mean talking to someone.

Maybe in the morning.

He glanced at his phone and groaned. Hopefully closer to *afternoon* than morning.

He didn't have pyjamas, either, but he didn't want to sleep naked in an unfamiliar place. He reluctantly pulled his sweaty grass and probably bug-covered underwear back on. It completely undid taking a shower, but he was too tired to care.

He thought about texting Charles — who would be awake, but at the club with his phone on silent. He could send him a text for him to read later, but he didn't want to get into the day's events, not yet, and he also, selfishly, didn't want to risk Charles waking him up when he replied. He wanted to get as much sleep as possible. He'd text Charles when he got back to the city.

* * * *

Hamilton called him at ten a.m. — a whole hour later than usual. Hamilton must have been tired.

Harlan groaned and rolled out of bed. He was glad that he didn't have to worry about packing anything. He only had his clothes, which he wished he could have cleaned before putting them back on.

He lingered in the room, spinning in slow circles and feeling like he was forgetting something, even though he knew there was nothing to forget.

He found Hamilton in the hotel's restaurant, devouring eggs and toast in front of a window. Tired as he was, Harlan had to admit the view was beautiful — trees in the distance and the river that had probably powered the mill beneath them. That was how mills worked, right? He momentarily considered asking the ghost he'd seen the night before.

He definitely needed more sleep, and he hoped Hamilton didn't plan on them working their shift when they got back to Toronto.

Hamilton grunted by way of greeting and kept eating.

A few minutes later a waiter brought a bowl of oatmeal and fresh raspberries and put it in front of Harlan — one of his comfort foods. He was puzzled for a moment, just tired enough to wonder if he'd ordered it without remembering or if someone had read his mind — a useful skill in a restaurant — or it had been an amazing coincidence, then realized Hamilton must have ordered for him.

Someone else might have found it patronizing, but Harlan was honestly relieved Hamilton had taken care of that one small interaction for him, especially because of how gross and tired he felt.

He actually teared up a little at this small gesture. Hamilton had known how much Harlan liked this for breakfast. Harlan didn't remember telling him. Well…he would make a great detective someday.

Harlan couldn't hold back a little laugh, but it wasn't a very happy one. He knew he'd probably be assigned to a new partner when Hamilton was inevitably promoted.

Hamilton looked up at him and raised an eyebrow. When Harlan didn't offer to explain the joke, he looked back down at his plate.

There was no sign of Morgan yet, unless they'd chosen to eat at another table or left early. Harlan wouldn't have blamed them. They hadn't asked to be dragged into this.

Just as Hamilton was starting to look restless, Morgan walked into the restaurant. They glanced at the empty tables but sat with Harlan and Hamilton.

Their clothes — the same ones as the night before, of course — were rumpled but clean...unlike Harlan's. Hamilton's uniform hid any dirt, but its normally razor-sharp creases were looking a little flat.

There were dark circles under Morgan's eyes, and they turned a little green when the waiter returned to ask if they wanted breakfast, but they still looked better than Harlan felt.

After Morgan told the waiter they didn't want anything, Hamilton said, "All right, kiddos, let's get the hell outta here." He stood, brushed off his hands and marched towards the front door. He didn't pay, and Harlan assumed that he wasn't doing a dine-and-dash and that either the OPP or the Toronto Police Service would cover the bill.

Morgan and Harlan fell in line behind him like good little zombie ducklings and followed him to the car.

"You can sit up front," Harlan offered.

They just silently shook their head and climbed into the back seat. They stretched out across both seats, made themself the comfiest nest they could and closed their eyes. *Damn.* Harlan wished he'd thought of that and called dibs. Feeling a little cheated, he plopped down in his usual seat beside Hamilton.

Hamilton turned to glance at Morgan. "Before you fall asleep, what's your address?"

They told him and Hamilton started the car.

"Are you okay to drive?" Harlan asked nervously.

"Oh, yeah. I've done way more with less sleep."

Not exactly comforting.

"Besides"—Hamilton held up a truly enormous travel mug with the Mill's logo on it—"I have *this*." Grinning a little maniacally, he peeled out of the parking lot.

Morgan let out a little groan but didn't open their eyes or move.

Harlan was beginning to think that their decision not to eat breakfast had been a good one. Oatmeal was supposed to be gentle on the stomach, but it just felt like a solid lump, banging around whenever Hamilton turned or changed lanes.

He had no memory of the route they'd taken to get there in the dark the night before—he'd got horribly turned around on the country roads, even before they'd driven to the Mill—so he could only trust that Hamilton had got directions before he'd come downstairs or that he remembered the way back. Hopefully a shorter, less circuitous way.

Hamilton didn't check the map on his phone, which made Harlan nervous.

They pulled onto the highway. He could already hear Morgan's gentle snores on the other side of the mesh. He hadn't expected to fall asleep, but his eyes started drifting shut and, after a thorough glance at Hamilton to make sure he didn't look like *he* would fall asleep too, he gave in.

* * * *

"We're here." Hamilton's voice was uncharacteristically gentle, and Harlan realized he was talking to Morgan.

He yawned, stretching as much as he could in his seat. Being in the car for so long during the last two days was bad enough, but he'd also spent the trip out there holding himself very tense and forced to keep constant contact with Morgan. Combined with sleeping in an unfamiliar bed followed by a car, he was stiff all over. He was used to driving all over the GTA to hunt ghosts and spending hours in the car, but this was different.

They were outside an unfamiliar apartment building, and for a terrible moment Harlan was afraid it was another haunting they had been assigned to deal with, but when he saw Morgan sit up in the rear-view mirror, he realized it must be where they lived. He hoped.

Morgan opened and closed their mouth a few times, clearly trying to think of what to say in this situation. Finally they settled on, "Thank you," and pulled the door handle. It didn't open, and a brief look of panic crossed their face before it was smoothed away.

"Oh, shit, sorry, I'll have to come around and open it for you. Hang on." Hamilton opened the door from the outside and Morgan spilled out onto the sidewalk.

Morgan's old, red-brick building was eerily similar to Harlan's. Had the Centre rented it for them, the way they'd set up an apartment for Harlan, and they hadn't bothered to move, or had they chosen it themself and it was a coincidence?

"Thank you," Morgan said again, their gaze darting between Hamilton and their apartment building.

"You'll be okay?" Hamilton asked in his talking-to-shocked-witnesses voice, which Harlan so rarely heard. "You've got someone to talk to if you need to?"

"Yeah. Someone... Yeah, I'll be fine."

"Hmph. Here." Hamilton reached into his chest pocket and pulled out a business card.

Harlan hadn't even known he *had* business cards.

Morgan stared at it like it was a dead animal, clearly not wanting to touch it.

"Here." Harlan held out his hand.

Hamilton passed it to him with just a moment's hesitation.

Taking it, Harlan fished a pen out of Hamilton's immaculately organized glove compartment. He might drive like a maniac and be a little rough on it, but he loved his car and it was always pristine.

Harlan scribbled his number on the back, then passed it back to Hamilton, who offered it to Morgan again.

This time they took it, clutching it to their chest.

"Call us—either of us—if you need anything," Hamilton told them.

Harlan nodded.

Morgan managed a faint smile. "I will. Promise." They turned and fled towards their apartment.

A moment later, Harlan got a text. It was Morgan, confirming they had the right number and giving theirs to Harlan in case he needed to contact them.

Hamilton leaned back in his seat with a groan, then slumped forward, actually resting his head on the steering wheel for a moment.

Harlan had never seen Hamilton look this tired. Before he could think better of it, he blurted, "I thought you and that Olympic-size swimming pool of coffee have been through worse."

Hamilton laughed, flipping him off. "Yeah, yeah. Smartass. I'm getting too old for this shit." He started the car and pulled out into traffic a little more smoothly than usual.

Does he actually drive better when he's tired?

"Ready?"

"For what?"

"For the first ghost of the day."

Now it was Harlan's turn to groan.

"Ha. Sucker. You should see the look on your face. Nah, I'm shitting you. I'm taking you home."

Harlan had never been so relieved in his life.

The drive seemed twice as long as it should have been, and Harlan cursed silently every time they got stuck in traffic or at an especially long light. And they *all* seemed especially long.

Finally, they pulled up in front of Harlan's apartment.

About to get out, he glanced at Hamilton. He looked tired and, while Harlan thought he was only a decade or so older than him, he *did* look "*too old for this shit*".

"D-Do you want to come upstairs?" Harlan offered, surprising himself.

"What?" Hamilton's head whipped around to stare at him.

"You could crash on the couch. Or the bed. I could be on the—"

"I'll take a rain check. I texted him last night, but I'm sure Matthew's worried about me. Ugh. I guess he won't be home. Fuck. I'll see you tomorrow, 'kay?"

Harlan nodded, shooting one last glance at Hamilton before going into his building.

He'd never been so happy to see Libby, the black-and-white floor tile, the shiny brass elevator doors...

He practically skipped out of the elevator, down the hall and into his suite—his beautiful, ghost-warded haven, with the comforting sounds of traffic and construction outside. He barely took the time to peel off his clothing before collapsing into bed.

It's good to be back in the city.

Chapter Eleven

Harlan's phone alarm went off. He rolled away from Charles to look at it and groaned. "I just want to stay in bed with you," he told Charles, "but my coffee with the other mediums is in an hour." There were three police mediums in the Greater Toronto Area besides Harlan — Beth, Benjamin and Leo.

"I should shower and get dressed soon. I could skip it, but I really... I think I need to talk to them...about Monica."

Charles sat up, trailing his fingers down Harlan's back. "Hey. It's all right. You don't have to explain yourself to me. If you need — if you *want* to go, you should go. I'll see you later?"

"Yeah." He had a thought. Charles' hand was still on his shoulder and he put his own on top of it, turning to look at Charles. "You could come with me," he said, very softly.

"What?" Charles laughed.

Harlan shook his head, sliding back down so he was sitting between Charles' legs with his head tipped back and resting on Charles' shoulder. "No, really. You said to Morgan the other day that you have an ability, and you're right. You do. And if it's not mediumship, it's pretty fucking close."

Charles stroked Harlan's hair thoughtfully. "I guess," he said slowly, "but isn't this meeting for *police* mediums?"

"It's not really a meeting," Harlan assured him. He liked this plan more and more as he tried to convince Charles. "And you've met them. Well, you've met one of them. I don't know if you remember him." They'd met right after the incident with Samuel Harkness, but Charles had been in and out of consciousness.

"You don't think they'd mind?"

Harlan shook his head.

"I'll give you a *ride*," Charles told him, "and I'll at least come inside with you. But if I get the feeling anyone doesn't want me there, I'm leaving, okay?"

Harlan nodded eagerly. "Wanna shower with me?"

Charles laughed again, kissing the top of Harlan's head. "If we do that, I think we'll be late…if we make it there at all."

"I know you're right, but…"

"Later, babe. Promise."

It wasn't until he was soaping his armpits that it occurred to Harlan that he didn't think Charles had called him a pet name before. Definitely not 'babe'.

Grinning, he hummed softly to himself as he rinsed off.

* * * *

"So, this is it, huh?"

Harlan paused with his hand on the door handle. "What were you expecting?"

"I don't know...something more mystical, I guess? Some hole-in-the-wall place with scarves over the lights and crystals everywhere. Definitely not Tim Hortons."

Harlan couldn't help laughing at the image. "No. Beth would hate that. She likes a place she can, and I quote, *'just walk in and buy a coffee without learning fucking Italian or something'* and knowing what she's going to get. But," he admitted, "we do occasionally meet at Starbucks or, like you said, some indie place, when we know she's not gonna be around."

Charles grinned. "I see."

Beth waved from a table in the corner. She didn't look all that surprised to see Charles, and she definitely did not look upset. "Called it!" she crowed. "Pay up."

Groaning, Benjamin pulled out his wallet, slapped a five-dollar bill on the table, and slid it over to Beth.

"Uh..." Harlan glanced between the two of them.

"We had a bet about how long it would take for you to bring him. Hi, Charles," Benjamin said.

"Hi," Charles answered, friendly but off balance.

"You probably don't remember me. I'm Benjamin, and this is Beth."

Beth waved again. "Welcome. We're glad you *finally* joined us."

"You don't mind?" Harlan asked.

"Mind? He's a medium in our books," Beth told him. "A really fucking useful one. Thought about joining the force?"

"Thanks. I've got enough on my plate," Charles said dryly, squeezing Harlan's hand.

"All right. Well, we're here if you change your mind!"

Smiling, Charles shook hands with the two mediums.

Taking a seat, Harlan frowned. "Where's Leo?" He leaned back so he could look at the line of people at the counter, but he didn't see her there either.

Benjamin and Beth glanced at each other, all traces of humour gone from their faces.

"What?" Harlan asked.

"You haven't heard from her, have you?"

"N-No? Why? Should I have?"

"That's just it—none of us have. Neither has Detective Taylor—Leo's partner. Leo's girlfriend says she hasn't been home for days. She hasn't replied to any of our calls or texts."

"It's not like her to just disappear like this," Benjamin added. "Miss work. We were really hoping she'd show up here today and explain what's going on."

"Sorry, no, I haven't heard from her. *Shit*."

"Yeah." Benjamin turned to Charles. "Sorry. You guys don't have to stick around. We're usually at least a little more fun than this."

Charles spoke up before Harlan had to. "Of course not! What can we do to help?"

"Well, not *you*…" Benjamin began slowly.

"But him, yeah," Beth continued.

"Me?" Harlan asked.

"You…and your friend Mx. Vermeer."

Beth grinned at the surprised look on Harlan's face. "Yeah, you can keep that kinda thing out of the press, but cops talk—*especially* in front of us, like we're so tuned into the fucking 'mystical energies' or whatever

142

bullshit that we don't hear them fart. We heard all about how you found that poor girl."

The two of them stared at him almost hungrily.

"I-I guess I could ask them," Harlan said, slowly. Even though he could understand their fear over Leo, he had a really bad feeling about bringing Morgan into this. His ability combined with theirs could help solve a lot of cases, but Morgan wasn't a cop. He found it extremely unlikely that they wanted to become one, especially after their experience. They'd been reluctant enough the first time, when they'd been personally involved. To drop all this on them again... He could still picture how pale they'd been the night they'd found Monica.

"Please," Benjamin said. "Just ask them. If they say no, that's it."

Harlan sighed. "All right. I'll ask." He retreated outside so he'd have some privacy. He felt a little guilty about leaving Charles alone with people he'd just met—something Harlan would have hated if their positions were reversed—but when he glanced through the window, he saw Charles talking away. *Of course.* Charles made friends wherever he went. He was good at listening to people, putting them at ease.

Harlan had started typing *Hey, Morgan* when he realized this was really more of an actual phone call situation. He gritted his teeth. Talking to people face to face was bad enough. He *hated* talking on the phone.

Morgan answered on the second ring. "Harlan! This is a surprise. Is everything okay?"

"Well... No. Not really."

"Oh, shit. What happened?"

"There's another missing person."

A moment of frosty silence, or maybe Harlan was reading too much into it. "So? Call the canine unit."

No, definitely not reading too much into it. He heard them take several long, slow breaths, again in a familiar pattern.

"I'm sorry. I shouldn't have snapped at you. It's just... I was sick for three days after last time, Harlan — vomiting, chills. I almost had to go to the hospital. I couldn't keep anything down, and I was sweating so much. And that girl... Oh, fuck, I didn't even see her face, not her real, dead face, but it's all I can see."

"I'm sorry. I shouldn't have called."

Morgan sighed. "Is it a kid?"

"N-No. No. It's another medium. A police medium... Leo." Harlan was still so rattled by the news that Leo was missing that his thoughts felt thick and slow and heavy, like he was underwater.

"Can't you guys, like, sense each other? I think I read something like that."

"We can, normally."

"How long?"

"What?"

"How long has he been *missing*?"

"He? Oh. *She*. She's been missing a couple of days, I think. I'd have to go inside and ask."

"You know the police won't even start looking for an adult until they've been gone for like seventy-two hours, right?"

"I, um... I don't think that's true in Ontario." He nibbled some dry skin on his lip. "And...I'm not asking as the police." Hopefully he could make that call and he wasn't unintentionally lying to them.

"Fuck. Okay. I can... We can at least try to find out if she's alive or dead. I am *not* committing to another ghost chase."

"No, of course not. Thank you. *Thank you.*"

"She has a significant other?"

"Yes. A girlfriend. We'll pick you up. You're at home?"

"Yeah." They hung up without saying goodbye. He couldn't blame them.

He texted Hamilton. Luckily he remembered their address, so he didn't have to call them again.

Both the other mediums and Charles turned to look at him as he walked back in and sat at their table.

Beth was the first to break the silence. "Well?"

"They agreed to try."

Harlan found his almost-untouched Iced Capp pressed into his hand then he was being rushed right back out the door somehow. He wouldn't have minded sitting for a minute, but apparently that wasn't happening. He glanced at Charles. *No.* He knew that if Charles was missing, he wouldn't want to wait, either. He hadn't known Leo as long as the other two, but he wanted to try to find out where she was.

Benjamin gave Harlan Leo's address and then got in Beth's car.

Charles took Harlan to pick up Morgan.

"You doing okay?" Charles asked, taking one hand off the wheel and giving Harlan's thigh a brief squeeze.

"Yeah. Yeah, I think so." He nibbled his finger for a few seconds. "I'll be *better* when we..."

Charles nodded. "Of course. Hey, how's Morgan? I know you didn't talk long, but you told me they were pretty freaked out after last time. I know what it's like, being dragged into all of this."

Harlan stiffened in his seat.

Charles glanced at him. "Shit, I'm sorry. I didn't mean it like that. You made the right call to bring me in. James would have died if you hadn't, and Samuel might have got away to keep killing." James had been Samuel's prisoner when Harlan had found him. He would have been Samuel's next victim, but he, Charles and Hamilton had managed to save the man.

Charles sounded so *certain* that Harlan's eyes filled with tears. "*You made the right call.*" He felt like a part of him, a part he hadn't known existed or had at least buried way down deep, had needed to hear those words. To hear *Charles* say those words.

"You're sure? You're not just saying that to make me feel better?"

"I'm not just saying that to make you feel better," Charles promised, and what choice did Harlan have but to believe him?

"I could've got *you* killed," Harlan said, very slowly. Somehow, Leo's disappearance had made that possibility real in a way it hadn't been before.

"Do you want me to stop for a second so we can talk about this?" Charles asked gently.

Harlan shook his head without looking at Charles. He did and he didn't, but right now they needed to help find Leo.

Charles sighed. "Yeah. I could've died. And I'm definitely not in a hurry to go through anything like that again." He laughed. "But I *didn't* die. We can't think about what *might* have happened." He exhaled. "*You* might have died," he pointed out. "But we're both here, and we're both safe—and so is James." He gave Harlan's thigh another squeeze, longer this time. "I'd do the same thing again."

"You mean it? Really?" Harlan sniffed, pulling a Kleenex out of Charles' glove compartment and blowing his nose.

"Yeah. Yeah, I do. Hey, pass me one of those tissues, would you?"

Chapter Twelve

Morgan answered the front door just as Charles was about to press the buzzer.

"It's good to see you again, Morgan," Charles told them. "I'm sorry it's because..."

Morgan laughed, a little dryly but warmer than they'd sounded on the phone. "Yeah. Me too. But it *is* good to see you again."

They drove the rest of the way in near silence. Charles eventually turned on the radio, but Harlan couldn't have said what they listened to. Morgan seemed poised and nervous in front of him, and he felt the same. He thought about Leo, wondering which would be worse — that he and Morgan would be able to summon her ghost...or that they *wouldn't*.

Leo's building was ultra-modern, not at all like his or Morgan's. He wasn't sure if she'd gone through the Centre or not. He realized he didn't know all that much about her personal life — or any of the other mediums' — despite their coffees together. Harlan didn't ask questions about people—not like Charles, who engaged with everyone he met.

"I'd better stay in the car," Charles said. "Just in case... Well."

It hadn't even occurred to Harlan that Charles wouldn't be able to come in with them, but he was right. "Sorry," he said, more to himself than to Charles. He would definitely have preferred having Charles beside him, especially in this situation.

"It's okay. I've got my phone— I've got the entirety of human knowledge here with me."

"You're sure? You could go, and we could find our own way back?"

Charles shook his head, grinning at Harlan. "I'm fine. Go do your thing."

"Thanks," Harlan murmured.

Benjamin was outside having a smoke when they pulled up. He waved at them lazily, then stubbed out his cigarette and offered Morgan a hand. "Mx. Vermeer?"

They nodded.

"Benjamin Xun. Thank you so much for doing this. We really appreciate it."

They nodded again, more stiffly this time, but shook Benjamin's hand. "Just Morgan is fine."

"Please, come on in."

Leo's girlfriend, Cassandra, was a short white woman with brightly coloured sleeve tattoos. She thanked Harlan and Morgan for coming, asking if they'd like a drink, a sandwich, anything...

They both politely declined. Harlan, for his part, knew he didn't want to spend any more time there than he needed to.

Beth, standing near Cassandra, gave her a firm hug.

Morgan cleared their throat to get everyone's attention, but she was focused on Cassandra. "I'm not sure what you've been told about my power."

Cassandra took a tiny step away from Beth, grabbed her elbows with her opposite hands and gave her head a tiny shake.

Morgan smiled at her. "Okay. So, basically I'm a shapeshifter, but my power works in a very specific way. I can only turn into the person you love most. Okay?"

Cassandra nodded, managing a tiny smile in return.

It wasn't quite the same way they'd described their power to Harlan, but it was probably better under the circumstances.

"With your permission, I'm going to turn into Leo."

The corner of Cassandra's mouth twitched, but she nodded again.

"Then, Harlan and I are going to try to use our new ability to find her."

They didn't add *ghost*, and again Harlan thought that was very tactful.

"I can't promise you anything, but we'll try. Are you ready?" Morgan asked, gently.

"Do I need to do anything?"

They shook their head. "Just picture Leo standing here with you." Morgan gave Cassandra a soft smile. "Picture her in as much detail as you can. Think about your love."

Harlan knew he wouldn't have been able to say something like that with a straight face, but somehow Morgan made it sound genuine and pure.

"Anything else?" Cassandra looked almost disappointed, which Harlan thought he could understand. He was sure that if Charles were missing, he'd feel helpless and useless—even more so than usual. He'd want to be involved even in some small way, and he'd want something to do.

"Close your eyes and focus on Leo."

Cassandra nodded after a moment, sitting on the couch and closing her eyes.

Morgan rolled their shoulders, and between one blink and the next they were gone and Leo stood in their place.

"Holy fuck," Beth gasped.

Opening her eyes, Cassandra cried out, surging off the couch and taking a step towards Morgan before stopping herself. She had one hand over her mouth and the other over her heart as she slowly shook her head back and forth.

"This is Leo?" Morgan asked softly.

Cassandra nodded. "What does this mean? Is Leo alive? Is she…?"

"It doesn't mean anything yet," Morgan told her, "except that you two love each other very much. Harlan?" They held out a hand.

Oh, fuck, he didn't want to do this, not in front of the other mediums. What if this new power repulsed them, frightened them? He wasn't sure what, exactly, his relationship with them was, but he knew he didn't want to lose them.

Not in front of Cassandra, who looked like she was in danger of shattering into a thousand pieces at any second—and who could blame her?

The tip of his forefinger brushed the ball of Morgan's thumb just for an instant. He pulled away as though he'd been shocked.

Morgan—still looking like Leo—cleared their throat, thrusting their hand at him more forcefully.

Harlan took it this time, closing his eyes like a coward. No one made a sound. He opened his eyes. Morgan still looked like Leo. There was no ghost in the room.

Beth snapped her fingers. "Oh, shit. Duh. This place is ghost-warded."

Pulling his hand away from Morgan's, Harlan did the special *blink* that allowed him to interact with ghosts and see ghost wards. The apartment shone like a beacon, and he quickly closed his eyes. It didn't help. He wasn't seeing them with his eyes, not really, so the 'light' shone right through his eyelids. He blinked again and again until his vision returned to normal.

Morgan shook their head. "We did it in your apartment earlier, and the ghost wards didn't matter there."

"You're right." He held out his hand for Morgan this time.

They took it quickly, grasping it tight.

Once again, nothing happened.

After a long moment, just to be sure, he let go of Morgan's hand. He flexed his own discreetly — they'd been squeezing it hard and it was a little numb.

"No ghost," Benjamin said, looking around. It almost came out as a question.

"No ghost," Harlan agreed.

"What does that mean?" Cassandra asked, looking between Harlan and Morgan.

"This is still new — really, really new," Morgan cautioned her. "But...I think it means Leo isn't... That she is alive." They glanced at Harlan, as though for confirmation, and he nodded.

"Okay. Okay." Cassandra half-sat, half-fell onto an armchair. "So? Now what?" She looked to Beth.

"Now we keep looking," Beth assured her, "in more conventional ways. And I know we'll all be keeping our feelers out to see if we can sense her. In the meantime...do you want me to stay with you?"

Cassandra wiped her eyes on the back of her hand, sniffling. "No. No, that's fine. Thank you. Thank *all* of you." She aimed a weak smile at Harlan and Morgan in particular.

Morgan smiled back at her. "Of course."

Chapter Thirteen

Libby had broken her usual pattern — stand at the lobby window, step, step, bite her nails, disappear and repeat — and was frantically waving at someone outside, someone he couldn't see. He tried looking past her, but all he could see through the window was thick grey fog.

He opened his eyes. Libby was still there, floating at the foot of his bed.

He screamed, pulling the covers up over himself like a little kid. He *felt* like a little kid. He wasn't Harlan Brand, police medium. He was just Harlan, tiny and alone and afraid in a world where no one believed he could see ghosts at all.

This couldn't be happening. He hadn't woken up to find a ghost beside him since he was a child, before his parents left him at the Centre. Since then, he'd always slept behind ghost wards, with the exception of his time at Charles' apartment — which didn't really count — and his single night in Elora.

Silence. Stillness. He could sense that Libby was still there, but she hadn't moved closer or tried to interact with him in any way. It didn't seem like she was trying to frighten him—at least not yet.

He slowly pulled the blanket back down. He was shaking so hard that his teeth were chattering.

She hadn't moved from her place at the foot of the bed, and he got the sense that she was being carefully still so she wouldn't frighten him—more than she had already just by being in his room.

"Wh-What do you want?" The muscles in his jaw were so tight that he could hardly get the words out.

She smiled and slowly approached the head of the bed.

Harlan's breathing sped up, becoming dangerously shallow. *Fuck.* She hadn't threatened him in any way, hadn't done *anything*, but he was still losing it.

She retreated slightly, holding up her hands.

Fuck this. He *wasn't* that scared little boy anymore. He'd dealt with ghosts that would have swallowed him whole—with her as an appetizer—if he'd let them. He *knew* her. He'd lived with her for almost a year. She was his neighbour—not that neighbours couldn't turn out to be monsters, of course, and by most definitions she *was* a monster, no matter how sweet she looked and acted, but...

He threw off the blanket, feeling a little queasy as it passed straight through her and dropped to the floor, more slowly where it 'touched' her, or maybe that was just his imagination.

He immediately regretted it, since it left him completely naked in front of her.

She didn't react to his nudity.

"What do you *want*?" he asked again, relieved that he sounded more tired and annoyed than frightened this time.

She tilted her head as though thinking about his question. She slowly held out one hand, then curled her fingers towards her palm. She had to repeat the gesture a few times, a little faster with each repetition, before he understood. She was beckoning him.

"You want me to follow you?"

She nodded eagerly, motioning with both hands now.

He stood. "All right, all right. Give me a sec to let me put some pants on." He was halfway through pulling on a pair of pyjama bottoms when a spike of white-hot pain crashed through the left side of his body, and he was flat on his back on the floor with no memory of falling.

Libby rushed towards him, her mouth open in a silent scream.

He threw up both hands to protect himself and closed his eyes as he waited for her to strike, but before she reached him, there was another burst of energy and she was gone. He could tell that even with his eyes closed.

He opened them. No trace of her remained.

He got to his feet, distantly aware of being in pain from the fall. He'd feel it more later, he was sure, but he was so full of adrenaline that he could brush it aside.

He pulled his pants on and ran downstairs, only realizing he'd left his door unlocked when he was two floors down. He wasn't even sure he'd closed it. Normally this would have made him incredibly anxious, but it hardly fazed him. He had more important things to worry about. Besides, it was the middle of the night. No one was up except him.

The lobby was empty of both living people and ghosts. There was no Libby pacing back and forth in front of the window where she was supposed to be.

He extended his senses outward, feeling the brush of a familiar ghost a few blocks away.

No Libby. He reached out farther, as far as he could, stretching his ability until it *hurt*, touching dozens of spirits as he passed, but he couldn't feel her energy at all.

He was half naked, shivering and standing in the middle of the lobby in the middle of the night. He felt out of control, and it frightened him.

He glanced at the door leading to the stairwell, then at the elevator. He was exhausted but also rattled enough that his old fear of elevators had returned and he didn't want to shut himself inside a claustrophobic box.

Exhaustion won out—or maybe stubbornness. He didn't want to use the elevator, so he had to.

Nothing happened on the way up.

He locked his door behind himself—he had left it partially open—but he still didn't feel safe, not the way he usually did once he was barricaded inside his apartment. It wasn't just Libby's intrusion. It was something more. Something...

He stumbled away from the door, his eyes wide and feeling numb with horror. He could barely focus long enough to do the mental shift that allowed him to see ghost wards.

The wards on the door were intact, but instinct made him turn. To his right, along the inner wall of the apartment, the wards stretched away clean and unbroken. To the left... The ward that spanned the outer wall of his living room was *gone*, along with a chunk in the corner facing the hallway. That had to be how Libby had got in.

He followed the outer wall into the kitchen, the bedroom, the bathroom. The wards had disappeared from *all* the outer walls. He had a corner apartment, so *two* of his bedroom walls were affected. All the interior walls, along with the floor and ceiling, were intact.

Unlike what he'd seen at the Centre, the edges of this breach weren't clean. Where the last ward looked like it had been removed with surgical precision, this looked like an animal had ripped it to shreds, tearing off great chunks but leaving messy tendrils behind.

He was shivering again, and his body was beginning to ache from the fall and the unexplained jolt of energy that had caused it. His left side flashed between tingly pins-and-needles numbness and hot bolts of pain that made him cry out involuntarily and double over.

What is happening? What did this? His wards had been retouched barely three weeks before. They'd all been glowing powerfully when he'd checked a few days earlier, as he did at least a few times a week. It should have taken a very powerful ghost days, if not weeks, of pounding against them to so much as make a hole large enough to get *through*, never mind...this. And he would have noticed any ghost who tried.

He needed help. Who should he call first? No ghost wards...Charles. He pulled out his phone and glanced at the time. Not quite four a.m. Charles would still be at the club, either with his phone muted or not on him. Either way, he probably wouldn't see Harlan's text until at least seven, when he usually finished work. More often than not lately he'd been coming straight to

Harlan's after work so they could cuddle—and sometimes a little more—before Hamilton picked Harlan up at nine for the beginning of their shift. He'd been thinking about asking if he could change his hours to more closely match Charles'. The ghosts didn't care what time he was dispatched to deal with them. The only thing that had held him back was the fact that he might lose Hamilton as a partner if he changed his shift. Nine months ago, the thought would have been a relief, but now it was a real consideration. He didn't want a new partner.

He was getting distracted. He texted Charles anyway—*Need help when you get this* and a kiss emoji.

What was the next step? He felt like there were *physical* holes in his walls that anything could blow through, leaving him cold, exposed and vulnerable. If that were the case, he would call someone to patch those holes with plywood until they could be repaired properly. The equivalent would be a ward-painter. He had no idea how to contact one, and he suspected he wouldn't be able to just google it and find out. He gave it a shot. *Ward-painter Toronto* gave him a few results, but all of them seemed sketchy, like they'd just come, paint some olive oil on his walls and charge him a thousand dollars...or more. He knew getting wards painted was expensive, but he'd never actually seen the bill.

He groaned, his sleep-deprived brain crashing as he came down from his adrenaline high. Part of him was tempted to just crawl back into bed and deal with anything else that happened in the morning, but he knew he couldn't.

Tom. Tom had called a ward-painter to the Centre. And he *had* told Harlan to call him if he ever needed anything — something Harlan had tried to avoid.

He sighed and dialled Tom's number. He suspected that, if he texted, Tom would know he was using it as a cop-out to not talk on the phone and call him anyway.

The line rang and rang. Tom didn't answer, and it didn't go to voicemail. Finally Harlan hung up, frustrated. Who else might be able to help?

Beth or Benjamin? Worth a shot. He texted *hey* to each of them. Neither responded, but it was the middle of the night, and who knew when they'd got off work? The more experienced police mediums didn't just do crime-scene cleanup. They also 'interrogated' the ghosts of victims.

The only other person who came to mind was Hamilton. He had a pretty good idea of how pleased his partner would be if he called him at this hour, but he didn't know what else to do. He could call the non-emergency police line and hopefully be able to convince them he was a police medium and actually needed a ward-painter, but that seemed like it would take a long time and a lot of energy he didn't have.

He called Hamilton rather than texting like he normally would. Even though there were probably good explanations why no one else had replied to him, he was starting to get a little freaked out and he needed to hear someone's voice, reassure himself that he wasn't all alone except for the ghosts.

"Brand. You'd better have a really fucking good reason for this."

He could hear Matthew in the background asking who it was.

"It's Harlan. Go back to sleep," Hamilton told his boyfriend in a much gentler tone.

Harlan heard fabric rustling and a door close.

"What?"

"You remember how the ghost ward at the Centre failed?"

"Yeah." Harlan wasn't sure how Hamilton managed to make that single word sound like 'get to the point', but it was impressive.

"Mine failed tonight."

A sharp intake of breath. He knew he had Hamilton's attention.

"*Fuck.* Why? How?"

"I have no idea. I can't get a hold of Charles—he's working—or anyone else. Do you know how to contact a ward-painter?"

"Give me a couple minutes." He hung up.

Harlan realized he'd unconsciously made his way to the corner of his living room where two interior walls met, the farthest he could get from the un-warded walls. He didn't like that he'd done that without thinking about it, so he forced himself to go sit on his couch while he waited for Hamilton to call back.

Even though he'd been expecting it, he'd got distracted wondering what had happened to Libby. The abrupt noise of his ringtone in the silence of his apartment startled him. He dropped his phone on the rug and only managed to push it under the couch as he scrambled to pick it up. He finally had to drop to his knees and reach beneath the couch to get it, even though he couldn't shake the feeling that hands would grab him or he'd see a face leering at him from under the furniture.

There was nothing there.

"Hello?"

"Jesus, took you long enough." Hamilton sounded fully awake now, which was more than Harlan could say.

"Sorry. I dropped —"

"It's not just you."

"What?"

"Wards are down all over the city."

"What?" Harlan jumped to his feet and started pacing, hoping Hamilton couldn't hear him gnawing his forefinger.

"You're on a list to get re-warded, but you're not high on it."

"I understand." He hated it, but he understood. He could protect himself for the time being. Other people who needed to be behind wards might not be safe.

"And…"

"What?" he asked, for the third time.

"Nothing. Never mind. You've got enough to deal with right now." His voice was almost as gentle as it had been with Matthew, which made Harlan think something *really* bad was going on or had already happened.

"Hamilton, please. What's going on?"

Hamilton sighed. "The wards at the Centre fell. All of them."

"Oh, shit." *Those poor kids*. They might never feel safe there again. He knew he wouldn't.

"Harlan…"

Fuck. Hamilton *never* called him 'Harlan.'

"One of them is dead."

"One of who?"

"One of the kids."

Harlan's head swam, and he sank down onto the couch. "Dead?"

"Yeah."

"What happened?"

"I don't know, exactly. Everything's kinda…crazy right now. Xun and Wilson are already there."

It took Harlan a second to realize that he meant Benjamin and Beth.

No wonder they hadn't replied to his texts. Even though he didn't really want to get involved, he couldn't help feeling a little hurt that he hadn't been called in.

"What can I— What can *we* do?"

"Dunno. Sit tight, I guess. Wait to see if anyone needs us or needs help with the aftermath."

"That's it?"

"'fraid so, kiddo."

Harlan let his head fall back so it was resting on the couch and he was looking straight up at the ceiling.

"You'll be okay? Do you need me to come over?" Hamilton asked.

"No. I'll be fine."

"Bye." Hamilton didn't wait for Harlan to reply before he hung up, but he usually didn't even say goodbye.

Chapter Fourteen

Harlan felt restless and itchy, like spectral insects were crawling up and down his arms, prickling along his spine. He got up and started pacing again. Every ghost ward at the Centre had failed — at the same time, or close enough. One of the children was dead. Who — or what — could be doing this? How had things gone so terribly wrong all across the city?

His phone went off and he let out a little yelp. It took him a moment to realize it was Charles' special ringtone, and he quickly answered.

"Hey, Harlan. Sorry. I just got your message. Is everything okay?"

No. It really isn't. "I'm fine," he reassured Charles. "But...my ghost wards were broken."

"Holy shit, you're sure you're okay? Do you need me to come over until they can send someone?"

Yes. He wanted that so badly, wanted nothing more than to sink into Charles' warm, strong arms and know he was safe, but he knew that was selfish. There were people who needed Charles more than him. "No, but you need to go to the Centre." So far, Harlan was the only medium who Charles' power completely blocked, but hopefully he could suppress ghosts around the kids. Harlan probably didn't have the authority to make that call, but he'd deal with any possible fallout later.

Or make Hamilton do it.

"The Centre? Why?"

"Their wards failed too. One of the kids is dead."

"Oh my God! I'll go right away."

Harlan couldn't help smiling. It was just so *Charles* to immediately agree to help out however he could.

"Do you need me to pick you up?"

"No, I'll take a cab. I'll meet you there. Shit!" Harlan ducked and flinched as something flew past his head, just inches from his left ear, followed quickly by a crash.

"Harlan? What was that noise? Are you okay?"

Harlan leaned forward so he could see past the couch. An ugly vase—one that had come with the apartment and he hadn't got around to throwing away—was smashed on the floor. He glanced in the direction it had come from, unsurprised to see a ghost floating there. "Yeah. I'm fine. I'll see you soon." He hung up.

The ghost yanked one of the generic pictures off the wall hard enough to break the wire that held it in place. It got ready to throw it at Harlan, grinning malevolently.

At least this gave him an excuse to actually do some redecorating.

The ghost was familiar—he'd never actually seen it before, but he recognized its presence. He'd at least 'brushed' every ghost in a ten-block radius around his apartment to make sure none of them were dangerous.

The site this one haunted—its locus—was several blocks away. Why had it come all the way here, and why was it acting so violent? It hadn't registered as at all dangerous, or Harlan would've dealt with it earlier.

It threw the painting.

Harlan sidestepped and glass shattered around him. It had been an ugly painting, but it was *his*, and now Harlan was annoyed. "Cut. That. Out," he growled, backing up each word with some of his power.

The ghost fought him, trying to grab anything else it could reach to throw at him. He held it in place.

When it realized it couldn't attack him, it tried to escape.

He gave it a sharp *yank*, throwing it down onto the ghost-warded floor, which it wouldn't be able to simply sink through.

"What is *wrong* with you?" he demanded, beads of sweat appearing on his forehead as he struggled to control its flailing ectoplasmic limbs.

It shook its head, growling at him.

"Fine!" he snapped. "No more Mr. Nice-Medium." He tightened his grip with his left hand so hard he felt his bones creak and his knuckles looked like they might cut through his skin, but it freed his right hand. He slammed it on the floor beside him. A shimmering portal appeared and he had to close his eyes and scramble back a few inches so he wouldn't get disoriented and fall in. The brief glance he'd got of the other side was turned ninety degrees to his perspective, making his head swim. He usually made openings vertical, on a wall or upright in the middle of a room. He'd never made one on the floor before.

From what he'd seen, this particular ghost's afterlife didn't look hellish. While he suspected that something or someone had made this ghost turn malevolent through no fault of its own, he was still annoyed enough with it that he was disappointed there wasn't *any* fire and not even a whiff of brimstone.

"Now, get *in*." He filled the words with power, yanking his handful of ghost towards the hole.

It fought him, spitting and cursing as he dragged it closer and closer, inch by inch, to the doorway he'd created. The instant a trailing edge of its form touched the portal, the ghost froze. There was a sharp *clap* that Harlan felt more than heard, a smaller echo of the explosion that had knocked him over earlier.

Harlan held on grimly, not easing up his grip on the ghost even a fraction, in case this was some sort of trick.

"I…" The ghost lost its wild, ominous shape and swirled down into a mostly human form. "Where am I? What happened?"

Harlan took advantage of the spirit's confusion and distraction to drag it to the edge of the opening, so one good tug would pull it down and it wouldn't be Harlan's problem anymore. He didn't quite pull it in, though. He'd always thought it was better for ghosts to choose to leave on their own whenever possible. They didn't always leave him that choice. Hopefully it wasn't just fucking with him.

And, he had to admit that he was curious to see how the ghost explained itself.

"What's your name?" he asked.

"Miles. Miles Cavendish."

"Mr. Cavendish, what's the last thing you remember?" It was more convenient for Harlan if he remembered that he'd died, that he'd been a ghost before tonight. He hated having to tell people they were dead.

"I was with— No, that's not right. We were— No, no."

Harlan wasn't sure if the confusion was left over from whatever had made Miles leave his haunting ground and attack him or if it was the normal kind a lot of ghosts had when questioned. There was an art to it, asking them things without overwhelming them or influencing their answers.

"No. No, I remember. I was—I *am*—dead. I was at my corner…where I died. Where I've been since… I haven't been able to leave there, not until tonight. I haven't been anywhere *new* in so long," he said, with an edge of hunger Harlan didn't like.

None of what he said was very useful. It didn't give Harlan any idea of what had gone wrong with the wards or the ghosts. "It's time for you to move on, Mr. Cavendish." He inclined his head in the direction of the portal without releasing his grip.

Miles leaned over and peered down it. "Oh. Oh, that *is* beautiful! Is it…?"

"Yes. It's for you," Harlan assured him. Quickly, because he wanted to get this over with.

"Is it—?"

Before Miles could finish his second question, another bolt of pain struck Harlan. He lost his grip on the ghost when his left hand spasmed.

Miles didn't pull away. He doubled over, screaming from the same pain Harlan had just felt.

The portal caught Harlan's eye. The edges were…pulsing, flashing with bursts of bright purple, green and shades he couldn't name because they weren't meant for human eyes to see. "Hurry!" he shouted over the sudden rush of sourceless wind. "Get in the portal, *now*!"

"But what if I...?"

"It's where you belong!" Harlan told him. He wanted to lie and say he *knew* there was a good place waiting for him on the other side, but he knew at least what he'd said was true—whatever was waiting for him, it was where Miles belonged—where he should have gone when he'd died and was only catching up to him now.

"Please. Hurry." The portal was fighting him, struggling to open wider. Hot blood poured from his nose, pooling on his upper lip, then running down his chin and dripping on the floor. He was down on all fours now, with no energy or concentration to spare on anything but the portal. He had no idea what was wrong with it, only that it seemed almost... contaminated.

His whole body was shaking. His vision was going dark at the edges and his ears rang. He knew he might black out at any moment, and that he had to close the portal before he did—with the ghost trapped here on Earth or where he belonged. He'd never tried to open a gateway for the same ghost a second time. He wasn't actually sure it was possible. He *wanted* to help Miles cross over, but his first priority was making sure he didn't lose complete control of the portal.

"But—"

"Get. In. *Now*." Harlan pushed his hands closer together on the floor, using the physical motion to reinforce what he was doing with his power to keep it from growing.

Miles looked at the opening, then back at Harlan. He was clearly afraid—and Harlan couldn't blame him for that, no matter how inconvenient it was for him personally—but he finally stepped through and immediately vanished. As soon as he was gone, the portal tried to close on its own, the way it was supposed to, but something was still blocking it.

Harlan slammed a palm on the floor on either side of it.

The edges of the portal shivered, and for an awful moment it continued expanding.

Harlan screamed, frenzied and primal, pouring every ounce of himself — his will, his soul — into closing it.

The edges met and the portal closed, the sudden burst of energy knocking Harlan backwards and toppling a bookshelf behind him. He watched as books he hadn't chosen and would probably never read bounced and skittered across the floor in every direction.

He realized he was smiling and wondered if he had a concussion — or the magical equivalent. He felt... fried.

He lay where he'd been thrown, flat on his back, staring up at the ceiling. Its ghost wards were still intact. He groaned. They were blinding-bright, but even the effort of a *regular* blink seemed like too much, never mind one he had to concentrate on.

It took him several tries — which had never happened before — but he finally got the patterns to fade.

He sat bolt upright as something occurred to him. The wards on the floor, like the ceiling, were still intact. If he *hadn't* opened the portal on the floor, if he'd made it in the air the way he normally did... He shivered, wrapping his arms around his knees. He'd barely been able to close it, even with the wards supporting him.

If he'd tried it on one of the outer, de-warded walls...

He started shaking, and he couldn't stop. He felt, again, like his walls were physically gone and an icy wind was blowing through the apartment. He was beaded with sweat, his pyjama bottoms soaked through, even as his bare upper body rapidly cooled. He wanted to have a shower, crawl into bed and let the world take care of itself, just for one night.

A siren screamed past, sounding like it was right outside his window.

He groaned again, releasing his knees and allowing himself to fall back, his arms sprawled at his sides. He closed his eyes. He wasn't sure if he'd made it easier or more difficult to get up.

Just sitting straight up again seemed impossible, but he managed to flop onto his side. From there he got one elbow under himself and used it to lever himself into a sitting position again. He slid both legs to one side and rocked forward onto his knees. Then he just had to push himself up with his hands, and he was on his feet. *Triumph!* And it had only taken four or five times longer than it should have.

He staggered into the bedroom, staring into the bathroom longingly. He knew he couldn't risk showering. It would take more energy than he could spare.

He strongly considered just pulling on a shirt and staying in his PJs, but he forced himself to take them off and actually get dressed. With his pyjama bottoms off, he could see a nasty bruise forming on his left hip where he'd fallen. He quickly pulled up his jeans so he wouldn't have to look at it.

More sirens passed. It wasn't an uncommon occurrence in Toronto, but it did seem like more than usual — or maybe he was just noticing them more. He couldn't fix the whole city — not tonight, not on his own — but he knew he couldn't just sit quietly in his apartment either. He thought he could do the most good at the Centre, but he had to *get* there somehow. There was no way he had enough energy to walk, and he didn't think his odds of getting a cab or bus on this night were very good. Maybe he also didn't want to tie up a cab if someone needed it more than him. Taking the subway was out of the question. He could barely handle it on a good day, when ghosts weren't running wild.

He didn't want to call Charles, who was hopefully at the Centre and protecting the kids already, so that left Hamilton. That was, unfortunately, an actual *call* situation, not something he could do by text.

Hamilton answered on the tail of the first ring. "Finally! I've been waiting for you to call."

"You…have? You said you were — "

"I told 'em you'd need me tonight. What're we doing?"

"Going to the Centre."

"Great. I'll be there in… As soon as I can." Hamilton hung up with his usual abruptness.

Harlan's brain felt slow and clunky, like there were rocks in its gears.

He didn't have a coffee maker, and he didn't think this was the kind of tired caffeine could help, but there had to be something he could do. He remembered that Charles had 'left behind' a box of energy bars. Harlan suspected he'd left them on purpose so Harlan would have something to eat when he wasn't up for making something as simple as a decision and Charles wasn't around to feed him. He devoured one in three bites and shoved a few more into his pocket.

Chapter Fifteen

Normally Harlan would've waited in his apartment as long as possible, but with his ghost wards destroyed anyway, he figured he might as well just wait downstairs.

He'd hoped to find Libby in her usual spot in the lobby, but she wasn't there. Was she really, finally gone? Who or what had taken her? She hadn't passed on the way she was supposed to, but he didn't know what *had* happened.

He shouldered the heavy wooden door open and stepped outside.

Ghosts were on the move all around him in the darkness. Their usual haunting grounds weren't holding them in place. They were free to roam the city.

Most of them seemed to just be travelling, ignoring the living they passed. Most of the living didn't seem to notice the ghosts passing right by — or sometimes through — them, except for an occasional shiver or glance over their shoulders.

Harlan was relieved. He was so drained that the most he could have done was yell at a ghost and hope it worked. Maybe he wouldn't actually be of any use at the Centre, but he had a feeling he was needed there, so he was going to try.

Across the street, a ghost lifted a woman's skirt, holding it up while he had a good, long look.

She spun, crying out when she didn't see anyone behind her. The ghost simply followed her around, not letting go of her skirt.

"Hey!" Harlan shouted, clapping his hands hard enough to hurt.

The ghost released her and started floating towards Harlan.

Harlan pointed a warning finger at it, and it drifted off — probably in search of a better victim, but he didn't have the strength to deal with it right now. Harlan was just relieved it hadn't taken more to make it leave.

He watched until it vanished, hoping it wouldn't keep assaulting people, but he couldn't go after every ghost he saw, not by himself. If this...phenomenon didn't stop and the ghosts weren't forced to return to the places they normally haunted, he and the other mediums would have to hunt them down one by one, but he had bigger problems to deal with. Hopefully he and the others would be able to figure out what had caused this disturbance in the ghosts and wards of the city — or beyond. How far had this effect spread? How far *would* it spread, if they couldn't stop it or find the source?

Hamilton pulled up beside him, lights flashing but with the siren off. "Holy shit. What's going *on* out here?" He peeled away from the curb as soon as Harlan got in, making Harlan feel like he'd left his stomach behind.

Harlan just shook his head. He knew it wasn't a helpful answer, but it was the best he had.

There were so many ghosts prowling the streets that it made him feel like he was fraying at the seams. He couldn't focus on just one voice, one presence, in the crowd surrounding him.

Hamilton screeched to a sudden halt, cursing, when the light abruptly changed right in front of them, going straight from green to red. "Fuck. They've been doing shit like this all night. I passed so many accidents on the way here..." He glanced at Harlan almost accusingly, but quickly looked away.

Harlan could see goosebumps on Hamilton's arms—and a wild-looking ghost crouched on the pole holding the swinging traffic lights. "I'm sure you did," he said grimly, wishing he had time to stop and fix this, but he knew that if he tried, they'd never reach the Centre.

They drove in silence, weaving in and out of slow-moving traffic. Hamilton used strategic bursts of the siren to help clear a path. They passed many other emergency-response vehicles.

Suddenly, Harlan's eyes widened and he grabbed his armrest. "No. No, no, no."

"What, kid? What is it? You're scaring me."

"Stop."

"What?"

"Stop!"

"Brand, we can't—"

"Stop for every ghost, I *know*. Stop the car. *Now!*" His skin was crawling. He had always thought that was just

176

a saying, but it felt entirely too real. He had to close his eyes and focus on his breathing so he wouldn't be sick.

"All right, all right, all right, I'm stopping — not that we're getting anyplace in a hurry." Hamilton pulled over as soon as he could — but not nearly soon enough for Harlan.

Harlan jumped out of the car, running blind, following only his psychic senses.

Hamilton followed more cautiously, but he ran and grabbed Harlan's sleeve before he could go into the pitch-black entrance of an alleyway. "Brand! You're running into a back alley during a fucking...ghost-pocalypse! This is exactly how Batman's parents died! Stop. Think. At *least* tell me what's going on." He exhaled, then added, "Please."

It was the 'please' that caught Harlan's attention and made him pause. Had he ever heard Hamilton say it before? Not often, certainly.

He stopped pulling against Hamilton, ignoring a wave of panic when Hamilton took the opportunity to grab Harlan's wrist. He hadn't been able to catch much of Harlan's sleeve, and it had threatened to slide out of his hand.

Hamilton's fingers felt like a warm, living handcuff, and just as unyielding. And, he suspected, he'd need a damn good 'key' to get out of it. The words weren't coming, just the dread, the *urgency*, closing in around him.

How could he *make* Hamilton understand? He couldn't think past the sickening waves of *wrongness* pouring out of the alley. He couldn't focus on Hamilton. He kept looking over his shoulder before looking back at Hamilton again.

Hamilton sighed. He set his free hand on Harlan's shoulder, then let go of his wrist, putting that hand on Harlan's other shoulder. "What? Just... Just tell me. Three words or less, Lassie. Then I'll let you go — *if* you can convince me you need to do this. Right now."

Harlan gulped, feeling like he needed to clear his ears after a pressure change, but it wasn't a physical force bearing down on him.

He could only manage one word — "Possession." He locked eyes with Hamilton, trying to *will* him to understand what was happening, how desperately he was needed, how little time they had.

"Poss —? Oh, shit." Hamilton let go, almost unconsciously.

Harlan took a step back, then nodded. He wasn't sure if Hamilton would stop him or not if he moved any farther away.

"I'm coming with you."

Hamilton said it as though Harlan might refuse his help, but — coward that he was — he didn't want to face whatever was in that alley alone.

"Please do."

Possession was — fortunately — extremely rare. He'd seen videos of it at the Centre, read about cases in his textbooks, but he'd never seen one in real life or, as far as he was aware, known a medium who had. While some of the other mediumship students had been excited at the thought of such a challenge, Harlan could have quite happily lived out the rest of his life without encountering a spirit powerful and determined enough to attempt such a twisted act. Apparently, he wasn't that lucky.

As he approached the gaping black mouth of the alley, all he could feel was *wrongness*. Against the natural order or…something. A violation.

He crept down the alleyway, Hamilton right behind him.

There. On the other side of a dumpster stood a white man in an expensive-looking suit, his skin sickly pale despite his light tan. His blond hair was stuck to his forehead with sweat. Under better conditions, Harlan thought he might be handsome.

His arms hung limply at his sides. His head was rolled back on his neck, so he was staring straight up at the overcast night sky, his pale eyes just as clouded over, unfocused and unseeing.

As Harlan stepped closer, he saw that the man was leaning against the wall behind him — probably the only thing keeping him on his feet. Usually a ghost could only take over someone who was already unconscious or badly injured, but since the man was standing, Harlan suspected that he'd been taken fully aware. The ghost had subdued him somehow, but the man was still fighting feebly. Every few seconds an arm or leg would spasm violently or his facial muscles would twitch into a violent grimace or a pained 'smile'. His knuckles were bleeding from hitting the wall. The sight of it almost made the energy bar Harlan had eaten come back up. He swallowed hard, clenching his fists.

The air in front of him — in front of the ghost and its prey — crackled and shimmered. The ghost had spread itself like a shroud, losing any trace of human form as it stretched wider and wider, engulfing the man.

For a moment Harlan could only stare, caught between horror and wonder. The alley was lit only by the spirit's otherworldly glow, rapidly shifting through all the colours of the human spectrum and sending out sparks of shocking pink, green and violet.

Totally ignoring Harlan, if it had even noticed him, it pressed forward. It touched the man's forehead, quickly wrapping around his face like plastic, but Harlan didn't think the man would suffocate. Something much worse than simple *death* was about to happen to him.

"Hey!" Hamilton yelled, pushing forward to stand beside Harlan, his head sweeping from side to side. He couldn't see the ghost, but he knew it was there.

Harlan had forgot Hamilton was with him. His shout scared the shit out of Harlan, but it was more than *he* was doing. If nothing else, it snapped Harlan out of his mesmerized state. He could feel Hamilton practically vibrating. He could tell his partner wanted to be in front of him, protecting him, not just beside him, but there was nothing he could do but watch Harlan.

Watch Harlan do…nothing.

He shook himself. If Hamilton wasn't there, would he have been captured like the businessman? He didn't want to imagine what a ghost could do with his body, his power.

The trailing, veil-shaped ghost snapped into a roughly human figure so quickly that there was an audible sound. Apparently, it had taken energy to force itself out of its natural form and flatten out.

It was still misty and indistinct. Harlan couldn't make out any features, but it had a rough head-shape, wispy arms and a large central mass. It turned.

It looked exactly the same on the front as it did from behind, at least until an impossibly wide hole opened on its 'face', stretching wider and wider like the yawning mouth of the dumpster beside them. A wave of putrid decay spilled out, the scent of week-old death making Harlan's eyes water as he choked, trying to fill his lungs with living air.

"Ha!"

Harlan wasn't expecting the sudden sharp burst of laughter from Hamilton. If it had come from anyone else, he would have turned to look, certain the sight and smell had made the other person unhinged, but he wasn't worried about Hamilton's sanity. Well, he wasn't worried about Hamilton losing his mind with fear, at least.

"Nice try! You'll have to do better than that!" Hamilton shouted.

Harlan gritted his teeth. He could have gone *without* challenging an already-powerful and extremely malicious spirit.

It screamed, howled, roared and shrieked, raking at them with wicked shadow-claws that suddenly appeared at the ends of its limbs.

"Whoa!" Hamilton jumped back a step, pulling Harlan down into a crouch beside him. The talons passed just over their heads.

It didn't advance…yet. It had driven them back and it didn't press its advantage.

The businessman's head slumped forward bonelessly, his already-pale skin fading to dead white.

Harlan knew he was running out of time. He knew there was no way he could talk this spirit down enough to get it to leave on its own…certainly not before it drained the man completely or managed to possess him and walk away inside his body.

He gritted his teeth again. He'd just have to do this the hard way.

He rolled up his left sleeve, leaving his hand and a good portion of his forearm bare. It ached in anticipation. He knew he'd have to grab the damn ghost, and he wouldn't be surprised if it caused more permanent nerve damage in that hand. He might even finally lose all sensation in that pinkie. Doctors had warned him for years that this would happen, and he knew it was only a matter of time.

Still, he had a job to do. There was no one else who could stop this. If it meant losing sensation or even movement in his left hand, that was a price he was willing to pay.

He surged upward, trying not to give away any sign, even to Hamilton, that he was about to move. He wrapped both arms around the ghost's shapeless lower half, making sure his left side made the most contact. He screamed when he pulled the ghost too close and it touched his face. His cheek felt like he'd pressed it against frozen metal that also burned and sent a jolt of electricity down his neck.

"Brand!" Hamilton shouted.

Harlan couldn't spare enough concentration to look in his direction or speak. He shook his head and hoped Hamilton wouldn't do anything stupid, like trying to rescue him.

He began pulling down, slowly sinking to his knees and hauling the spirit with him.

It fought, twisting wildly and trying to phase out of his grip.

"No. You. Fucking. *Don't*," he snarled between deep, panting breaths.

Realizing it couldn't break free, couldn't pass through him the way it could with other people, it began attacking rather than trying to escape. It raked him with spectral claws longer than his hand. They bit deep into his shoulders and scalp. They drew little blood, but he knew the damage was far worse and deeper than a normal cut. Numbness spread everywhere they touched — numbness, and a bone-deep cold.

It would be so easy to stop fighting. He just had to close his eyes and give in.

He —

"Harlan!"

He opened his eyes.

Hamilton was pacing just outside the ghost's reach, poised for action he couldn't actually take.

Harlan growled when he realized how close he'd got to losing himself. The pain and visceral horror of its touch had given it a way in, but he wouldn't let his guard down a second time.

He dug his nails into the ghost's 'flesh,' capturing one 'wrist' as it swung at him again.

It shrieked with rage.

While it was distracted, Harlan grabbed its other arm and pinned both of them to its sides.

Now for the fun part.

Fully on his knees, he shifted his right hand across the front of the ghost until it touched his left. He felt something cold, wet and unpleasantly chunky soaking into his jeans from the pavement. *Great.*

"Hey, fucker!" he shouted to distract it.

It hesitated, just for an instant, and he pressed both of its 'hands' into his left and clamped down for dear life. His hand burned briefly, then went icy numb, but he didn't dare let go.

Only held by two points now, the spirit began to twist and thrash again.

Fighting it for every inch, Harlan pulled it lower and lower until the straining fingertips of his right hand met the pavement beneath them. Fortunately, whatever he was kneeling in hadn't pooled that far.

He wished he could take even a moment's rest. It was almost over. He was almost done. He just had to open a portal. And he'd have to drag the ghost through it.

No. I'm so close. He had to tell himself that, try to convince himself that he just needed to hold on a little longer.

He felt the portal slowly spreading from his right hand. *So close.*

It stopped growing. He couldn't force it any wider, and there was no way he'd be able to cram a ghost through a hole smaller than an orange while it fought him tooth and nail—not without more strength than he had in him, maybe more than he *ever* had in him.

The portal began to shrink, its edges pulling back toward his hand—the source—like a drawstring pouch being pulled shut.

His heart was pounding. The alley was absolutely silent—or could he just not hear anymore?

He couldn't keep the portal open *and* hold the ghost.

He had to do both.

He couldn't.

Knowing he might not—probably would not—have enough strength to open it again, he released the hole, letting reality fill in again beneath his hand. He wrapped his right arm around the ghost, barely noticing the biting chill as its trailing edge brushed his face. He couldn't keep this, any of this, up for long. He was a little surprised he'd managed this long, but he knew he couldn't let go. He had a job to do.

Each breath—the only sound in the world—was nearly a sob. He dropped his right hand and tried again. A tiny opening, no bigger around than a pencil.

Gasping, he let it close, adjusted his grip on the ghost.

Dropped his hand again. *Nothing at all this time.* He didn't have enough strength left to break through the veil. Between the ghost in his apartment and fighting this entity, he'd burned through everything he had.

He had nothing left.

He shook his head, his right arm dangling uselessly at his side as the relentless chill from direct contact with the ghost marched up his left. He knew that when it reached his heart, he'd die.

He felt giddy, almost drunk. He'd lost. He'd *failed*. He wasn't strong enough, and now he was going to die and so was the man, and he didn't even know his name, and—

"Harlan."

Hamilton's voice in his ear, surprisingly gentle. And he'd called him 'Harlan', not 'Brand'. Yep, he was already dead.

He opened his eyes. He hadn't realized they were closed.

Hamilton was crouched beside him, a hand resting on his thigh. He couldn't see the ghost crackling above them. Luckily it was too distracted by trying to get away from Harlan to notice him.

"Harlan," he said again, confirming that Harlan hadn't imagined it.

Harlan wasn't worried about crying in front of Hamilton—not really, not now—but the tears were blurring his vision and annoying him. He shook his head, blinking furiously.

"I can't do it. I can't hold on to it *and* open the gate." His voice was rough and harsh, sounding like he hadn't spoken for weeks. "I can't... I don't know if I could open a portal even if I let go right now. Every second I hold on... I don't have many more."

"Brand. You can *do* this." Hamilton sounded more certain than Harlan had ever felt in his entire life.

"I *can't*," he wailed. It was just too hard. He was too weak.

"Yes. You can. Listen to me." Hamilton grabbed his right forearm. "You *can*."

A surge of warmth, of strength, shot up Harlan's arm, then another. His shoulder, which had gone numb, burst into a riot of pins and needles. "What?"

Hamilton immediately let go, eyes wide. "What?"

The numbness crept back. "Please, don't let go."

Hamilton barely hesitated before grabbing him again. "Like this?"

Hamilton's energy drained into Harlan where their skin met. It wasn't much. Hamilton didn't have much mediumship power, but he had plenty of a different kind of strength to share. Maybe, just *maybe*, it would be enough.

Harlan spread the fingers of his right hand and the veil opened to him. Concentrating his own dwindling strength on holding the ghost, he used his body as a conduit, pouring Hamilton's energy into opening the portal wider. It blossomed until it was large enough to send the ghost through. Harlan held his breath. The edges quivered but stayed in place. It was secure — for now. He'd have to act quickly.

He lifted his right hand from the pavement, relieved when Hamilton moved with him without breaking contact. He grabbed the ghost's trailing bottom edge and started heaving with both hands. His left was still numb, and he was worried it would stay that way. He had to hurry, before his hand spasmed and let go, while he still had some chance of saving it, before the ghost broke free.

His right hand was cold, so cold, but hot spikes of living energy pulsed through it in time with Hamilton's heartbeat.

He was crouched over the opening he'd made, staring down into infinite darkness. There was no fire or brimstone, but it clearly wasn't a place of light and warmth like Miles' destination. *Good.*

It didn't try to pull him in, but it was a vertigo-inducing view. Closing his eyes didn't help. He could still feel it yawning beneath him.

Harlan took a deep breath and yanked the ghost down even harder.

It shrieked when it first made contact with the hole, writhing and twisting desperately, but Harlan wasn't going to give in — not now that he was finally this close.

Harlan didn't think Hamilton could actually see the ghost, but he seemed to be able to feel or sense it in some way. He shuffled back and out of the way as Harlan pulled more and more of the ghost down towards them. Without ever breaking contact with Harlan's skin, he stood and stepped behind Harlan, touching the back of his neck instead of his arm.

Harlan had got about half of the ghost into the hole when it suddenly *stuck*, like a cork in a bottle, and refused to go any deeper.

"Fuck!" He didn't have the energy to spare for this shit. Looking to the side, he saw that the ghost had shot out a tendril and was leeching from Mr. Power-Suit. It wasn't much — the man had very little energy left — but at this point in the battle it would probably be enough.

Harlan coughed. "Hamilton!" He could barely manage a desperate whisper.

"Yeah?"

"The connection..."

"What?"

"The ghost...attached...man. Have to break... connection."

"Kid, I can't see it. How am I supposed to — ?"

"I know. But you can *feel* it." At least he hoped his hunch was right. If Hamilton couldn't find and break the connection in some way, they were done for.

"All right. Yeah. I think so. Are you sure I can let go of you now?"

Unable to summon the energy to speak, Harlan nodded. He wasn't sure, not at all, but they were out of options.

Hamilton slowly uncurled his fingers from the back of Harlan's neck and straightened.

Harlan felt the blood rush back into the places Hamilton's nails had dug in. He couldn't look up to see what Hamilton was doing. Every fibre of his being was focused on keeping the ghost where it was. He might not be able to force it deeper, not until Hamilton succeeded, but he was damned if he was going to lose any ground to it either.

"I can feel it," Hamilton crowed. "I *hear* it."

"Good." It was more a grunt of effort than a word.

"Now what?"

"Break it!"

"Wh — How?"

Harlan growled with frustration. *He* would probably have torn it apart, stretching the connection between his hands until it snapped, but Hamilton... He was sure Hamilton would do it differently. "Hit it! Punch it! Rip it apart— *chew* through it if you have to. Anything... Whatever it takes!"

He felt the impact of a blow travelling through the spirit and rattling his teeth. "Again! Keep going! You'll know when it breaks." At least he *hoped* Hamilton would sense it.

Another blow.

"It's not... This isn't working. I'm just flailing at it blindly." Hamilton was panting now, a dangerous sign.

Harlan risked closing his eyes, just for an instant, so he could think. Hamilton had said he could *hear* the connection.

"You have to...interrupt it. The sound!" This was unlike any mediumship he'd ever done or heard about, so he hoped he was on the right track.

"Right. That makes sense. Kinda. So, what, do I scream at it?"

"Hamilton, I don't know! This one is up to you. Please, just hurry!" The numbness in his left arm had almost reached his shoulder. They were running out of time.

"Interrupt it... *Fuck*."

"What?" Harlan asked.

"I think I'm gonna have to sing."

The tiniest corner of Harlan's mouth turned up. He'd never even imagined Hamilton singing, but unfortunately, he couldn't take the time to savour it right now. "Yes! Do that!" he said as confidently as possible while the ghost strained against him and his arms shook.

Despite the circumstances, Hamilton's voice was steady and warm. Harlan spared just a moment to wonder if Hamilton actually *enjoyed* singing and did it regularly.

There was also something familiar about the song, but he couldn't quite place it...

Harlan could *see* when the music hit the ghostly connection and began to interrupt it, just a little. Each note sent a tremor through the spirit, the shockwave rolling down into Harlan as well. Where it made the ghost weaker, it filled Harlan with Hamilton's strength.

"Keep going!" Harlan encouraged him.

Hamilton kept singing.

Buffeted by sound, the ghost lost some of its grim concentration and Harlan was able to force more of it through the opening.

While Hamilton sang, Harlan kept pulling. The instant the top of the ghost's 'head' disappeared into the portal, Harlan slammed it shut so quickly that he almost fell on his face. He rocked back so he was kneeling again, brushing the alley filth off his hands with a grimace. He could feel blood running down his face, but he didn't want to wipe it off until his hands were cleaner. He thought Hamilton kept some wet wipes in his glove compartment, but he wasn't sure even that would be enough.

Hamilton, who had his hands braced on his knees, straightened with a groan. "All right. We've gotta get him" – he pointed to the man in the suit – "to a hospital, and you...also to a hospital."

Harlan gritted his teeth. He didn't want to go to the hospital. He wanted to go to the Centre even less, but he knew what he had to do. "No."

Hamilton hobbled over to the businessman, who was now slumped against the wall like a puppet with its strings cut. While checking the man's pulse, he looked back at Harlan, frowning. "No?"

"No. The plan was to go to the Centre. We're going to the Centre."

Harlan had never seen Hamilton look so surprised. He could only stand there and blink at Harlan.

Harlan held up a finger. "First, he'll be safe there, because Charles is there." He held up another. "Second, I'm drained. It's not something the hospital can help me with. Third, I doubt we can get an ambulance here right now, and we're closer to the Centre than a hospital. The school nurse might be there. Let's get him there, so he's at least safe... Safer than he is in this alley. We can try calling an ambulance from there. Fourth, it...it's where I'm needed."

"Kid..." Hamilton stepped closer. "You said it yourself. You've got nothin' left. What are you going to do when we get there? You're drained. Outta juice. Running on em—"

"Okay, I get it. I'm out of power!" Harlan snapped. He sighed, immediately regretting his outburst. "I'm sorry. This isn't... I know I shouldn't take it out on you. I'm just frustrated because..." He rubbed his temples. "Because...I *know* that's where I'm supposed to be, but I won't be able to do any fucking good, even if I do *make* it there. I'm useless!"

"Hey. Useless for *now*, not useless."

"Oh, yeah, thanks. That really makes me feel so much better."

"Good," Hamilton said, ignoring the sarcasm. "Let's go."

"Where?"

"The Centre! Chop-chop, we've got ass to kick, and you won't find it moping around here! Help me carry this guy to the car." He looped an arm under each of the man's arms, motioning with his head for Harlan to take his feet. Harlan hoped that was the lighter end. Knowing Hamilton, it probably was.

Harlan picked up the man's legs, only to have one slip and hit the ground, dragging for a moment before Hamilton stopped and frowned at him.

Harlan was shaking with exhaustion, his hands were still numb and wet and slimy, the man's suit pants were made of a very slippery material, and he was completely dead weight in their arms.

He grabbed the man's ankle again and lifted.

With Hamilton taking almost all the weight, they managed to half-carry, half-drag the man to the cruiser and load him into the back seat.

"I'm pretty sure 'chop-chop' is actually racist," Harlan panted, resting his sweaty forehead on the cool roof of the car.

"Really? Shit, I had no idea. Won't say that again." Hamilton got into the front seat.

"...Did you sing the *Firefly* theme?"

"Yes! Shut up. It's the first thing I thought of!"

As they drove, Harlan felt a few very, very faint tugs — tugs which probably would have been stronger if he'd had any power left at all — but none that gave him the skin-crawling feeling of the possession. He gritted his teeth, closed his eyes and ignored them.

Not that he'd be able to do anything but watch, even if he *did* come across another possession.

He was so drained that the ghosts they passed seemed to flicker in and out of existence. He shivered. He'd never been this weak before. He wished he was at full strength — stronger, even. He'd never needed it more.

A stray thought brushed his mind. *Someone is testing us.* But that was crazy, wasn't it? It was just...an anomaly, some sort of power fluctuation, maybe an accident. No medium would create this chaos on purpose, would they? *Could* they?

He shivered again. The amount of raw power it would take...

In any case, if it was a test, he'd failed. He could only hope the other mediums had succeeded, or at the very least that Charles' power was strong enough to protect the Centre for the whole wild, chaotic night—and that it would *only* be one night.

Light poured from every window in the Centre, as though that would keep the ghosts at bay. Harlan knew from experience that it didn't work that way.

Benjamin outside smoking. The harsh floodlights above the front door brought out the lines on his face, making him look old. And he looked tired, as tired as Harlan felt.

Waving at them, Benjamin threw down his cigarette and stomped on it a little harder than necessary. Every movement was sharp and deliberate. Whatever had happened there, Harlan got the feeling it had taken a toll on him.

Hamilton glanced between the two mediums, then crooked a finger at Benjamin. "Gimme a hand with this guy."

Benjamin frowned deepened, but he followed Hamilton to the back of the car. "What ha—?" He recoiled as soon as he touched the man's skin, turning away as though he might be sick.

Harlan just nodded.

The man was still limp. His eyes were glazed and staring at nothing, completely unfocused. He was still dead weight, and he didn't struggle or even move as Hamilton and Benjamin supported him between them.

Harlan felt like he'd been struck by the worst flu of his life. On top of that, he still hadn't recovered full feeling in his left hand, and he was worried he might not this time. The scratches the ghost had left with its raking claws were red and raised and itchy.

He was happy to just trudge after them, carrying nothing but himself.

And the man's briefcase.

Chapter Sixteen

The Centre should have been dark, with all the students in bed and most of the staff at home. It was alarming to see it so brightly lit at that hour.

They passed a few ghosts. They were harmless, but Harlan felt dangerously close to a panic attack every time he saw one inside the Centre itself—what had been his sanctuary.

Benjamin sent the spirits on their way with a tiny burst of power, like a small electric shock. As far as Harlan could tell, Benjamin wasn't terribly drained, but it made sense for him to conserve his strength in case they needed it later.

After a few wrong turns, Benjamin led them to the infirmary, and Harlan's pulse sped up. Were a lot of students injured? He remembered Hamilton telling him there'd been a death an eternity ago in his apartment.

As soon as he pushed the swinging doors open for Hamilton, Benjamin and the still-limp man they were carrying, Harlan could see why they'd chosen this room for what he tried not to think of as their last stand. Of course, the second he thought it he couldn't get it out of his head.

The infirmary was one of the largest rooms, besides the gym and the dining hall, and there were cots for sick or injured students. Someone had dragged a few extra mattresses in from the nearby bedrooms. Every bed was full, occupied by wide-eyed children and teens. Some sat alone, but most were huddled together with a friend or two. All the lights were on and only a few were lying down, let alone sleeping. The staff moved among them, talking to them quietly and probably trying to reassure them.

All eyes turned to Harlan and the others when they entered. Harlan ducked his head and shifted a little so he was beside Hamilton instead of at the front of the group.

Charles was sitting on a chair in the middle of the room like a pillar, silently supporting everyone, his power reaching out to surround and protect them. He looked tired, with dark circles under his eyes and beads of sweat on his forehead. His power was usually passive, but he'd never had to use it this long or this intensely. Harlan wondered how many ghosts Charles had turned away already.

Harlan ran over to him, standing a few inches away without touching him so he wouldn't break Charles' concentration if he needed it.

Charles wrapped his arms around Harlan's waist and pulled him close, burying his nose in Harlan's chest and inhaling deeply. "You're here. You're okay."

"Yeah." 'Okay' was a bit of a stretch, but he wasn't going to tell Charles that, not now. He was used to leaning on Charles, and while he very much wanted to, he knew that Charles needed his support more at this moment than the other way around. Whether he liked it or not, his part in the night was finished. He had nothing left to give.

"You?"

Charles shrugged. "I'm all right. A lot of ghosts have been trying to get in here, but so far I've been able to hold them off."

He had no idea when Charles would be able to stop and rest. He could only hope it was before exhaustion *forced* him to stop. Harlan kept thinking, *we just need to make it till dawn*, though he had no logical reason to think anything would change with sunrise. Ghosts were just as active during the day as at night. Still, he couldn't shake the thought.

"Do you need anything?" he asked Charles.

Charles shook his head, then nodded. "Water?"

"Of course." He grabbed one of Charles' hands and gave it a firm squeeze. He let go reluctantly, one finger at a time, only releasing it when he heard one of the children behind him giggle.

"There's water in the fridge," a man told Harlan.

Harlan nodded gratefully. He didn't know the man, so he must have joined the faculty after Harlan had left.

Weaving his way between the overcrowded beds — and trying not to make eye contact with anyone — Harlan grabbed a water bottle. He was about to close the fridge when he heard Charles' voice in his head telling him he needed to drink too. It was something that happened all the time when they played. Charles would offer him some water, Harlan would insist he wasn't thirsty but take it reluctantly, and before he knew it, the bottle would be empty.

Charles grinned when he saw the second bottle, giving Harlan's hand a quick squeeze. He drained half his bottle in one swallow, gasping when he came up for air. "Thanks." He already looked a little better, and he quickly finished the rest of the water.

Harlan nodded, taking a sip of his own. He hadn't noticed how dry his mouth was, and soon his bottle was empty as well.

Before he could ask Charles if he needed anything else or if there was some way he could help, he slowly realized there was a commotion behind him.

Someone had either brought in another mattress or shooed some children off one of the beds that were already there to make room for the man Harlan and Hamilton had brought with them. He'd woken up, and he was struggling against Hamilton's restraining grip on his shoulder.

"Sir? You need to calm down," Hamilton told him in his 'cop voice'.

Harlan wondered if telling someone to calm down had ever worked. Maybe cops had a script of their own, like the one the Centre had drilled into him for talking the ghosts—the one he'd mostly stopped using.

"No! What is this? Where am I? Who are you people?"

He almost sounded like a ghost—the same confusion, the same questions.

"You're at the Centre for Psychic Education and Research." It was the Centre's full name, but no one ever called it that. "You're safe." Hamilton kept his voice level and even, not matching the man's intensity—a strategy Harlan used when dealing with ghosts.

"The Centre!" A look of disgust crossed his face, there and gone so quickly that Harlan wasn't sure he'd seen it at all or if it was only the reaction he would have expected from a man in an expensive suit.

The man looked around and saw all the children staring back at him. "Why am I here?" he asked more softly. "Why do I feel... What happened to me?"

"You were involved in a" — Hamilton caught Harlan's eyes for a moment — "spectral incident."

Harlan could tell he was talking out of his ass, but he didn't think anyone else would.

"A what?"

"You need to just lie down. Rest. You've been through a traumatic experience. We can discuss the details later." When the man looked like he might protest, Hamilton shoved an already-open bottle of water into his shaking hands.

The man drank, but he was still looking around nervously — not that Harlan could blame him.

After giving Harlan a warm smile, the school nurse moved in to check the man's vitals.

Harlan blushed. He'd had a bit of a crush on the young nurse while he was still at the Centre, and Harlan had faked being sick several times so he'd have an excuse to see him.

He saw that Beth and Benjamin were talking, their heads close together. She glanced at Harlan, then shook her head.

A hot spike of anxiety shot through Harlan's guts. Were they talking about him? Had he done something wrong?

Beth motioned for him to come over, which he did reluctantly.

"The two of us have been taking turns patrolling," she said, "trying to keep at least a few ghosts away from Charles so he doesn't have to handle as much. I was going to leave when you got here, but...you look like shit."

"You're drained," Benjamin added.

Harlan nodded. He hated admitting his weakness, but he knew it was obvious to all three of them.

"You need to sit the fuck down before you *fall* down," Beth told him, not unkindly. She wrinkled her nose. "But first, let's get you cleaned up a little."

Harlan yawned. He passively allowed Beth to steer him to the bathroom, then to an empty bed. It was still warm from whoever they'd kicked out of it.

Too busy to babysit him for long, Benjamin had left the infirmary, probably to patrol.

Beth grabbed two bottles of water from the fridge. She gulped one down and passed the other to Harlan.

"Is that your boyfriend?"

Harlan looked up to see a little girl perched on the bed in front of his, leaning forward with her elbows on her knees. She pointed at Charles.

"Uh...yeah." Was that inappropriate? Harlan didn't have much experience with children and was never really sure how to talk to them. How old was she — four? Twelve? Fuck, he was bad at this.

"He's good." She nodded, like a matchmaker who was pleased with her work.

"Yeah, he is."

"He's keeping us safe. I'm Mandy."

He was so tired that it took him a moment to realize he was supposed to reply. "Harlan."

"I've heard of you! You're a policeman, right?"

"Not quite. I'm a police medium." He yawned again, but this time it was partly for show. He hoped she'd take the hint and stop talking to him.

"Do you work with that guy?" Now she pointed at Hamilton.

"Yeah. That's Hamilton, my partner." Apparently he was having an entire conversation now.

Attracted by the sound of voices, a little boy climbed onto the bed beside Mandy, sitting cross legged and staring at Harlan with wide eyes.

Harlan wasn't sure what was making him so interesting to these kids, but he wished it would stop.

Another girl approached slowly, from the side. Something about her seemed familiar, and he realized that he recognized the battered stuffed rabbit she was carrying. She was the girl he'd met the last time he'd been to the Centre. He didn't remember her name, if he'd even heard it. He gave her a tiny, awkward wave.

She nodded, a little pitifully, in response, keeping her head low, her eyes downcast. She reminded him so much of himself as a child that it nearly hurt, but he knew her behaviour wasn't universal in mediums. Beth was about as extroverted as it was possible to be.

He was surprised when she climbed onto the bed beside him and pressed against his side. He could feel her trembling.

Looking up, he happened to catch Hamilton's eyes. The other man mouthed, *So cute!* and mimed taking a picture.

Harlan frowned at him, then turned back to the three children—no, there were *five* now, but only Rabbit Girl was bold enough to sit beside him. Although 'bold' probably wasn't the right word, in her case. Mandy and the other three were all crammed together on Mandy's bed.

He had no idea what to say to them, especially to Rabbit Girl, who was still glued to his side. Did she expect him to comfort her? If so, she had definitely come to the wrong adult.

"You should go to sleep," Rabbit Girl said in her strangely serious little voice, barely above a whisper. "You'll feel better in the morning."

It seemed like a weirdly adult thing for her to say, and he wondered if she was repeating something someone had told her—a parent? Someone at the Centre? Had she been left here by her family, the way he had? Was that why she reminded him of himself? Or was he reading too much into it? His mind had slowed to a crawl, and he could practically hear the gears grinding.

She slid down from the bed, took his hand and pulled until he stopped resisting and lay down. She gave one brisk nod of approval and tried to cover as much of him as she could with the child-size blanket.

He was already curled almost double to fit on the tiny mattress. He reached up to help her, but she just said, "Sleep!" sternly.

He closed his eyes. It was too bright in the room, too bright and too loud. And he was worried about Charles. He took a deep breath, then another.

Chapter Seventeen

It was morning when he woke up, and there was a strange but very much welcome sense of lightness in the air. The sun shone through the uncovered windows, and he could hear a bird singing nearby. He couldn't help smiling to himself. They'd survived the night.

"Hey." Charles' voice was gravelly but warm.

Rolling over, Harlan saw that Charles was lying on a cot that had been pulled up next to his mattress. Charles looked tired — as tired as Harlan felt, lightness or not — but he was smiling.

After glancing around to make sure that no one was watching them, he reached out and entwined his fingers with Charles'. It wasn't that there were children around — or not *just* that. He wasn't comfortable with PDA around *anyone*.

Charles squeezed back, his grin broadening.

Harlan yawned. "Sorry I fell asleep before we could really talk…" He felt like an asshole for finally making it to the Centre and passing out without doing anything helpful, while Charles had already been standing guard before he got there and had still kept watch after he'd fallen asleep.

Charles frowned, and for a moment Harlan's stomach tightened. Then Charles shook his head, his expression softening again. "Hey. Did you think I was mad at you for falling asleep while I stayed up?"

"...No," Harlan said, looking away from him.

Charles cleared his throat.

"Maybe. Yes," Harlan admitted.

Charles squeezed Harlan's hand a little tighter. "Of course I'm not! You were exhausted!"

He laughed, and Harlan realized he hadn't really been *frowning*, he'd just been confused about why Harlan was apologizing. Once again, Harlan had read too much into it.

"I'm sure you were — are! — too," Harlan protested.

"I am," Charles agreed. He slid onto Harlan's mattress and took Harlan's hand, pulling him closer so he could kiss it. "But that doesn't mean you weren't, too. And I got some rest." He ran a hand through Harlan's hair, just once.

"Ugh. I don't know how you can stand to touch me. I must look like shit." He could feel that his hair was standing up in sweaty spikes, and he knew it needed to be cut.

"You look fine. Especially — Hamilton told me some of what you two went through. No one expects you to be runway-model perfect after that."

"Maybe *I* do," Harlan grumbled.

"Besides, I'm sure I smell like ass. The thought of a shower and clean clothes is what got me through the night."

"I like the way you smell." Harlan closed his eyes and soaked in Charles' scent, his warmth, his nearness. He wanted, more than anything, to just curl up with Charles and shut out the world for a while. He was too tired to even think about *going* to either of their apartments — he just wanted to *be* there. Unfortunately, he knew he had things to deal with.

He heard Hamilton clear his throat. He scrambled away from Charles and sat up, painfully aware he was blushing. He balled his hands in his lap.

Hamilton pulled up a chair and sat in front of Harlan's mattress.

Harlan wasn't sure where to look, and he ended up looking at the wall between the two men — which, he knew, was the worst of both worlds, but now he felt like he had to commit to his bad decision.

Harlan carefully kept his hands in his lap, resisting the urge to reach down and grab Charles' hand, even though it was oh-so-temptingly close.

Hamilton was staring at him way too intensely, especially for this early in the morning. Was it early? It *felt* early. How long had he slept? He was still exhausted, but he realized that a little of his power had 'recharged' while he'd slept. As much as he'd sometimes wished he didn't have it — though less and less frequently — being *without* it, even temporarily, had been awful. He definitely wasn't at full strength yet, probably wouldn't be for a few days, at least, but he wasn't completely drained anymore. His whole body ached, both from falling in his apartment and from exerting himself so hard.

"What, uh... What happened after I fell asleep?"

Hamilton and Charles exchanged glances, and Harlan was surprised when Hamilton nodded, deferring to Charles.

"It was weird. At dawn it just...stopped. The ghosts stopped trying to get in and just...drifted away."

Harlan shook his head. "That doesn't make sense."

Hamilton snorted. "*None* of this makes sense."

"No—I mean, *yes*, you're right, but..." Harlan massaged his left temple, as though he could physically mold his brain back into working order. He had a massive headache already and he suspected it was only going to get worse. "There's nothing special about dawn—not when it comes to ghosts."

Charles shrugged. "But that's what happened."

Both of them were watching Harlan, and he found himself staring at the wall again so he wouldn't have to look at either of them.

"I...I think I need to go outside."

"Are you okay?" Charles asked, covering one of Harlan's tense fists with his broad hand.

"I'm fine." He sighed. He could be honest with these two. "Well, as fine as I can be. I just have a headache, but that's not why I need to go outside."

"I'll get you some water and painkillers." Charles patted his thigh and left.

"Why do you want to go outside?" Hamilton asked, waiting for Charles' return.

"The ghost wards are gone, so I can sense things outside the building, but I'm still weak. It's dumb, but sometimes it helps if I can physically look around, get my bearings. I want to know what's happening out there myself."

Hamilton nodded. "Makes sense...kinda."

Charles came back and offered the water and pills to Harlan, who swallowed them gratefully.

Harlan glanced out the window again. The sunlight still had an early morning quality. Charles had said 'dawn', so it had to be later than that, though he had no idea what time it actually was. He fumbled his phone out of his pocket — *barely six-thirty*. "Charles, you stay here and rest. You must have got, what, two hours of sleep? At most?"

"Something like that," Charles reluctantly agreed.

He tugged at the hem of Charles' shirt and pulled him onto the mattress.

Charles sank back down, not fighting Harlan at all.

Harlan turned to Hamilton. "How much sleep did *you* get?"

"Some." Hamilton yawned.

"Uh-huh."

"You're not going outside alone," Hamilton said gruffly, but Harlan knew him well enough to recognize that the gruffness really meant concern.

Harlan rolled his eyes. "Fine. You can come with me. But only because I know it's the fastest way to get you back to sleep."

Hamilton waved a hand dismissively, but Harlan thought he looked relieved.

Harlan stood up unsteadily. He felt both of them tense and forced himself to straighten. "I'm fine." All three of them knew that wasn't true, but he did his best to look determined and neither of them tried to stop him. Hamilton followed him to the emergency exit at the back of the infirmary. It didn't occur to Harlan that it might set off an alarm until he'd already opened it, but nothing happened. He propped the door open with a chair so it wouldn't lock behind him and Hamilton, who was at his heels, and stepped outside. He'd never come out this door before, so he was a little turned around until he realized he was in the staff parking lot.

He looked at his surroundings with his eyes and with his power, extending his senses as far as they could go. It wasn't nearly as far as usual, but there was nothing he could do about that but rest. Hopefully he'd be able to do that once he got back inside. At the very least, he was going to insist that Hamilton and Charles sit down for a while if he couldn't make them sleep.

He could tell that Charles was right. The crushing, oppressive feeling from the night before had just...vanished. He could feel ghosts several blocks away, but they showed no interest in him or leaving their places. It didn't make sense. The sun wasn't some magical, purifying force. Something else had happened, and dawn had nothing to do with it. It was just a coincidence. But *what* else?

He heard Hamilton yawn, and when he turned to look at him, Hamilton contorted his face as he tried to hide it.

Harlan shook his head. "I'm not... There's nothing out there, nothing that's telling me what happened. Let's go back in." He pretended not to see Hamilton's relief.

When he got back inside, Beth and Benjamin were standing close together, talking quietly. Benjamin waved him and Hamilton over.

"The city just called. A ward-painter is on the way. The Centre is one of their highest priorities. We're going to stay here and keep an eye on things until they're finished, unless we get an urgent call. You're all right to stay too?" Benjamin asked.

Harlan couldn't help shooting a longing glance at Charles, who, in the short time Harlan had been gone, had fallen asleep sprawled across the mattress Harlan had slept on, but he nodded. "I'll stay."

Beth yawned, absentmindedly patting both their shoulders. "Good. You guys get on that. I've gotta pass out for a while. Wake me up in…as much time as possible or if the shit hits the fan. Again." She staggered off to an unoccupied cot.

"Where did all the kids go?" Harlan asked, realizing how much emptier the infirmary was than when he'd gone to sleep.

"We started moving them back to their rooms after things calmed down."

Benjamin couldn't have got much more sleep than the others. He certainly looked as exhausted. Once again Harlan felt weak and useless. "Are you sure you don't want to lie down?" he offered. "I know this place really well. I could patrol and make sure everything's okay."

Benjamin shook his head with a thin-lipped smile. "No. I'll feel more comfortable if two of us are out there. But, if you don't mind, I'll swap with Beth in a few hours."

"Of course." Harlan hoped they'd be *done* in a few hours, but realistically if they were waiting until the ward-painter had done just the outer walls, it could be several days. *Ughhh…* He just wanted to go home with Charles.

He forced himself to get moving and started plodding through the hallways.

His phone rang, startling him. It was Benjamin. He glanced at the time. It had been about an hour and a half since they'd separated — not nearly enough time to replace the wards, but he couldn't help a little surge of hope, anyway.

"Hello?"

"The cafeteria just delivered some breakfast for us. I haven't seen anything unusual, and I assume you haven't either, so I think we can take a few minutes to eat."

All of a sudden Harlan was *ravenous*. He didn't normally eat breakfast. He tended to roll directly out of bed and into Hamilton's patrol car. Sometimes he ate the granola bars Hamilton had suddenly started keeping in the glove compartment after Harlan mentioned that he didn't ever eat before work.

Hamilton had never said anything about it, and Harlan didn't think he ever would.

Harlan passed Beth on his way to the infirmary to eat. She'd wrapped a handful of breakfast sausages in a few pancakes and said she was off to get 'the lay of the land'.

Harlan devoured his own plate of pancakes and sausages and was considering going back for more when Beth ran in.

She was breathing heavily and her face was pale except for a bright-red spot on each of her cheeks. "You" — she pointed at Hamilton and Charles — "get the kids outta here. *All* the way out. Off the Centre grounds completely." She turned to Harlan and Benjamin. "Come with me. *Now*."

Even though he still looked exhausted, Hamilton was on his feet before she'd even finished speaking. "Is this a ghost thing? Do you need my help?"

Beth shook her head. "You can help by getting the kids out."

Hamilton nodded at Charles and they left, headed in the direction of the dormitory.

Satisfied, Beth motioned for Benjamin and Harlan to follow her, then turned and ran back the way she came.

Harlan didn't want to go, not at all, not in the direction of whatever had frightened Beth so badly, but Benjamin was already headed for the door.

Wishing he hadn't eaten quite so much, Harlan hurried after them.

Chapter Eighteen

Beth led them down a flight of stairs and into the labs beneath the Centre. Harlan didn't know that part of the complex, and it only made him more afraid. In any other part of the Centre, he could have guessed where they were going, but there he was just as lost as the others.

More so. Beth clearly had a destination in mind.

She led them down a hallway. There was a heavy metal door lying on the floor, and there was a trail of drywall dust and scrapes in the direction it must have come.

There was a room partway down the hall with a ragged hole where the door should have been.

Why would a ghost bother removing the door when the wards were down and it could simply pass through?

The room beyond was pitch black.

Beth clicked on a flashlight, quickly followed by Benjamin. They did it so naturally and automatically that Harlan found himself feeling at his waist, but of course there was nothing there.

Beth clicked her tongue. "Guess we forgot to tell you that one. Rule one of being a medium — always have a flashlight."

Pulling out his phone, Harlan turned on its flashlight. It was pitifully dim compared to the others. He noticed that their flashlights were encased in a kind of silvery mesh.

Benjamin held his up so Harlan could see it. "It keeps ghosts from being able to drain the batteries."

Harlan nodded, feeling even more stupid.

"C'mon," Beth murmured. "*Quietly*," she added, motioning with her palm down.

Harlan had expected her to lead the way, but it was Benjamin who stepped through into the darkness, the beam of his flashlight slowly, methodically sweeping the room from side to side. They wouldn't need the light to see ghosts. Harlan assumed that was the problem, but Beth still hadn't said.

The light revealed a nightmare scene in strobe — there, a white flash of bare bone. A head flat on the floor with nothing attached, hair in wild disarray above wide, still, shockingly blue eyes.

And everywhere, with each pass of the flashlight, were bright splashes of fresh blood. The room stank of it...and worse.

Harlan whipped his head around, looking away and closing his eyes. He could taste the maple syrup from his breakfast, and he was barely able to keep it down. He choked down a scream at the same time.

He took a few long, slow, deep breaths before forcing himself to open his eyes again. He tried to ignore the individual parts he was seeing and just let his eyes glaze over to take in the room as one whole image, breathing shallowly through his mouth. Even so, he could feel panic bubbling up inside him, waiting to burst out.

"Oh, fuck," Benjamin whispered. He'd barely finished speaking when he was pulled into the darkness ahead of them, the flashlight dropping from his hand.

It spun in lazy circles on the floor, showing more bodies and body parts, before finally coming to a stop facing the doorway.

Beth screamed, "Benjamin!" and threw herself forward.

To his surprise, Harlan found himself following her, stopping only to grab the flashlight Benjamin had dropped. He'd only been thinking about getting the light out of his eyes, but he realized a shielded source of light was better anyway. Then he realized that he was holding his cell phone in one hand, the flashlight in the other. *Useless.* He barely remembered to turn off his phone's light before dropping it in his pocket and forging ahead after Beth, who'd already got quite far ahead of him. He tried to ignore what he saw as passed, tried to think in terms of *obstacles* rather than parts that used to be human.

Beth was leaving a trail of bloody footprints, making her easy to follow.

So was he. He didn't want to step in it, but there was so much blood on the floor that it was impossible to avoid.

He heard a man's scream — Benjamin?

Beth sped up, running into the darkness in the direction of the scream.

He was too much of a coward to follow her. He knew that, but his feet kept carrying him forward.

He caught Beth disappearing through a doorway, then around a corner. He ran faster. No, he realized, he was too much of a coward to stay *away* from her. If he lost sight of her, he'd be alone in the building with whatever had done this—assuming this thing was alone and that Charles and Hamilton had got the children out safely.

Beth stopped so abruptly that he ran into her. She didn't scream the way Harlan knew he would have. She turned to glare at him briefly before lifting a finger to her lips and pointing into the room ahead of them.

The small room had counters and a fridge, so Harlan wasn't sure if it was another lab or a break room. It was full of...something. It looked almost like spider webs, if the webs were as thick as his wrist and glowing, pulsating purple and red.

Between their combined flashlight beams, they pinned down Benjamin in one corner. His head was slumped on his chest and he wasn't moving. He was covered in blood, like the rest of the room, but Harlan wasn't sure if any of it was his.

He also couldn't tell if Benjamin was alive, and he didn't have time to check. Beth's light continued up the wall. There, at the top of the 'web', was the spider.

No, not a spider. It had a human head and human legs, but far too many and stuck on seemingly at random. There was a cluster of grasping, straining arms and torsos melted together.

"What the fuck?" Beth gasped. She took a big step back and put an arm across Harlan's chest to pull him back with her.

A hand emerged from beneath a shattered workstation.

Harlan shrieked, but Beth's flashlight revealed that it was attached to a living woman.

Ducking low, Harlan ran behind the table, sliding the last few feet on his knees. Beth was right behind him.

The woman had her back pressed against what had been the underside of the table, keeping out of the spider's view as much as possible. Harlan and Beth quickly did the same.

The woman, who looked East Indian, wore a torn and bloody lab coat. "I'm Dr. Pahwa, one of the researchers here," she whispered. "You two are mediums?"

Beth nodded for both of them.

"Good. You can help—"

"What is that thing?" Beth interrupted. "Sorry. It was a long night. But I need to know what that is. Did you create it here, in this lab?" she asked, sounding disgusted.

"Certainly not!" Dr. Pahwa looked both horrified and a little insulted. "That creature created itself. When the wards fell, all the extremely dangerous ghosts we study here broke free and started killing my colleagues. Once there wasn't enough…prey for them, they began to turn on each other. They tore the weaker ones to bits, consuming them or adding parts of them to themselves. That thing is the victor. It is no longer simply one spirit. It is an abomination."

The temperature plummeted.

"Dr. Pahwa, are any of your colleagues still alive down here?" Beth asked.

She shook her head. "I don't believe so, no."

"Do you think you can make it to the stairs if we create a distraction?"

"I'm not just going to leave you here to face that thing alone!" Dr. Pahwa protested.

"The best way you can help us is getting out of here alive and getting more people down here to help us," Beth snapped.

Dr. Pahwa nodded reluctantly.

"Good." Beth turned to Harlan. "I think I can hold that fucker. You'll have to separate the pieces and send them on one at a time. I know it will be a lot of portals in a short time, and under a shit-ton of pressure, but you have to do it, and *fast*. The only thing in your favour is that the parts don't *want* to be together."

"Okay." It wasn't, not at all, but what choice did he have? Harlan breathed in deeply, then out.

Beth slowly stood.

The temperature dropped even further. Harlan's teeth started chattering and he hoped he'd be able to concentrate enough to complete his part of the task.

Harlan stood just in time to see the misshapen thing drop from its 'web' and skitter across the walls and floor towards them. The mouth on its single head was open and screaming. Harlan wanted to cover his ears and block out the infernal sound, but he needed his hands free.

Beth stepped around to the front of the table, her hands held out in front of her.

Harlan could feel Beth's power building, but he could also feel the cold, deadly power that was keeping this thing together. He hoped their combined strength would be enough to destroy it.

Beth allowed the beast to get far closer than Harlan would have, calmly watching it approach. When it was only a few feet from her, she reached out and grabbed a hand rising from one of its many backbones.

Harlan hoped he wouldn't have to touch the thing.

The creature went still, but Harlan felt how much power Beth was forcing into it. She wouldn't be able to keep it up for long. Harlan knew he would have to work quickly. He followed Beth to the front of the table.

"Dr. Pahwa, this is your chance to escape," Beth gritted out.

The doctor ran.

Harlan could see sweat beading on Beth's forehead already as she strained to keep the thing in place.

"Any…time now," Beth growled at him.

Harlan nodded briskly, trying to convince himself he knew what he was doing. He did the special *blink* that allowed him to touch ghosts and see them more clearly. The places where the disjointed parts met suddenly snapped into sharp relief.

He didn't want to touch the ghost and get more nerve damage, and he decided to try something else. He imagined his power in the shape of the pocketknife Charles always carried, narrowing it and honing it into a sharp blade to cut the thing apart. The thought of the knife, and of Charles, made him feel safe and like he had even a small chance of surviving this.

He twisted the knife of his power and brought it down where a thigh connected to a lower arm. They split with a blinding flash of light.

"Good! Now, send the pieces on, quickly!"

Harlan had never sent only *part* of a ghost over, but he thought that in some ways it might be easier. The pieces wouldn't be able to beg or attack him very well — or ask him endless questions.

He picked up the severed arm, its hand writhing and trying to grab him. Ignoring it, he opened a portal and tossed it through. It was easier than dealing with whole ghosts.

Now he just had to do it fifty or a hundred more times.

He sent the chunk of leg on its way, then moved on to the next junction and split it. He could feel Beth growing weaker and tried to go faster, faster, but it still took him about fifteen minutes to completely disassemble the 'spider' and send its bits to their various afterlives. Would pieces that belonged to the same ghost find each other on the other side, or would they stay in arm or leg Heaven?

He realized he was feeling a little giddy.

"It's done. You can stop," Beth told him.

He nodded, then abruptly found himself sitting in the middle of the floor. A moment later Beth was beside him, limp and already snoring.

Chapter Nineteen

"Harlan!"

He opened his eyes and saw a ghostly woman smiling down at him. There was something familiar about her, but why? Why would he recognize a ghost?

He recoiled, scrambling backwards on all fours as quickly as he could. He bumped into something and let out a muffled yelp. He dropped the flashlight and sent it rolling and spinning away, leaving him completely in the dark except for random flashes. He wanted to grab it, clutch it to his chest out of an instinctive human fear of darkness, but he also didn't want to take any of his attention away from the ghost.

"It's just me. Beth."

His heart was still pounding and he couldn't believe he'd been so stupid — passing out in an un-warded area where they'd just faced a dangerous ghost. For all he knew, there were more. Sure, Beth was more experienced, she'd fallen asleep first, and they'd both been exhausted, but Harlan had woken up to *a ghost,* and it was only through the grace of whatever that neither of them had been attacked or even possessed.

Pushing Harlan aside, Beth yanked open the veil with one hand and shoved the ghost into it with the other, practically slamming it shut behind her.

The ghost didn't resist at all, just gave Harlan a sad smile before she disappeared.

It was so abrupt, so sudden, Harlan felt like he'd had the wind knocked out of him. He shook his head, trying to clear it. Why had she looked so familiar? He'd only been to this part of the Centre once, when he first—

That was it. She was the ghost the director of the Centre had used to test him, to make sure he was actually a medium and not just...crazy or something.

He turned to face Beth, frowning. "Why did you do that?"

"What?"

Harlan wanted to snap at Beth, but he knew they were both tired and he didn't want to take it out on her, not really. She hadn't done anything *wrong*, it was just... "She wasn't doing anything."

"What are you talking about?"

"She didn't attack us or anything. She was just... She said my name."

"Creepy." Beth hauled herself to her feet, relying heavily on the wall.

Harlan shook his head. "No, it wasn't like that. She knew me. We knew each other. Why did you send her on like that without even talking to her?"

After working the kinks out of her neck and arms, Beth shrugged. "She was a ghost. Our job is to get rid of ghosts."

Harlan opened his mouth to respond. Closed it. He was so tired that he didn't think he could explain himself well enough for Beth to understand.

Beth offered him a hand up and there was a moment when Harlan was worried he'd pull her down on top of him, but then they were both on their feet.

She turned in a slow circle, and Harlan suspected, by the way her eyes were unfocused, that she was looking for any other ghosts. Normally he'd be able to feel what she was doing, but he was too drained.

When she didn't see any, she hurried over to Benjamin.

Harlan wanted to join her, but the distance between them seemed to stretch out farther and farther and he was barely standing as it was.

"He's alive!" Beth shouted, startling Harlan a little. She took out her flashlight and lifted Benjamin's eyelids one at a time to check his pupils.

Benjamin groaned and slowly raised a hand to bat her away.

"We should get back to the others. They're probably worried about us. Come give me a hand with him."

Harlan staggered over, and between them they managed to get Benjamin up. It seemed to take forever to get back to the stairs. They heard footsteps coming down just as they were about to go up. It was Dr. Pahwa, Charles and Hamilton.

"Harlan!" Charles threw an arm over the shoulder Harlan wasn't using to support Benjamin, pulling him close.

"Ow," Harlan wheezed.

"Sorry!" Charles pulled away, wincing. His eyes widened when he saw the blood on Harlan's clothes. "Oh my God. Are you hurt?"

"Not...badly." He managed a weak grin for Charles.

"Here." Charles slid his arm beneath Benjamin's, taking the weight from Harlan.

Hamilton did the same on the other side with Beth.

Charles and Hamilton still didn't look great, but they looked better than they had earlier, and certainly better than he felt or Beth looked.

"I'm sorry I didn't return earlier," Dr. Pahwa apologized. "We weren't sure if it was safe to do so."

"I tried calling and texting you —" Charles began.

"So did I," Hamilton added. "But we couldn't get through."

That was odd. Harlan was sure he had his phone on him and that it was charged. He pulled it out of his pocket and tapped the screen. It didn't respond. "I think the ghost must have drained it." Looking more closely, he saw that the screen was cracked, and he was sure he hadn't dropped it or fallen on it. And now that he thought about it, he *did* remember feeling a spike of intense cold on his leg at one point, but there had been so much going on that he'd barely noticed.

Beth shook her head, holding up her own phone and turning it on. It was covered in the same silvery mesh as her flashlight. "Gotta get one of these, too. Didn't anyone tell you about these?"

He shook his head and turned back to Charles and Hamilton. "I'm so sorry. You must have been frantic! I... We passed out. We should have come upstairs right away, but I was so tired..."

Hamilton and Charles glanced at each other across Benjamin.

"Of course we were worried, but you both clearly needed the rest," Charles said. "C'mon. Let's get you guys upstairs."

Charles and Hamilton supported Benjamin up the steps, with Dr. Pahwa following behind Beth and Harlan, probably to make sure they didn't fall. Which was good, because Harlan could feel his whole body shaking. Charles either hadn't noticed or, more likely, didn't say anything.

Harlan came to a stop when he realized they were going to the infirmary, shaking his head.

Charles touched his arm. "Hey. What's wrong?"

Harlan gestured down at himself. He'd walked far enough that he wasn't leaving bloody footprints anymore, but his sneakers were still soaked and almost entirely red. He had random red smears across his T-shirt that he didn't remember getting. The lower legs of his jeans were spattered with blood, and his knees each had a spreading red stain from hiding behind the table. "I…" He closed his eyes so he wouldn't have to look at it anymore, and tried to ignore the tacky feeling of bloody fabric drying against his skin. "I really, really need to get this off. Now." He could feel that wild panic building up inside his chest again, and he was afraid he was going to lose it right there, right in front of Charles and the others.

The infirmary door opened, and Harlan could smell food. He swallowed hard so he wouldn't be sick. He had to do it a second time. He wasn't sure how long he'd be able to keep doing it before he actually threw up. *Not much longer.*

"Okay. All right."

Someone came out of the infirmary, and Charles passed Benjamin off to them before sliding an arm around Harlan's waist to hold him up.

T. Strange

Beth gave Harlan a little pat on the back, which Harlan acknowledged with a rigid nod, then she went inside with Benjamin.

Harlan rested his head on Charles' shoulder. He closed his eyes, but his mind flashed back to what he'd seen in the basement. He opened them again, staring at the floor tiles. They were shiny and clean and a completely different pattern than the ones in the lab below.

Charles jiggled his shoulder just a little to get Harlan's attention. "What do you need?"

"I—" Harlan had to fight to get his thoughts in any kind of working order. "A shower?"

"Okay. I'm sure there's one around here somewhere." Charles laughed. "I guess you'd know better than me, eh?"

"The gym. That way." Harlan tried to lift his hand to point, but his arm wouldn't respond. He angled his head instead.

Charles walked them down the hall.

"Sorry I worried you."

"That's okay. Don't worry about that. You're all right?"

"Yeah." He wasn't all right, not at all, but he didn't want to get into that now. He didn't really want to tell Charles about it at all. Maybe his therapist, later.

"You?"

Charles laughed softly. "I'm tired, but okay. Better than I was earlier. You're all right? Sorry. I already asked that. I was just really worried. Dr. Pahwa and I wanted to go look for you, but Hamilton said it wasn't safe, especially because we couldn't call you."

"I'm sorry. Things got...bad down there, then we both fell asleep, and my phone was dead..."

"I know. It's okay."

"This is the gym." Harlan directed him to the boys' shower room. The gym itself was dark and cool and took the edge off Harlan's panic. He used to go there alone at night as a kind of meditation.

Charles sat him on a bench against one wall and turned on a shower for him. Luckily there were individual stalls, rather than out in the open the way he'd seen locker rooms in movies.

"There." Charles got him on his feet again and helped him across the tiled floor. "Do you want me to come in with you?"

Harlan shook his head. He was still afraid he'd throw up and he didn't want Charles to hear him. Didn't want Charles to see… He wasn't sure what. "I'll be okay." The stall was small enough that he could lean against a wall and still be in the spray, or he could sit down if he really needed to, and just let the water pour over him for a while.

Charles gave him a skeptical look but nodded. "Do you want help getting undressed?"

So many questions…! Harlan knew Charles had really only asked a few, but he felt himself getting overwhelmed. He swallowed hard, shaking his head again. "Would you —" His words cut off in a choking sob, and he had to take several deep breaths before he could speak again. "Would you wait outside?"

"Outside the changing room?"

Harlan nodded, the motion making his head swim. He hoped Charles couldn't tell how dizzy he was.

"Of course. I'll be right outside. Just shout if you need me."

Harlan stumbled into the shower stall, shutting and locking the door behind him without replying. It was rude, but he knew Charles would understand. A moment later, he heard the locker-room door swing open then shut. He relaxed, slumping against one of the chilly tile walls, soaking up the coolness, even through his shirt.

The water spraying him was warm — too warm. *Warm like blood.*

He pressed his forehead to the tile and concentrated like hell on his breathing until he was pretty sure he wouldn't throw up. He turned the water as cold as he could stand it and let it wash over him. He tried taking off his shirt, but the blood was making it stick to his skin and what little chest hair he had. He winced at the slight pain, then he was shaking and shaking and shaking.

He adjusted the water, making it a little warmer. He could slip out of his shirt. He threw it on the floor and fumbled with the button and zipper of his jeans. They stuck a little at his knees because there was *so much* blood, but he managed to slide out of them and his underwear. He toed his shoes off, but couldn't quite manage to do the same with his socks. They'd started out white and they weren't quite as soaked as his sneakers, so they were pink rather than pure red — pink like the water running off him and down the drain.

He closed his eyes and let himself slide down the wall until he was hunched on the floor, one foot on either side of the drain. With his eyes still closed, he ran his hands down his shins until his fingers brushed the top of his socks. He managed to pull them off, flinging them away. He heard them land somewhere with a wet plop.

He sat like that for a long time, just letting the water run down his naked body, until he remembered that

Charles was waiting outside and probably worried about him. He was a little surprised Charles hadn't knocked or tried to come in already. How long had it actually been? He had no idea.

Somehow he made it to his feet, and he ran his fingers through his hair beneath the water, shuddering when they caught in a section that was flattened to his head with dried blood.

When he was sure he'd got all of it off, he reached out and turned off the shower. He stepped out of the stall and called out, "Charles?"

The door immediately swung open, just a crack. "Yeah?"

"I'm… You can come in."

Charles passed him a towel but let him dry off on his own. He set down a bundle of clothing and a pair of clean shoes on the bench.

Harlan snorted. "Where did you get all that?"

Charles grinned at him, shrugging one shoulder. "Stole it from the girls' locker room. Y'know, it's not really a *locker* room if none of the lockers have locks on them."

Chin almost on his chest, Harlan managed a tiny smile. "Yeah, well, we—the Centre's never really had a problem with thieves. Until *now*." He thought for a moment. "It helps that almost every student here would have some way of figuring out who the thief was."

"I'll make it up to them later," Charles promised.

Once he was dry, Harlan pulled on the sweatpants and T-shirt with the Centre's logo Charles had brought him. The shoes were a little tight and there were no socks, but it would have to do. He didn't plan on walking far.

"There, uh, were underwear, but I didn't think you'd like them," Charles said sheepishly.

"This is fine. Thank you." Harlan wasn't sure he'd ever meant it quite so much in his life.

"You wanna get out of here?"

He nodded, pressing a hand to his forehead when the movement hurt. "We can go home—to my apartment?"

"Yeah. Let's go."

Chapter Twenty

The next day was Saturday. No work, thank God. He was still so drained that he would have been useless anyway, but at least he wouldn't have to pretend.

He hoped he'd be ready by Monday, but he was *not* ready yet.

He picked up his phone to do his BoosterBuddy mental health app and maybe call Charles, who had spent the night but had to leave early—after asking Harlan, repeatedly, if he would be okay on his own.

He'd plugged his phone in overnight, but the screen stayed black, no matter how many times he poked it or what buttons he pressed. *Shit. Right.* The fucking ghost had drained his battery. He had to get one of those mesh things—and possibly a new phone. Well, he'd take it in and get it looked at.

He got up and ate a bagel, both so he could have his pills and so he'd stop poking his phone every few seconds. After washing the dishes and putting them away, he went to the place where he bought his phone.

"Yeah, it should have turned on by now," the tech agreed. "I think it's dead. What did you say happened to it?"

Shit. "It, uh, got frozen?"

"It's the middle of summer."

"I dropped it in a freezer, and I didn't realize it was there for, like, an hour?" He knew he sounded like a total ditz, but he didn't want to explain what had actually happened.

The tech sighed. "I'm going to write it in so it's covered by your warranty and give you a replacement. Just...be careful around freezers, okay?"

"Thank you!"

He left, clutching his new phone. He *would* be careful around freezers. And by that he meant ghosts. He made a mental note to ask Beth where to get a phone protector.

Sunday afternoon Harlan got a text from Hamilton — *Lucky you have Monday off*

Why? he replied. He'd never heard from Hamilton on the weekend before, and he'd never just...got the day off.

Hamilton took a long time to respond, which didn't help Harlan's anxiety.

When Hamilton did reply, his message was simply three emojis — a present, a horse and some kissy lips. *What?* Harlan puzzled over it, then groaned — *Don't look a gift horse in the mouth.*

But looking was in Harlan's nature. He needed to...check the teeth — or whatever that saying was about.

He gritted his own teeth. He knew what he had to do, but he didn't like it.

He tapped Hamilton's name at the top of the screen. Pressed *Audio* when it popped up. Yes, he, Harlan Brand, was making a phone call…to Hamilton…when it wasn't an emergency.

It rang for a long time, until he didn't think Hamilton was going to answer.

"Hello?" More distantly, as though he was holding the phone away from himself, Hamilton added, "It's fine, Matthew. I'm okay."

"Hamilton?"

A sigh. "Yeah."

Harlan bit his lip. "Is…everything okay?"

"Yeah." Hamilton seemed even more monosyllabic than usual.

"It's just that… About Monday?"

Another sigh, even heavier than the first. "Okay, you're right. I'm sorry. I should tell you what's going on. I was a little freaked out by what happened the other day."

Harlan swallowed hard. A *lot* had happened. "Which part?" he asked, not sure he really wanted to know the answer.

"The part where you used me like a battery," Hamilton said flatly.

Harlan heard someone — he assumed Matthew — say something in the background, but he couldn't make out the words.

"Yeah, I know." Hamilton's voice was distant again, replying to Matthew. "I know it's not your fault," he told Harlan, "and I honestly don't think there's anything else we could have done, but I need a little more time to deal with it."

"Of course." Harlan felt sick. He'd fucked up and freaked out one of the few people who liked him and wanted him around.

"I'll see you Tuesday," Hamilton said gently.

Great. And now Hamilton was trying to make *him* feel better, when it should have been the other way around. "Yeah."

"Matthew says hi. And, uh, say hi to Charles from both of us. We'll have to have you over again soon." The last part was said in such a rush that Harlan thought he might have imagined it.

"For sure," Harlan said with as much fake enthusiasm as he could. He didn't want to make Hamilton feel even worse.

"Tuesday." Hamilton hung up.

Harlan groaned and tipped his head back to stare straight up at his living-room ceiling. He really needed some good news—or at least something to cheer himself up.

Charles appeared in his mind and he couldn't help smiling.

Monday.

Charles.

Monday.

There was something there, something good.

Monday and Tuesday were Charles' days off! Normally Harlan was working during the day so they could only see each other in the evenings, but this meant they could spend all of Monday together!

He texted Charles right away. When he didn't get a response immediately, he couldn't help dreading that Charles wanted to distance himself too, even though he knew Charles was probably at Rattling Chains getting ready for the night.

The little dots that meant Charles was typing appeared and Harlan started breathing again.

What's up?

Just found out I have Monday off.

Cool. Everything okay?

Yeah.

Shit, what should he say?

Ham's taking a sick day.

There. That was close enough to the truth that he wasn't lying to Charles, which he definitely didn't want to do, but vague enough that he wasn't giving away anything about Hamilton's personal life.

He didn't notice that it had autocorrected to 'Ham' until after he sent it, but he thought it was pretty funny.

He's okay tho???

He's fine. Just tired and everything.

Good!

I was hoping I could see you?

An eggplant emoji followed by a peach emoji. Harlan felt his cheeks flush. It was amazing how easily Charles could fluster him. And, as much as he was looking forward to sex, he was almost more excited to hold Charles and talk afterward.

* * * *

Charles came over right after closing the club on Monday morning, at about seven. Harlan was used to this and barely stirred as Charles, still smelling pleasantly of leather, crawled into bed with him. They slept for a few hours until Harlan woke up to Charles poking him from behind. He rolled over and gave Charles a slow, gentle stroke.

Charles groaned deeply and wrapped his arms around Harlan, pulling him close for a kiss.

Harlan kept his hand where it was and the kiss got sloppier.

"Lube?" Charles offered.

Harlan nodded. He was reluctant to let go of his wonderful hot handful, but he knew he'd get something even better when Charles came back.

Charles flipped the cap open but stopped before pouring lube onto his palm. "Heads or tails?"

Harlan grinned. "I don't think it's 'heads' you're after with that." He nodded at the bottle.

Charles playfully rolled his eyes. "All right, Mr. Technical — top or bottom? Does *that* work for you?" he teased.

Harlan frowned. He hated making decisions at the best of times, when his blood was flowing freely to his brain and not monopolized in another area. It didn't make him feel like much of a top in the BDSM sense.

"Well, if you don't mind, I pick top, then."

"I don't mind at all," Harlan breathed, happy to have the choice taken from him.

Charles rolled away from Harlan and off the bed, and Harlan let out a little sound in protest.

Shaking his head fondly, Charles smiled down at him. "Oh, don't look at me like that. I'll give you what you want as soon as I can. Scootch over here," he said, patting the side of the bed.

Harlan rolled onto his back and used his elbows and legs to rotate so he was lying across the bed, with his ass end closest to Charles.

"Perfect." Charles sighed in a very satisfied way. He grabbed Harlan's ankles and pulled him closer to the side of the bed, so his ass was perched on the very edge. He spread Harlan's knees and hummed with obvious pleasure. "What a lovely view."

Harlan couldn't help blushing, but he did manage to keep himself from closing his legs again, silently watching Charles admire him — and maybe wishing, at least a little, that he'd just get on with it. He was already fully erect, and he wanted sex more than admiration.

Charles poured some of the lube into his hand, courteously warming it for a moment before reaching down and tracing a finger over Harlan's opening.

Harlan shivered, even though it was warm from Charles' hand, feeling goosebumps raise on his thighs.

"Ready?" Charles asked.

Harlan nodded eagerly, lifting his knees almost to his chest, offering himself. He was glad that neither of them expected Harlan to be a top all the time because that was their BDSM dynamic. He loved fucking Charles, but he also loved Charles fucking him.

"Good." Charles blew him a kiss and rested his free hand on Harlan's thigh. He gently slid his lubed finger past the tight ring of muscle.

Harlan groaned, fighting the urge to clench down, forcing himself to relax and take it. Even one of Charles' thick fingers was a lot to start with, but it meant that he didn't have to spend much time opening Harlan for his cock.

Slowly, steadily, Charles slid his finger deeper. He kept his eyes locked on Harlan's face the whole time, looking for any sign of discomfort. Harlan tended to go non-verbal during sex, so Charles usually noticed if it was too much before Harlan said anything.

When Charles' finger bottomed out, Harlan had his usual feeling of deep bliss at his centre, his core, and it radiated out through his body. He grinned up at Charles, nodding.

Slowly, Charles began to move his finger — sliding it in and out, then curling it deep inside him.

Harlan cried out, grabbing the sheets and twisting them. He nodded again, harder, hoping Charles would understand without words that he was ready, that he wanted *more*.

Charles slid his finger almost all the way out and Harlan made a soft unhappy noise at being suddenly empty, but Charles quickly added a second.

This was more of a stretch, and Harlan had to concentrate on keeping himself relaxed again, breathing through the sensation and staying loose. It was definitely worth it when he felt two of Charles' fingers slide down to the bottom knuckle and curl deep inside him. They were going a little more quickly than usual, but Harlan was wild with urgency, and he could tell Charles felt the same.

"You're ready?"

Harlan nodded, pleading with his eyes and spreading his legs even wider to tempt Charles in.

Not that he had to. Charles slid his fingers out, and a moment later his slick cock was lined up with Harlan's entrance.

"Ready?" he asked again.

Harlan replied by rocking his hips, trying to press Charles deeper by sheer force of will.

"All right, all right." Charles laughed. "I'll take that as a yes."

Even after taking two of Charles' fingers, his thick cock was a bit of a stretch, but Harlan *wanted* it. He lay flat on his back with his eyes closed and concentrated on his breathing.

"More?" Charles' voice was already tight with need.

Harlan pushed down again. He wanted to swallow Charles whole.

Charles gave him what he wanted, sliding deeper and deeper until their bodies met.

Harlan let out a long groan, and Charles' hand tightened on his hip quickly, then released.

"Ready," Harlan managed to say, smiling dreamily up at Charles…his boyfriend. His grin got even wider. *Boyfriend.* He liked that thought.

Nodding, Charles supported one of Harlan's calves in each hand and began to pull out slowly, stopping well before they were in danger of him popping out. He pressed deep again, setting a slow, gentle rhythm.

Harlan was content to lie back and let Charles take care of him for a few minutes, keeping his hand away from his cock so he wouldn't finish too quickly, just concentrating on the sensation of Charles inside him, filling him. It wasn't long before he started rocking his hips again, wordlessly begging Charles for more, faster, harder.

Charles grinned, pulling out more roughly and quickly slamming home. Without giving Harlan time to breathe, he thrusted again.

The sped-up rhythm soon had Harlan gasping and moaning, and he couldn't resist touching himself any longer—though from the way Charles was going, Harlan suspected it wouldn't take much more for him, either. They didn't normally fuck quite this hard, and Harlan thought he'd be a little sore later, but *oh*, would it be worth it! He laughed with joy, beaming at Charles as Charles pounded him.

He wrapped one hand around his shaft, the other one still knotted in the blankets. The pre-cum beading at his tip wasn't quite enough. He managed to gasp, "Lube?" in between thrusts.

Charles poured a little on his outstretched hand—sensibly, he'd kept the bottle within reach in case they needed more. Charles was, after all, a sensible man, and Harlan appreciated that about him.

Harlan stroked himself with his slick hand, loosely following the pace Charles had set.

Looking down at him, Charles shivered. "Close," he grunted.

Harlan nodded. He could *feel* how close Charles was, and he couldn't wait to feel Charles spill inside him. He wanted to finish at close to the same time, and he started stroking himself a little more quickly. Charles nudged that place deep inside of him and Harlan's head flew back and his mouth opened in a silent scream as pleasure flooded his body and swept him away. Charles' thrusts became jerky and erratic as he came too, filling Harlan and making him cry out.

Finished, Harlan went limp, and a moment later Charles pulled out and gave them both a wipe with tissues from a box Harlan kept near the bed.

"Wow," Harlan groaned, shifting over and rotating to make room for Charles.

"Wow," Charles agreed. He lay flat on his back, and Harlan puddled against his side with his head resting on Charles' shoulder.

"Thanks for going to the Centre the other day." The words were out before Harlan could stop them. It wasn't great pillow talk, and he wasn't really sure why he'd said it, especially now, of all times. He just knew that something had been bothering him and he needed to let it out.

Charles turned to kiss Harlan's temple. "Of course."

Harlan groaned. Charles was too forgiving. "But...you shouldn't have had to."

Charles propped himself up on one elbow, frowning slightly. "Maybe not, but it was kind of an 'all-hands-on-deck' situation."

Harlan covered his eyes with the back of one hand and groaned again, louder. "I *know*. It's just..."

"You worry about me?"

"Yeah."

"You think I don't worry about you?"

Harlan blinked. He hadn't thought about it like that before. Ghosts, even dangerous ones, were just his life. But Charles...? "Oh, God."

Charles sat up farther, looking down at Harlan with concern. "What? What's wrong?"

"It's...*me*."

"What's you?" Charles asked with a concerned, confused smile.

Sitting up as well, Harlan balled his hands in the sheets and tried to put his thoughts into words. "Had you ever seen a ghost? Before you met me, I mean?"

"No, I hadn't." Charles shifted so he was leaning against the headboard and softly stroked Harlan's lower back. "Ah. I think I see where you're going with this."

Harlan leaned forward and wrapped his arms around his knees. It meant Charles wasn't touching him anymore, which wasn't what he wanted, but it was what he deserved. "I've put you in *so* much danger," he whispered. He was such a coward that he couldn't even look at Charles as he said it.

And he still hadn't told Charles what they'd found in the Centre's basement.

"We talked about this before," Charles said gently.

Harlan snorted. "Yeah. About the *last* time I almost got you killed. If it wasn't for me, you wouldn't have been pulled into all this…ghost stuff. You would have just been safe at the club."

Charles reached out and gave Harlan's knee a brief squeeze before pulling his hand away again. Harlan got the feeling it was an invitation to be touched, but he was giving Harlan the choice.

Harlan stayed away from him.

"Yeah, I might have."

Harlan felt a cold spike of dread in his guts.

"But…you and Hamilton might have died, and Samuel's victim, James. And Samuel might have got away and kept killing."

Harlan opened his mouth, but Charles cut him off.

"*And*, most importantly, I wouldn't have met you."

"Am I really worth dying for?" He said it without thinking and was immediately horrified. "Oh, God, Charles, I didn't—"

"Yes."

"Please, please don't answer that, I didn't mean…" Harlan curled up even tighter, resting his forehead on his knees.

"I know. My answer is still the same — yes. I would rather die having met you than live without you in my life." Charles laughed, wiping his eye with the back of his hand. "But I'm not exactly in a hurry for that, either."

"Good. We agree. No more ghosts for you." Harlan crossed his arms over his chest to emphasize his point.

"Harlan...like I said, do you think I don't worry about you?"

Harlan stiffened. "But...that's different! That's my *job*!"

"Do you think it would make any difference to me if ghosts killed you on or off the job? 'Cause, like it or not, ghosts are part of the Harlan package. And I think I just admitted how much I like that particular package."

"No, that's not..." Harlan pulled in the entire blanket and scrunched it into a ball in front of him.

"I worry about you. Fuck, I was *terrified* the other night, when you and Hamilton showed up looking like...well, ghosts, and again when you went off after Beth and I couldn't reach you. I worry, but I know that's part of dating you." Charles leaned forward and rubbed slow circles on Harlan's lower back again.

"I don't *want* it to be part of dating me. That thing I saw in the basement..." He shook his head. He'd honestly been trying not to think about it. "It could just as easily have gone upstairs and come after you. You were *there* because of me."

Charles' hand went still. "What are you saying?"

"I don't know! That...that I want to keep you away from all this ghost stuff."

He heard Charles start saying something a few times, but he kept cutting himself off.

Finally, he said, "*You're* not going to quit, are you?"

Harlan shook his head, letting it drop onto his blanket ball. "And I know that makes me a huge hypocrite, but…"

Charles slid his hand up Harlan's spine to the back of his neck and gave it a gentle squeeze. "It doesn't make you a hypocrite. It makes you a concerned boyfriend. Okay." He sighed. "How about this? I'll do my best to stay away from 'ghost stuff'."

Harlan nodded eagerly, leaning back against Charles' chest and looking up at his face from below. Because he was taller than Charles, it wasn't a perspective he got to see often.

"*But,* I'm still an adult and I make my own choices. And I'm not going to leave someone in danger if I can help prevent it."

Harlan frowned at him upside down, not sure what he meant.

Charles kissed his chin. "If there's a situation that I think will be less dangerous if I'm there, I'm not going to 'just be safe at the club'. Got it?"

"Yes." Harlan planned on never letting that happen again, but he didn't say that.

"Good." Charles' stomach rumbled, and he grinned. "On that note, as much as I would love to spend the day in bed with you, we should eat so you can take your pills."

Harlan nodded a little reluctantly.

Charles glanced at his phone and laughed. "I guess it's *brunch* at this point. But after that…I might have a little surprise for you."

"What kind of surprise?"

"Let's just say I'm considering getting some new toys for the club, and I need your help picking the best ones. And, of course, it would just be irresponsible of me to hand them out without testing them on myself first. I'd do it on my own if I could, but..." Charles heaved a dramatic sigh.

Harlan grinned. "Oh, of course. *Anything* to help your business."

"Y'know, I thought you might say that." He slid out of bed before Harlan could catch him. "*After* breakfast!"

Harlan lazily stayed in bed, just a little longer, listening to Charles putter around in the kitchen.

"Oh, shit!" Charles' shout snapped him out of his doze. "Oh! Oh, fuck!" He heard Charles retch.

He ran out of the bedroom and into the kitchen.

Charles was standing a few feet away from the fridge, staring at it in horror like it might attack him.

"What is it? What's wrong?" Harlan wished he'd at least stopped to put on boxers. Whatever had frightened Charles that badly was probably something he didn't want to face with his dick hanging out.

Charles didn't answer, just shook his head and pointed at the fridge.

Was it a raccoon or something? A rat? Harlan picked up a spatula from the counter and, holding it in front of him, slowly advanced on the fridge. He threw the door open hard enough that it banged against the wall. A sickening wave of odour poured out, as if the fridge had been unplugged and shut for years.

"Oh, fuck!" Harlan doubled over, gagging and barely keeping himself from throwing up.

Charles nodded, not looking much better.

Using the spatula, Harlan reached out and slammed the fridge closed. The smell didn't go away, not completely, but they could breathe again and at least no more was coming out.

Charles went around opening windows while Harlan, after pulling on some underwear, watched gratefully and tried to convince his stomach contents to stay put. This was definitely a dick-covered situation.

"Whew," Charles said, returning to the kitchen. He kept one wary eye on the fridge. "I know you sometimes skip a meal or two when I'm not around, but this…!"

Harlan shook his head. He felt pale and shaky, and he wasn't sure if it was from the lingering smell or what he was beginning to suspect had happened. "I bought those groceries last week, and I cleaned out the fridge when I brought them home."

"You might want to switch grocery stores."

"No, I don't think it's that. Let me check something." He grabbed one of his Centre mediumship textbooks — the only books that hadn't been in the apartment when he moved in — and flipped through it. "Ah, here it is." He closed it decisively.

"Gonna share with the class?" Charles laughed humorlessly.

"Sorry. I've never seen it in person, but I remembered reading about it. Um, basically, some ghosts can contaminate or rot food. They can even —" He took a deep breath, immediately regretted it and opened the fridge again. *Yep. Maggots.*

"Garbage bag?" he wheezed, trying not to look too closely at the foul, writhing mass inside.

Charles passed him not only two trash bags, one inside the other, but a pair of rubber dish gloves. It took another double bag, but they got the whole mess, maggots and all, wrapped up. Holding them at arm's length, Harlan ran down the stairs and out to the dumpster. He didn't want to get that smell in the elevator. He caught his neighbour, the one Charles said was into him, giving him some major stink eye.

Not that he could blame him.

He threw out the gloves for good measure, ran back upstairs and frantically washed his hands.

Charles had Febrezed the shit out of the kitchen, to the point that it was probably more aerosol than air, but between that and the open windows, the stench was contained.

"It must have been that ghost from the other night," Harlan said apologetically. "One last 'fuck you', I guess." He glanced around the kitchen, looking for inspiration and trying not to think about whatever yummy thing Charles would have made. "Um, oatmeal?" he offered. He wasn't really hungry anymore, and he doubted Charles was either, but Charles was right. He did need to eat before he had his pills, and it was already later in the day than he was supposed to take them.

"Sure."

Harlan opened the cupboard a little cautiously, but everything inside looked normal. He picked up a box of oatmeal packets and shook it. It sounded normal. He tore just the corner off one of them, then recoiled. "Oh, come on!" The oats were black and crumbly like they'd been hit by one of the plagues of Egypt. The smell wasn't as bad as the meat and vegetables in the fridge, but it seemed to coat the inside of his nostrils. He had a feeling he'd be smelling it for a month. Hopefully none of his neighbours would complain. He was tempted to get some plastic sheets and just seal off the whole kitchen indefinitely.

The sugar was crawling with maggots, and even the honey was black and putrid.

He'd thought honey and sugar couldn't go bad. Hadn't they found some honey in the pyramids that was still edible? Why couldn't the pyramids be haunted instead of his apartment?

Charles was right there with another garbage bag. They didn't bother checking anything else, just shoved every scrap of food into bags and took them downstairs immediately.

He had to go to the store, talk to people and buy groceries less than a week after going through all that already! And he'd have to buy *everything*, not just a few staples. He groaned.

"Hey." Charles took his hand and gave it a gentle, reassuring squeeze. "I guess we're going out for breakfast."

Chapter Twenty-One

Despite thinking that he'd never want to eat again, Harlan enjoyed their brunch of waffles and bacon, and he was feeling a lot better by the time they got back to his apartment. The smell seemed to be gone, but he couldn't bring himself to even look in the direction of the kitchen.

"Ready for your surprise?" Charles asked.

Harlan blinked, then grinned. "Oh, right!" The day had got off to a weird start, but he thought that brunch, combined with whatever Charles had planned, would be enough to turn it around.

"The toy bag is already in the bedroom."

Harlan gave him a light swat on the butt. "Let's go to the bedroom, then." He'd meant to sound sexy and dominant, but he wasn't sure he'd pulled it off.

Charles skipped ahead of him and was already halfway undressed by the time Harlan caught up.

"Because we enjoyed it so much last time, when I was first introducing you to toys, I picked out one toy from each of the main food groups — a flogger, a crop, a paddle and a cane — to try. I mean, for the *club* to try, of course." Charles grinned, then rummaged in the bag he'd brought and set four toys on the bed.

Harlan walked over to look at them. The last time they'd played this game, he'd never held a BDSM toy before, but he'd got a lot of experience since then. He still felt a little nervous at first, but they were all similar to toys he'd used before. There was nothing too difficult or strange, nothing that made him worry he'd hurt Charles for real before he'd tried it a few times — not that Charles would want those sorts of toys in his club. People were free to bring in their own, but most of Rattling Chains' toys were pretty basic. Charles also had to be able to disinfect all of them, which narrowed his options.

The paddle was rectangular and made of red leather. The flogger was also red leather, with wide, flat falls with rounded tips. The cane was black, basically a riding crop without a tab at the end. The actual crop looked a little more unusual.

"What's this one?" he asked Charles.

Charles grinned. "That's a jockey bat. It's one of my favourite toys, so I thought I'd try one out and see if the club likes it."

"The club selection committee that's just you and me?" Harlan teased.

"Yep!"

Harlan picked up the jockey bat. The handle and flat piece at the end were more or less the same as other riding crops he'd used, except that the tip was firm instead of just being a folded-over piece of leather. The shaft was very different. It was made of flexible rubber in a candy-cane-stripe pattern of red and black. He gave it a gentle swish through the air. It was much heavier than a normal riding crop, and the rubber made it more flexible. He could make a much larger arc using the same amount of swing.

Once he was satisfied with his equipment, he turned back to Charles. He tapped two places on the end of the bed with the tip of the crop. They were far apart and would put Charles off balance. "Put one hand there and the other there." To make it even more difficult, he indicated two more places for Charles' feet where they'd be spread nice and wide.

Charles obeyed without question, grinning and eager.

Harlan laid out the ground rules. "Ten strikes with each toy, each strike harder than the last. I want you to count each strike out loud. After every toy, I want a 'yes, Sir' or a 'no, Sir.' Or a 'maybe', I guess." *Rats...* He'd lost his Dom role for a moment there. "Understood?" he added firmly.

"Yes, Sir," Charles purred, raising his ass invitingly.

"Mmm." Harlan couldn't help taking a second to just appreciate the view — Charles' well-furred, muscular ass cheeks, with just a teasing peek of what hid between them, and the dark shadow of his heavy balls underneath. Maybe one day he'd get used to seeing all of Charles laid out in front of him — just for *him* — but so far he was still in awe each time he saw Charles naked.

He couldn't decide between starting with the flogger or the paddle, so he gave in and played eenie-meenie-minie-moe. He landed on the paddle. It had grooves in the handle that fit his hand nicely, and he gently stroked Charles' left cheek with one edge. He was delighted when Charles' skin immediately got goosebumps.

A long shiver rolled down Charles' spine, and he let out a soft, "Ohhhh."

Harlan waited until Charles was nice and relaxed again before lifting the paddle for his first strike.

Charles let out a breathy shout, his whole body rocking with the impact, even though it hadn't been that hard. He immediately shifted his ass back towards Harlan, offering himself for another strike.

"Well?" Harlan asked softly, grinning to himself.

"'Well'?" Charles repeated. "Oh! One, Sir."

"That's better." He hadn't asked Charles to call him 'Sir' after each blow, only after each toy, but he had to admit he liked it.

Harlan stroked Charles' ass cheek with his free hand, lingering on the slightly red mark the paddle had left. He could already feel Charles' skin getting hot.

He rewarded Charles with a second blow on the same spot as the first — but harder, as he'd promised.

Charles waited just long enough to take a breath before saying, "Two, Sir."

A third strike, and this one was a little above the last two. Harlan decided that he'd use the paddle on one cheek and switch back and forth for the other toys, so he wouldn't overwhelm either side of Charles' ass and he'd be able to see the marks each toy made. After all, they were at least pretending to choose toys, not just playing for fun.

He gave another few blows, one after the other, barely giving Charles time to call out the number before the next one landed. Harlan was hitting a little harder each time, and Charles' ass was getting nice and pink, but Harlan wasn't anywhere near going all out. They still had three more toys to go.

"Ten! Sir!" Charles called out proudly, turning to grin at Harlan before sinking a little farther forward on his elbows. "And that one is a 'yes', Sir."

"Good," Harlan praised him, lightly stroking his extra-warm ass cheek. He set the paddle down and picked up the flogger. "Ready?"

"Yes, Sir." Charles settled himself, his ass raised as high as it could go.

Harlan hated not being able to keep touching Charles, but he had to take a step back so he could swing the flogger and not hit both cheeks. He wouldn't be able to keep a hand on Charles with the next two toys, either, but he could always give him a stroke in between.

He snapped the flogger in the air a few times, getting used to its weight and the length of its falls.

Charles let out a little moan every time he heard it crack.

When he was ready, Harlan brought it down on Charles' right cheek.

Charles cried out, spreading his legs wider to brace himself — and, Harlan thought, to give more of his ass for him to hit.

Harlan waited a moment, then cleared his throat just as Charles said, "Two, Sir."

He swung three times without pausing between them, not giving Charles time to count.

"Six, Sir?" Charles asked after Harlan lowered the flogger.

Harlan grinned and shook his head. "Nope, that was only five. Should we start over?" It was up to Charles —

if he wanted to just keep going from where they'd left off, that was fine with Harlan.

Charles thought a moment, then said, "Yes, Sir."

"All right." Harlan stepped closer so he could stroke Charles' lower back, feeling Charles shiver with happiness beneath him, then lined up to flog him again. This time he had mercy and gave Charles plenty of time to answer between swings.

Charles hissed softly and pulled away at the tenth strike, but he quickly said, "Ten, Sir."

"Sorry, was that too much?" Harlan hadn't been swinging full force even at the end, but it was still ten — no, fifteen — blows pretty much on top of each other. He ran a hand over Charles' hot skin. There were a few darker spots of colour — not quite welts, but close.

Charles shook his head without lifting it from the mattress. "No. No. The last one just wrapped a bit."

Harlan winced. "Ooh, I'm sorry!" 'Wrapping' was when a flogger's falls went around the curve of a hip or other body part and struck extra hard on the other side. He looked, and there were a few small welts on Charles' thigh. "Do you want to stop?"

"No way. Not yet. Not until we've tried all of these," Charles insisted. His voice already sounded a little dreamy, and Harlan was pretty sure he'd be in subspace by the time he was finished with Charles. Charles was *adorable* when he was in subspace. "That one's also a 'yes', Sir."

"All right." Harlan stroked Charles' ass a little longer, giving him time to recover before putting the flogger down. "Which toy next?"

"Cane," Charles answered immediately.

Harlan grinned as he picked it up. "That didn't take you long."

"Canes *sting*, and I like jockey bats. I'm saving the best for last."

"Oh, you've used a jockey bat?" Harlan teased. "I guess we don't have to try this one today."

"No! It's different!" Charles insisted.

Harlan was tempted to ask how—in detail—it was different, but he took mercy on Charles again...in a manner of speaking.

He quickly drew back the cane and lashed Charles' left cheek.

Charles cried out and rocked forward again, but before Harlan could even raise the cane a second time Charles was back in place. "One, Sir," he said breathlessly.

"Good," Harlan told him, then brought the cane down again. Normally he liked to layer his cane-marks on top of each other and see how clean he could make a single line, but he'd already used the paddle on this cheek, and it was still pretty red. He spaced his cane-marks out, leaving a series of pink stripes while Charles counted. Charles gasped and moaned, getting Harlan more and more excited. He couldn't resist hitting almost full force with his tenth strike. There was only one toy left, and it would be on the other cheek. He knew Charles could take it.

"Ten!" Charles panted, shifting his knees and elbows to get comfortable again.

"Ten," Harlan agreed. He didn't scold Charles for not saying 'Sir' after the number, since it was something Charles had started doing on his own, after all, not something Harlan had asked him to do— otherwise, he would have insisted.

If he'd remembered, in his own excitement.

Charles didn't give his opinion of the toy, so Harlan gently prompted him, "What did you think of that one?"

"Mm-m? Oh! 'Yes', Sir."

"Good. Ready?" Harlan picked up the jockey bat.

Charles nodded, keeping his head low.

It was a good thing it was the last toy. Charles seemed close to his limit and Harlan was getting tired too. Impact play was surprisingly exhausting for both people.

He rubbed Charles' ass in slow circles with his hand, wandering his fingers across both cheeks. "The left is so much warmer," he murmured, sliding his palm from one cheek to the other.

"We'll just have to even them out, won't we?" Charles laughed.

"Yes, we will." Harlan grinned. "That sounds like someone who's ready for the next toy." He took a reluctant step back, lightly stroking Charles' ass with the tip of the jockey bat. He knew it was much cooler than his hand on Charles' flushed skin, and he liked watching Charles shiver a little.

"Ready?" he asked again, waiting for Charles' nod before taking his first swing.

It left a perfect rectangular mark that quickly faded into the redness of Charles' ass.

"One, Sir!"

"Good. You're taking it so well," Harlan praised him. He struck again, then twice more, but he left Charles enough time to count in between. He fell into a steady rhythm, and only Charles saying, "Nine, Sir," reminded him that they were almost done.

"Last one. This'll be the hardest," Harlan warned him, also giving Charles a chance to tell him if he wanted something different. "Ready?"

Charles nodded, his head barely moving, then added, "Yes, Sir."

Harlan lined himself up carefully, aiming for a part of Charles' ass that didn't have a rectangle yet. He didn't hit as hard as he could, but it was the hardest of the day. He shivered with pleasure at the solid *smack!* and the way the impact vibrated back up the rubber shaft of the toy into his hand.

Charles cried out, his body tensing then going completely limp, with only his knees and elbows supporting him — and they looked like they might give out at any moment. "Ten, Sir," he sighed. "And also very much 'yes', Sir."

Harlan grinned down at his sweaty back. "That was amazing." He'd momentarily forgot that he'd asked Charles to give him a yes or no after each toy. He was impressed that Charles had remembered.

He helped Charles roll onto his back, then sit against the headboard.

"So, which ones are you going to get for the club?" Harlan teased. "I'm pretty sure I heard four yeses."

Charles groaned, his head loose on his neck. "*All* of them," he drawled, grinning.

"Yeah, I thought that's what you'd say."

"I'll be right back."

Harlan let out a little needy moan, reaching for him.

Charles laughed but shook his head firmly. "I'll be *right* back," he promised.

He returned with a chocolate bar for each of them that he'd got from his bag and two glasses of water.

"Don't worry. I filled them from the bathroom sink, not the kitchen."

Usually this was Harlan's job after they played — the only time he fed Charles, rather than the other way around — but he was glad he hadn't had to go into the kitchen.

Harlan always meant to have drinks and snacks ready *before* they started playing, but they usually got too excited and forgot.

"Which one was your favourite?" Harlan asked, once they'd both eaten and had some water and he'd got Charles tucked in. He sat on the edge of the bed beside Charles, stroking Charles' thick chest hair.

"The jockey bat."

"Right, you said that already."

"Which one was *your* favourite?" Charles beamed up at him.

"Hmm. I'm not sure. I liked the jockey bat too."

"*You're* my favourite."

Harlan blushed. Charles' eyes were already closed. "You're my favourite too," he murmured. Before Charles could fully fall asleep, Harlan asked softly, "Would you mind grocery shopping with me?" Buying literally everything was a little less overwhelming with the thought of Charles beside him.

"'Course not."

Hopefully Charles would remember when he came down from subspace. If not, Harlan was sure he'd say yes again.

* * * *

When he wasn't distracted by Charles, Harlan spent all day Monday worrying that he'd get a call or text from Hamilton saying that he was still too freaked out by Harlan to work with him. He woke up at six-o-three a.m. on Tuesday, way earlier than he needed to be awake, and checked his phone. No messages from Hamilton. His phone stayed silent, and when he went downstairs at eight fifty-nine, Hamilton's patrol car was waiting for him.

He didn't say anything about his absence the day before, and Harlan didn't question it. He hoped he was imagining the new distance between them, the way Hamilton didn't make eye contact and seemed to be leaning away from him.

Whether he was imagining it or not, Hamilton appeared to relax over the course of the day. By the time they'd handled their third ghost, things felt back to normal, and Harlan finally felt like he could breathe again.

The phone rang almost as soon as Harlan got home. He didn't like answering the phone, even when it was a number he recognized, and he was quite happy to ignore an unknown caller. They left a voicemail. He tried to decipher the transcription, but it was a garbled mess. Sighing, he listened to the message. The voice sounded vaguely familiar, but he couldn't place it.

"Hi. Is this Harlan? Fuck, I hope I have the right number. I called the Centre and this is the number they gave me. This is Michael…Michael Clark. Right, you don't know my name. I'm, uh… I'm the guy you saved from the…yeah. I left the Centre while you were asleep, so I didn't get a chance to thank you. Then I needed some time to… Well, you get it. Anyway, I wanted to thank you for rescuing me, and I was wondering if you'd like to go out for dinner or something. No, dinner's probably too much, isn't it? Maybe coffee?

Anyway, it'd be great to hear from you. Just…call me back! Okay? Bye."

Harlan was relieved to hear that the man — *Michael,* he reminded himself — was all right. He hadn't honestly given him much thought, never mind tried to contact him.

He was just about to step into the shower when he was startled by an unfamiliar text tone. It wasn't the ones he'd set for Charles or Hamilton, and really, the only other texts he got were spam.

He tapped his phone screen and glanced at the text.

Hey. It's Michael. I thought I'd text you too in case you're not someone who does voice calls lol
Like I said, I'd really like to thank you in person sometime.

Harlan set his phone down, then picked it up again. The guy had been through something really traumatic, and Harlan had been there when it happened. He could understand why Michael would want to reach out to him.

He started typing a few times before he was ready to send.

Hey, it's Harlan. Just wanted to let you know you have the right number. I'm really busy with work right now, but we could meet for coffee sometime.

He had no intention of actually following up on that, but it was better than just saying no outright. Or maybe it was worse, and Harlan was just a coward. Hopefully Michael would forget about it in a few days.

He was about to put his phone down again when he saw that Michael was typing a reply already. *Wow, eager*. It was a little much, but Harlan also remembered thinking that, under better circumstances, Michael might be hot. Harlan had fantasized about being with more than one man before, but had never really thought he'd have a chance to try it in real life. He definitely hadn't discussed it with Charles, so he had no idea how Charles felt about being poly.

Maybe coffee wasn't such a bad idea. With Charles there, of course.

I'd love that! Hope to see you soon.

Harlan didn't reply. That seemed like the end of the conversation.

Chapter Twenty-Two

Harlan caught glimpses of a woman running through a forest. She screamed and he tried to run closer, but fog closed in, leaving him alone while her cries echoed around him.

He was in a bare concrete room, lit only by a single, uncovered fluorescent strip. It flickered and went out and he heard a muffled cry.

The light came back on, and he saw Leo tied to a chair with a gag in her mouth. She didn't seem injured, but she was pale and thin. Her dark hair hung in limp, greasy strands over her eyes.

Harlan looked down. Surrounding the chair were neat rows of symbols. They almost looked like the ones ghost-warders used, except they were subtly wrong. They made his skin crawl. He thought he might be sick. He couldn't imagine being surrounded by them for...however long Leo had been there.

He closed his eyes to blink away the sick feeling. Opening them, he focused on Leo again. "Where are you?" he whispered, not wanting to attract the attention of who or what had captured her.

She slowly lifted her head, her unfocused eyes darting around the room. He thought she could hear him but not see him.

Her eyes widened as she stared at something behind him, screaming into her gag and frantically pulling at the chains binding her.

Harlan reached for her, but then his phone rang—

He opened his eyes. He was drenched in sweat. The room was pitch black except for the red glow of the alarm clock. And the light from his phone, which was still ringing.

"I think I was here-ish," Charles mumbled, clearly still asleep. He rolled away from the sound.

Harlan grabbed his phone and slid the ringer to silent without answering it. Whatever it was, it could wait until morning.

It started vibrating in his hand again before he could put it down, and he gave in and looked at who was calling. It was Morgan.

He slid out of bed as carefully as possible, trying not to jostle Charles. He padded into the living room, shutting the bedroom door behind him before answering.

"Hello?"

"Oh, thank fuck. I was really worried you weren't going to answer. I'm freaking out and I didn't know who else to call. I just had the craziest dream."

Harlan froze, feeling goosebumps prickle his skin and making the hair on the back of his neck stand up. "About Leo."

"Y-Yeah. How did you…? Oh, fuck, you had it too, didn't you? What should we do?"

Harlan got up and started pacing. "Okay. We have to assume she's reaching out to us. She didn't seem dead, at least not in the dream, but maybe she's dying, and we made a connection when we were searching for her before."

Morgan sighed. "We have to do the thing again, don't we?"

Harlan held out his phone so he could see the time. It was almost three a.m. "Yeah. I think so."

"Shit. I was afraid you were going to say that."

"I'll get us a ride," Harlan told them before hanging up. Neither of them had a driver's license. Harlan was trying to keep Charles away from ghost business. They could call a cab, but who knew how far they might have to follow Leo? Harlan sighed. That left only one option.

"Holy shit, this had better be good, Brand."

Harlan heard Hamilton murmur something to Matthew, then scuffling sounds as he got up.

"It is," Harlan promised. "Or rather, bad." He explained their identical dreams.

"Oh, good, I get to chauffeur the Murder Twins again."

Harlan frowned at the phone.

Hamilton sighed. "Sorry. It's just too fucking early. I know Leo's a friend of yours, and I've known her a long time. I'm happy to help. See you in fifteen." He hung up.

Harlan texted Morgan to let them know the plan, then crept back into the bedroom to grab some clothes. He left a note on Charles' phone where he'd see it when he turned it on. He was glad Charles had shown him how to unlock it.

He just wanted to crawl back into bed with him.

Instead, he forced himself to get dressed, put on deodorant and head downstairs. The others would just have to deal with his unbrushed teeth.

Hamilton, always punctual, arrived exactly fourteen minutes and thirty-seven seconds after he'd hung up. He was driving his personal car, which Harlan had never seen before. Harlan didn't know much about cars, but it was fancier than Harlan would have expected for him. Maybe it was Matthew's.

Neither of them spoke during the drive, which wasn't unusual, but Harlan kept feeling an uncharacteristic urge to break the silence. He'd thought things had got a little less strained between him and Hamilton over the course of the week, but he still felt tension in the air — or imagined he did. He hadn't mentioned it. He assumed Hamilton would just laugh it off and tell him he was being paranoid or something, whether it was true or not.

Morgan was waiting outside their building, pacing a few steps in one direction before pivoting and taking a few steps back the way they'd come. They reminded Harlan of Libby, and his heart ached when he remembered she was gone.

Was it sad that he was coming to the realization that a simple repeater who hadn't even known he'd existed and he knew nothing about was one of his closest friends?

He shook off that thought and climbed into the back seat beside Morgan.

"Ready?" Morgan held out their hand.

After covering a yawn with the back of his right hand, Harlan held out his left and braced himself for whatever might appear.

Nothing happened. The street was still deserted, no humans or ghosts in sight. He squeezed a little tighter just as Morgan's fingers clenched on his hand.

They turned to each other, blinking and drowsy.

Hamilton frowned at them in the rear-view mirror. "Oh, for...! Really? I got out of bed for *that*?" He groaned, pressing his forehead against the steering wheel. "Okay. How about this? We drive by Leo's place, see if we can pick up the trail from there."

Still not releasing Harlan's hand, Morgan nodded slowly. "That...might work."

The dream hadn't shown Harlan—or, he assumed, Morgan—a specific, identifiable place to begin their search. Hamilton's plan was the best one they had, and he seemed to be thinking the most clearly of the three of them. "Sounds good." He glanced at Hamilton's reflection, hoping he'd imagined how quickly Hamilton looked away.

Morgan yawned, and Harlan did the same a moment later.

Hamilton's jaw shifted from side to side, but he didn't give in.

"There!"

Hamilton slammed on the brakes.

Harlan's head snapped up from where it had been resting on Morgan's shoulder. He didn't remember putting it there or falling asleep. He was about to apologize to them when he saw what they'd already spotted—a shimmering, translucent apparition of Leo. Somehow he hadn't let go of their hand.

Leo's ghost showed no obvious signs of how she'd died.

"Here we go again," Hamilton muttered, but he was grinning and leaning forward eagerly. "Do we need to let her know we're here?"

Harlan and Morgan glanced at each other.

"I'm...not sure." Morgan started rolling down their window.

Harlan wondered if they were going to stick their hand out the window and wave, but he didn't have any better ideas.

Slowly, Leo turned. She was facing their car now, but not looking directly at them. Unlike Monica, she didn't seem to be aware she was being followed. She drifted down the middle of the road without purpose, as though simply carried along by the wind, but the night air was still through Morgan's open window.

"All right, I guess we're playing another round of 'follow that ghost'." Hamilton swept the car around and followed her shimmering outline.

Luckily there wasn't much traffic as they crept along quiet side streets.

"Shit." Hamilton stopped, craning his head to look in every direction. "I don't see her. Do you?"

Morgan shook their head.

Harlan couldn't see her, either. His hand was beginning to cramp from being locked in Morgan's. He didn't want to risk breaking the connection—though he thought it might already be too late.

The three of them sat quietly, Hamilton humming a song Harlan didn't know. Harlan felt Morgan jerk a few times as they started falling asleep. Maybe if he closed his eyes just for a second, he could—

"There!" Morgan shouted again, pointing through their still-open window.

Leo's ghost had appeared far ahead of them. If she'd become visible even a moment later, she'd have been around the corner and out of sight.

Hamilton easily caught up with her, then they were back to a crawl as they followed her.

She flickered out of existence again.

Harlan glanced down at his hand, as though he'd broken contact with Morgan, but their fingers were still tightly entwined. He saw them do the same.

"Shit." Hamilton pulled over. He turned to face the back seat. "Well?"

Morgan turned to look at Harlan.

He bit his lip. "We keep driving," he said as confidently as he could manage. "She might reappear." He was terrified that, even if she did appear, it would be on another street or even behind them, but he wasn't ready to give up yet.

Morgan gave his hand a little squeeze.

Hamilton nodded and started the car.

She suddenly appeared beside Harlan's window, and he shrieked. He instinctively tried to jerk his hand free of Morgan's, but they held on.

They followed Leo for another three blocks before she disappeared, but she was back a moment later in the same place. Then she was gone again, but this time felt...different. Something tight in Harlan's chest loosened and he let out a long, slow breath. "She's gone."

Morgan nodded. They freed their hand and shook it.

Harlan did the same.

"Now what? We keep driving?"

Harlan could tell Hamilton was getting tired. He watched them in the rear-view mirror rather than turning around.

Harlan shook his head. "She's gone."

Hamilton sighed. "Yeah, you said that. What does it mean?"

Harlan glanced at Morgan, relieved when they answered for both of them.

"We've lost the connection. I don't think we'll see her again tonight."

Harlan nodded, covering a yawn with the back of his hand. He sensed the same thing.

"Great. This was for nothing. Okay. What does losing the connection mean?"

Again, Morgan glanced at Harlan.

"I'm not totally sure. She didn't...feel like a normal ghost."

"Uh-huh. What is she, then?"

"I don't know."

Sighing again, Hamilton glanced at the clock on the dashboard. "There's a twenty-four-hour Tim Hortons around here. Let's sit down and figure this out. Coffee's on me."

Harlan ordered his usual Iced Capp.

Morgan ordered herbal tea.

Hamilton, who ordered a large double-double, paid for it all with a laugh. "I should make you two pay for your drinks, since they're not actually coffee." He also bought three donuts, then led them to a table.

Morgan immediately snagged a donut, then grinned. "Or are these for cops only?" they teased him.

"Ha-ha. If this keeps happening, *you'll* be on the payroll soon enough."

Their hand froze halfway between the box and their mouth. They didn't sound at all playful when they said, "No. Oh, no. I don't want that."

Harlan cleared his throat, frowning and shaking his head at Hamilton when Morgan wasn't looking. "Leo."

Hamilton nodded and dug his notebook and pencil out of his pocket, flipping to a blank page. "Yeah. Brainstorm. What went wrong?"

Harlan and Morgan frowned at him.

He threw up his hands. "Okay, okay, let me rephrase that! Why did we lose her?"

Harlan thought back to what he'd seen and felt. "I don't think it was a problem with my connection to Morgan," he said slowly.

"Me neither." Morgan stirred sugar into their tea. They already had a pile of empty packets on the table in front of them, and Harlan wondered whether they had a sweet tooth or just needed something to do with their hands.

Hamilton nodded, writing something down. "What other reasons could there be?"

Harlan took a long, thoughtful sip of his drink. He had no idea, and his tired brain wasn't offering any suggestions. He had to look at it logically. If the problem *wasn't* on their end, what did that leave? He'd thought earlier that there was something wrong with Leo. What could make her flicker in and out like that?

No. Not what was *wrong* with Leo. What was *right* with her.

Eyes wide, he looked up and saw that Morgan's expression was identical to his. They'd come to the same conclusion.

"She's alive," Harlan breathed.

"Alive? How is that possible? Weren't you guys just following her ghost?"

"I think she was *near* death but not actually dead. She must have...stabilized or something. That's why she disappeared, and we can't feel her anymore."

"Great."

Morgan glared at him.

"Hey, I'm glad she's alive! But it would have been nice to find her and see if her disappearance is connected to everything else that's going on."

Hamilton stirred his coffee thoughtfully. "So, just to be clear, you guys can't follow her right now."

"Right," Harlan agreed.

Hamilton swiped a hand backwards through his short sandy-blond hair, groaning. "So this is a dead end."

"For now, yes." Harlan was as frustrated as Hamilton. He wanted to find Leo alive, but he also wanted to know what was going on in his city.

Chapter Twenty-Three

"Hey," Hamilton greeted Harlan as he got into the patrol car. "I've got something you might find interesting." He passed Harlan an article clipped out of a newspaper.

"You get the paper?"

Hamilton snorted. "No! Of course not. I'm not *that* old." He scratched his jaw, nails scraping against his stubble.

Harlan shivered happily. The sound always gave him a pleasant tingling sensation up his spine.

Hamilton sighed. "*Matthew* reads it and he pointed this out to me. Just...shut up and read it."

Local Medium Missing

Bradley St. James, a privately practicing medium in the Toronto area, went missing Sunday night. Authorities are seeking anyone with any information...

"That's a second missing medium."

"Yep."

"Is anyone else looking into this?"

Hamilton shrugged. "As a missing person case, but not in connection to Leo or anything else."

Nodding distractedly, Harlan skimmed the rest of the article. "It says he owned an occult shop right around here."

"Seems like a good place to start. That was where he was last seen." Hamilton snorted again. "Believe it or not, I actually *did* read the whole article before handing it to you."

"Right. Sorry. Of course you did. If he died there, he might be able to tell us what happened. If not...maybe Morgan and I can find him."

"Yeah." Hamilton sounded skeptical.

"Yeah," Harlan agreed. He was reluctant to put them through that again.

The shop's display window was full of crystals and fairy statuettes.

"Man, I bet it just *reeks* of incense in there," Hamilton laughed, shaking his head. "After you."

He held out an arm and Harlan pushed past it to open the door. As Hamilton had predicted, a wave of patchouli poured out onto the sidewalk. Harlan ignored it and stepped inside, but not before he saw Hamilton stifle a laugh by pretending to cough into his fist.

A woman wearing a turquoise-blue headscarf looked up when the bell above the door jangled. "Hello, and welcome to— Oh, good, you're here!" She rushed out from behind the desk after she glanced past Harlan and saw Hamilton's uniform. "You're here about Bradley, right?"

Hamilton nodded, stepping up beside Harlan.

Harlan quickly tuned out the conversation. He turned in a slow circle, trying to get a sense of the place. The closest spirit was about a block away. It didn't feel like anyone had died in this place, never mind left a ghost behind. *Is that good or bad?* It could mean that Bradley was alive, or that he'd been killed somewhere else and he might or might not be haunting *that* place.

Or maybe mediums' spirits were entirely different. Maybe Bradley was there, watching him without Harlan being able to tell. He'd never met a medium's ghost, and the subject hadn't been brought up at the Centre. The instructors probably hadn't wanted the kids to think about their own deaths, which was great—but unhelpful.

Harlan closed his eyes and really focused, extending his awareness out as far as he could reach. He felt one other ghost on the very perimeter of his senses, but he couldn't pick up any trace of Bradley.

Opening his eyes, he saw Hamilton shoot him a questioning glance. He shook his head.

"Thank you for your time, Ms. Zaman." Hamilton handed her one of his cards and she tucked it away in her pocket. "If you think of anything, or you have any questions, please don't hesitate to call."

"Of course. I...I really hope he's okay." She swallowed hard and wiped her eye on her sleeve.

"As do we," Hamilton assured her, giving her a sympathetic smile. He flipped his notebook shut with a well-practiced motion and put it away.

A thought occurred to Harlan. "Ms. Zaman..." It felt strange calling her that, but he hadn't been paying attention when she'd introduced herself, so he hadn't caught her first name, only what Hamilton had called her. "Do you have Bradley's home address?" On the other hand, he only remembered Bradley's first name, so he couldn't sound as poised and professional as Hamilton.

"I think so." She pulled her phone out of her pocket and scrolled through it, frowning. "Ah. Here it is."

She turned her phone to face him but didn't actually hand it to him.

He started asking Hamilton, "Can I borrow your...?" when he realized he could just take a picture of the address with his own phone. Just because Hamilton was old-fashioned and wrote everything by hand in his notebook, it didn't mean that Harlan had to do the same.

"You done here?" Hamilton asked Harlan.

Harlan nodded, eager to get back into the fresh air. Now that he was only concentrating on the physical plane, the incense was getting overwhelming, and he didn't want to be rude and openly cough because of it.

"All right. I hope the rest of your day is better, Ms. Zaman." Hamilton tipped his hat at her, turned with military precision, and left.

Harlan followed, almost tripping on the welcome mat.

"You know we could've got the missing guy's address from the file, right?" Hamilton asked once they were in the car.

"Oh. Right." Harlan kept forgetting how much information he — or, rather, *Hamilton* — could access.

Bradley had lived close to the shop. *No — lives,* Harlan reminded himself. He was trying to be positive and not assume Bradley was dead.

"We'd need a warrant to get in," Hamilton reminded Harlan as they got out of the car. He leaned on the roof, resting his elbows against it.

"That won't be a problem. I don't need to go inside."

Hamilton waved a hand. "Fine. Do your thing, then we can call it a day." He frowned. "Unless you find something." He tapped the roof of the cruiser with his knuckles. "Don't find anything, all right?"

Harlan snorted. "I'll see what I can *not* do. And I'm pretty sure you're supposed to knock on *wood*," he teased.

"Yeah, I'll leave the magic stuff to you." He shooed Harlan with both hands.

How close *could* he get without needing a warrant? He could reach out and 'see' inside the building from the boulevard or the sidewalk, but closer was always better.

He stepped through the gate around the apartment building's postage-stamp-size front yard, then looked back at Hamilton. Hamilton was looking up and down the street, not paying attention to him, so Harlan boldly walked up the front steps and stood just in front of the door.

Almost immediately, it opened in his face and an annoyed-looking man pushed past him.

Harlan took a step back and to the side on the concrete landing, so he wasn't blocking the door. He made sure he was standing on the opposite side of the stoop from the bank of buzzers, because, with his luck, someone would need to use those while he was concentrating.

Satisfied that he wasn't in danger of falling or inconveniencing anyone, Harlan closed his eyes and reached out with his power.

No ghosts. No deaths, at least since the current apartment had been built.

He withdrew into himself and opened his eyes. Hamilton was watching him now, and Harlan shook his head as he walked back to the car. "If he died here, there's no sign of it. No sign of his ghost, either."

Hamilton didn't exactly look devastated. He was probably eager to get home to Matthew. "He might not even be dead," he pointed out.

"Might not," Harlan agreed, not really convinced.

"He might just be missing—or he ran off or something. There's a million places he could be, safe and sound."

Harlan nodded.

"And, unless you've got any other ideas, he's someone else's problem unless he turns up—or doesn't turn up."

"No. Nothing helpful. Not... Not without bringing Morgan in."

"I'll drive you home."

Chapter Twenty-Four

Harlan was half-watching some movie on Netflix and scrolling through Reddit on his phone when it rang, startling him as usual. The caller ID said *The Centre for Psychic Education and Research*.

Figuring it was Eileen with more information, or maybe Tom checking in, he answered. "Hello?"

"Hello?" It was a very faint voice, barely a whisper. It sounded like a little girl. "Is this Harlan?" She said his name very carefully, like she was afraid of getting it wrong.

"Yes." Harlan frowned. It was almost ten o'clock at night, he realized. Why would either of them be calling him now? "Who is this?"

"It's Caroline."

He blinked.

"From the Centre," she added.

Not helpful.

She huffed. "You came to my room when the wards broke."

He hated admitting when he didn't remember people, but to speed things along he asked, "You had a stuffed rabbit?"

"Yes!"

That was why the voice had sounded so strange. It *was* a little girl.

Fuck. He didn't know how to talk to kids. "Do you…have permission to be calling?"

"No! So we've gotta hurry. This is important!"

"O-Okay."

"Remember I told you about my friend Emily? She's the one who gave me the rabbit."

He didn't. "Yes."

A long inhale, followed by a rush of words. "Well, Mr. Addison told her she got accepted to a special school in Europe, and she told me she would write me, but she never did, and…and, I was really worried about her, so I called her parents. Mr. Addison told them the same thing, but they haven't heard from her since she went away, either. He told them she was just really busy, but she *promised* she'd send me a letter and it's been a really long time."

Harlan's blood ran cold. "Wait. You're saying no one's heard from her?"

"Uh-huh."

"Did you talk to T—Mr. Addison about it?"

"Uh-huh."

Harlan sighed. "And what did he say?" he prompted her.

"He just said she was really busy and she probably for-forgot about me, but I don't think she would."

"No. I don't think so, either," he said slowly. "Thank you, uh…"

"Caroline."

"Caroline."

He heard a voice in the background on the other end of the phone.

"Gotta go." She hung up.

Harlan set his phone down, rested his elbows on his knees and his chin on his folded hands. He felt like he'd just been handed something important, a clue, but he couldn't figure out what it was.

Time to call Hamilton. It was late, but he thought Hamilton would want to hear this sooner rather than later.

"I'm coming over," he said after Harlan told him what he'd just heard.

"What? Really? Now? Why?"

"I have a theory, and I think it'll make more sense if we both see this in person."

"Okay…"

Hamilton sighed when Harlan opened his apartment door. "I fucking hate you," he said, fondly.

Harlan blinked. "What?"

"Where's your Harkness stuff?"

"*What?*"

"Your…" Hamilton waved a hand. "Your maps and pins and shit."

Harlan raised an eyebrow. "I got rid of all that junk."

"What? Why? I'll set up here. Is there a corner store nearby?"

"Yeah, a 7-Eleven—"

"Go get a map. And some pins. And some fucking…red string."

"Are you serious? You made fun of me for doing this last time."

"Yes! Hurry the fuck up before I change my mind!"

Shaking his head, Harlan walked to the store and bought a map of Toronto, then one of Ontario, just in case. They didn't have string of any colour, but they did have dental floss. It would have to do.

When he got back, Hamilton had commandeered the coffee table and was hunched over his work laptop, typing at lightning speed.

Harlan unfolded the map on the remaining space and neatly centred the box of pins above it, taking off the lid so they were ready to place on the map. He hesitated before setting the floss down. "They didn't have—"

Hamilton held up a finger.

Harlan rolled his eyes. He sat and waited, fucking around on his phone.

"Okay. I think... I think I've got something." Hamilton looked at the map, then back at his screen, then the map again. "Yeah...okay." He opened the box of pins, then raised an eyebrow at Harlan. "Where's the string?"

"That's what I was trying to tell you. They didn't have any, so I got this." Harlan slid the plastic case of floss across the map.

Hamilton picked it up like it was a dead mouse. "Gross."

"It's not *used*!" Harlan laughed.

"I know that, rationally, but it's still...someone else's floss, y'know?" Hamilton shook his head. "Whatever... It'll do. Okay, you're the one who's done this before. You can put the pins in." He gestured grandly at the open box.

Harlan picked out a red pin.

"Put that one on the Centre."

He was about to stab it into the map when he realized there was nothing underneath it and he'd just put holes in his coffee table. It was ugly, but he didn't feel like buying a new one. He set the pin upside down with the metal point in the air.

"Really?" Hamilton shook his head. "Fine. Now the spot where you lost Leo. A different colour."

He arbitrarily chose a blue one, then realized he had no idea where to put it. "Uh…"

Hamilton sighed and told him the location. He consulted his computer, then tapped another spot on the map. "This is the occult shop. We don't know if that's where Mr. St James went missing, but it is his last known location."

Harlan set down another blue tack.

"Okay, ready? This is where things get interesting. While you were gone, I looked up the nine-one-one calls from that crazy night the wards failed. Use a colour that isn't red or blue. Colour-code them in order, so you can tell which was the first, second and so on."

There were only four colours—red, blue, green and yellow—but Harlan knew which one was the Centre, so he didn't think he'd get confused.

He grabbed a green one. "Okay."

"The first call came from here." Hamilton circled a finger over the map.

"Got it."

"The second one came from over here."

A yellow pin.

"Then here." This time Hamilton actually tapped the map, visibly excited, even though he was clearly trying to contain it. The pins wobbled, but none of them fell over or moved out of place.

Harlan placed another red pin.

Hamilton glanced at the map. "I think one more should be enough to make the pattern clear. Here." He stabbed his finger down.

Another green pin.

"Okay. What do you see?" Hamilton was grinning from ear to ear.

Harlan licked his lips nervously—what if he couldn't solve the puzzle, even though Hamilton thought it was really easy? What if it was a test and he failed, and Hamilton would know he was really an idiot?

He forced himself to take a deep breath. They were *partners*. If he was really stuck, Hamilton would help him out.

He might make fun of him for it, but he'd help him out.

Harlan stared at the map, at the pins. He was so close that he could almost see it...

"Okay, okay, I can't wait any longer." Hamilton was practically vibrating. "I'll give you a hint—imagine each pin as a ring in a concentric circle. A ripple, if you will."

When he still didn't see it after several seconds of staring, Hamilton picked up the container of floss again, wrinkling his nose at it. He unspooled a few inches of it, looked at the map and its face-up pins, then sighed. "This is completely useless."

"Yeah. It is."

"Here." Hamilton took out his pen and traced a circle in the air over the map—not with each dot in the centre of its own circle, the way Harlan had been picturing it, but using each point as the outer edge of a circle.

Harlan's mouth dropped open. He pointed at the red pin that represented the Centre, then each nine-one-one call in the order Hamilton had relayed them. "Holy shit." They *were* ripples. Ripples leading outwards from where the stone had dropped—the Centre.

"And look where you lost Leo." Hamilton touched the first blue pin. "And here's her apartment, where you started following her." He took a pin out of the box and placed it himself.

Once it was all laid out for him, it was obvious. She'd been leading them to the Centre, but someone or something had cut her off.

"We need to get in there."

"Uh, yeah, no shit."

Harlan shook his head. "But me, Beth and Benjamin were all over the place when we were there last time. We would have seen or felt something...wouldn't we?"

Hamilton shrugged. "That's your department, man. It sounds stupid, but maybe there's a hidden door or something else you missed."

"We need to get in there," Harlan said again.

"As previously stated, no shit. You know people there, like that guy, Mr...." Hamilton mimed flipping through a notebook.

"Addison. Tom." Harlan actually had his phone out and was about to dial when something clicked into place. Harlan froze, trying to make sure he was remembering the *exact* details, which wasn't always easy for him.

Hamilton leaned forward like a cadaver dog straining at the leash. "What? You thought of something. What have you got?"

Harlan held up his hands. "I might be totally wrong. I might be misremembering. He might have just had the day off or something."

"Yeah, yeah, okay, now I've heard the disclaimer." Hamilton rolled his hand in a *hurry up* motion. "*What?*"

"Well...I didn't see Tom the night the wards failed." As he said it aloud, Harlan felt more certain he was remembering it right. "Which is weird. *Really* weird. He was *always* around when lived there. And," Harlan remembered, getting excited, "he's the *director* now! Even if he was off campus or wasn't working that day, shouldn't he have come back for an emergency that big?"

"Maybe he was out of town," Hamilton said, not looking convinced by his own words.

"Maybe." Harlan tossed his phone from hand to hand, staring down at his lap. "It doesn't make sense, though. Tom was our history teacher. He doesn't have a psychic ability, at least that I know of. Whoever did this has to be really powerful—stronger than me, for sure. Maybe he's working with someone?" He sighed. "Well, he's still the best lead we've got right now."

Hamilton nodded. "Hey, I've learned to trust your gut. So, what do we do? Call him? Put some pressure on him?"

Harlan nibbled his lip for a moment, then shook his head. "No. If he is...involved, I don't want him to know we're investigating him." And maybe he was just *involved*, a naïve part of Harlan's brain hoped. Or maybe he'd been trying to do something helpful, good and it went horribly wrong. "We can't let him know we're investigating him, especially if he's got the missing mediums. He might...hurt them."

Hamilton grimaced. "It'll be hard for me to get a search warrant with just what we've got."

Harlan thought for a moment. "Well, we could ask Eileen, the librarian, but I don't want to jeopardize her job." He grinned. "Actually, I might know another way."

Chapter Twenty-Five

Skye had been a student at the Centre at the same time as Harlan. She was a few years younger than him, but she'd chosen to leave at eighteen, rather than waiting until twenty-one—like Harlan—and being *required* to go.

It was easier to text Skye, but she was the only person Harlan preferred to video chat with. It was a good way for him to practice his sign language, and somehow calls were less stressful without speaking and with the other person mostly focusing on his hands rather than his face. Realizing he'd need both hands free, he quickly built a little phone-stand out of a few books.

Skye answered with a grin and her name-sign for Harlan—an H followed by the sign for ghost.

He greeted her, rushing through the conversation a little. *"We need to get into the Centre secretly. Your way. Can you — ?"*

She cut him off, her movements large and excited. *"Of course. When?"*

"*As soon as possible. Tomorrow?*"

"*Done.*"

"*Do you still have your keys?*"

"*My what?*"

Harlan realized he'd screwed up the sign for *keys* and he couldn't remember how to do it properly. He resorted to fingerspelling. "*Your K-E-Y-S.*"

She laughed. "*That is* not *what you said,*" she signed, using her pinky to emphasize the word 'not'. "*Of course I do.*"

They arranged a time and place to meet.

"*I'll take you out for coffee or something to thank you,*" he promised. "*I'm sorry I don't call more.*"

"*We're both adults, and we're both busy with work. But I will hold you to that.*" She hesitated a moment, then asked, "*Why are we doing this? Or will you have to kill me if you tell me?*" She laughed again.

Harlan started signing several times, but he quickly realized that explaining it was way beyond his limited ASL vocabulary and it would take forever to finger spell, which he was bad at doing anyway.

The question was, could he trust her with this information, trust that she wouldn't tip off Mr. Addison? He wasn't usually this paranoid, and he hated it already.

Yes, he decided, they could trust her. There had been no love lost between her and Tom. She had seen through his saccharine façade way earlier than Harlan, and she'd taught Harlan some colourful signs while they were making fun of their teacher.

"*I'll text you after we hang up.*"

They said goodbye.

"Are you going to—?" Hamilton began.

Harlan held up a hand and started typing up a brief version of why they needed to sneak into the Centre.

Skye replied with a grinning emoji. She'd always had a mischievous streak.

"Well?" Hamilton asked impatiently after Harlan looked up from his phone.

"That was my friend Skye. She was always sneaking out of the Centre to go to parties and stuff, and she told me she made copies of every key in the place." He laughed. "Everyone treated her like this fragile, innocent thing because she's deaf, and she played along...while picking their pockets."

"You don't think they'll've changed the keys since then? At least in the higher-security areas?"

Harlan shook his head. "I don't think so. The Centre has never been rolling in money, and Skye was always really careful. I doubt any of the staff ever even realized she had keys."

Hamilton sighed, rubbing his forehead. "I don't love this. We're on pretty shaky legal ground, but you're right. If he's got the mediums, we have to get them out without tipping him — or whoever's responsible," he amended, glancing at Harlan, "off." He thought for a moment. "Well, we'll have Charles with us. If we get caught, we can just say you wanted to show your boyfriend and your cop buddy your old haunting grounds. Heh."

Harlan frowned. "Why would we bring Charles?"

"Uh, duh, in case we have to deal with more nasty ghosties than you can handle alone. You said yourself whoever did this has a lot of power."

Harlan looked away. "I'm kinda trying to keep Charles out of...all this."

"What? Why? Is he okay?" Hamilton asked rapid fire, like Harlan was a perp he was interrogating and trying to throw off balance. Or maybe Harlan just watched too much TV.

"He's fine. I just...don't want to put him in any more danger. He doesn't need to be part of this side of my life. I don't *want* him to be. He'll only get hurt again."

"Harlan, he's —" Hamilton stopped when he saw the look on Harlan's face, holding up his hands in defeat. "All right, all right, shutting up. No Charles."

Harlan nodded decisively. *No Charles.*

"Go get some sleep. Sleep in, actually. I'll cover for you tomorrow so you'll be nice and fresh for our little break-in."

"It's not a — Fine. I'll see you tomorrow."

After Hamilton left, Harlan flopped on his bed. He tried to follow Hamilton's advice and sleep, but his mind was racing. He was still fucking around on his phone after midnight. It vibrated without making a sound — his nighttime do-not-disturb setting had kicked in. He would have liked to keep his phone on silent all the time, but the vibration alone wasn't usually enough to get his attention unless he was already holding it.

The text was from Charles.

U still awake?

Yep

Go 2 sleep! Followed by the tongue-out emoji.

Harlan started typing *I wish you were here*, but he knew that wouldn't be fair. He was sure Charles would rather be there with him — and wasn't *that* thrilling! — but he knew Charles had to work.

He deleted it and typed something else instead.

Miss you

The response appeared right away, and Harlan smiled.

Miss u 2
Get together 2morrow nite?

It was followed by the familiar eggplant and peach emojis, along with a smirking face.

Fuck. He'd completely forgot. The next day was Monday — one of Charles' days off and one of the few days they could play together. Harlan hated wasting one, but he didn't want to delay his 'mission' with Hamilton.

He typed *Can't* then paused. He didn't want to *lie* to Charles, but he was pretty sure Charles would want to come along if Harlan told him what he had planned. and he didn't want that for Charles.

On the other hand, it was probably a good idea to tell someone where they were going in case something went wrong.

Me and H are going to the Centre to follow a lead.

A long pause, long enough that Harlan started to worry, and then a single word —

Okay.

Harlan's guts twisted. The word 'okay' in texts, with no indicator of mood, always set off his anxiety.

I'll text you when we're done.

This time Charles replied right away.

Can't wait, followed by several kissy faces.

Harlan heaved a deep sigh of relief, pressing his phone against his chest. *Okay*. Charles didn't seem upset with him, and he'd make it up to Charles — after he and Hamilton figured out what was going on at the Centre.

He said goodnight and finally fell asleep.

Chapter Twenty-Six

"We're *really* not bringing Charles?" Hamilton asked when he picked Harlan up, actually looking behind Harlan in case he was back there.

Harlan shook his head firmly.

Hamilton squared his shoulders, but he let out a long sigh. He closed his eyes, visibly relaxed, and took a slow, deep breath. Harlan could almost hear him counting to ten in his head. "All right. It's your call," he said, with a forced grin. "Let's go."

They picked up the keys from Skye, who was disappointed that she couldn't join them. She didn't give Harlan a hug, even though she clearly wanted to, and he appreciated that.

"How are we going to keep Tom from catching on?" Harlan asked. Talking was a helpful distraction while Hamilton was at the wheel. He wished he had a harness like a race-car driver instead of a seatbelt.

Hamilton grinned. "I've already taken care of that."

"What did you do?" Harlan asked, slightly horrified.

"Oh, c'mon. I just had one of our colleagues" — Harlan liked his use of 'our' — "bring him in to discuss the possibility of adding a police presence at the school, just in case someone from the outside is trying to sabotage it or whatever."

"That's...actually a really good idea."

"Gee, thanks. I do have 'em from time to time." Hamilton tapped the side of his head. "I'm not just handsome. I'm the total package."

Harlan couldn't help laughing. "You don't think he'll get suspicious?"

Hamilton shrugged one shoulder and took a swig of his Tim Hortons coffee — thankfully without taking his eyes off the road. "Even if he does, I trust Wright to keep him there as long as we need. She's *wily*," he said with a great deal of admiration.

"Cool. So we're free to search his office and the basement?"

"Yep. That's the plan. We've even got a warrant. Of course, I might have let them assume someone was *officially* letting us in, but... Well, let's just hope we find something — or *nothing* — and no one has to ask any questions."

They drove the rest of the way in silence. Harlan tried to imagine what they'd find, what they'd be up against and what he'd be able to do about it, if anything. Was Hamilton right? *Should* he have brought Charles? So far Tom — or who or whatever was causing this — seemed to only be targeting mediums rather than using ghosts, so Charles' ability probably wouldn't help them, anyway. He suspected that the ghost in his apartment, the horror in the Centre's basement, the one that had possessed the businessman and others elsewhere in the city had been freed accidentally, and the chaos they'd caused was only a by-product of whatever 'Tom' was trying to do.

A large part of Harlan hoped that Hamilton's fake scenario—that an outsider was attacking the school—was true. He didn't want Tom to be responsible. It wasn't that he especially *liked* Tom. He just didn't want the safe foundation, the only solid thing he'd had for most of his life, to have been a lie.

"We're here."

The large gate across the entrance road was closed, and they didn't have a pass to wave at the scanner so it would let them through.

"I don't think any of these keys will open that, but there's a man-gate we should be able to get through."

"It's probably less suspicious if we don't park inside the Centre compound where the car can be seen, anyway," Hamilton pointed out. He dropped Harlan off and parked up the street.

None of the keys looked the right size or shape, and he was still flipping through them when Hamilton got back.

Hamilton tried the handle. It swung open.

Harlan realized part of him had been hoping they couldn't open it and they'd have an excuse to stop before they'd even started.

"After you," Hamilton said, right before brushing past him.

"I don't think that means what you think it does," Harlan muttered, lengthening his stride to keep up with him. Hamilton could move amazingly quickly, despite being shorter than him, and he didn't want to let Hamilton get too far ahead.

The whole 'campus' seemed darker than usual... creepier. The shadows between the various wings and smaller scattered buildings could be hiding anything, with the leaden sky above them... Okay, now he was just scaring himself.

He focused on Hamilton, who was charging ahead with a great deal of gusto, even though he had no idea where he was going.

"The office is that way," Harlan told him quietly.

Hamilton corrected his course with Harlan trailing behind. Hoping to attract less attention than going through the main entrance, they unlocked a side door with one of Skye's keys, which Hamilton had taken possession of at the gate.

Hamilton unlocked the director's office and stepped inside.

Harlan froze. "What if we're walking into a trap?"

"Will you relax and stop being so paranoid?" Hamilton huffed. "Why would he suspect anything?"

"I don't know. I just..." Well, Hamilton was already inside and he hadn't...blown up or set off an alarm or anything.

Maybe it was only triggered by mediums. Well, mediums stronger than Hamilton.

Hamilton was staring at him, waiting, and that was almost worse than being blown up. It certainly lasted longer.

Harlan took a deep breath, closed his eyes and stepped over the threshold.

Nothing happened.

"See?" Hamilton nudged him with his elbow, but Harlan didn't think he was imagining the brief look of relief that flashed across Hamilton's face. "Perfectly safe. Put these on." He handed Harlan a pair of latex gloves, then pulled on his own. "Now, what are we looking for?"

Harlan, who had been just about to ask the same thing, frowned at him. "You're the cop. Shouldn't you know what we're looking for?"

"You're the medium. Shouldn't *you* know what we're looking for?" Hamilton retorted, looking like he was close to sticking his tongue out and saying, '*Nyah nyah.*'

"I guess we're looking for...anything suspicious?"

"Obviously." Hamilton rolled his eyes. "All right, you put out your ghost feelers—"

"That's not—"

"And I call going through the desk drawers. That's why I became a cop."

Harlan snorted, trying to cover the sound with a cough so he wouldn't encourage Hamilton. "Really?"

"Oh, yeah. I *loved* snooping as a kid. I was undetectable." He shook his head. "I could have got my siblings in so much shit so many times... Of course, then I would've had to admit how I knew... I couldn't exactly leave an anonymous tip in my own house."

Harlan tried to imagine young Hamilton keeping tabs on his siblings—siblings he'd never mentioned before and probably writing everything in a notebook or journal. Yeah, he could see it.

He sent out his ghost—nope! He wasn't going to start thinking of them that way. He 'opened himself to the spectral realm' and searched the room.

"Nothing."

"Shit, really? I was hoping it would be that easy."

"If it were, I would've noticed last time we were here."

"True. All right. You can search those filing cabinets. I'm keeping the desk drawers. That's where the good stuff always is."

Harlan laughed. "Sure. You go right ahead."

The top three drawers of the first filing cabinet contained students' files, past and present. The director didn't have a secretary, so everything was kept in his office.

They were alphabetical by last name. Harlan flipped through the As, slowing down when he got to the Bs. He wouldn't want to miss anything… Aha, there was his file. He slowly lifted it out, freezing when Hamilton cleared his throat behind him.

"Uh-uh. Put that back. Unless you're feeling some serious ghostly vibes from that, it's not important right now." Hamilton sighed. "Trust me. You probably don't want to know what it says, anyway."

Harlan felt his face grow hot—how had Hamilton *known*?

He slid the folder back into place and kept flipping, pausing only when a thought occurred to him. It sounded like Hamilton had read one of his own files before. Well, he had admitted he liked snooping, and he'd left Calgary to move to Toronto. He'd probably seen something…unflattering…in his Calgary Police file. Or maybe Harlan was reading too much into it.

"Nothing interesting," he reported, closing the third drawer after glancing at the last file — Zentai, H. It made him think of 'Zen' and 'hentai' combined, and the mental image made it hard to keep a straight face when he turned back to Hamilton.

Hamilton grunted. "Me neither. *Very* disappointing."

"I mean, I think it's probably for the best that the principal of a school that teaches mediums *isn't* responsible for kidnapping them."

"Yeah, yeah, Captain Buzzkill. Keep looking."

Harlan tugged at the bottom drawer. It didn't budge. He slid the little metal stud beside the handle, but it still wouldn't open. "It's locked! I don't suppose your apparently misspent youth included learning how to pick locks?"

"Hey, I never got into trouble! But I never could get the hang of anything more complicated than one of those diary locks, and you can practically sneeze those open. Try the other cabinet."

Harlan tried to imagine Hamilton keeping one of the pastel-coloured journals with a picture of a unicorn or a kitten on the cover that came with a little lock and key, but he couldn't. Maybe it had belonged to one of Hamilton's never-before-mentioned siblings.

After glaring at the locked drawer like he could intimidate it into opening—which might work for Hamilton, but never for him—Harlan drifted over to the second cabinet. He checked all four drawers first, and they all slid open. "This is all accounting stuff and blank forms."

"Hmm. There *could* be something there, but we don't have time to look through it all. Do any of the tabs on the folders look suspicious?"

"Like, do any of them say 'Here Is My Evil Plan'? No."

"Oh, shut up. *Shit!*"

Harlan jerked back from the folders he'd been thumbing through. "What? Did you find something?"

"Nah. Just that this desk drawer is locked, too."

"Shit," Harlan agreed softly, hoping Hamilton hadn't realized how much he'd startled him.

"Wait a sec…" Hamilton opened each of the drawers above it again, then took a step back to study them from the side.

"What are you doing?"

Hamilton looked at him like he'd just asked why the sky was blue. "I'm looking for false bottoms."

"What, really? Is that a thing people actually do?"

"Yeah, all the time! Wait, you *don't* have a false-bottom drawer in your desk?"

"I don't have a desk."

"Well, you really should get one. And put a false bottom in at least one of your drawers."

"Why, so you can snoop through it? I'll get right on that."

"Aha!" Hamilton swayed back and forth, looking between the front and side of the second drawer. He looked like a robin sizing up a juicy worm. The Centre's grounds were always covered in robins in the spring and watching them through the window had been more interesting than paying attention in class.

Hamilton suddenly shoved the drawer's contents aside and tapped the bottom. "Yep. Here we go."

Harlan was surprised. He wouldn't have thought Tom was handy enough to build a secret compartment, and what was the point of having one if someone else knew about it? He remembered Tom teaching his class about pharaohs and emperors killing the people who built and designed their tombs so no one would know the way in. Maybe he'd taken a page out of his own history book.

Hamilton scrabbled around for a moment, then lifted a panel out of the drawer. Reaching inside the hidden space, he held up a small key triumphantly. "It fits in the locked drawer..." They were both so quiet that Harlan could hear the soft *click* of it opening. "And it's...full of booze."

"What?" Harlan hurried behind the desk to peer over Hamilton's shoulder.

"Yep." Hamilton lifted out a few bottles, whistling with admiration. "This is some *very* nice Scotch. I'd keep it locked up, too. Probably not in a school, though."

"Not exactly what we're looking for."

"No," Hamilton agreed. He eyed the bottle before gently slotting it back into place. He closed and locked the drawer, and he was about to put the key back when Harlan stopped him.

"Maybe it works on the filing cabinet, too."

Hamilton did his one-shoulder shrug. "Maybe. Give it a try." He passed the key to Harlan and started rifling through the drawers on the right-hand side of the desk.

Practically holding his breath with anticipation, Harlan slid the key into the lock. It fit, but didn't turn, no matter how he wiggled it. He even tried the thumping trick from the old door of his apartment. "Nope."

"Shit. Well, I'm just going to pretend that whatever we need *isn't* in there. Go check the closet."

The door was unlocked. There were shelves on one side and a closet bar on the other. The shelves mostly held standard office supplies — packages of printer paper, neatly arranged boxes of pens, staples and paperclips.

There were a few suit jackets, shirts and pants hanging on the bar. Harlan went through the pockets, just in case. *Completely empty, not even a stray Kleenex or receipt.*

"Nothing," he called out to Hamilton.

"Tap the back wall, especially down near the baseboard."

"Really? Do you *really* think — ?"

"Hey, we've already found one. Can't hurt to look."

Shaking his head, Harlan knelt on the closet floor and started tapping. When he didn't find anything in the closet, he checked the wall on either side of it. As far as he could tell, it was all solid. "Nothing," he said again.

"Me neither." Hamilton sounded dejected. He came into the closet and tapped a few places to check Harlan's work, but Harlan didn't think his heart was in it. "Shit. I was really hoping we'd find something in here." He walked out of the closet and stared at the desk, one arm across his chest with the opposite elbow braced on it, hand on his chin. "It's pretty pretentious to have a picture of yourself over your desk, don't you think?"

Harlan followed him out, then laughed. He'd had the same thought the last time they had been here. "Yeah, I'd say so."

"Fuck. Well, I guess let's check out the creepy basement again."

"Wait a second..." Harlan stared harder at the picture, looking at it in more detail than before.

It was an outdoor shot of a serious-looking Tom, wearing a very natty suit and standing in front of a house.

Harlan felt something come together in his mind. "I know that house."

"You've been to the principal's house? Man, private school is really — "

"The director, not the principal. And no, I've never been inside. But it's on the Centre's grounds."

Hamilton whistled, jostling Harlan with his elbow. "I think you might be on to something. I'm sure that place has a lot fewer people going in and out than his office — or the basement. Let's check it out."

It was dusk when they got back outside, but somehow the semi-darkness made the place seem less creepy than it had been a few hours earlier. Harlan practically jogged to the house, only making a few wrong turns.

Morgan and Charles were standing by the front steps.

Morgan tapped an invisible watch on their wrist. "Took you guys long enough."

"Wha — What are you doing here?" Harlan babbled, looking back and forth between them.

Charles shot Harlan an apologetic look. "Morgan called me — "

"I tried calling *you* first — both of you — but it said your phones were 'out of service'," Morgan interrupted.

Harlan frowned. He wasn't always great about remembering to charge his phone, but he'd specifically done it before coming here. He pulled it out of his pocket and touched the screen. It stayed black. He tapped it again, then hit the power button. Still nothing.

Hamilton took his phone out and did the same, then shook his head. "Mine's dead too."

"Something drained them both without us noticing." Harlan shivered. "We really need to get those special phone cases."

"I mean, you might have just forgot to charge them," Morgan suggested.

Harlan shook his head. "If it was just mine, sure, but Hamilton's is *always* charged. I'm pretty sure it was plugged in on the way here." He glanced at Hamilton.

Hamilton nodded. "It was fully charged when we went in."

"I didn't feel a cold spot or anything. This…this isn't good. And now *you're* here…" They hadn't really had much of a plan to begin with, and Harlan could feel it unravelling.

Charles raised an eyebrow.

Harlan sighed deeply. "I mean, I'm happy to see you, of course, but I didn't want you here."

Morgan glanced at Charles, then at Harlan. "Is everything okay between you two?"

"We're fine."

"Yeah…" Charles stepped closer to Harlan. "Can we talk for a minute?"

Harlan glanced at Hamilton, hoping he'd say they didn't have time for this. He was terrified of whatever Charles was going to say, and he knew he'd only work himself up more and more if he waited to hear it, but he didn't want to deal with this. Not yet.

Hamilton whistled under his breath, staring at the ground. Obviously *he* wasn't going to be any help.

Morgan just stared at him steadily. "I'll pick the lock while we wait."

"Ooh, can you teach me?" Hamilton hurried up the steps beside Morgan, clearly relieved to get away from the others.

"Let's talk over here." Charles led the way around the corner of the nearest building, out of sight and, hopefully, earshot of the others.

"It's not that I don't want you here," he began. "It's just that I—"

"Don't want me here?"

"…Yeah."

Charles sighed. "Harlan, we talked about this."

"I know, I know. It's just—"

With a wry grin, Charles reached out and took Harlan's hand. "Do you remember how we met?"

"Of course I do!" *Why did that stupid delivery driver have to die in Charles' club and make me get rid of him?*

On the other hand, he couldn't think of any other possible way he might have met Charles. Most of the time it felt like a blessing. When he was so afraid for Charles, of losing Charles, he couldn't help wishing it hadn't happened at all.

"We met because of a ghost. I don't think it's possible to have a ghost-free relationship with you."

Harlan's breath caught in his throat.

Charles took his other hand, holding them in front of him. "And I *want* to be in a *relationship* with you."

Harlan swallowed hard, feeling tears prickling at the corners of his eyes. He nodded with his head lowered. "I'm glad you're here," he said softly. "We could use your help. Hamilton wasn't happy that I didn't bring you along in the first place." He took a deep, steadying breath. "Just…don't die, okay?"

"I can't promise that, but I promise," Charles assured him. "If that makes sense."

Harlan nodded again, hoping Charles didn't see him wipe his eyes on his shoulders. He squeezed Charles' hands. He didn't like it, as he'd said, but Charles was there already. At that point, it was *way* too late to try untangling Charles from the ghostly part of his life. And Charles was an adult. He could make his own decisions, even if Harlan didn't like them.

Even if he hated them.

"We should…get back to the others."

"Yeah." Charles pulled Harlan closer, wrapped both arms around him, and kissed him deeply. "Now we can." He raised an eyebrow at Harlan. "We're never having this conversation again, right?"

Harlan nodded decisively. "Right."

Chapter Twenty-Seven

"How did you two end up here in the first place?" Harlan asked as they walked back to the house.

"Well, like they said, Morgan called me. Leo appeared to them again. When Morgan couldn't reach either of you, they called me and said they needed a ride. I didn't realize there was a ghost involved. I don't know how or why, but I could see Leo. It took a few hours, but she finally led us here. Straight to this house."

Morgan opened the door with a flourish just as they reached the front steps. *"Et voila. Entrez, s'il vous plait."* It was completely dark inside. "I guess we shouldn't turn the lights on, huh?"

"Probably not," Hamilton agreed, pulling his flashlight off his belt and clicking it on. "I guess this'll have to do."

Charles and Morgan turned on their phone flashlights.

Part of Harlan was afraid that the door would slam shut and lock behind them as soon as they were inside, but nothing happened.

Morgan, the last one in, closed the door. "We should split up and give the whole house a quick check, then we can all go down to the basement," they whispered. "That's probably where he's keeping the prisoners, right?"

Harlan had seen way too many horror movies to think splitting up was a good idea. "I don't think that's—"

"Charles, you come with me. Harlan, you go with Hamilton."

Harlan opened his mouth to protest. If they had to split up, he at least wanted to be with Charles, but Morgan was already heading upstairs with Charles just behind them.

"Shouldn't *you* be in charge?" Harlan asked Hamilton.

Hamilton grinned, putting his hands up. "Hey, don't look at me, I'm just a beat cop." He glanced in the direction the other two had gone. "I should probably call for backup before we get too much farther." He thumbed the 'talk' button on his shoulder-mounted radio, but nothing happened. There was no static. "Shit." He pulled the radio off his belt and tried speaking directly into that. Silence. He popped the battery out and rammed it back in. "*Shit!*" he repeated, more emphatically, but still keeping his voice lowered. "I guess it's just us, unless Morgan or Charles can get a call out."

Two little lights bobbed towards them through the darkness.

"We checked upstairs. There's nobody there, but there were some freaky drawings and books in the bedroom that look like seriously bad news," Morgan reported. "Have you two looked at all?"

"We've got a problem. My radio is dead. Do either of you have a signal?"

Morgan glanced at their phone. "I do. Should I call nine-one-one?"

Hamilton nodded.

They got out the word 'hello' before their light went out. "No, no, no..." They tapped their screen and clicked the power button repeatedly, but the phone didn't light up again.

"Fuck!" Hamilton's flashlight went out a moment later, and no amount of thumping or fiddling with the batteries made it turn on again.

All three of them glanced at Charles.

"I don't know if I should try. This is the only light we have."

"Could something...mechanical be doing this?" Morgan asked, looking at Harlan. "Something besides a ghost?"

Harlan shook his head. "I-I don't know. I don't think so."

They turned to Hamilton.

"Why are you all looking at me? I don't know anything about this shit!" He sighed. "*Maybe*. But I doubt that a school principal would have access to that kind of tech."

"So it's probably ghosts?" Morgan asked.

"So it's probably ghosts," Hamilton agreed. He looked at each of them, one at a time. "We can still leave now. We're potentially walking into a highly dangerous situation without backup, with no certain way to contact the outside world. If any of you want out, I would understand. More than understand. I might—"

There was a muffled scream from below. Charles' phone went dark at the same moment.

The house seemed to devour what little light came through the windows, but maybe that was just Harlan's fear.

He dimly saw Hamilton unsnap his holster and draw his gun.

"Shit. Okay. I *have* to go down there now, but the rest of you don't. You can—"

"We're not leaving." Despite Morgan's words, Harlan could see them trembling even in the near-darkness.

Harlan glanced at them. "Maybe you should go. The three of us—"

They shook their head. "I know my skillset doesn't exactly lend itself to this situation, but I don't want to just turn tail and run."

"You could go back to the main building and call for help," Harlan suggested.

They shook their head again. "And let that creep catch me alone? No way. At this point, I think we're safer as a group."

"Charles?" Hamilton asked.

"I'm coming." Charles straightened his shoulders and rolled up the sleeves of his Rattling Chains T-shirt.

Harlan's face tightened, but he didn't say anything.

"Harlan?" Hamilton turned to him last. "You're not technically a police officer. You don't *have* to come," he said, gently.

Harlan looked at the other three. He was terrified, but he couldn't let them go alone—not when his ability might mean the difference between life and death. "I'm in," he said shakily.

Charles reached out and squeezed his hand. Harlan squeezed back, ashamed that Charles could probably feel him shaking.

"Everyone stay behind me," Hamilton ordered.

They followed him as he felt, stumbled and cursed his way through the kitchen and living room before he found the basement door. He turned the handle. "Locked." He sighed deeply, then motioned Morgan forward. "I've always wanted to kick a door in or shoot out the lock, but I think we should stay as stealthy as we can for as long as possible."

Morgan set to work with their tools, and a few minutes later they turned the knob.

The door opened silently. Harlan had almost expected an ominous creak.

"Okay, stay *behind* me," Hamilton hissed. He crept down the stairs like a big cat, holding his gun up near his ear.

Harlan was hardly breathing as he watched Hamilton turn a corner. He could only see Hamilton's silhouette.

After what felt like an eternity but was probably only a few seconds, Hamilton padded back up the stairs. "There's another door at the bottom," he murmured. "I can hear people moving around on the other side. If I can hear *them*, they'd probably hear Morgan picking the lock." He grinned. "So I think it's my turn. Stay back until I come and get you or I call out that it's safe. Clear?"

Harlan nodded.

Hamilton sighed. "Look... I can't see what any of you are doing. Are you clear about the plan?"

"Clear," Morgan said, followed by Charles, then Harlan a moment later.

"Good. There's a little bit of light coming from the crack under the door. I think there are some candles or something inside, so hopefully we'll be able to see once we're in." Lifting his gun again, he made his slow, careful way back down the stairs.

This time the wait was even worse. Harlan kept expecting to hear... Well, he wasn't sure what. Gunshots? Screams?

Silence.

A sudden *bang!* made him cry out, and he wasn't the only one. He jumped sideways and heard Charles hiss as he stepped on his foot. They found each other's hands in the dark, and a moment later he felt Morgan's hand on his arm.

It must have been Hamilton breaking the door down, Harlan realized when nothing else happened.

He was surprised Hamilton hadn't fallen and broken his neck on the way down the stairs in the darkness.

A foul stench wafted up the stairs, a combination of sweat, urine and feces. The door must have been well sealed to keep it out of the rest of the house.

Morgan retched, looking like they might bolt. Harlan wouldn't have blamed them. He coughed, his eyes burning. Charles grimaced but managed not to make a sound.

"You guys coming?" Hamilton called up. "I could really use your help down here."

The three of them looked at each other.

Harlan was surprised when Morgan stepped forward first—after looking over their shoulder and taking in a deep breath of fresh air.

Charles held on to Harlan as they made their way down the stairs and, as Hamilton had said, there was light at the bottom.

Through the splintered doorway he could see a small concrete room with four chairs bolted to the floor. He was a little disappointed that they were right there in the open and not in a hidden chamber. There were candles scattered around, a source of light that ghosts couldn't drain — though they could, with effort, extinguish them.

There were people in three of the chairs.

Hamilton was kneeling beside the smallest shadowy figure.

Once his eyes adjusted to the light, Harlan could see that it was a little girl, bound and gagged. Her eyes were open and enormous.

He hurried over to her while Charles and Morgan each went to one of the others. "Are you...?" *Shit, what did Rabbit Girl say her roommate's name was? What is Rabbit Girl's name?* Harlan couldn't think through his choking fear. "Are you friends with...Carol?" He was almost sure that was it.

She nodded, straining against the metal cuffs digging into her wrists and ankles.

"Leo?" Charles asked softly from the other side of the room.

Harlan heard a muffled sound in response. Since Hamilton was taking care of the girl, he went to help Charles with Leo. Morgan was reassuring a pale Caucasian man Harlan assumed was Bradley from the occult shop. There hadn't been a picture with the newspaper article Hamilton had shown him.

"It's okay. We're here to get you out," Charles assured Leo. He worked at the tight knot holding her gag in place.

Leo shook her head, trying to say something, but it was too muffled to understand. When she realized they couldn't tell what she was saying, she frantically jerked her head in Harlan's direction.

"It's too tight. It's been tied too long, and it's damp," Charles said apologetically, letting go of the gag.

Harlan, who knew how good Charles was with knots, was sure it would be useless for him to offer to help.

"I can use my pocketknife, but I'd be worried about cutting your face. It might be easier and safer to take it off once we've uncuffed you."

Leo let out a sharp "Mmm!" of protest, shaking her head wildly.

"Okay. I'll try." Charles pulled the knife he always had on him out of his pocket and held it up where Leo could see it.

She nodded.

"I'll be as careful as I can, but I still might hurt you."

She said something muffled, then nodded again.

Charles began cautiously sawing at the knot, murmuring to her reassuringly the whole time.

Hamilton had got out his handcuff key. He tried it in the little girl's cuff, then swore. "It won't turn."

Tears ran down her cheeks, mingling with the dampness already on her gag.

Harlan heard a gasp behind him, and he turned just in time to see Leo's gag fall onto her lap. She opened her mouth to speak but nothing came out. She coughed, hard, then said, "Harlan, you can't be here." Her voice was hoarse, and he wondered when she'd last spoken. "He'll—"

Above them, a door slammed.

Chapter Twenty-Eight

Leo shook her head, over and over again. "Too late. *Run.*"

Hamilton glanced at the stairway, then around the room. He could see, just as Harlan did, that there was nowhere to go. "Fuck," he whispered under his breath.

The little girl screamed, muffled by the gag, and shook her head. She grabbed Hamilton's pants in a tight, desperate fist with her free hand.

Stone-faced, Hamilton peeled her fingers loose and stepped out of her reach. "I'll try to shoot him," he said grimly. "Everyone else, your priority is to get out of here, no matter what happens."

Morgan opened their mouth to argue, but Hamilton cut them off with a look.

Harlan heard footsteps above them, then light flooded down the stairs.

Hamilton gestured sharply for them to move back, then he ran through the doorway and disappeared around the corner.

Harlan heard Hamilton cry out and his limp body rolled down the stairs. He could see a ghost crouched on top of Hamilton with its bony, spectral hands wrapped around his throat.

Tom appeared, his hands raised, the veins on his neck popping with exertion. He kicked Hamilton aside and stepped over him. It didn't make sense. Tom wasn't a medium, but he was clearly commanding the spirit.

"Kill him," Tom said, without even glancing at the ghost or its victim.

"*No!*" Harlan screamed. He didn't realize he'd taken a step forward until he felt Charles' hand on his elbow, trying to pull him back.

Tom smiled, then snapped his fingers. "Wait. He might still be useful. *Take* him."

Leo, Bradley and the little girl inhaled simultaneously, their spines straightening painfully until all three were staring up at the ceiling with wide, unseeing eyes.

Harlan tried to rush forward, to do *something*, but he couldn't escape Charles' grip. He knew Charles was only trying to protect him, but he was forced to watch as the ghost possessed Hamilton. It was slow, and it looked like it would have been agonizing if Hamilton weren't unconscious. He'd never seen anything so horrible, but he couldn't force himself to look away.

When it was finally over, a long twitch rolled down Hamilton's body from head to toe. He sat up unnaturally, like a horror-movie monster. He climbed to his feet, each movement jerky and erratic as the ghost relearned how to operate a physical body. It stood in the same spot Hamilton had fallen, watching…waiting. There was an unfamiliar expression on Hamilton's familiar face, a stranger looking out through his eyes. Tom hadn't commanded it to do anything yet, but it was clearly waiting to attack. At least it didn't have Hamilton's gun. He must have lost it on the stairs.

Once Tom was certain that Hamilton — the most immediate threat — was taken care of, he turned to look at the rest of the room. "Isn't this a nice little reunion? Morgan… Harlan…" He nodded at each of them. "And you must be Charles." His voice was so calm, so familiar. It made Harlan sick. How many hours had he spent listening to Mr. Addison teach him about the French Revolution and ancient Greece? How many times had Mr. Addison come to him with help or advice? Harlan had always been mistrustful of adults, but Mr. Addison had been the one he'd trusted most.

Charles. Harlan's mind raced. Something here didn't make sense. It shouldn't be possible for ghosts to even appear with Charles there, never mind possess anyone.

Harlan had never been good at hiding his expressions, and he was sure Tom could easily read the confusion on his face.

Tom's smile twisted, becoming even crueler. "Wondering how I'm able to work around your little friend here?"

Tom's gaze slowly drifted downwards, and Harlan's eyes automatically followed.

Harlan had been too busy trying to help the prisoners to look at the rest of the room. There was a circle painted on the floor. It was the exact bright-red colour of fresh blood. Harlan didn't want to know who or what the blood had come from. He couldn't see any visible wounds on the prisoners, at least.

But, no, that couldn't be possible. For the blood to look that fresh, Tom would have had to *just* finished painting it, recently enough that they would have seen him do it. Unless...the spell, or whatever it was, kept the blood from coagulating.

It wasn't just a circle. From the solid outer edge there were concentric rings of symbols and glyphs — similar to ghost wards, but somehow...wrong. Harlan realized he could see them without needing to blink, unlike ghost wards, which faded away from normal sight once they were painted and activated.

These markings made his skin crawl and his scalp prickle, and he wanted to turn and run as far from them as possible.

You still can, a dark, selfish side of him whispered. *If you leave the others, you can run now. Let him be someone else's problem. You can even take Charles if you're quick and careful and lucky. Start a new life with him, far from here.*

Harlan was no saint. He couldn't deny that he was tempted. But...

He looked up, locked eyes with the little girl who was bound to a chair. No way he could just leave her, or Hamilton, or the others.

He sighed, the sound slowly turning into a groan. Without Charles' ability to protect them, he'd have to try something else.

"What do you want, Tom?" he asked, wearily. He just wanted to hear Tom's crazy plan and get it over with so they could fight or...whatever was going to happen.

"What do I *want*?" Tom snorted. He slapped the wall behind him, making his prisoners flinch.

Harlan wasn't sure he believed in hell, but when he saw how badly Tom frightened them, he hoped Tom was headed there — sooner rather than later.

"All you kids ever do is *bitch*." Tom was silent for a long moment, staring at Harlan and Morgan.

When Morgan didn't speak, Harlan asked, "What do you mean?"

"You're handed power — *real* power — and all you do is shit on it."

Harlan blinked. It was strange to hear Tom swear. He was afraid he'd have to ask another question to get Tom to continue, but the man carried right on. It was as though he'd been carrying these thoughts a long time and was relieved to finally let them out. Harlan could relate to that, though he wished *he* wasn't the one who had to hear these.

"All day long, I've got kids coming to me and bitching about their powers. 'Oh, wah, I can make things levitate! I can speak to the dead! I can'" — he frowned at Morgan — "whatever the fuck it is *you* do." He balled his fists, the veins on the backs of his hairy hands popping.

"There are people who would kill for even a *fraction* of your power," he said softly, almost reverently, glancing at his prisoners as he spoke.

Harlan knew he'd been guilty of Tom's 'accusation'. He'd wished that he was a normal boy, that he'd only ever seen ghosts in movies. He hadn't complained much or often, especially compared to some of the kids he'd grown up with. He hadn't trusted adults enough to confide in them — but he'd occasionally joined in with the other students when they talked about the ways having powers had screwed up their lives — and some of them had got to the Centre in even more fucked-up ways than Harlan.

On a few occasions an adult had caught Harlan crying in a bathroom or some other remote, out-of-the-way corner of the Centre and he'd had to explain what he was upset about. He remembered several times that it had been Tom who'd found him. Tom had listened to him, reassured him that he was all right, that he wasn't a freak and he wasn't broken.

The memory made Harlan's guts twist. What an idiot he'd been to trust this man. The whole time, kind 'Mr. Addison' had been laughing behind his back about how pathetic and weak Harlan was. He'd been hungering for the power Harlan didn't even want.

Harlan licked his lips as the entire foundation of his life tipped sideways.

Did that mean that he *was* pathetic and weak and broken, the way he'd always suspected? If no one had ever really believed in him, had he been right about himself all along?

His gaze darted sideways and landed on Charles. Charles, who was here with him and knew all his fears and flaws and stayed *anyway*.

He looked at Hamilton — well, Hamilton's body. He could only hope that Hamilton was still in there, fighting from the inside.

He'd had to work like hell to earn Hamilton's trust. Hamilton would never tell him sweet lies just to make him feel better. Hamilton said he trusted Harlan, so he'd meant it.

Harlan straightened. *No.* His dark thoughts were wrong. Tom was wrong. He had people who *truly* supported and cared about him now.

"So what?" Morgan snapped, all but tapping their toe with impatience — and, Harlan suspected, to draw attention back away from Harlan, which he appreciated.

Tom turned to them with a smile, like they were a good student who'd just answered a question correctly. "So I found power of my own."

A hot rush of anger pulled the words out of Harlan's mouth — and Tom had just looked away from him, too. "It isn't your power! You're taking it from *them*, aren't you?" His arm swept out in a slashing arc, taking in the three prisoners. "How?"

Tom shrugged one shoulder. "It's mine now. Does it matter how I got it?" He closed his eyes.

Harlan knew he should take advantage of Tom's distraction, but before he could move — before Charles or Morgan could, either — the blood on the floor began to glow.

A wall of red mist rose from the glyphs and surrounded Tom. With his eyes still closed, he breathed it in. When he exhaled, Harlan expected it to be red, but there was nothing.

Tom opened his eyes. They glowed with the same baleful red light as the blood. He pointed at Hamilton and said something in a grating language that made Harlan's skin prickle.

Once he'd spoken the words, he gasped, blinking until his eyes returned to normal.

For a moment Harlan thought nothing had happened. Then Hamilton's body jerked and stiffened, his spine going completely straight and rigid, his open mouth pointed at the ceiling in a silent scream.

Harlan took an involuntary step back, sure they were about to be attacked.

Some brave but stupid part of Charles seemed to activate. He stepped in front of Harlan and Morgan, blocking them with his body, even though he was shorter than both of them and Tom had proven Charles couldn't shield them against ghosts.

Of course, he was also a lot physically stronger than either of them, and probably had more experience fighting.

Maybe.

Hamilton's body didn't attack.

Harlan could...see? Feel? Neither one was right. Perceive? That was the closest.

He could *perceive* Tom drawing Hamilton's small flicker of mediumship out of him, draining it until nothing was left. The shock and horror of it pulled the breath from Harlan's lungs.

It was over quickly. Hamilton didn't have much to take.

Tom gasped, his eyes briefly glowing red before dimming again as he absorbed the last of Hamilton's ability.

Once it was over, Hamilton's body slumped for a moment. His parasite straightened again with a toothy grin that looked completely wrong on Hamilton's face.

It shocked Harlan out of his stupor. He didn't have to stand there and watch. He had power—his *own* power. Tom hadn't drained him yet, so there was still a tiny sliver of hope.

First things first. He had to get rid of the ghost inside Hamilton. Hopefully that would distract Tom enough that he wouldn't just try to drain Harlan to stop him, and it would take away Tom's only ally.

Harlan could feel his power inside him, a deep, cool wellspring at his core. Now that he was paying attention to it, he could feel that something was keeping it contained—probably part of what the circle on the floor was meant to do. It felt like a nasty film surrounding a secret part of him, trying to contain what should be free, like an impermeable skin trapping his ability inside him. There was a fluttering panicky sensation in his chest as he realized there was nothing he could do.

No...that isn't entirely true. There was a tear in the sac, an opening so small he hadn't noticed it at first, so small that Tom had overlooked it. It was probably too small to be much of an advantage, but it was all he had. He didn't know what had created it, but that didn't matter.

Time seemed to slow down.

He could see, as if it were happening to someone else, Tom raise his hands, palms up, at him. He heard him speak a few syllables of that guttural language.

Harlan frantically tried to focus on that tear, to direct his power from a formless pool down into a narrow stream so it could escape. It was slow, so slow. Tom had said several words now. It wouldn't be enough. Nothing he did was ever enough, and now he was going to get Charles, Hamilton and Morgan killed, and who knew how many others? Harlan knew he couldn't draw enough of his power to be useful in time to save them, and he couldn't tear the hole any wider, no matter how hard he strained.

Distantly he heard Morgan say, "Charles, look at me. Think about—"

The air around them shimmered, and Harlan was standing in their place.

He blinked. When he opened his eyes, he was still standing there, looking exactly like himself, even down to the clothes he was wearing.

No, not exactly like himself. He wasn't that handsome. He didn't look that confident.

Do I?

"Wha—?" Tom stopped chanting, looking between the two of them with confusion and dawning fear. "How are you...?"

"Hey!" The other Harlan clapped his hands, getting Tom's attention on him. "You didn't see this coming, did you, idiot? Yeah. I'm Harlan Fucking Brand and I'm going to stop you. Right *now*!"

Harlan realized the last part was meant for him. He had to act while Tom was still distracted.

There was no time for subtlety. He *ripped* the ghost out of Hamilton's body before Tom could realize what he was doing and stop him. Tom had the power of three mediums, plus what he'd just taken from Hamilton, to draw on, and Harlan only had his trickle.

Hamilton's back arched and he screamed, then collapsed on the floor with his limbs sprawled around him.

Harlan wanted to rush over to him, make sure he was okay, but there was no time.

Tom turned away from Morgan at the sound of the scream, looking at the real Harlan.

Before he could start speaking again, Harlan threw the power he'd managed to pull out of himself at Tom's psychic shields, testing for weaknesses for any opening, no matter how small, that he could pour himself through.

There wasn't one.

No. It wasn't a hole, not an opening, but *something*. He could feel the flow of power Tom was still drawing from his prisoners. Unlike Hamilton, they had too much to drain all at once—or maybe Tom enjoyed torturing them.

If Harlan could break those streams, sever those ties, he'd cut off the source of Tom's stolen power.

Before he could try to find a way in, to chip away at those streams until he could join their flow, then sweep up into Tom and take him from the inside, Tom slammed him with a wave of power that dropped him to his knees. He could taste blood and feel a little of it running from his left nostril.

"How are you doing that?" Tom demanded, and Harlan almost answered him as if he were in class.

Harlan only smiled in response. It had been stupid of Tom to break his concentration and ask the question — not that Harlan would tell him that.

Words and movement were only distractions this deep in the flow of power.

It bought Harlan another second, at most, but that second was all he needed. He realized that he, too, was connected to Tom by a stream. After all, the film containing his power had come from Tom.

Following the thread binding them together, Harlan changed his strategy. He realized that cutting Tom off from the mediums was too much to start with, too big. Now that they had a point of contact, he could feel that Tom had spread himself across the city, reaching out farther and farther — but also spreading himself thinner and thinner. That was where Harlan had to start.

He closed his eyes and focused on the energy moving between them. He imagined it widening and finally felt the membrane holding him back tear farther, letting more of his power spill out, driving him along in front of it, into Tom.

"No! What are you doing?"

Harlan smiled. He couldn't blame Tom. He was so new at this. He was used to being right, knowing what to do, being in control. It had probably been years since he'd been this inexperienced at something.

Not that Harlan was in control. He was riding the edges of their energy, barely clinging on. He knew that if he fell he'd die and take the others with him, so he held on. He managed just enough control to keep Tom's power from strengthening the barrier around Harlan's mediumship.

Reaching deep inside Tom, he could feel the network of Tom's stolen power draped over the city like a diseased spiderweb. There were vulnerable points, places it hadn't quite settled yet, hadn't fully taken root—the places he'd colonized most recently. Harlan knew that was where he had to begin. He chose one 'line' of power and followed it out to its tip, where it was weakest. He imagined it as a ball of yarn that had come unravelled, and he began rolling it back towards them. He pulled it through Tom and past him, into himself, and swallowed it down.

Tom tried to fight back, but he hadn't spent his whole life earning his energy, working with it, learning to control it, honing it, fighting it and *hating* it. Harlan had never done anything like this, but he knew mediumship like he knew how to breathe—more than that, deeper. Breathing was automatic, something everyone did without thinking about it. This was his true, deepest self, something that was his and his alone. Tom had more raw power, but Harlan knew how to shape what he had, and now he was going to fucking use it against Tom, turning his own strength against him until he broke.

Stop! Tom's voice was in his head. He ignored it.

Now that he'd freed one strand, Harlan traced his way back along the web, dancing from line to line as he sought out the next-newest. He found it and began digging at its tip, ripping it loose and drinking it down.

Tom was wary now, and he tried to stop Harlan when he raced out along the next stream of energy.

They struggled, but Harlan knew what he was doing — not really, but enough. He forced his way past Tom and out along the thread. This one was older, more deeply rooted, but when it did snap free, it released more power than the others, power that Harlan neatly stole before Tom could absorb it, then he was on to the next. Each strand was harder to free, but also gave him more strength to attack the next.

Harlan was only distantly aware of his body, just enough to know his heart was pounding and he was fighting for each breath. He knew he was on his knees, so he didn't have to worry about falling, at least not very far.

He was gaining ground, slowly, but he wasn't sure he could reach the tipping point before his body gave out. Stolen or not, this was Tom's power, and it was already in place. Harlan was at a disadvantage. He was trying to undo what Tom had done, but until he was finished, Tom could draw on what remained to fight him.

Harlan grasped yet another tendril of power, tore it free and gathered it up into himself. This time, its energy didn't feel like Tom, or at least not him alone. Something from Leo, her essence, was mixed in with it.

Harlan hoped it was a sign that Tom was getting weaker, but he couldn't slow down and think about it. He had to keep moving — keep moving or be swept away and lost forever. Tom's web was shrinking as Harlan yanked its loosely staked outer edges back towards them, but the lines were thicker closer to the centre — more deeply entrenched, more resistant. They didn't want Harlan to take them. They wanted to return to Tom. If Harlan had thought removing them had been difficult before, now it was agony. He had to wrest every scrap of power he could from Tom so he could divert it to himself. It roiled within him uneasily, like he'd eaten rotten meat. It wanted back up, back out, and he kept having to choke it down. He was slowly pulling ahead, but now Tom was making up lost ground. More and more of the energy Harlan was unweaving was flowing back into Tom and staying there.

Far away, Harlan felt his body fall, but Charles was there to catch him. He felt a wave of solidity pour through him at Charles' touch. It had nothing to do with mediumship. There were no ghosts around to control, even if Tom's blood-circle hadn't shut down Charles' power. It had everything to do with trust and affection and the sheer *belief* that Harlan would succeed and Tom would fail — belief like Harlan had never known from anyone, especially himself. He could feel the strength of that conviction like a warm hand caressing his face, or something deeper — his soul?

He knew he could do it, because he had to, because Charles knew he could. He couldn't disappoint Charles, couldn't let him know that he wasn't as strong or as brave or as good as Charles thought he was. He had to keep trying to be the man Charles thought he was.

Another vine of power sprang loose, almost on its own, and Harlan managed to snatch all its released energy before Tom had even realized it had broken.

Far in the distance, Charles shouted, "*Yes!*"

Tom shot out another roil of energy that made Harlan's limp body twitch and jerk in Charles' arms, forcing him back from the next thread, forcing him to regroup and gather his strength instead of pushing ahead. He surveyed the remaining web, briefly overwhelmed by its vastness, how tangled and twisted and knotted and *evil* it was. It felt like he had hardly removed any of it, and he realized that he needed to stop picking at its edges and go for the heart.

Gathering all the strength he had, all the strength he'd taken back from Tom, all the strength Charles poured into him, he turned it against Tom himself, pouring it all down the connection between them and slamming it open. He felt the bag containing his power burst, and he cried out in silent joy as he was finally set free.

Too late, he realized that Tom had changed tactics. He was still putting up a token struggle, but he was letting Harlan reel in the web while he worked on his actual goal—strengthening his connections to the imprisoned mediums—allowing Harlan to take the city while he consolidated his real power.

Harlan reluctantly released the spoke of energy he'd been chiseling at. The web could wait. He had to focus on Tom.

He could feel Tom draining the mediums faster now, knew they'd die if Tom continued taking so much from them so quickly, knew he had to stop him. But how?

Before he could make up his mind, Tom decided for him. He reached out along what remained of his network of power blanketing the city and reeled in the darkest spirit he could find.

Kill. Tom's thought-command was strong enough to burn, strong enough that Harlan recoiled.

Tom turned the spirit on Charles.

It brushed Charles' face with the tip of one spectral finger, leaving behind a dark ectoplasmic smear. Charles, who had never seen a ghost before he met Harlan... Charles, who would have been safe — should *be* safe — if not for Harlan...

He felt Charles twist and writhe as he held Harlan's body, heard Charles cry out.

He suddenly knew, with unshakable certainty, that Charles had meant what he'd said. He wanted to be a part of Harlan's life, even the dark parts. He knew Charles would rather die here and now than go on without having ever met him. That ghost shit followed Harlan everywhere, but Charles was willing to risk that to be with him.

The ghost pressed a hand into Charles' chest, just above his heart. Charles screamed, and Harlan screamed with him.

Harlan's power burned up its connection to Tom, out and past him and into the other mediums. He could feel that they'd given up after the days or weeks they'd been imprisoned, allowed Tom to drain their power so that they might live to see the next day, and he couldn't blame them. It hurt so much less to surrender, but he didn't have that option — not while Charles was hurting, not while Charles might die.

He lashed them with his power over and over, even the little girl, trying to rally them to join him and turn against Tom, even though he could feel his own life-force flickering and fading along with theirs. *Weak.* They were all too weak, and Tom was so strong and getting stronger with each heartbeat. Charles deserved someone strong, someone who could save him, but all he had was Harlan.

Harlan felt when the ghost's icy fingertips brushed Charles' heart, as if it was his own. He felt Charles' light begin to dim.

He couldn't let that happen. It didn't matter what happened to him, didn't matter if he died, as long as he saved Charles. The world was a better, warmer place with Charles in it.

He unleashed all his power at once, burning up everything he'd ever held back, leaving nothing in reserve, and he felt the other mediums break free and join him. He opened himself completely, turning their joint strength into a blunt weapon to smash against Tom all at once. Tom was stronger, but Harlan's energy had been building up his whole life. Tom couldn't bring his full might to bear against Harlan, to shield himself, before Harlan and the others struck with everything they had.

He felt something in Tom's body break, something irreparable, and Tom's power instantly faded away to nothing. *No, not nothing.* That power had to go somewhere. Energy was not created or destroyed. It burned its way into Harlan, filling him to the brim and spilling over and out of him, feeding back into the lines of power Tom had etched on the city and changing them so they were *Harlan's*.

He felt the ghost touching Charles disintegrate, not moving on to the next world but simply annihilated from this one.

He felt warmth return to Charles' still form.

There, poised in that crystalline moment, Harlan could see it all—how easy it would be to spin his *own* web of power and set it over the city. His would be neater, of course, less rushed, less...sloppy. He knew how to use his power in a way Tom never could have. He could tie every ghost in Toronto to him, using them as his eyes and ears and sources of power, a vast network all feeding back to him. It would be so *easy*, easier than trying to fight it. He could use it to protect the city, to keep anything like this from happening again and he knew it — knew it in his blood and his bones and his soul. All of this could be his, but he'd do it *right*. To help people, not to hurt them. To bind, not rip apart.

His awareness spread, larger than his body, larger than the Centre, down through the streets and sewers and walls of Toronto. He felt every ghost he passed and every living thing — for, what were the living but vessels for the spirit? He couldn't control the living, not directly, but he knew he could use their fear, their helplessness, to direct them.

He felt himself brush something familiar. It slowed him down, drawing him into a single focused point again.

What?

A face. A familiar form. *Libby.*

Harlan laughed with delight, and the city laughed with him. He'd thought he'd never see her again.

Her mouth opened and she waved her arms frantically, but he couldn't quite hear her. Not over the pulse and roar of listening to — of *being* — everywhere, everyone...

He forced himself down even smaller so he could focus on her and —

No, don't do it what are you doing. Stop!

He blinked, in the way a city blinked. A brief hesitation before life moved on, messy and imperfect and beautiful.

Stop? Why should I stop? I'm trying to help.

Libby rushed towards him, but he wasn't afraid of her. What did he have to be afraid of now?

She placed her cool hands on him and closed her eyes.

A vision swept over him. The cool blue knots and swirls of power he'd woven across the city flashed and disappeared, replaced by ragged, poorly spun skeins of knotted purple, red and black.

He recoiled from her and she smiled her sad, faded smile. He sent her a wordless wave of gratitude, but she was gone before he knew if she'd received it.

Chapter Twenty-Nine

First, there was pain—white-hot, red-hot, black pain. He felt like he was being rebuilt from his core, agony spiraling out from his guts, through his marrow, until it finally reached his skin and there it was worst of all, but it could at least move out of him, past him, through him. It felt like every nerve ending was being scorched at once, but he knew from the pain that he'd survive.

He screamed. Maybe with his mouth and lips and lungs, maybe with something more. Something...else. All he knew was that he was screaming.

Some *force*—or maybe it was still him, just another part of him—slammed him back into his body, like hitting warm water after falling from space. He gasped and choked and tried to remember how to breathe, tried to remember how to *be*, to exist only as himself and nothing more and nothing less. He was aware of sound and movement on either side of him—aware only physically—but that wasn't important...not yet.

First he had to remember how to be human, in a human body. Real. Alive.

Vomiting.

The smell, the taste, was so visceral, so animal. Revolting. *This, this is a part of me? Happening inside me all the time? Disgusting.*

The scent, the act, was so primitive, so barbaric, that it taught him how to move again. He scrambled backwards on all fours until there was no risk of the vile liquid spreading far enough to reach his hands.

His hands...

They hurt. All of him hurt, but his hands were small enough to focus on, and right in front of him, on either side of where his head was hanging down until it almost touched the floor.

He turned one hand over. His palm was bloody and raw. His nails were ragged and broken and there was blood underneath them, like he'd torn at the concrete floor while he was...gone, while he'd been everywhere.

There was blood on the floor. It wasn't his blood. It was dry and brown with age.

A wave of profound revulsion rolled through him at the sight, and *that* taught him how to stand, struggling to his feet like a newborn animal on shaky legs.

Everything else caught up to him then, a wave of sound that nearly knocked him over again.

"No, don't stand up!" Charles.

"Harlan!" Morgan called.

"Jesus fucking— Someone catch him!" Hamilton's voice, but too low.

Harlan moved just his eyeballs —*even that hurts*— and saw that Hamilton was sprawled on his side, trying desperately to get up, even though Harlan could tell he was still too weak to do so. Enough of Harlan was still connected to the web around them, the web he'd torn away from so he could cram himself back into his singular, weak body, that he could see just how much strength was inside Hamilton.

He turned to Charles and saw just as much strength, but a very different kind.

Morgan glowed like a beacon, so bright that he had to look away.

He blinked, realizing his eyes had been open too long. When he opened them again, the awareness was gone. Hamilton was just Hamilton, Charles was just Charles, he could look at Morgan and they were themself again, and he was just…him.

"Gotcha."

He felt Charles' strong arms around him, keeping him steady, keeping him from falling—like he always did.

He wanted to insist that he was fine, that he could stand on his own, but he couldn't even summon the energy to do that.

He surrendered himself to Charles, letting Charles slowly lower him back down until he was sitting against a wall.

He leaned forward in sudden desperation, fighting Charles' grip on his shoulders. "Tom!"

A strange expression crossed Charles' face, one Harlan couldn't read. He glanced over at someone— Hamilton, Harlan suspected—before answering. "You don't have to worry about him."

"What are you talking about? We—"

"He's dead," Charles said, very softly.

"What?"

Charles gritted his teeth, opening his mouth to speak but changing his mind and closing it again several times. "Never mind that now. You're safe. We're safe. Just…rest."

Harlan tried again. "We have to —"

"He's dead. You killed him." Hamilton's voice was also soft, but without Charles' gentleness.

"I…" Harlan managed to shake his head, just barely.

"We *agreed* that we weren't going to tell him that yet." Now there was steel in Charles' voice too. He sat beside Harlan, one arm draped protectively across his shoulders, drawing him close.

Hamilton shrugged. "I'm not gonna lie to him."

"It's not — Never mind. Harlan. What matters now is that everyone is safe."

Harlan nodded, slowly. *Safe.* It was good to be safe. He felt a little giddy now that he was fully inside himself again.

"You three should go." Hamilton had managed to sit up, which was good, but he still wasn't on his feet. "Backup is on the way."

"Go? What about…?" Harlan nodded in the direction of the three prisoners. They were all unconscious — at least he *hoped* they were just unconscious. "We can't just leave —"

"I'll stay with 'em."

Charles snorted but wisely didn't say anything.

"Why don't you just use your…?" *Shit.* Harlan couldn't think of the word. He mimed turning a key. "…On their cuffs, so we can *all* get out of here?"

"I tried that. It didn't work."

Harlan was pleased to see Hamilton haul himself to his feet, but he was very unsteady and had to lean against the wall.

"Oh, for —" Morgan strode over to Hamilton and held out an elbow for him to grab.

Hamilton hesitated, just for a moment, then took it with a grateful smile. "Thanks."

"No problem." Muttering something that sounded suspiciously like 'dumbass', they escorted Hamilton across the room.

"Like I said before, it's no good. This fucker didn't use regular handcuffs. They're some kinda shackles. Fucking...whack-job! We'll have to cut these off. My key won't work."

Of course it couldn't be that easy. Harlan tipped his head back, letting it rest against the wall. The ceiling was painted a beautiful periwinkle blue that didn't match the evil-cult vibe of the rest of the room at all.

"You three go," Hamilton repeated, stiffly letting go of Morgan's arm and standing on his own. His face was tight with pain. He must have really been hurting if he looked like that while he was clearly trying to hide it.

"Fuck that."

Hamilton turned to Morgan with surprise.

"Either we all go together, or we all stay here." Morgan crossed their arms to make their point extra clear.

"Until backup gets here, I'm in charge of this scene, and I'm not leaving. Until backup gets here — I'm not leaving." Seeming to realize he'd got stuck in a loop, Hamilton abruptly shut his mouth, but he still looked rigidly determined.

Morgan snorted. "Right now, you're not in charge of your own butt." They softened their tone. "We're not leaving you here alone, and you and Harlan aren't in any shape to go anywhere."

Hamilton growled but lowered his head in what could have been interpreted as a nod. Now that he'd given in, he allowed himself to slide down the wall, sitting on the opposite side of the room from Harlan.

Morgan visibly relaxed. Then, clearly in triage mode, they turned to the prisoners. "Should I...?" they asked Hamilton.

Hamilton's only response was a rumbling snore so loud that it jerked him awake.

"Never mind."

"Never mind *what*?" Hamilton demanded.

"Nothing." Morgan waited until Hamilton was still again before approaching Leo. They touched the side of her face softly, and when she didn't respond in any way, they slid their hand down to her neck. "Her pulse is faint, but it's there," they said quietly.

Harlan would have slumped with relief if he wasn't already basically a pile of mush supported only by the wall and Charles. He managed a shaky thumbs-up.

Morgan moved on to the next victim, Bradley, but before they could touch him, Harlan heard heavy bootsteps above them.

Hamilton instantly snapped awake, but he didn't even try to stand again. "Hallelujah, the cavalry's here," he groaned. "Fuck, I'm thirsty. Hope they brought some water."

A few minutes later — Harlan assumed they'd had to do a thorough check of the rest of the house before coming to the rescue — several people wearing full riot gear came through the door and quickly secured the room.

One of them nudged Tom's body with the toe of her boot. He flopped bonelessly, and for a moment Harlan was afraid he'd throw up again, especially when Tom's head came unstuck from the puddle of blood beneath it with a wet squelching sound and his face came briefly into view. Harlan could see that at least some of the blood had come from his nose. That wasn't uncommon when someone exerted their psychic power, but Tom had also bled from his mouth, ears and eyes. The whites of his eyes were red where blood vessels had burst.

Harlan somehow saw all of this in an instant. Tom's head lolled back to the side, mercifully facing away from him, but not before Harlan saw a single drop of blood fall, thick and heavy, from the tip of Tom's nose.

Harlan looked away so quickly that it made his head spin. He squeezed his eyes shut and sank his teeth into his forearm to keep himself from vomiting or screaming, forcing himself to just breathe and concentrate on the fresh air pouring down the stairs through the open door.

Probably seeing how upset Harlan was, Charles wrapped his other arm around him, pulling him close and burying Harlan's face in his chest.

Harlan couldn't keep himself from thinking.

How had Tom died? Hamilton had said Harlan had killed him—how? Shouldn't he remember that sort of thing, killing a person? He remembered struggling for control, then the next thing he knew, he was engulfing the city with his power. If he'd caused Tom's death, it had been a blip, if that, and Harlan was horrified. If he could kill so easily once, what was to stop him from doing it again—to someone who didn't deserve it?

By accident.

His downward spiral was interrupted by EMTs rushing into the room. One of them was carrying a saw, which confused him until he remembered Hamilton saying they'd have to cut the shackles off.

The one with the saw hurried over to the little girl, while the other three went to Leo and Bradley.

Harlan started drifting off—as Hamilton had said, the cavalry was here. They were safe. He didn't have to do anything more...not now, not yet.

He didn't think Hamilton could get him out of the paperwork of *killing* someone, but that was a problem for future-Harlan.

A sudden commotion made his eyes snap open. All four EMTs surrounded Bradley.

"There's no pulse."

"He's not breathing."

Leo, who was conscious now, thrashed against the chains holding her in place. "No, no, no, he can't—!"

The paramedics did what they could, which was limited by him being chained to a chair, but it soon became clear to everyone in the room that he was gone—and had been for a while.

One by one, they stepped away from the body to tend to the living.

It became even clearer to Harlan when he saw Bradley floating near his body, staring down at it.

Harlan wanted to go over to him, talk to him, but there was too much happening. Bradley would have to figure it out on his own, at least for now.

Harlan drew his legs up against his chest and turned to face the open door. As much as he wanted to just stay curled up in Charles' arms, it wasn't very professional. He also didn't want to see anything in the room.

Chapter Thirty

Between the police team and the EMTs, they managed to get the two mediums — and Bradley's body — up the stairs. Morgan went with them.

They had just returned for Hamilton, who was protesting loudly that he wouldn't leave until Harlan and Charles did, when Beth strode down the stairs.

She turned to the officer in charge. "Give us a few minutes alone."

Hamilton looked like he was about to protest, and the officer went over and talked to him quietly. Hamilton's jawline was tight, but he left, leaning heavily on the officer.

With Charles' help, Harlan managed to stand. He started following the rest of the group, but Beth stopped him.

Charles hung back, but she practically pushed him out of the room. It was just her and Harlan.

"No. You can stay and help me," she told him.

"Help you with what?"

She pointed at Bradley's ghost. "With him."

Harlan just wanted to leave. Couldn't they do this later? Couldn't someone *else* do it later?

Without waiting for a response, she closed the door at the bottom of the stairs.

"What...what are you doing?"

She didn't reply.

"I just want to get out of here," he said, actually raising his voice a little.

She sighed. "I know. But this will be easier with you here. You have a connection to him. He trusts you."

Harlan took an involuntary step back—away from her, but also away from the door, his only way out. He suspected she'd stayed in front of it on purpose, to block his path.

"What are *we* doing?"

Bradley's ghost drifted past Harlan to hover over Beth. Bradley had just died, but Harlan could feel that he was more powerful than most new ghosts, that he was more focused and directed.

Harlan had never encountered a medium's ghost before. He had honestly tried not to think about the possibility of a medium becoming a ghost. He wondered if they were all...precocious.

"We're going to send him on." The *obviously* was unspoken but clear.

"What? Why?" Harlan suddenly wished Bradley's ghost would drift away, escape before Beth could claim him, but he knew it didn't work that way. Ghosts were bound to a place—usually their graves or where they'd died. It took something very unusual to allow them to leave, and precocious or not, Bradley had been a ghost for barely an hour. He was as stuck in that basement as Harlan was.

"He just died! If he was meant to move on right away, wouldn't he have? Can't we let him adjust just a little before — ?"

She shrugged. "Who knows why some people leave on their own and some stick around? My orders are to send him on, *now*."

"Orders?"

She nodded.

Bradley seemed to panic. He flew at the closest wall and bounced off, wincing as though it physically hurt — and maybe it had.

He rocketed towards the ceiling, struck it and fell far enough that he almost hit the floor. He quickly tried the other three walls, the door and the floor, one after another, ricocheting around the room like a deranged pinball.

Harlan had to duck several times to avoid him, and he shivered when he miscalculated Bradley's angle and the ghost passed through him.

"Are you finished?" Beth asked, tapping her foot.

Bradley finally settled down, keeping Harlan between him and Beth.

Harlan wanted to tell Bradley he wouldn't be able to protect him, but he couldn't.

"Good. You don't belong here." She rolled her eyes. "Harlan, would you do the honors so we can hopefully cut down on any further dramatics?"

He slowly, haltingly shook his head. "He just died," he repeated. "It's not like he's going anywhere — as you just saw — and it's not like there are any living people in the house he's going to inconvenience." Well, except for crime-scene techs… Harlan was sure the house was going to be picked over brick by brick before anyone was allowed to live in it again. "If he bothers anyone working here, we can—"

"No. I have my orders, and none of us are leaving here until they're followed. As they say, we can do this the easy way or the hard way."

Harlan shivered. He could guess what the hard way was—forcing Bradley to pass through the veil rather than choosing to go on his own. Harlan had done it to spirits before, but he'd always hated it and tried his best to avoid it, especially if the ghost wasn't dangerous. It probably didn't matter once they got to the other side, but Harlan didn't want someone's last experience on Earth to be traumatic, especially because Bradley had just died after being held prisoner. The end of his life had been very traumatic, and Harlan didn't want to add to that. Bradley had been through enough. If Harlan could, he'd let Bradley pass through on his own. It wasn't much of a choice, but Bradley deserved to make it for himself.

He turned to face the ghost behind him, the hairs on the back of his neck prickling as he took his eyes off Beth. "Well?"

Bradley looked at him, then at Beth, then back to him. He shook his head and reached out a translucent hand, his fingers passing through Harlan's arm.

He felt Beth begin drawing in power behind him, and he turned to look at her with his hands up. "It's okay. I don't think he's going to hurt me." *And fuck, won't those be ironic last words for my tombstone if I'm wrong?*

He looked back at Bradley, doing the special *blink* that would let Bradley actually touch him.

Bradley looked relieved. He reached out again and lightly touched Harlan's bare forearm—his left one, luckily.

I don't think she can hear us like this. His voice echoed softly in Harlan's mind.

Harlan had never spoken to a ghost this way before, not while he was fully awake and conscious, anyway. He wondered if all ghosts could do this—or just dead mediums.

He wasn't in any hurry to find out.

"I—" he said out loud, trying to figure out how to silently reply to Bradley. He felt Beth tense behind him again.

I don't think so, he thought as loudly as he could, still moving his lips.

Good. You can 'hear' me. I...I'm not ready to go.

I know.

I don't have a choice, though, do I?

No. I don't think we do. She's stronger than me, even if I did— He wasn't willing to try challenging Beth and ruining his career—not for Bradley. He hoped Bradley hadn't been able to hear that particular thought.

"Harlan? What are you doing?" Beth asked, almost sing-song.

I'm— No, that wasn't right. "I'm trying to convince him."

"Well, hurry it up. This place is creepy as fuck, and it stinks."

Harlan had got so used to the smell that he hadn't noticed it until she'd pointed it out, but it suddenly became overwhelming. Just keeping three people prisoner would have reeked, but death had left its own stench behind. "I'm *trying*."

"My way would be a lot faster. And I'm sure you're tired."

"I've *got* this." He managed to keep himself from snapping at her, but just barely. He was so tired. He hoped the veil would be thin and Bradley wouldn't fight him at all.

Time to go? Bradley asked.

Harlan nodded.

Will you pass on a message for me?

Sure, Harlan agreed, hoping he hadn't just volunteered to do something that would take a long time or involve talking to a lot of people.

Tell Amira my will is in the shop's safe. I'm leaving the shop to her – and all my assets. He shook his head. *It's all in there. Tell her... Tell her, 'thank you'. It's not enough, but I don't know what else to say.* Bradley somehow managed to sigh in the silence of their minds. *There... There isn't really anyone else. It's pretty pathetic, I guess.*

It's not pathetic, Harlan told him. Privately, he thought it was at least *sad* that he had nothing and no one but his magic shop and his employee – he assumed Amira was the woman he'd met in the shop – but that wasn't important.

Were you happy? he asked. He didn't know what else to say, and he hoped it was the right thing.

Bradley nodded. *Very.*

Harlan smiled. *Then that's enough, I think. Have you ever sent someone through the veil? Or seen it?*

No.

Obviously I've never been there, but I think that happiness will continue on the other side. It would have sounded completely cheesy if he'd said it out loud, but he found himself tearing up a little. *It's beautiful. Are you ready to look?* he asked Bradley.

Bradley jerked his head in Beth's direction. *Do I have much of a choice?* he asked bitterly.

Not much.

Do it.

Harlan gently pulled free of Bradley's grip. There was a bright-red patch on his arm, and he gritted his teeth as sensation slowly returned to the freezing-cold area.

He ignored the pain and his ever-present worry about further nerve damage. He reached out until he found that tiny snag, almost like an invisible zipper, that was meant only for Bradley. He tugged it open. He didn't turn to look at what was inside, but he could see multicoloured, unearthly light dancing on his hands and the wall behind Bradley.

Wow. It's –

He went through abruptly enough that Harlan suspected Beth had at least given him a push, but he couldn't prove it.

He closed the portal, then turned around.

"Well… That took a little longer than it should have, but you got the job done. Good work, Brand." She stepped away from the door, grandly gesturing *after you*.

Harlan stepped as far around her as he could. He wasn't sure who he hated more – her or himself.

As they left, Harlan stared at the ground. He didn't want to see the bloody circles Tom had drawn on the floor, but it was better than looking at Beth.

Just before he passed through the door at the bottom of the stairs, he saw how he'd managed to break through Tom's control and what had caused the tiny 'hole' he'd felt – there was a scuffmark through one of the symbols. A careless footstep, probably Harlan's own, that had broken the circle *just enough* for Harlan to squeeze through. *An accident.*

That's why you should always use real ward paint! he thought gleefully, then he was crying and he couldn't stop. Didn't want to stop.

Charles was waiting for him just outside the house, his shoulders already draped with a Victim Blanket.

He rushed forward into Charles' arms. He was too weak to put up more than a token resistance when the EMTs tried to remove him so they could check him for injuries and wrap him in a blanket of his own. He could see Morgan sitting on the back of an ambulance, talking to another pair of EMTs and also wearing a blanket. He didn't see Hamilton, but he'd been in pretty bad shape. They'd probably already taken him to the hospital.

Two hearses pulled up.

"It's okay. Let them take care of you. I'll stay with you," Charles murmured, reaching up to stroke Harlan's hair. It was plastered to his head with sweat and maybe worse things, but Harlan couldn't find the strength to worry about Charles seeing him like that.

He nodded, reluctantly, and allowed them to peel him away from Charles, who stayed close enough to hold his hand the whole time.

They didn't find any serious injuries, but they wanted him to go to the hospital for overnight observation. He shook his head, silently pleading with Charles with his eyes alone.

Charles sighed and shook his head, wrapping an arm around Harlan's waist and pulling him close again. Harlan could feel Charles' warm, strong hand rubbing his lower back.

"I'll take him home and keep an eye on him. If he needs to go to the hospital later, I'll take him."

Once he was in Charles' car, Harlan allowed himself to drift away, a soft smile on his lips. He was going home with Charles, and that was all that mattered.

Chapter Thirty-One

The police found old books and papers behind a hidden panel in Tom's bathroom wall. They depicted the symbols he'd drawn on the floor and used to drain the mediums. Harlan wanted to watch the materials get destroyed personally, but he had to take Hamilton's word that they were gone.

Harlan was suspended with pay while Tom's death was investigated. As he'd suspected, this time Hamilton wasn't able to take care of all the backlash for him. He was questioned — borderline interrogated — several times. He repeated his story over and over, telling his accusers in detail what he remembered and insisting that he didn't remember killing Tom. They never seemed to believe him. They seemed to think that he'd intentionally killed Tom. He *hadn't*. He'd wanted to stop him with every fibre of his being, but he hadn't been trying to *kill* him.

The investigators didn't seem to think there was much of a difference, and maybe there wasn't, but it was important to Harlan.

"It's bullshit," Hamilton told him.

It meant a lot to Harlan that Hamilton believed him. He knew Charles did, too.

Hamilton was also suspended. Harlan could tell he needed the break. He'd admitted to Harlan that he was in counselling to deal with the aftereffects of being possessed. Knowing only a fraction of what Hamilton had seen and been through during his time as a policeman, Harlan could only imagine how bad it had to be to make him seek therapy for *that*. He was just glad Hamilton had accepted that he needed help dealing with it.

Hamilton hadn't recovered the trickle of mediumship Tom had stolen from them. Neither of the surviving mediums had recovered theirs, either.

Leo and her girlfriend, Cassandra, had invited Harlan, Hamilton, Morgan and Charles over for breakfast one day. He'd been worried that it might be awkward, since *he* had been the one to drain the last of Leo's power, but she honestly seemed relieved. She talked about going to university and getting a degree in psychology.

He hadn't spoken to Rabbit Girl's friend.

He'd kept his promise and passed on Bradley's final message. Ms. Zaman had thanked him, and he'd left before things could get too emotional.

He didn't have any more nerve damage in his arm than before. Once again, he'd got lucky, but he knew his luck would probably run out sometime.

Libby had been back in her usual spot in the lobby when he got home, but that time she'd turned and smiled at him as he passed. He waved back at her, relieved that she wasn't gone forever.

Hamilton invited him for coffee, something they'd never done before, but now they both had a lot of free time. It had also felt strange to Harlan for them to be apart so long, and he was secretly pleased that Hamilton apparently felt the same way.

Harlan squirmed uncomfortably. He knew he was going to have to tell Hamilton something that had been building in him for a while. He'd told Hamilton—and no one else, not even Charles—what had happened in the basement with Bradley's ghost and Beth.

"I'm thinking of leaving the police force."

Hamilton blinked at him, then nodded slowly. "Yeah, I was kinda waiting for you to say something like that."

"What, really?"

"Yeah. I know this whole thing has really pissed you off—"

"I'm not pissed off!"

Hamilton raised an eyebrow.

"I'm *not*," Harlan insisted. "I'm just…upset."

"Yeah, well, however you put it, you're feeling a lot of *emotions* about this."

Harlan couldn't help laughing. "Therapy's really been helping, huh?"

"Oh, shut up." Grinning, Hamilton flicked a sugar packet across the table at him.

"You know I think it's great that you're going," Harlan quickly added.

Hamilton waved a hand dismissively. "Yeah, yeah, I know you're just teasing. It really *has* been helping, though. Anyway, you were saying?"

"I just…" Even though Harlan had been thinking about it a lot—almost obsessively—he still struggled to put his thoughts into words. "I'm really glad I started there, and I learned a lot, but I think… I think it might be time for me to move on."

"I'm sure you've already thought of this, but if you'll let me play the devil's advocate for a moment?"

Harlan nodded, a little reluctantly. He wasn't sure where Hamilton was going with this.

"With Leo out of the game, they're already short a police medium. This would leave only Benjamin and Beth. You and I both know they were already stretched pretty thin when they had four."

The back of Harlan's neck prickled at Beth's name. He hadn't admitted it to Hamilton, but she was another reason he wanted to leave. It might be cowardly, but he knew he couldn't work with her after what had happened in the basement.

He nodded again. "I know." Maybe he was selfish for even thinking about leaving them in the lurch, but he knew he had to take care of himself too. "But I'm not planning on just abandoning them."

"What *are* you planning?"

"I still want to help with the city's ghosts. I just don't want to do it the way I *have* been doing it. The police way. I want to be proactive, not just reactive."

Hamilton whistled. "Those are some sixty-four-thousand-dollar words."

"I might have talked about this with my therapist," Harlan admitted.

"But, yeah, I think I know what you mean."

"I don't want to just go around 'cleaning up' ghosts. They were people. They deserve to be treated like people. Respectfully, not just rushing from one to another to another like they're… I don't know" — he waved his hands — "just a nuisance. I want to find them, talk to them — *before* they become problems." He shook his head. "Not that they're *problems*… I just…"

"Breathe, kid. I'm with ya."

"I want to help people *and* ghosts."

"So, what are you thinking?"

"Well, I don't have all the details figured out yet…" Harlan said slowly.

"That's okay."

Harlan sighed. He knew it was going to sound really stupid. "I want to open a kind of…detective agency? So I can look for ghosts and help them move on — which would take some of the workload off of Beth and Benjamin — and people can ask for help with ghosts. And" — this was the part he *really* wasn't sure about — "finding missing people."

"I assume you're thinking of collaborating with Morgan?"

"Yeah."

"Have you talked to them yet?"

"…No."

"Do you want me to be there when you do?"

"You'd really do that?"

Hamilton shrugged one shoulder. "Eh. I've got nothing better to do right now. So, how are you going to pay the bills?"

"I don't know yet," he admitted.

Harlan didn't like the thought of asking grieving people for money, and the ghosts certainly couldn't pay him, but he knew he couldn't live on goodwill alone. His expenses wouldn't be very high if he met clients in his apartment. He didn't like the idea, but he thought he could mentally barricade the living room so he wouldn't feel like his home was being invaded. He didn't use the living room that much, anyway. He'd rather be in his bedroom.

Besides... He hadn't felt completely comfortable — completely *safe* — in his apartment since the ghost had got in, even though it had been re-warded and, with Tom dead and his research destroyed, there was little-to-no chance of something similar happening again.

Hamilton grinned at him. "So, are you hiring?"

"I just said I don't know where I'm going to get money from, and that's your first question?" Harlan laughed. When Hamilton's expression didn't change, he blinked. "Wait. You're serious?"

"Yeah. You're not the only one who's been doing some thinking with all this downtime, you know."

"*You're* thinking about quitting the police?"

"Yeah. I am." He shrugged. "Really, Matthew makes enough money that I could just stay home and be a househus — Well, I don't *need* to work."

It took Harlan a moment to adjust to what Hamilton had just told him. Finally he said, "I wouldn't want it any other way," since they were apparently being emotionally honest with each other, at least temporarily.

"Good. I'm hired."

"Then...your first job is to help me try to recruit Morgan." It was crazy. It was all happening so fast, and Harlan knew he should have been anxious, if not terrified, but it all felt...right.

"I accept."

Matthew joined them once they were done with their shop talk. Charles would have, too, but he was sleeping before his night of work.

* * * *

Morgan primly set their cup of tea on their saucer, then set both on their Queen Anne-style coffee table. "You're asking me to work with the two of you?"

To his surprise, Harlan found himself speaking before Hamilton could. "Yes."

"After everything we went through, everything I saw, you're here to ask more of me."

Harlan frowned—despite what they were saying, they weren't giving an outright no. "Yes," he repeated.

It also sounded a little like they might quoting *The Godfather*. He hadn't actually seen it, but he'd heard lots of references to it.

They crossed their legs, braced their elbows on one knee and rested their chin on their folded hands, looking back and forth from Harlan to Hamilton, steady as a metronome. "You're sure about this."

The words caught in Harlan's throat—he was never that sure about *anything*—but Hamilton was there to save him.

"Yes. We're doing this, and we could really use your help. *Other* people could use your help."

"Oh, shut up," they said breezily. "I don't need your ham-handed attempts to appeal to my better nature."

Hamilton grinned. "Fair."

They sighed. "I'll admit, work has felt a little…dull lately."

Hamilton's grin widened. "Ahh…! C'mon, you know you want to."

They held up a finger. "On a part-time, trial basis. I am *not* quitting my day job for this little venture, no matter how bored I get—not until I see results. Also, I'm never doing field work ever, ever again." They frowned thoughtfully. "Okay, beyond holding hands with him" — they jerked their head at Harlan — "to follow ghosts. That is *it*."

Never say never, Harlan thought but didn't say. He didn't remind them that they'd *chosen* to follow him and Hamilton. He exchanged a very brief glance with Hamilton, who nodded. "That would be perfect," he assured them. It was more than he'd worried they might offer.

They picked up their teacup, pausing with it halfway to their lips. "But not yet," they said, very softly. "I need…time."

Hamilton nodded right away. "So do I. So does Harlan. We're not announcing anything until we're both off suspension. We're putting plans in place, but we don't want to rush this." He snorted. "Well, maybe I do — maybe he does too — but we're *trying* not to."

They took a long sip of tea, their expression somehow turning harder and softening at the same time. "And I suppose the two of you know exactly how you're going to finance this project?"

"Not…exactly," Harlan admitted, staring at the floral-pattern rug between his shoes.

"I thought as much. So you came to me for financial advice?" they asked, a little coolness creeping into their voice.

"No! Nothing like that." Harlan's mind raced. *Right. They're an accountant.* He'd completely forgot. "I wasn't even thinking about your…day job when I asked you. We're working on that. We just want you to help us by using your ability."

They nodded. "All right, I believe you. And I think I can be a little more help than that. I'm betting there are some grants or other funding we can apply for — and by *we*, I mean *me*. I'm sure you two are great at filling out police paperwork, but when it comes to shuffling money around, I'm clearly the most experienced."

"Hey, I'm not going to turn down that kind of help," Hamilton assured them. "And he's not even good at *that* paperwork."

Harlan wanted to protest, but he knew Hamilton was right. "Thank you," was all he said.

"Oh, don't thank me yet. You haven't worked with me, not really. I have *very* high standards."

"I think that's just what we need on the team," Hamilton assured them, and Harlan nodded.

* * * *

"Morgan agreed to join us," Harlan told Charles excitedly.

"Hey, that's great! Not that I'm surprised. I had a feeling they would." Charles was driving them to his weekly boardgame night with his friends.

Harlan was still nervous about meeting them — what if they didn't like him, and their dislike made Charles like him less? Charles had known them a lot longer than he'd known Harlan, after all. Their opinions would probably be more important than someone Charles had only met within the past year.

He forced himself to stop that train of thought. He closed his eyes.

Breathe in.
Breathe out.
Breathe in, deep.
Breathe out, deeper.

He liked Charles. Charles liked him. Charles liked his friends. Harlan would like Charles' friends, and they'd like him. It was as simple as that.

Or so he tried to convince himself, without much success.

"We're here." Charles pulled up in front of a duplex and got out.

Harlan wasn't sure what he'd been expecting—something a bit more suburban, maybe?—but this was pleasantly down to earth. He followed Charles up the front walk, trying to keep enough distance between them that it didn't look like he was hiding behind Charles—which he definitely was.

Just before they got to the door, Charles turned to Harlan with a strange look on his face.

Uh oh. This is it. He's going to tell me not to be too weird, or mention ghosts or…something. He's going to tell me not to be myself in front of them, and who could blame him?

"There's something I've been meaning—wanting—to tell you, and I don't know why, but now seems like as good a time as any, and I worry that if I don't do it right now, I won't be brave enough to do it again for a long time—and I really want to say it."

Oh, fuck. It was even *worse* than that. Was he going to tell Harlan he regretted inviting him?

That he wanted to break up with him?

"I think I knew it before, but when I saw Morgan turn into you, I realized…I love you."

Harlan actually staggered back a step, one hand on his chest and one on his cheek, like Charles had hit him.

"Oh. Oh, God, I'm so sorry! I shouldn't have said that here, or now. Maybe I wasn't just being spontaneous. Maybe I subconsciously chose to do it here because I knew you'd be trapped. Please. Just…forget I said anything."

Harlan took a step forward again.

Charles visibly tensed.

Harlan stepped even closer, reaching down to put a hand on the back of Charles' neck and gently pull him up for a kiss. "I love you, too," he admitted, before he could chicken out. "And...Morgan turned into you when I first saw them again. I didn't want to tell you in case you'd think it was weird, but... Yeah."

Charles gasped, doubling over with his hands braced on his knees. "Oh. Thank God. Oh, fuck. Oh, Harlan, I was so scared I'd fucked everything up. You have no idea."

Harlan grinned down at him. "Well, if you did, I did too."

Charles grinned back. "Yeah. I guess it does." He shook his head. "I can't believe you didn't tell me Morgan turned into me!" He took Harlan's hand, then rang the doorbell.

The door opened, and they stepped inside together.

Want to see more from this author?
Here's a taster for you to enjoy!

Bound to the Spirits: Laid to Rest
T. Strange

Coming December 2022

Excerpt

"Where do you want this box?" Morgan asked.

"Um, anywhere over there is fine." Harlan gestured vaguely in the direction of the kitchen. He had no idea what was in the particular box they were holding, but he was feeling too flustered to check. He knew his 'system'—or, rather, complete *lack* of one—would bite him on the ass later when he was actually trying to unpack and organize, but putting it off felt better than dealing with it at the moment.

"You know you don't have to help with this part, right?" he told them. "Moving *my* stuff, not the business stuff? I mean, you didn't really have to help with that, either. It's not part of your job description—"

"Please. The 'business stuff' was like three boxes. And I write my own damn job description—unless you've come up with a written statement of what my duties entail?"

Wide-eyed, Harlan shook his head.

"Yeah, I didn't think so," they laughed, setting the box down on a pile.

Charles swooped in and glanced at it. "Mm-m, that's a bathroom one."

Morgan frowned at him.

"I'll take it," he assured them.

Harlan sighed. Of course Charles could keep track of everything.

Harlan knew it was stupid to move his business out of his apartment—all three boxes of it, as Morgan had just pointed out—immediately followed by moving in with Charles, but that was how the timing had worked out with renting an office and Charles' lease on his old apartment running out. Technically there was no hurry on his end—Harlan's apartment was his as long as he wanted it—but it had seemed silly for Charles to move all his things and get them all unpacked, only for Harlan to dump a fresh pile of boxes on some nebulous future date. Not that Harlan had that many personal possessions... At least he'd *thought* he didn't, but there had been a surprising amount to pack up and load into the truck Charles had borrowed from a friend.

"Hey, does that mean I didn't have to help, either?" Hamilton—now Harlan's business partner at Laid to Rest Investigations—laughed.

Shit. Harlan swallowed hard. "Of course not. I'm sorry—"

"Hey." Hamilton clapped him on the shoulder. "Sorry... I was just kidding. I'm happy to help you two out. Matthew would have been here, too, but he had to work." He hurried back outside, probably to grab more boxes.

"Are you okay?" Charles asked, setting down the plastic tote he was holding.

Harlan noticed that Morgan was also giving him a concerned look. "Yeah. Sorry. I'm fine. It's just—a lot."

Charles nodded, giving Harlan a quick hug. "I know. But the end is in sight!" He turned in a slow circle, taking in the boxes covering every horizontal surface. "Well, the end of *moving*. Then it'll just be unpacking—and we can go at our own pace."

Yeah. As long as we don't want to sit on the couch or find anything, Harlan thought.

He just nodded at Charles, doing his best to smile.

"I think it's just a few more, then we can go for beer and pizza."

Harlan nodded again. He turned to leave the apartment to at least get some air and pretend to be useful by carrying something back inside, but his path was blocked by Hamilton, who was carrying a stack of boxes.

"Did I hear beer and pizza?"

"You did," Charles agreed. "As soon as the truck is empty."

Hamilton set the stack haphazardly by the door. "Then it's beer and pizza o'clock. These are the last boxes."

Charles whooped, grinning at the room. "Good work, team! I thought it would take us at least a few more hours."

Morgan snorted. "It would have gone a lot more quickly if you didn't have *so many* BDSM toys."

"Ha. Just be glad Harlan hasn't really started collecting his own yet or there'd be twice as many."

Harlan found that difficult to imagine. Charles already had one of every kind of whip, flogger, paddle and cane imaginable—if not multiples.

Charles mimed dusting his hands together. "Alright, if that's it, let's get out of here. Why don't you just take one car?"

Harlan's stomach sank. He was already feeling really peopled out—which was sad, because these were the people he was closest to in the world—and there would only be *more* people at the restaurant. He'd been looking forward to at least driving over with just Charles.

"You guys go ahead. I'm gonna drop the truck off. Phil can give me a ride, and I'll meet you there. Harlan, you can order for me, okay?" Charles gave his shoulder a gentle squeeze.

Great. Now he wouldn't even have Charles in the car with him? And he would have to order not only for himself but for Charles as well? Usually, it was the other way around. It made him feel like an immature jerk and a hot mess, but their system worked for them.

"Don't worry." Charles leaned over to kiss his cheek. "I wrote my order down for you."

Well, that's something, anyway.

Charles did that magical thing Harlan still couldn't figure out how to do that sent something directly from his phone to Harlan's.

"We can take my car," Morgan offered. "Hamilton's smells like thirty-year-old Tim Hortons."

Harlan wrinkled his nose. They weren't wrong.

Hamilton laughed. "Hey, I've spilled lots of *other* kinds of coffee in there! I don't think the stuff at the precinct is even 'no name'. It's...somehow even sketchier than that. It's probably not even real coffee."

"Yeah, you probably shouldn't be drinking that." Morgan shook their head, laughing.

Harlan found himself swept out the door and into Morgan's car. He barely had a chance to wave goodbye to Charles before he was gone.

* * * *

Morgan and Hamilton put in their beer and pizza orders almost as soon as they sat down at the restaurant, leaving Harlan frantically flipping through the menu. He chose the first thing that sounded edible and didn't have too many weird specialty ingredients. He ordered Charles' pizza, and he was about to tell the waiter what beer Charles wanted, but Hamilton shook his head.

"Nah, wait 'til he gets here so it'll still be cold."

Harlan nodded, feeling his cheeks flush a little. He was relieved when their drinks came. It meant that he had something to do with his hands, and he didn't have to talk.

He'd ordered Pepsi. He didn't drink alcohol — or only rarely. It tended to fuck with his mood the next day.

He downed his first drink quickly and accepted a refill when the waiter came around again. Having that much caffeine so late in the day would probably fuck with his *sleep*, but he didn't want to switch to Sprite or something else. With a dark-coloured drink, he could at least pretend he was drinking beer like the others.

For the most part, Morgan and Hamilton were happy just talking to each other and leaving Harlan alone, which Harlan appreciated. Even knowing that they *knew* him and wouldn't expect him to carry the conversation, he still worked himself up sometimes.

He slowly relaxed. Luckily their booth was in a quiet corner, away from other groups, so he didn't feel *completely* overwhelmed.

The pizza arrived before Charles did. Harlan wondered if they should wait for him, but the other two started eating right away. Of course, they'd been helping move boxes for hours, whereas Harlan felt like he'd just sort of drifted around getting in the way.

He was starting to worry that Charles' food would get cold when Charles slid into the booth beside him, giving him a quick peck on the cheek before grabbing a slice and inhaling it.

Of course Charles' mouth was full when the waiter came around for his drink order.

Harlan fumbled in his pocket for his phone, which he'd put away because he knew it was rude to have it out while socializing. Though, again, he didn't think Hamilton and Morgan would really care.

Hamilton waved a hand at him. "It's okay. I've got this." He ordered for Charles, glancing at him for confirmation.

Harlan wasn't sure if it was even the right thing, but he gave up trying to get his phone.

Charles nodded, his lips slightly parted as he tried to swallow the too-hot sauce and cheese.

Harlan groaned inwardly. Hamilton could remember what his boyfriend liked to drink, and he couldn't?

Everyone else wolfed down their food while Harlan picked at his pizza and drank soda after soda.

"Oof, I'm stuffed." Charles leaned back with a groan, his hands folded on his stomach. Making sure Harlan was looking at him, he cocked his head in the direction of the door — his silent way of asking if Harlan wanted to leave.

Harlan nodded, moving his head as little as possible and hoping the others wouldn't pick up on their little exchange. That would have felt rude. He appreciated that Charles had come up with this little system for them. Again, he was pretty sure Hamilton and Morgan wouldn't actually mind, but this way he didn't have to say it himself. And he really did want to go home. Well, back to the box-choked apartment. *Ugh.*

At least he didn't have to work the next day. Laid to Rest didn't have any open cases, which was great for having time to move and unpack but not so great for his wallet or peace of mind.

What was I thinking, trying to start my own business?

* * * *

"Knock knock!" Benjamin Xun, one of the two remaining Toronto police mediums, stepped into the tiny Laid to Rest office, his hand raised as though he had been actually going to knock. The door was open. The office got really hot and stuffy with both Harlan and Hamilton inside, and the solitary window didn't open.

Hamilton grinned at him. "Oh, *please* tell me you have a case for us."

Harlan leaned forward. He was glad Hamilton had said it, because he'd sure as fuck been thinking it.

Benjamin shook his head. "No, sorry, guys. I just wanted to drop off some 'congratulations on starting a new business' presents. I know it's a little late, but they were on back-order and… Anyway…here." He set four gift bags down on Hamilton's desk, which was closest to the door. "They're for you two, Morgan and Charles. Charles told me what kind of phones you all have." He cleared his throat, looking away from Harlan. "They're, uh, from Beth, too, but she wasn't sure if you'd want to see her."

She was right, but Harlan didn't say it out loud. "You'll have to, um, thank her for us."

Hamilton pounced on the pile of presents and started rooting around in one of them. He frowned as he held up its contents. "Oh, great. A weird-looking phone case and a flashlight. Thanks."

Harlan got up to take a closer look. "Really? Thank you!" He picked up the bag with his name on it and held it against his chest.

Hamilton snorted. "Jeez, kid, if I'd known you were that hard-up for a phone case, I would've gotten you one."

Harlan shook his head. "No, these are special."

Nodding, Benjamin pulled out his phone, which was already in a similar case. "The mesh on the back keeps ghosts from draining the battery, and" — he plucked the package out of Hamilton's hands — "it also comes with a warded screen protector so they can't get in that way, either. The flashlight is protected by the same mesh."

Hamilton whistled, leaning back in his chair with his hands laced behind his head. "Wow. Those must've cost you a pretty penny."

Harlan gulped. He hadn't realized that a warded screen protector was part of the case. Warding was expensive. "You really shouldn't have." He put the bag back on Hamilton's desk.

"Hey, don't worry about it. I was there when you learned how much it sucks for a ghost to drain your phone and light. I — *we're* — happy to help."

"Thank you so much." Realizing he should probably say something more and that he actually knew very little about Benjamin outside of their shared mediumship work, Harlan asked, "How are things going for you two?"

Benjamin let out a soft huff of laughter. "Well, I won't lie. It has been busy without you and Leo." Leo had been the Toronto Police Service's fourth medium until she'd lost her abilities six months earlier. "But we're managing." He smiled at Harlan. "It *has* helped that you guys are handling the less serious cases and we can just concentrate on murders."

Harlan shuddered. He definitely did *not* miss that part of being a police medium. Most of the ghosts he'd dealt with through Laid to Rest had died of natural causes or accidents. They tended to look more intact than murder victims, even if their deaths had been fairly gruesome.

"Anyway"—Benjamin patted the top of a gift bag with one hand—"I'll let you get back to it. Keep up the good work!"

Harlan and Hamilton glanced at each other. Harlan could see that Hamilton's computer screen only had a game of Solitaire on it. Harlan had been looking at Tumblr before Benjamin had come in.

"Thanks, we will!" Hamilton assured him, already trying to work open the plastic clamshell package on his new phone case.

"Say…say hi to Beth from us," Harlan added. He wasn't sure that he really meant it, but it seemed like the polite thing to do.

"I will." Benjamin waved at them and left.

"You're going to cut your finger off!" Harlan laughed, watching Hamilton saw at the packaging with his pocketknife.

"Mm-m, that sounds like someone who doesn't want his new flashlight and phone case," Hamilton said airily. "Besides, I'm just the muscle. I don't need all my fingers. In *fact*, I'm probably scarier *without* all my fingers!" He held up his left hand, his ring finger tucked against his palm so Harlan couldn't see it and wiggled his others.

"Yes, very scary." Harlan rolled his eyes. "You won't be able to marry Matthew without that particular finger, though," he pointed out.

"Oh, true." Hamilton let his finger pop up again. "I'll just have to make sure to cut off a different one, then."

Hamilton and his boyfriend weren't officially engaged yet, but Hamilton had confessed that he thought it was going to happen soon.

"And you're more than just the muscle," Harlan assured him, even though he knew Hamilton wasn't completely wrong. Hamilton had lost his small mediumship ability at the same time Leo had.

Harlan cleared his throat and quickly changed the subject. "We should have some scissors around here somewhere… Maybe…" Harlan went back to his own desk and dug through the drawers. "I don't. Do you?" *Great.* Another thing he'd have to buy for the business.

"Don't need 'em," Hamilton said without looking up from tearing the package open. He pulled out his phone, transferred it to the new case and applied the screen protector, which was completely transparent. Once they'd been painted, warding runes were invisible unless a medium was looking for them. "Eh. Not the most stylish thing, is it? Does this actually work?"

Harlan nodded. "They kept Benjamin and Beth's phones from getting drained when mine did, and their flashlights still worked."

Hamilton wrinkled his nose, tossing his phone down on his desk and beginning to attack the flashlight's package. "Well, hopefully we won't ever have to put that to the test."

"Agreed." Since it was unlikely that a rampaging ghost would appear in the office, Harlan decided he'd open his with Charles when he got home.

He and Hamilton had debated having the tiny office ghost warded but decided against it—in large part because of the cost, but also because they wanted *friendly* spirits to be able to come in. That was one of the main reasons they'd started Laid to Rest, after all. Harlan—and Hamilton and Morgan—wanted to work *with* ghosts as much as possible, rather than seeing them as a nuisance to the living and just getting rid of them.

Of course, it was unlikely that a ghost of any kind would show up. Most spirits were bound to the place they'd died, where they'd been buried or somewhere that had been important to them in life. Once they began haunting a place, it was very difficult for them to leave it.

Hamilton took out his new flashlight, loaded the batteries and clicked it on and off a few times…then a few more.

He groaned. "Would you mind if I take off early?"

Harlan shook his head. "No. I'm sure I can handle—"

"Don't say that! You'll jinx it!"

"I don't think anyone's coming in today. Better?"

Hamilton nodded.

"Besides, I told you that you don't have to be here at your desk all day. I can just call you if —*when*—I need you."

"Nope. This old workhorse needs to be in harness." He rapped the desk with both hands in fists, presumably as hooves. "Besides…Matthew's at work all day, and otherwise I'd just be kicking around the condo by myself."

"Oh, yeahhhh. Because sitting around *here* with me all day in an empty office is *so* much less sad!" Harlan teased him.

"Shut up. It is. I'm leaving now, but that doesn't change what I just said."

"Uh-huh. Say hi to Matthew for me."

"Will do. You say hi to Charles for me."

Harlan nodded and waved Hamilton out of the office.

He sighed, highly considering following Hamilton out the door. But where would he go except home, which was cluttered with all his junk and Charles', and if he wanted to sit down or find anything, he'd have to unpack. He didn't want to do that.

Besides…he kinda wanted to be alone after spending the day with Hamilton and Benjamin's unexpected visit, and Charles would be there until he left for work, probably six at the earliest.

It wasn't that he didn't want to see Charles! He just wasn't used to having someone else around *all* the time, and he hadn't realized how much he'd gotten used to having his own space.

It was fine. He'd adjusted to living alone. But he'd adjusted to working with Hamilton every day, so he'd adjust to living with Charles.

It was fine.

He looked at the clock on the wall. It had come with the office, but it made him feel more legit, somehow, so he'd kept it. It was only three-thirty, and they were officially open until five—later by appointment—but there hadn't been a single phone call or anything all day. A few other occupants of the office building had stopped by, curious about the new agency. Harlan made a mental note to return the plate that someone had brought them 'welcome' cookies on. Hopefully Hamilton would remember who they'd said they were and where they worked.

He shook his head. *Return a plate.*

When had he become such an adult?

About the Author

T. Strange didn't want to learn how to read, but literacy prevailed and she hasn't stopped reading—or writing—since. She's been published since 2013, and she writes M/M romance in multiple genres, including paranormal and BDSM. T.'s other interests include cross stitching, gardening, watching terrible horror movies, playing video games, and finding injured pigeons to rescue. Originally from White Rock, BC, she lives on the Canadian prairies, where she shares her home with her wife, cats, guinea pigs and other creatures of all shapes and sizes. She's very easy to bribe with free food and drinks—especially wine.

T. Strange loves to hear from readers. You can find her contact information, website details and author profile page at https://www.pride-publishing.com

PUBLISHING

Sign up for our newsletter and find out about all our romance book releases, eBook sales and promotions, sneak peeks and FREE romance books!